CALL
of the Sea

Chani Lynn Feener

ALSO BY CHANI LYNN FEENER

*For a list of YA books by this author, please check her website. All of the books listed below are Adult.

Bad Things Play Here

Gods of Mist and Mayhem

A Bright Celestial Sea

A Sea of Endless Light

A Whisper in the Dark Trilogy
You Will Never Know
Don't Breathe a Word
Don't Let Me Go

Abandoned Things

Between the Devil and the Sea

Echo

These Silent Stars

His Dark Paradox
Under the name Avery Tu

CALL of the Sea

Chani Lynn Feener

CHANI LYNN FEENER

This is a work of fiction. Names, characters, places, and incidents are the product of the author's imagination, and any resemblance to actual events or persons, living or dead, is entirely coincidental.

Call of the Sea

Copyright @ 2023 by Chani Lynn Feener.

All rights reserved. No part of this book may be reproduced, distributed, or transmitted in any form without written permission from the author.

Front Cover design by the.ravens.touch.

Cover Character Art by Olga Panfilova.

Edited by Jen Young.

Printed in the United States of America.

First Edition—2023

AUTHOR'S NOTE

Dear Reader,

STOP! No, really. Even if you've read one of my books before, please do not skip this note. As some of these triggers couldn't be included on the books main page, I wanted to take the time to include them here.

This book is a Dark MM Romance, and as such it contains certain situations and themes not suitable for all readers. Sila Varun is not a good person. He isn't a hidden prince charming or a misunderstood guy waiting for the right person to come along to turn him into a hero. There is no redemption here. Some of the things he does are seriously vile and depraved. He's a psychopath who doesn't feel guilt or remorse—even toward his love interest. Bay Delmar suffers from emotional detachment, and this causes him to also do questionable things throughout the story. Neither of them are saints. Both of them are sinners. This book does have a HEA, but please mind your triggers.

I want to be clear that I in no way condone anything that takes place in this book in real life. This book is purely fiction. These characters are not real and this takes place on a made-up planet in a made-up galaxy. None of my characters are human, though I sometimes use the word humanoid, and this galaxy is nowhere near ours. If you or someone you know is ever in a toxic relationship, please seek help. You deserve better.

One thing I want to be very forthcoming with is the topic of suicide in this book. While it never happens, there is mention of attempts, as well as one attempt mildly shown on page. It is not graphic by any means, but if suicide is triggering for you, I suggest possibly putting this book down and choosing something else instead. The main character, Bay, suffers from emotional detachment which has caused him to feel numb inside. Basically, he coasts through life as more of a ghost than a living person, and this has left him feeling empty and bleak. He is not depressed, and there's no self-hatred in this book. His thoughts and attempts at ending his life come purely from a place of feeling like life is too boring to bother with.

Also, I would like to point out more bluntly, this book has non con. There is non con in this book. Non con will happen, and you will see it, if you continue reading. Bay Delmar is a masochist, who ends up enjoying rougher sex throughout, however, that doesn't take away from the fact there is non con in this book. If this isn't for you, totally understandable. If it is, please continue to the rest of the list.

Now onto the other triggers. **If you aren't easily triggered or you want to avoid potential spoilers, feel free to skip the rest of this note.**

I tried to list all of the triggers I could think of, but please be aware I might have missed one or two. Your mental health is important, if any of these don't sound appealing or may put you at risk, please skip this book. I have other MM books that don't fall under the dark category and may be better suited for you.

Most, but possibly not all, notable triggers include: Non con (I'm serious), dub con, primal play, consensual non-consent, masochism, sadomasochism, bondage, blood play, fear play, knife play, breath play, asphyxiation, torture, violence, death, drugging of characters, sexual assault, psychopaths, sociopaths, and graphic sex scenes. Finally, lube is used all of one time. I know this is a big one for some people. Please practice safe sex in real life, and remember this is completely fiction and these characters are not human.

Again, **this book does have a HEA**. That being said, this relationship is...Look it's not okay. Nothing about it really. Despite all of the trigger warnings listed above that sound like I'm referencing legitimate kink play, this isn't that. There is no contract or understanding beforehand between the characters about boundaries, and there are definitely no safe words. There is absolutely nothing to be ashamed of when it comes to kinks, however, I implore all of you to explore in a *safe* setting, ideally with experienced partners or even professionals. Sila is, for lack of a better word, a devil. I in no way, shape, or form condone anything mentioned above in real life. This is purely fiction.

This book is intended for a mature adult audience only.

Remember, your mental health and well-being is more important than reading this book. Always put yourself first and be responsible for your triggers. You're worth it and you matter.

BLURB:

The Devils of Vitality always catch their prey.

Bay Delmar is pretty done with life.

There's a reason even his friends refer to him as the Undead or Robot. It's been years since Bay's been able to feel anything other than emptiness when he isn't straddling a hoverbike and risking his neck in one of Vitality's infamous street races. By day, he's Professor Delmar, the reputable—yet stony—youngest staff member at the prestigious Vail University. But by night, he's either racing or sneaking off to the Seaside Cinema where he partakes in other…questionable pastimes. The fact that he suffers from emotional detachment, likes fast bikes and violent porn, aren't even his biggest secret. No, the one thing Bay can never risk the world finding out is that he has an obsession. With a student.

Sila Varun is an apex predator.

Being a genius and all-around perfect specimen sort of ensured from the get-go he would be. He's lived his life at the top of the food chain, and the best way to get prey to let down their guard? Give them a false sense of security. The mask he wears on a daily basis provides him and his brother with a layer of protection, but boredom is always there, scratching at the back of his psyche. Until he discovers Bay Delmar lurking in the shadows—both literally and figuratively. What was meant to be a quickly handled task soon turns into a fixation. Sila's never grown attached to anything before, and he has no intention of doing so now, so what harm could playing a long game bring?

Bay is shocked, and admittedly a little thrilled when the person he's been secretly yearning for suddenly shows an interest in him, only it's clear from the start that Sila isn't the kindhearted boy next door type he's led the planet to believe. His psychopathic nature is revealed the very first night the two of them share together, and the worst possible thing that could happen does. Bay realizes that only makes him like the younger man more. Since his emotions went dormant, he needs constant stimulation—of both the pain and pleasure sort—in order to feel anything, and Sila's vicious nature easily calls to the soul Bay thought was gone forever. This psychopath may be the only thing that can breathe life back into him. But how can he convince Sila he's worth more alive to him than dead?

Sila's always in control, always in charge. He plays everyone like pieces in a game of chess.

So why does he feel like he's stumbled onto someone else's board? And why is he suddenly wondering if the Devil kills the King after all, or if perhaps he lays claim to him instead?

CHANI LYNN FEENER

PROLOGUE:

"You said you'd handle it," his brother's annoyed voice came through the earbud in Sila's right ear a second before a loud male moan reverberated through the surround-sound speakers set high on the walls on either side of him. There was a pause and then, "Are you watching porn right now?"

"No." Sila's eyes stayed locked on the large movie theater screen, tracking the movements of the person depicted on it. One of his hands drifted down his stomach to settle absently over the very large bulge in his pants, but he didn't allow himself to take things further than that.

"Are you lying?" his brother asked.

"I'd never lie to you."

There was another pause, followed by a weighted sigh. "You're watching the real deal aren't you? Damn peeping Tom."

The corner of Sila's mouth twitched. His brother was always reprimanding him for something but he never really meant it.

"At least tell me this person knows you're

watching?"

Sila remained silent.

"Fucking unbelievable," his brother said, and Sila could practically hear his eyes rolling.

"We're safe," he reassured before shifting forward in the leather seat, edging a little closer to the screen.

"Where are you?"

"Seaside." The Seaside Cinema was well known for their private viewing rooms, though typically they were reserved for people to watch porn. That's what the guy next door was using it for; Sila knew because he'd installed cameras before his arrival to ensure he'd get to catch the show.

It wasn't the same as being in the same room as him, but Sila was taking things slowly, only allowing himself crumbs to lead up to the main course.

Something his brother clearly lacked an appreciation for.

"You're watching someone have sex at the Seaside?" his brother snorted. "Weird but okay."

"He's not having sex."

"Ah," he picked up on his meaning quickly, "he's fucking himself. Sounds like the type of thing you'd be into."

"Because it is." There was something thrilling about watching someone's private moment, getting to witness the way the man on screen scrunched his brow and bit down on his lower lip as he got close to climax. Since this wasn't the first time Sila had spied on him like this, he'd already picked up on the man's tells.

And that was what he personally got off on. Sila liked the power that came with controlling others, the rush it gave him knowing he could make someone dance in the palm of his hand. Even better if he did it without them knowing, like he was right now. He'd pulled a dozen strings to ensure his prey wound up exactly where he was right now in this moment.

His brother was ruining all his hard work with his grumbling.

But Sila wouldn't tell him that. That was the one person he'd never try to control or manipulate. Doing so would be no different that controlling or manipulating himself, and that would be counterintuitive.

"Classes start next week," his brother reminded.

"I've polished my Vail University pin," Sila said, knowing he'd understand the meaning of that statement as well.

"I'll start at the Academy. Make sure you handle this like you promised."

"When have I ever broken a promise?"

"To me?" his brother sighed again. "Never. Just hurry up with your new pet project so you can get back to work."

His brother hung up on him before Sila could let him know they were actually one in the same, but that was probably for the best. He doubted he was ready to hear it, and he wasn't exactly ready to share. The two of them may be intrinsically linked, but that didn't mean they didn't also have their own lives.

Half the reason they'd escaped to this planet was so they'd have the chance to explore their own identities without the pomp and circumstance that came with being identical twins. It was proving more difficult than either of them had imagined, but they were trying, and at the end of the day, having their own vices was beneficial toward that goal.

So, no, for now Sila would be keeping the writhing, moaning man on the screen across from him a secret, in part because he wasn't yet willing to share, but also because his brother would no doubt have a conniption when he discovered the man's identity.

He leaned forward, gaze locked on the massive movie theater screen ten feet away, resting his elbows on his knees.

Another sound of pleasure echoed from the speakers, followed by a sharp cry as the writhing body on screen quickened the movements of their fingers buried deep inside their ass. They were kneeling on the ground in front of a plush leather seat similar to the one Sila was on, a screen in front of them playing a dirty film of two guys roughly fucking in the woods.

There'd been a chase and some bloodshed

—more than Sila would expect from a scripted pornographic video. It certainly wasn't the type of thing most people would be getting off to.

Not that the man pleasuring himself was paying attention to it. His head was tipped down, eyes on a picture projected from his multi-slate.

Sila had set up the best spyware he could get his hands on in the adjoining private show room, but even it was unable to capture the image on the man's multi-slate. The picture was too tiny, kept small so the man could keep it close to him as he worked himself into a frenzy.

Not that Sila needed to see to take a guess what the picture could be of. Earlier that afternoon he'd posted a shot of himself sitting on the edge of the Vail University pool. He'd been shirtless and still dripping from the swim, his head tilted to the side suggestively, one hand brushing his hair back. Sila had posted it for this very reason, to be used in this exact way.

Baiting this particular prey was child's play. It would have been tedious even, if not for all the hidden skeletons the man on screen kept tucked in his closet.

The man gasped, one hand behind him, fingers pushing in deep, the other wrapped around his cock. His pastel blue hair was damp at the sides, no doubt from the rainstorm taking place outside, but he'd shed his wet clothes as soon as he'd entered, the tailored two-piece suit tossed carelessly over the leather armrest behind him.

He'd left the tie on though, the long black length of fabric brushing against the thin gray carpet with each pump of his fist.

If he were in there with him, Sila would enjoy grabbing hold of it and yanking—

He cut that thought short and forced his hand away from between his legs. Now wasn't the time for that either.

All good things were worth the wait.

"Not that anyone would call you good," Sila murmured to the blue haired man. "At least, not once they actually got to know you." He was curious how many people had snuck a peek under the mask, or if anyone ever had at all. Was he the first?

"Bay Delmar," he tested the name on his tongue for what must have been the hundredth time. When Sila's brother had pointed out they had a secret admirer, neither of them ever would have guessed it was Bay of all people. Since they hadn't had any classes with him and were new to the school, neither had recognized him as a teacher.

Initially, when his brother had told him about the unwanted attention, Sila had expected another boring exchange with a fellow student. He'd find them, turn them down, move on with his life.

And if the person insisted on sticking around even after having been warned?

Sila would kill them.

Problem solved, end of story.

Only, it hadn't been another student his brother had noticed gazing from afar.

Bay Delmar, the youngest member on staff at Vail University, was lithe and about a head shorter than Sila. His hair was naturally a soft cotton candy blue shade, styled in a soft part with an asymmetrical fringe. It looked like he rolled out of bed like that and merely finger combed those blue locks, but Sila knew that was a lie. Bay must take time every morning to get it perfect like that. So, appearance was important to him.

He wore thin rimmed glasses that practically swallowed his face with how big they were, but the golden rims did help highlight the intensity of his eyes. They were gold as well, like shiny coins dropped in a crystal-clear stream. Pretty even. Standing amongst the throngs, he could easily be mistaken as another student.

Though, with how skillfully he was working his ass and his weeping dick, he wasn't exactly the picture of a strict professor either.

Prior to catching him at the illegal races held at the docks, it'd been almost laughable that a man as boring and unimpressive as Bay could believe for even a second he stood a chance with one of the Varun twins. Apparently, he'd been watching for a while too, at least over the course of the past semester, if his brother's timeline was correct. He'd asked Sila to deal with it, afraid he'd do something stupid and lose his cool if he did so himself, and Sila had been more than willing to oblige.

He'd do anything for his brother. Keeping him safe ensured keeping himself safe as well. All their lives, the Varun twins had been a unit. There was no Sila without Rin and vice versa.

After spending the entire first year on this planet as the quiet, studious nobody he'd been known as back on their home world, Sila had already decided it was time for a personality overhaul. This gave him the perfect excuse for it too, so in a way, he should be thanking the fascinating professor.

Sila had already put his plans in action and had spent most of the summer at the clubs and bars, never turning down an invitation to a party. He'd reinvented himself as friendly and flirtatious, building a friend group practically from scratch. It'd been easy, but he'd had to work subtly to avoid any suspicions and to keep his brother from realizing the full extent of his plot.

All of this just to get a better handle on their would-be stalker.

"You're already so much work, Professor," Sila said to the screen. "I wonder how you'll be once the game really begins?"

He'd realized Bay was an illegal racer at the end of last semester, too late for him to do anything to the older man before school ended for the year. Since they'd be parted for the next three months during break, Sila had needed a way to keep himself in Bay's mind even with distance between them. Posting on the social media app—once known as Inspire, newly named Imagine—had been the obvious solution.

Before, he'd been relatively unknown on the app, but he'd grown his following rather quickly. As far as he knew, the professor wasn't one of them, but he'd purposefully set his account to public, calculating that Bay wouldn't want to risk being caught by openly following. This way he could still see every one of Sila's posts without having to and, in turn, Sila could keep him on the hook.

His brother would be livid if he knew that instead of getting rid of their stalker, Sila was out here luring him closer, but there were no rules to *how* he handled the problem, so technically he was doing nothing wrong.

It'd been so long since the last time he'd had any real fun too, all of last year spent on getting the lay of the land, learning the social hierarchy. He'd considered playing with the Devils of Vitality, university students and cadets same as him, but his brother had caught wind early on and put a stop to those notions.

Sila was annoyed about it, but he had to admit it was for the best. They couldn't risk ruining their overall plan, which was to find a way to free themselves from their sanctimonious father.

A man who would toss his sons out on the streets if he ever caught wind of what they really were.

Different.
Broken.
Unique.

It varied depending on someone's perspective, but no matter what label was put on it, the truth would always remain the same. The Varun twins had been born to a species that valued emotional stability above all else.

And that was the one thing they were lacking.

His brother's problem was he felt too much. Sila was the flipside to that same coin. He didn't feel enough. More than half of the expressions he wore on any given day he'd carefully learned by mimicking others. When they'd been younger, his brother had spent hours sitting across from him, showing him the same one over and over again until he could perfectly mirror it.

As soon as they'd realized they were different, they could have turned on one another to get ahead, but they hadn't. Their instincts had been to grapple closer. To take comfort and trust in only each other. The result was an odd, almost overly dependent relationship between them. They were aware of that fact as well, which was why they'd fought so hard to come to Vitality for a fresh start.

Sila didn't feel things like worry or doubt, but he did experience boredom and whenever that happened things got dangerous. If they'd stayed much longer on their home planet, that boredom was bound to lead him to slip and make a mistake. He'd put them both at risk then. They'd agreed they'd needed a new outlet. Needed to try a different approach without their father and the threat of those who already knew them hovering.

There'd been the very real chance things would simply repeat themselves here, of course, but as of late, Sila hadn't been feeling bored at all.

There was nothing boring about Bay Delmar. The man was an amalgamation of differing parts that didn't belong anywhere near each other. A professor who moonlighted as a street racer with a penchant for filthy sex theaters and getting off to photos of his student?

Name something more interesting.

He did a good job at staying hidden, but not good enough. If he hadn't stalked the Varuns first, his secret could have remained just that, so really, this was Bay's own fault.

Once he'd been made aware of the situation, it'd been almost laughably easy for Sila to identify the man. He'd been mildly intrigued over how a professor neither of them had a class with even knew of their existence, but then that curiosity had bloomed when Sila had tracked him downtown to the docks.

The illegal hoverbike races that took place there at least a couple of times a month had never interested him before, but that night, watching Bay don a disguise and win several races in a row...

Sila had suddenly seen the appeal.

He'd been back many times since, placing bets on the professor, riding his coattails and lining his own pockets with Bay none-the-wiser. If they kept things up, Sila might even have enough money soon for him and his brother to ditch their original plan and get off this planet before graduation.

The races had been Bay's first uncovered secret. The Seaside had been his second. They'd done this dance as well, Sila and Bay at the theater in adjoining rooms, the professor having no idea he was being filmed and watched. That his moans and the tiny pleas he made to himself were being recorded.

That all of the filthy, hardcore and sometimes degrading plots of the pornographic videos Bay chose were being noted and studied.

Sila's kink was manipulation. Emotional. Psychological. Physical. Didn't matter. He was into them all. He'd never had a sexual preference other than having to be in control of his partner, and had never had an interest in exploring the various types of sexual deviancies out there.

In that sense, Bay had opened his eyes to a whole new world he would have otherwise not bothered with. There were a few things he was even curious about trying himself, things he could picture himself doing with the professor. But that would have to wait.

These secrets weren't enough. Sure, he could

implode Bay's life with them, but then it would all be over.

Week after week, he kept coming here and setting up the hidden cameras. The video files were stored on his tablet at home, some kept on his multi-slate. On more than one occasion, Sila had even found himself watching them.

Bay Delmar was a novelty, one that had managed to do the unthinkable and keep Sila's interested for months now.

Maybe that said something about all of this, something Sila should be paying closer attention to…Maybe it didn't. He didn't so much care. So long as he got to do what he felt like doing when he felt like doing it, he didn't try all that hard at questioning the why behind any of it.

He was who he was. End of story.

"Who are you though?" he asked the image of Bay. "What kind of pervert saves pictures of a student at their school and jerks off to them like this?"

Sila had already been on the phone with his brother when Bay had stormed into the room next door. The professor had made quick work of things, wasting no time to select a film before stripping down to nothing but the tie. He'd pulled a small bottle of lube from the pocket of his pants and removed his multi-slate, setting the device on the ground. The photo had only just barely flickered to life before he'd slathered a glob of lube between his cheeks and started playing with himself.

"Someone's had a bad day," Sila mussed, steepling his fingers. "Eager to blow off some steam, Professor?"

There was no response since he'd ensured the audio was only one way. He could hear everything that took place in that room, but Bay couldn't hear him. Poor guy had no clue he was been watched, that someone other than himself now knew how badly he wanted to take it up the ass.

The corner of Sila's mouth tipped ever so slightly. Of course Bay's day had been bad. He'd ensured it would be, after all.

Bay's hovercar hadn't started this morning and he'd been almost twenty minutes late to work because of it. All of the staff at the university were required for a meeting about the upcoming semester, so his boss had been in the room when he'd arrived late. Then the repair guys had told him they were swamped and it would take them a full day and a half just to take a look. He'd had to get a rental over the lunch break, which had only soured his mood further because Bay didn't like using anything that he hadn't specifically chosen himself.

He was rigid and particular, monotonous. At least on the outside. Sila had wondered for a while over whether or not his outer appearance was a mask, the same way his was, but he'd come to the realization that it wasn't.

Bay lived his life studiously and had created a reputation for himself as an attractive, yet strict and aloof professor. He never got close to any of his students or fellow staff members and only seemed to have two friends. When people were looking, he was rigid, brow always slightly furrowed, full lips typically pressed in a straight line.

When no one was around, he was still much the same, only there was more to it. That was when his true feelings slipped through the cracks, almost as though he was unable to keep up the act when alone but still desperately tried.

He came off emotionless, cold, two things Sila could relate to, however he'd discovered the professor's secret in that regard as well.

Bay Delmar wasn't lacking emotion. He was drowning in it. And while Sila had never experienced it himself, he was pretty sure he'd managed to correctly place which emotion it was that kept the professor so down.

Grief.

It'd done something odd though, if Sila wasn't mistaken—and he'd been closely watching the professor for long enough now he was certain his theory was correct.

Bay was drowning in grief and nothing else. Unless he was here, holed up in this room violently screwing himself, or on the racetrack, he was nothing but a shell of a person. Dead yet unable to rest.

Like a zombie.

The corner of Sila's mouth tipped up ever so slightly. He'd never met anyone quite like Bay. Someone so empty, yet overflowing at the same time. Sila understood what it felt like not to feel, but then, he'd always been this way. He wondered how it was for Bay, someone who'd once experienced the full range of emotion possible, yet had lost his connection to it.

Did he miss it?

Was that why he was here, getting himself off to the sounds of one man screaming as another cut him and fucked him well past completion?

Even Sila hadn't known about half the kinky shit Bay seemed to be into, and he admittedly found the video selections every bit as enthralling as the man who chose them.

Bay was so cut off in every other setting it was impossible to reach him, which was why Sila had figured eventually he would need to come up with a way to pull this version out during the light of day. It wouldn't be any fun if he wasn't able to. Wouldn't be entertaining if he only got this wild, messy, twisted version of the professor in a movie theater. He needed to find ways to push him to his limits, to slowly break down those unfeeling walls so emotion could trickle back in.

The process might take a while, but then Sila was nothing if not patient and for the right prize…Waiting could be worth it. His attempts had started off small for this very reason. After making enough money to afford it, he'd orchestrated more and more races at the rocks between Bay and other skilled racers. It was an investment, and it seemed to be working.

The professor had gone from racing maybe once or twice a month to having at least one every week. Since it was summer break this was possible, though Sila was a little worried Bay would turn offers down once the school year began, citing he was too busy to participate. He'd cross that bridge if and when they came to it.

Constant exposure to sensation had knocked a bit of that dazed state of being loose, as Sila had hoped. Bay might not have noticed the change yet, but Sila saw it. Things that the professor would have overlooked before now irritated him more easily. Hatred and love were supposedly the two most powerful emotions, not that Sila had much experience—or any—with either. Whether that was true or not, Bay certainly seemed to be more susceptible to the first.

Sila's brother was like that as well. Quick to anger. Sometimes, that anger could grip him so tightly he lost control and gave into it. That's what Sila was hoping for with Bay.

Which was why he'd known from the start that a broken car and scolding from his boss wouldn't be nearly enough to back Bay into the corner Sila wanted him in.

Sila had also paid a student signing up for classes last minute to run into Bay in the hallway. He'd just returned from his break with his shitty car and the student had spilled their iced mocha latte down the front of his crisp white shirt, which was why he'd arrived to the theater wearing all black—in the spare shirt Sila had left in the teacher's lounge, unbeknownst to Bay.

Sila had assumed Bay's trips to the theater took place after he'd become desperate enough to give in to the need to chase after an emotion other than grief. The only times he'd managed to catch Bay *feeling* anything real had been before or after a race or when he was in here touching himself to the sound of aggressive fucking and Inspire posts of Sila.

The first time they'd done this, he'd thought perhaps the man would come in and sit down prim and properly, maybe put on a softcore porn movie—a straight one, despite his obvious obsession with the Varuns—and then go home.

He'd had no idea the man was going to fuck himself with such a harried passion, like his life was on the line and if he didn't come he'd die.

It was...fascinating.

The fact he'd done so to a picture he'd taken of Sila on campus? The icing on the cake.

"You don't feel and yet you feel too much," Sila mussed, rolling the concept around in his mind. It was almost as though Bay was the combination of both him and his brother, which was hard to wrap his head around. How could one experience too much of something and yet none of it at all?

Yes, grief was technically an emotion, but it was clear it'd beaten the professor so far down that the despair had morphed into something more akin to detachment. The rest of the world seemed to think he was simply aloof.

"What made you this way?" Sila asked the screen, clicking his tongue when Bay sobbed to himself. "Don't fret. I'll find out."

He wasn't sure exactly when this little game of his had turned into something more, when he'd gone from curiously watching to coveting a taste. It didn't really matter. Sila wasn't in the habit of denying himself the things he wanted and his twenty years of existence had taught him the best way to get people to dance to his tune was to figure out their weakness.

Figure out what they truly desired.

Bay should be easy. He spied on the Varuns whenever they were on campus. The problem was, he clearly couldn't tell them apart and assumed he was interested in the twin who attended the university. Since they swapped places every now and again, unbeknownst to everyone around them, it was impossible to say for sure which of them Bay actually wanted. Rin couldn't pinpoint the exact moment they'd caught Bay's attention, therefore they couldn't figure out which of them the professor had originally seen and instantly fallen for.

Considering he loved fast hoverbikes, that should have been another potential angle for Sila to work with, however, word on the street was Bay wasn't interested in upgrading his bike. Money wasn't his main concern either. He made a fat sum at the races and yet barely touched a single coin of it. It all just sat in his bank account gathering dust. There were many things he needed, like a new car and a better house, yet he didn't show any interest in upgrading his life despite having the means to do so.

Which meant something had made him that way. Had snuffed out the will to live in him.

Sila was confident that so long as he could uncover what that thing was, he could mold Bay to his liking with ease. It wasn't that the professor was special or anything, but he was interesting for now.

Bay's moans grew louder and he shifted on his knees to get more comfortable.

It was so tempting to slip his hand into his pants and palm his aching cock at the sight, but Sila refrained. The touch of his own flesh wasn't the same as skin to skin contact with another person. He tipped his head at the screen, considering.

"I wasn't sold before but," he licked his lips, "should we play soon, Kitten?"

Suddenly he was curious how Bay would feel crushed beneath him. Would he cry pretty like he was doing now, alone? Or would he be stubborn and try to hold the tears back? Since he'd never shed them himself, Sila had always held a mild enthrallment toward tears. It was too dark in the theater room, but he could see the wet glisten on Bay's cheeks reflecting from the light cast by the screen in front of him. He wished he had a better view.

If Sila walked in there right now, would he find the professor still wet and needy? Would Bay scream for help or be shocked into silence? Embarrassed at being caught, or excited that it was Sila who'd done the catching?

His brother would understand in the end, even if he was impatient now.

He was the only one who knew Sila's urges and how deeply they ran. How tightly in control he kept his inner devil. The one he could feel stretching beneath his skin in anticipation of the hunt.

How long had it been since he'd played properly? At least a couple of years. Their senior year of high school he'd been forced to behave to ensure he and his brother got to leave and their freshman year, on a new planet, he'd done the same. He wouldn't risk jeopardizing their new lives so soon. But now...

"Come quick, Kitten," Sila said to the screen. "Do us both a favor and end the show early before I do something we'll both regret."

Bay because Sila would hurt him.

Sila because once he did it would all be over.

There was still so much left to uncover and explore where the sneaky professor was concerned. He'd unearth all of the skeletons hidden in his closet, discover exactly what made the smaller man tick, before this was through.

The long game. That was Sila's style. So as much as a part of him wished he could enter the room next door right now and find out how good Bay's skin might feel against his own, he wouldn't.

Inhaling slowly, he calmed that inner devil and ordered in a tighter voice, "Come, baby."

"Varun!" Bay cried out, emptying into his palm as he came. He jerked a bit and collapsed into a heap on the ground, moaning slightly as he slipped his fingers free from his sloppy hole, his other hand still wrapped tightly around his now flaccid dick.

Sila had known that photo was of him.

After a moment, Bay dragged himself back onto his feet and got dressed, washing his hands in the small sink unit against the wall. He kept his head bowed the entire time, never once glancing anywhere near where the camera was hidden.

Completely unaware that the man whose name he'd just called out was watching from less than ten feet away.

Sila grinned and let some of his true self free from its hidden compartment, the sensation a lot like getting up to stretch after a long time lying down.

"Let the games begin."

CHAPTER 1:

The first day of the new semester required finesse. Altering his schedule had been a breeze, and Sila was on his way back from the class aid office when he spotted Rabbit Trace heading into the cafeteria. Last year, Rabbit had been the one friend he'd bothered to make, sticking to the older student during every lunch break. They were friends, but the kind that only hung out on campus and mostly in silence. It'd been nice actually, easy.

Too bad their relationship was going to have to undergo some changes.

The quiet and shy Sila had been an act through and through. Nothing about him was soft or demure, it was simply a façade used to help hide his and his brother's true personas from the world. But masks were only useful when they were used to hide the right things, and since Sila had spent all that effort recreating his image into one of a friendly and flirty individual, he was going to have to properly do away with the one he'd worn all last year.

Since Rabbit was the only one who'd gotten to know that fake version of himself, it made sense to nip that in the bud right away.

Sila followed, slipping into the cafeteria, hands casually in the front pockets of his black jeans. His shirt was a light gray, telling everyone who glanced his way as he walked in that he was a sophomore. The school's color-coded uniform system had made him chuckle when he'd first learned of it.

His brother had cursed and rolled his eyes, annoyed, but then every little thing could set him off.

Rabbit was already collecting his lunch tray from one of the workers serving behind the long bar to the left of the room, and Sila hung back just long enough to watch him select a table off to the side before he walked over and got his own meal.

He smiled at the lunch lady as she packed his tray, glancing over to the corner where he was certain he'd spotted Baikal Void sitting with a couple members of his Satellite—or as Sila liked to think of them, the Brumal Prince's cute little posse.

Sure enough, he found him there and, unsurprisingly, he was staring at Rabbit from afar.

Like a total creep.

Sila chuckled to himself and took his tray with a thank you. He admired that about Baikal, truthfully. The guy knew how to lay low and play his cards. Too bad for the future leader of the Brumal Mafia, Sila was going to have to stir the pot a bit to get things moving since he'd grown bored with being the only witness to the man's possessive glances from across the room. The only question was how...He'd yet to figure that part out. But it would come to him.

"Hey," he greeted Rabbit as he slid into the booth across from the older student, smiling widely, sure to keep his head tipped up to maintain eye contact.

Rabbit blinked at him, caught off guard by his boldness and then slowly lowered his fork. "Hi. Did you...have a good summer?"

"Yeah, it was great. I got to meet a lot of new people." Sila pretended to find interest in opening the can of soda on his tray and then took a slow sip, watching Rabbit closely over the top of the can as he did.

Rabbit Trace was a senior this year, not that he needed the degree from Vail to make it big in life. He was a musical prodigy who played a rare instrument called the beiska. It was made out of a local crystal and had some weird properties to it. He also happened to come from money, since his mother was a famous musician herself who spent most of her time touring throughout the galaxy.

Sila had gotten the sense there was animosity between mother and son, but he hadn't bothered to pry. Everyone had their secrets and so long as it didn't interest him, he wasn't about wasting time trying to uncover every tiny boring detail in other people's lives. He'd only even noticed because of all the time he'd spent around the older guy and the look that was constantly on his face.

It was a familiar look. Sometimes Sila's brother wore it when he thought no one was paying attention.

The look of feeling trapped.

Maybe that was why he kind of liked Rabbit for real. Why he'd never once considered trying to play with him.

"What about you?" Sila asked, popping a piece of fruit into his mouth. He could barely taste it but whatever. Some of the foods here were too bland for his liking. "Did you do anything fun?"

Rabbit dropped his gaze. "I spent the summer practicing."

He shouldn't care that Rabbit was a loser and had nothing going for him other than music, which was so obviously suffocating him it was a real wonder none of the professors had pulled him aside and warned him to take it easy. Sila wasn't the caring type. And yet…

Even if the emotions weren't the same, Rabbit reminded him a lot of his brother. Closed off and hiding. The latter was due to their circumstances, but the first wasn't necessary. In fact, blending in and fading into the background were two entirely different things. He wasn't above teaching his brother that lesson and it seemed Rabbit could do for a little instruction himself.

Besides. If he was going to be spending this

entire year with the older guy, Sila wasn't putting up with his melancholy mood. It was a drag.

"Hey, Sila!" Eager, a junior Sila had met at a party, waved at him from across the room before taking a seat with his friends.

Sila nodded at him in return then turned back to Rabbit who was watching him closely once more. "What?" he laughed. "I told you. I made friends. You should try it. A lot of the students here are really nice."

They were vapid and unintelligent, but close enough.

He kept his eyes on Rabbit, pretending not to notice when Baikal and his cousin walked by, even making sure to keep his voice steady and just loud enough to be overheard as he said, "You can't be a zombie forever, Trace. Should I set you up with someone? Tell me what you're into. I'm sure I can think of a good candidate."

Out of the corner of his eye he saw Baikal slow but forced the smirk back. Messing with the Brumal Prince was almost too easy. He'd expected a lot out of the man when he'd first arrived on planet and heard half the place was owned and run by a mafia. Since they were years apart, he'd had no reason to approach Baikal, unfortunately, so the two were still unacquainted, though that was probably for the best.

"Oh, no thank you," Rabbit shook his head. "I'm not in a position right now for a relationship. I've got too much work to focus on."

Baikal made a sound, maybe a grunt, Sila couldn't be sure, and finally moved off, his cousin Kazimir trailing behind him like the little bitch he was.

Sila checked his multi-slate for the time, noting to himself that Bay should be returning from his lunch break soon. He'd considered the best way to stage their first interaction—should he bump into him accidentally, knock on his office door and request a private meeting—in the end opting for his favorite route: shock value.

His multi-slate rang suddenly and he almost hit the ignore button before he noticed Rabbit curiously watching. He slid out the earbud attachment from the side of the rectangular device attached to his wrist and slipped it into his ear before accepting the call.

"Hey, Arlet, what's up?" He supposed if he had to waste time talking with someone she was as good a choice as any. She was smarter than the average student here, in any case, which was impressive considering she didn't even attend Vail.

"I'm outside the cafeteria on your campus and was wondering if you were in there?" Arlet's bubbly voice came through the line.

"You're here?" He got to his feet.

"Go," Rabbit said before he could say anything. "I'll empty your tray for you."

"Thanks." His smile was genuine this time. He might not be able to feel many emotions, but he still understood the importance of treating those who'd treated him well right in return.

His brother would kill him if he ever acted any differently.

"Are you coming out?" Arlet asked as he started for the doors.

"You can't come in here," he reminded lightly. "If campus security catches you they'll toss you out."

"I borrowed a pin from a friend. They'll never know. All I had to do was trade my dad's autograph and they loaned it to me for an hour." Arlet's father was a well-known composer.

Sila didn't bother pointing out they wouldn't need that long. He had class in ten minutes and he'd planned to arrive exactly two minutes late, so this conversation had to be fast.

He found Arlet standing at the bottom of the stone steps leading up to the side entrance of the cafeteria building and, to help speed things up, he decided to be nice. Ending the call he smiled as he approached, even accepting a hug when she offered it.

"Why'd you come all this way?" Sila asked once they'd separated, turning slightly so he could keep the walkways that led around the cafeteria and its neighboring building in his line of sight. "Meeting with someone?"

Him. She'd come all this way for him. He wasn't stupid, but it didn't hurt to pretend to be every now and again. Stupid was relatable. Go figure.

"Yeah, you." She batted at the side of his arm and giggled. Arlet wasn't unattractive in any sense of the word. Her hair was this pretty lilac shade and she was currently dressed in a plaid skirt in black and a white t-shirt, no doubt an outfit she'd thrown together in the hopes it'd pass as the school uniform.

She was cute, but not his type for more reasons than one.

He glanced at the time and then shifted so he was facing the walkway a bit more. Any minute now...

Bay came around the corner just then, shuffling a stack of physical papers as he mumbled something incoherent to himself. He seemed distracted, a frown furrowing his delicate brow.

That wouldn't do.

Sila laughed.

That did the trick. Bay stumbled and came to a complete standstill. Sila didn't have to check to know he was looking at him now.

The professor was known for being a tough, rule enforcing, take-no-shit teacher, but there were moments where Sila was able to catch him off guard, where his suave act slipped just a little and he came off more clumsy than not. He'd only gotten to try it out a few times before the semester had ended before the start of the summer and he found himself looking forward to giving it another go.

It shouldn't be nearly as entertaining as it

was.

"I'm flattered," Sila said, opting to get straight to the point since he knew Bay was on a tight schedule. He'd need to leave for his classroom in the next five minutes or risk being late, which wasn't something Bay was a fan of being.

"Oh." Arlet deflated some.

"No, it's not that. Don't take this the wrong way, you're gorgeous. But I guess you haven't heard." He ran a hand through the short hairs at the back of his neck sheepishly. Really laying on that boyish charm thick. He'd yet to be able to peg if that was part of the attraction for Bay. If he was interested because Sila was younger. Better safe than sorry and stick with the part for now.

"Heard?" Arlet frowned.

"I'm gay." A fact he'd known since he was twelve and one he'd been waiting for the right opportunity to inform Bay of. Knowing he was listening in on this conversation had Sila internally chuckling all over again. "Even if I wasn't though, I actually just had my heart broken."

"No, really?" Arlet rested a hand on his arm, clearly over her small crush instantly. "Are you okay?"

"I'll be fine. But he was…I don't want to speak ill of anyone." That was a lie. He really, really did and if she didn't stick to her predetermined role and ask him to elaborate he was going to have to rethink the whole keeping her around bit.

"Wait," she moved in closer, "did he hurt you?"

She was speaking too softly. He needed to be sure Bay overheard all of this.

"He hit me a couple of times," he admitted, keeping his voice light but loud enough. He shook his head. "It's fine. We broke up so I don't have to deal with August ever again. But it's still tough, you know? I've never been treated that poorly before."

"August?" She made a face. "August Bril?"

He was a sport major at Vail, popular enough that most people even at Gift, the arts school Arlet attended, knew him. Sila had made out with the guy a couple of times last week in the middle of the club, Fornication, though the two of them had never been an item and August hadn't even come close to hitting him.

He'd hit his past lovers though, Sila knew for a fact. Had selected August to be this particular experiment's guinea pig for that very reason. The best lies were the ones most closely rooted in truth.

August also happened to be a member of the Shepards, a ridiculously small gang that for some reason believed they were more important than they were or would ever be. Recently, Sila had made another discovery about Bay and he wanted to test a theory using one of those gang members.

An alarm beeped then and both Sila and Arlet turned to find Bay scrambling to shut it off.

The professor swore and fiddled with his multistate, cheeks staining an adorable shade of pink, and then he glanced at them, adjusted his glasses and sped off. He'd disappeared around the side of the cafeteria within seconds, but that was all right.

He'd heard everything Sila had wanted him to hear.

"Wow," Arlet was also staring in the direction he'd just vanished, "was that Professor Delmar? The rumors about him are true. He's so hot."

Bay was popular on campus—no doubt why he went to such extreme lengths to keep his helmet on and left his bike behind for someone else to drive off the docks for him. Students swooned over his looks and his cool demeanor, gushing over how firm with them and how uninterested in their attention he seemed to be.

If only they knew. Sila wondered what would be said about him if it was leaked he was obsessing over one of his male students.

"Are you taking one of his classes?" Arlet asked.

And that was more than enough of that.

"You know what, I remember you saying you were ready for a serious relationship. Have you considered Rabbit Trace?" Though he was annoyed at the way she'd practically drooled over Bay, Sila had to admit Arlet was helping to tie up all sorts of loose ends for him without even knowing it.

That certainly deserved a reward.

After he was finished with her, of course.

"Rabbit?" A dreamy look entered her eyes. "We've sadly never met. He's impossible to get in touch with since he never comes to any of the parties or the bars."

"Why don't you ask your dad to set you two up?" Sila suggested. "He's got to know Rabbit's mom, right? Your parents will probably love the idea of the two of you together."

Rabbit most likely wouldn't, but he'd go along with it if his mother told him to. On some level, Sila felt a little bad about using that against his friend, but Trace wasn't the only one who'd no doubt find this pairing upsetting.

Baikal Void needed a push? Sila would oblige.

And if the Brumal Prince didn't take the bait? Arlet was a sweet girl. If she and Rabbit did end up dating for real she'd probably be able to pull him out of his shell too. Win win.

"Maybe I should," Arlet considered. "Do you really think that'd be okay? Involving our parents?"

"These are different times," Sila said. "If the two of you meet and Rabbit ends up not feeling it, he can always opt out no matter what your parents have arranged. Same goes. You might meet him and change your mind. Besides, between you and me, his mom keeps him on a tight schedule. Setting this up with her so she allows it and gives him a break will be doing him a favor. He'll already be grateful and open to getting to know you after that, trust me."

"Still...Aren't the two of you friends?" she asked.

Knowing she was about to suggest he introduce them instead, Sila held up his multi-slate and tapped it. "Shit, I've got to go or I'll be late for class on the first day. Let me know how things go when you talk to your father. Later!"

He turned on his heel and bounded up the steps two at a time, practically racing around the cafeteria building, heading the same way Bay would have gone a few minutes ago. He'd held things off just long enough that he'd be exactly two minutes late to class as planned and slowed as soon as he'd entered the science building.

Intro to Criminal Psychology was being held on the top floor and he took his time getting there, pausing outside of the closed door to count to five before he sucked in a breath and burst through the door.

He heaved and pretended he'd just run here, hanging onto the door knob as the full class went quiet, all eyes turning to him.

The professor was standing at the front of the room, a few feet from the door, but his mouth dropped open when he spotted Sila.

"I'm sorry I'm late," Sila said, bowing low before he straightened. "There was a family emergency." He waited to see if Bay would call him on the lie, a bit disappointed when the other man continued to stare at him wordlessly. "Um, Professor?"

Bay blinked and seemed to get a hold of himself, clearing his throat and straightening his spine. "I believe you're mistaken. I've already gone through roll call and everyone is here."

"I transferred in this morning," Sila explained. "They probably haven't added my name yet." They hadn't because that wasn't done until the end of the day.

He almost grinned when a look of shock and dread flashed over the professor's face before he could help it. That was already more emotion than the professor was known for showing in public.

"Right." Bay pressed against the center of his glasses and then motioned to the desks. "Well then, since it's the first class I'll let this slide, this once, Mr....?"

If they'd been alone, he would have snorted. A week ago the guy had been moaning his name on the filthy floor of the Seaside Cinema and now he was acting like he didn't know it?

Cute.

"Sila Varun, Professor." He rushed forward and held out his hand. "It's a pleasure to make your acquaintance."

"Yes," Bay cleared his throat a second time, hesitating before taking his hand and giving it a delicate shake before pulling away. He motioned to an empty seat in the back once more. "Take a seat,

Mr. Varun. I was in the middle of going over the syllabus."

He flashed one last smile before he followed instruction, settling down at the single empty desk. Once he was situated he glanced back up to find Bay was still watching him.

The second their eyes met, the professor looked away and began talking about the class requirements, doing his best to pretend like he didn't know who Sila was and he hadn't just been caught off guard by his presence.

Oh yes. This was going to be so much fun, Sila could practically taste it.

CHAPTER 2:

Racing had always been a secret hobby for Bay. Before, it'd been because his grandmother would have forced him to stop if she'd ever learned her one and only grandchild was out "risking his neck on a death machine". When she'd passed however, it'd needed to be a secret for different reasons.

He'd only been teaching at Vail University for two years now, going on his third, and he'd developed a reputation for being an upstanding member of the staff. If the school ever discovered he was an illegal street racer? He'd be fired without a second thought, and then what? All he had were the names he was known by. If people stopped calling him professor…

Identity had always been a thing Bay struggled with. When he'd been a child growing up at the orphanage, that had been for obvious reasons. He'd been dropped off as a baby with no notes or indicators of who his parents might have been or why they were giving him up. Later, once he'd finally been adopted at the age of ten and given a name all his own, identity had still been an issue.

It'd surprised him at first, made him feel terribly ungrateful to the woman who'd been kind enough to take him in, but he'd been too young to make anything of the foreign name Bay Delmar and for years he'd struggled with wondering if he deserved it or not.

That was also why, even though he didn't like it, Bay clung to the professor title. To honor the woman who'd raised him. Since he could no longer feel sadness for her, it was the least he could do. Literally.

Idle Delmar had been the well-off owner of a three-bedroom home on the outskirts of the city when she'd woken up one day and randomly decided she no longer wanted to spend her life alone. She'd adopted Bay that same day and he'd gone from sharing a room with twelve other kids to having one all to himself. She was already considered past her prime, unable to run around the yard with him, but he hadn't cared about that.

While he'd never been mistreated, his life at the orphanage had been repetitious to the point he'd begun to wonder if there was even a purpose to living at all. Dark thoughts for a ten-year-old to have, and he'd often wondered how far down the rabbit hole they might have taken him if he hadn't been selected by Idle and given the gift of a second chance.

She may have been old, but that'd only

meant she'd been worldly. As a well-educated member of society, a retired professor no less, she'd had so many stories and facts to teach him. He'd been enthralled with every word that came out of her mouth, from tales of her travels on and off planet, to descriptions of the various creatures she'd seen. Through her, Bay had learned how vast the universe really was.

She'd taught him that life was greater than the four gray walls of the orphanage, too great to waste living boxed in by routine and monotony. He'd kept that lesson close to heart for the next twelve years he'd spent with her.

Everything had changed after she'd left him.

For as long as his grandmother lived, she'd made sure he was taken care of. That was why he'd agreed to study psychology when she'd asked and why he'd worked so hard at Vail University when he'd been a student there.

She'd never gotten to see him accept his diploma.

Her death had been sudden, catching him completely off guard, but that hadn't even been the half of it. He'd found out the day of the funeral that sometime before she'd died, she'd lost their house. When he'd checked her account with the bank, it was to find that was empty as well.

The amazing, intelligent woman he'd grown to respect and love had allegedly gambled away all of her assets at the end of her life.

Bay had refused to believe it when he'd first

been told. Refused to accept the police report when he'd filed with them claiming it was impossible. The house she'd cherished wasn't something she would have carelessly gambled away and yet all the evidence the Vitality police collected said otherwise.

It'd gotten worse from there. The autopsy showed that her cause of death had been heart failure and suddenly the police were speculating that she'd died from shame. Shock over losing her house and all of her money gambling at the Shepard's popup card stalls had supposedly driven her over the edge and killed her. Her heart couldn't take it, they'd said.

Over and over and over again. Like broken records.

It'd become hard to tell who exactly they were trying to convince, Bay, or themselves.

He'd tried to hire a lawyer, but the man had gone over the report and then concluded the same thing the police had. When he'd mentioned she'd been old enough for others to easily have coerced or taken advantage of her, the lawyer had given him an apologetic look then explained it wouldn't make a difference. The courts only cared about evidence, not theories.

In the blink of an eye Bay's perfect life had burst at the seams and left him right back at square one.

With nothing, no one, and no purpose to go on.

The diagnosis had been the final nail on the coffin for him. Emotional detachment brought on by extreme stress and trauma. Because of it, Bay hadn't been able to muster enough emotion to even really care that there was something intrinsically wrong with him. He stopped caring about everything.

Therapy had been a bust. He'd only even bothered with it at his friends' insistence. They'd wanted him to get better, to return to his old, upbeat self. When Bay accepted that was never going to happen, that's when he first made the decision to do them all a favor and just put a stop to it all.

He hadn't even been able to feel guilty toward them for not being present in their lives anymore. Wasn't able to connect and be happy or excited over anything with them, even the things they all used to love.

Bay had gone to the largest bridge in the city and leaned out over the edge, peering down at the murky water below. And for the first time since Idle's death, he'd felt a spark of *something* in his chest. It'd been too hard to tell if it'd been fear or excitement, either way, it was obvious where it was coming from.

He probably would have jumped if his friend Nate hadn't called him at that exact moment, begging him to come fill in at one of the races. After everything he'd put him through, Bay had figured he'd go and do him one last favor. It wasn't like the bridge was going anywhere.

But then, as he'd been racing down the narrow road, his opponent hot on his heals, it happened again.

That spark of sensation—that *feeling*.

The thought of death appealed to him. And not just as a means to end his numb existence. But as a way to revive it. Briefly, so briefly sometimes it didn't seem worth it, but catching glimpses of those old feelings, of his old self, became a sort of addiction to Bay.

He'd gotten a rush when he'd won that day, a big one since it'd been his first time against a seasoned opponent. He'd thought of all the amazing stories his grandmother had told him about her experiences and how they'd made her feel, had been reminded of her advice to live in the moment.

So that's what he'd decided to do. In honor of her memory, he'd do as she'd suggested. He'd live in the moment. It'd turned into a sort of morbid game he played with himself, one that no one knew of.

Bay raced and, if he won, he lived until the next time. If he lost, he'd head back to the bridge he'd been contemplating jumping off of before Nate had called him that night.

Two years later, he was an undefeated racer. He wasn't in the top tier, but he was close to it.

In the midst of what had to have been the worst time of his life, racing had become an intrinsic part of who he was. One of the few times he felt truly like himself, like he *existed,* was when he was hunched over and speeding down the pavement like he was right now.

He needed that zap of adrenaline and the fear of possible death to get him going, to kickstart his emotions and be able to feel through the internal fog. His closest friends, the three that had stuck with him through this, knew that much at least. That was why they all went out of their way to help him continue to race and keep his identity hidden.

Even though no one had ever said it out loud, Bay knew they all worried that he'd do something drastic if he was ever exposed.

They weren't wrong.

Bay ground his teeth as he took a sharp right curve, his body leaning heavily into it. He was ahead, but not by much, and this race was too important for him to botch due to distracting thoughts.

For nine months now, there was one other reason Bay had to keep living.

And that reason had posted a new photo to Inspire right before Bay had arrived at the docks. He'd had to prepare and as sort of extra incentive, had forced himself to hold off on looking at it. If he wanted to see it, he needed to make it out of this alive, which for him, meant winning.

It was sick, he was aware. That was why no one could ever know—about his secret game, or his secret crush. If either were ever discovered... He wasn't afraid of death, would welcome it, in fact, but he wanted to go on his own terms. Being ostracized from society? Not something he wanted.

Did that make him a hypocrite? If someone wanted to die, but was also afraid of being looked at with disgust, what did that say about them?

Was Bay a monster?

Or was he just broken?

If his typical state of being wasn't emptiness, maybe he would have taken the time to really pick his psyche apart to find the answer. As it were, he couldn't ever be bothered. As soon as this race ended—if he won—the thrill of the ride would start to wear off and before he even made it back home, he'd be in that place again.

That dark, hallow place, completely devoid of feelings and wants. He'd stay that way too.

Until he looked at pictures of Sila Varun.

Racing and Sila. The only things that could spark something inside of Bay. The only things that made it worth peeling himself out of bed in the mornings and returning to the lumpy mattress at night. Just when racing had started to lose its magic, Sila had appeared before him like a sign from above.

A sign to keep pushing, to keep breathing.

A sign that he was fucked up, and not just because he dreamed of the comforting embrace of the grim reaper.

Sila Varun was a *student*.

Bay could never have him.

The finish line was fast approaching and Bay put all his focus into it as he sped through the brightly lit backstreets. Rumor was the Emperor herself had a thing for these races and helped fund them, though no one had ever actually seen her face here before. Considering the pot on this particular race, someone with money and influence was certainly watching from somewhere.

His opponent was right behind him, but he knew even before he crossed the line he had this in the bag. As soon as his bike zoomed over it the crowd broke out in raucous howls and he grinned behind his helmet.

"Pandaveer! Pandaveer!" they cheered his nickname, and the high he got from the feeling filled him, easing all that empty space he typically carried around.

He'd gained the nickname by chance when he'd still been a rookie racer. His skills had drawn a small crowd his first couple of times out on the track and with his identity hidden even then—since he'd been a student and paranoid about being caught and ratted on—people had started to call him Pandaveer. He had no idea who had started it, but it'd stuck and grown on him. Bay had never seen one in real life before, but his grandmother had shown him a picture she'd taken of one once and for that reason he'd kept it.

He didn't stop even once he'd crossed the finish line, continuing down the straight road until he could exit off a dirt curve. Pretty soon he was going to need to come up with another exit.

Bay parked right at the edge of the forest, slipping off the bike and handing the keys over to the man waiting there.

"Killed it as usual," his friend and fellow racer, Nate, said with a smirk, patting him on the back.

If only he knew.

"Flix is waiting for you in the lot," Nate continued, pointing over his shoulder.

The handoff was typically done quickly so no one saw them and followed Bay, which was why he didn't bother verbally replying. With a wave he stepped into the forest, instantly swallowed by the trees. He kept the helmet on even then, heading through this shorter segment of woods until he came out the other side. The back parking lot, smaller than the main one and not attached to the actual event grounds, was empty aside from a single vehicle.

The man waiting for him was standing outside the black hovercar, arms crossed over his chest as he leaned back against the tinted passenger side window. Flix never bothered to hide when he came to pick Bay up, unlike his best friend Berga who seemed to enjoy playing secret agent.

Technically, Berga was the one Bay had been

friends with at the start of this two years ago, but whenever the twenty-two-year-old was caught up with one of his experiments, he sent Flix in his stead. Berga was loyal like that and would never leave Bay hanging. And Flix…

Bay still didn't really know enough about him to have formed an opinion other than to say he clearly cared an awful lot about Berga. Though, and this was just a guess made off the way the two had always interacted, the relationship was strictly platonic in nature.

Both of them were younger than Bay and they also happened to be prominent members of the Brumal Mafia. More aptly put, they were part of Baikal Void's Satellite.

Another reason Bay hadn't believed his grandmother gambled with the Shepards? Berga's family had lived right next door to them for the first seven years Bay had been there and Idle had gotten on pretty well with them. The fact they had dinners regularly at one another's houses was why Bay and Berga had become friends despite their age gap in the first place.

If she were going to suddenly fall into gambling, surely she would have chosen to play at one of the Brumal establishments instead. Gambling was legal on Vitality, and the Brumal were scary, but better the evil you knew. Idle knew Brumal members personally. It made no sense to Bay that she'd gone down the road to the Shepards shitty, barely in operation card game held in a pitch post tent.

He didn't want to think about this anymore. What was done was done and he'd given up a long time ago on ever getting answers. No matter what he believed, Idle's signature and thumb print had been on the official transfer of deed documents. The leader of the Shepards, Haroon Caddel, had supplied them as proof the second he'd been asked.

"How'd it go?" Flix asked as he approached.

Bay went straight to the back door and opened it, quickly stripping out of his racing leathers and helmet. He tossed them into the duffle bag on the floor and then pulled on the cherry red leather jacket and the black baseball cap that'd been left on the seat for him.

The cap helped conceal his blue hair—which had a tendency to stand out even on a planet such as Vitality where the color was common—and the brightness of the jacket gave off the appearance of someone not afraid to stand out, which ironically enough, typically had people losing interest in him.

"I won," Bay said a second before his multi-slate beeped. He unzipped the leather sleeve at his right forearm to expose the screen and saw the deposit notification that had just been made to his bank account.

As per usual, his body gave no reaction. Two years ago, he'd most likely have been elated. The kind of money he'd accumulated was already more than enough for him to quit his teaching job. But now…Money didn't matter.

Nothing did.

The app for Inspire stared back at him when he closed the bank notice and the corner of his mouth twitched.

Okay, one thing did.

Bay couldn't look at Sila's account now though, not with Flix standing right there. Both he and Berga were also students at Vail. They were seniors and wouldn't have any classes with Sila, but that didn't mean Flix wouldn't recognize him. Sila stood out, even more so lately.

A twitch of something—no doubt only possible due to the adrenaline stil pumping through his dead heart from winning—caused an itch at his chest and absently, he scratched at it. He'd been the jealous type before, but he was still caught off guard whenever he felt a flash of that familiar emotion now, after years of it being dormant.

It wasn't his fault though, really. Sila was the one who'd changed and caused this reaction. Over the summer something had caused the younger man to open up and become more flirtatious and charismatic. Bay simultaneously hated it and found it alluring.

The picture he'd posted earlier…had it been for someone else? Someone other than Bay? Some new man Sila was trying to attract and—

"I'm shocked," Flix drawled sarcastically, pulling Bay's attention off the device. "Come on, like I'd ever back a losing cat."

Pandaveers were rather large feline creatures, lithe and speedy, with pearlescent fur that gleamed in the light. There were certainly uglier things he could have been compared to instead, especially on this planet.

In exchange for their services on nights like these, Bay had promised Berga and Flix he'd help them earn money. All they had to do was place bets on him and he'd do the rest. In the beginning, it'd been imperative to bring someone like Flix on. A member of the Brumal betting on a nobody? It'd drawn attention just like they'd hoped. Now everyone knew the name Pandaveer and sponsors were frequently requesting him for impromptu races.

Some of those races had been tight and Bay had started to wonder in the past couple of months if there weren't someone out to get him. He'd even feared for a hot second that someone had somehow uncovered his secret game, but had soon realized how impossible that would be. He didn't keep anything like a diary and he'd never told a soul. It wasn't like there was a good way to slip "hey, if I lose one day, I'm going to kill myself" into a conversation.

"Speaking of backing," Flix straightened and then reached into his front pocket, "You helping Berga with one of his experiments again? He asked me to give you this." He held up a small glass vial and then carelessly tossed it at Bay. "He specifically told me to tell you that he upped the dosage, whatever the hell that means."

"You don't want to know," Bay stated, checking the contents of the vial. It was a small mixture of loose leaves the color of midnight. When they were mixed in with a tea blend no one would be able to tell the difference between them. This was the second batch Berga had concocted and given Bay to test out, though he was a little annoyed the future Butcher of the Brumal had shared that tidbit with Flix.

The less people who knew what Bay was up to, the better.

He may have given up on finding proof his grandmother had been taken advantage of, and he may go through life like the walking undead, but he'd never forgiven the Shepards. He'd left them alone only because he had no real way of getting back at them, and no strong urge to do so, but hearing Sila talk about August Bril had ignited some of that old hatred within him.

Sure, he couldn't take on the entire Shepard gang, but he could teach August a lesson. Those assholes already had his house. They weren't allowed to take Sila from him too.

Even if Bay technically could never be with the man either.

He'd gone to Berga and asked if he had any poisons that wouldn't leave a trace and Berga, the evil little devil that he was, had gleefully listed off all the new concoctions he'd been crafting in his off hours. Bay had offered to help him test them out and Berga had accepted without asking any questions. The only thing he'd said before handing over that first vial had been not to use it against a Brumal member.

The Shepards and the Brumal were enemies and Bay had been tempted to share who his target was, but had refrained. He couldn't risk anyone knowing and it ever getting out. If he were caught, they'd lock him up and then not only would he never get to ride again, he'd also be parted from Varun.

August had come into his office at the beginning of the week for a meeting—Bay had made up wanting to discuss their first pop quiz which he'd done poorly on—and Bay had slipped him the spiked tea then. The kid had stumbled from his office acting all out of sorts, but if anyone had seen him, they would have just figured he was tipsy on campus.

It wouldn't have been the first time for him, so it was more than believable.

There was no target in mind for this next batch, but Bay had asked for it just in case. He'd never admit it, but he'd gotten a sick twisted thrill when he'd seen August's face flush. Revenge had never been something he'd legitimately considered because it'd seemed so impossible but...

August wasn't the only Shepard who attended Vail and Bay would chase anything that made him feel something other than the dark, yawning empty state of being that was his normal, even drug students.

"Thanks." He pocketed the vial and then waved, about to leave.

Someone waited here for him so he could change, but he never rode in their car. It would be too easy to figure out his identity if he was caught with one of the Satellite. He was able to coast by with such a mild disguise because people actively knew not to look too closely at other spectators in the crowd since this event was illegal. If someone was spotted with Flix or Berga, however, the curiosity would be too great for anyone to ignore.

"I'll see you at school," Flix said before Bay started across the parking lot.

He had to travel through another short cropping of trees, a patch that was attached to the main forest, in order to reach the larger parking lot where most people parked. By the time he got there, the crowd had already started to arrive. He was careful to move with them and not draw attention to himself.

Typically, he ignored everyone else the same way he hoped to be ignored, but he was halfway to his car when he lifted his head slightly for no particular reason and caught sight of someone that gave him pause.

A tall man with broad shoulders dressed in black was walking in front of him, making his way through the throngs of people with confident steps. Bay couldn't catch a glimpse of his face, but the back of his head was familiar enough that after a moment he was eighty percent positive he was looking at Sila Varun.

Before he knew what he intended, he started moving again, rushing forward to follow the man, the timing was terrible, however, with more and more people making their way to their vehicles. It wasn't long before he lost sight of Sila and, no matter how hard he looked, he wasn't able to locate him again.

Swearing under his breath, Bay's shoulders slumped forward. What were the odds that was actually Sila anyway? He'd had a long day and the adrenaline rush from the race was still spurring him on. There was a very good chance he was seeing things and whoever that man had been, he'd simply seemed like Sila from behind.

Sila Varun was a straight A student on the honor roll, well rounded, with regular hobbies like reading and swimming. There was no reason for a guy like that to be here, at an illegal race that could easily wreck his entire future if they were raided and he was caught. And even if it were Sila...He was a *student. Bay's* student. If he'd run up to him, Sila would have recognized him for sure.

Shaking his head at his foolishness, Bay continued to his car, keeping his head tilted down and the cap pulled low just in case. He was so intent on making it there and getting out of here, that he'd already rounded his vehicle and unlocked the doors before he glanced up and saw someone had placed something on his hood.

A single long-stemmed bay rose greeted him, the vibrant blue and reds of the petals standing out against the black paintjob of his hovercar. He hadn't been named after the flower, but someone had taken to leaving them for him here after his past two races.

The first time he'd been in a panic over it, certain someone had discovered his identity. That may still be the case, but if they had, they weren't interested in using it against him just yet. Since there was nothing else for him to do but wait it out to see what this person might want, Bay had been forced to go with the flow.

Like he had the other times, Bay took the flower and placed it on the passenger seat when he got into his hovercar.

In a life that already wasn't all that worth living, he never said no to pretty things.

CHAPTER 3:

Was he looking at him?

Damn it. Of course he was. He was a student and Bay was his professor. Of course he was—

He wasn't looking.

Bay glanced away from Sila seated in the middle of the classroom, setting his gaze literally anywhere else. Two weeks into the first semester and he was still nervous every time this particular class was in session. Nervousness was good though. Nervousness meant he was still breathing and he had reason to keep doing so. It meant for one hour and thirty minutes two times a week, he was guaranteed to not feel dead inside.

He'd gotten the shock of his life when the object of his desire had waltzed through the door and lied to his face about why he was late. Sila had probably been worried about being reprimanded, not wanting to admit he'd lost track of time while he'd been talking with his friend. Since Bay hadn't wanted to embarrass him, he'd played along.

Sila Varun was the epitome of picture perfect through and through. His hair, a sandy color that sparkled like spun gold was always impeccably styled. It was longer at the front and sides, with an undercut. A little edgy, but still clean.

He had heterochromia, one eye a pale pastel blue, the other a seafoam green. Sila was bigger than Bay was, taller and broader, with a torso and legs that seemed to go on for miles. Last year, he'd looked like an angel in the freshman white, but this year as a sophomore he was required to wear light gray. If anything, the color only helped highlight the golden hue of his skin tone.

Bay had seen him smile at a passing student during freshmen orientation and that had been it for him. His heart had kicked into overdrive, a sensation he only experienced anymore when he was straddling his hoverbike. The rush he'd felt from simply *looking* at the guy…He'd instantly been obsessed.

With a man five years his junior.

And a student at the university where he taught.

He recognized it for what it truly was. Sila reminded Bay of the person he'd once been. A part of him had seen it instantly in the way he'd caried himself. Before his grandmother's death, before he'd turned into this undead thing, Bay had gotten on with most people as well. He'd been popular and fun.

People had liked him.

If he could muster up enough feeling to care

that they no longer did, he would, but as it were... Besides, he'd heard the whispers about him in the halls. He knew the students found his indifference attractive for one reason or another. They thought he was the quiet brooding type and that added a layer of mystery to him.

Only, there was nothing all that mysterious about him in the end. If anyone ever got close enough to see, they'd be disappointed in what they found.

Bay wasn't mysterious.
He was broken.
Empty.

Even his friends only stuck around now out of some sense of loyalty to the person he'd once been. He should be grateful since their help is what allowed him to continue racing despite the risks. Instead, he thanked them dispassionately and they pretended not to notice that he didn't really mean it.

Or, he meant it. He just couldn't feel the emotion behind what those words stood for.

He didn't dislike his friends, but he could no longer feel that caring or attachment toward them he knew he once had. He didn't get excited when they called or miss them when they didn't. He wasn't ever lonely or sad or disappointed being on his own. His house was just a place he stayed and the school was just a place he worked and sometimes, when the emptiness became too much, he escaped it by climbing on a hoverbike or sitting on a silicon cock.

Simple as that.

Tedious.

His entire existence was tedious.

Someone like Sila, who was vivacious and bold and had their whole future ahead of them, deserved better than being the object of a person like Bay's desire. He deserved the attention of someone who could feel with their whole being and who could love and cherish him the way he deserved to be.

Bay had kept his distance for this very reason, only watching from afar. It should have stayed that way this year as well, but for some reason Sila was here, in his class. He'd thought there'd been a mistake initially, had even been forced to address the issue and ask Sila what he was doing there when his name wasn't on the registry list.

Sila had merely flashed that bright, friendly smile and explained he was a late transfer in. Apparently, he'd taken a sudden interest in psychology and figured taking the class might help him later on down the line when he graduated and became a doctor.

He was a twenty-year-old kid already considering the wellbeing of his future patients. Further proof that he was too good for Bay, who couldn't even be considerate of his friends, let alone a stranger he may or may not meet in the future.

He was looking at him now. For real this time.

"Um," Bay cleared his throat and turned back to the projection screen, tapping away on the keyboard set in front of him, "right. Moving on."

Which was what he should be doing. Moving the fuck on. Because this was no longer an innocent imaginary tryst. Bay wasn't a good person and no one could ever find that out, least of all Sila. He should cut his losses now, end the risk of getting caught. But...

How?

It'd been a long time since he'd experienced an emotion this intense and he found he wasn't willing to let it go. Not just yet. Not when it was the only thing helping him get through his pathetic daily routine.

When it was starting to become his only reason for continuing on.

"We'll be discussing the different types of stalking you may or may not come into contact with throughout your lives," Bay said, forcing his voice to remain firm and his expression lax. He would never give away what he was feeling on the inside. He'd keep that a secret along with everything else. Though, it'd admittedly been easier to mask when he'd been feeling nothing. "Remember, if you or someone you know feels threatened, report it to the campus police or the Vitality Police immediately. These types of situations can escalate at a rapid pace, before you even realize you may be in danger."

Bay risked another glance at Sila, but the student was jotting down notes, back to looking away from him. "There are many different reasons someone begins stalking another person, but what it all boils down to is they want something."

"Like sex?" Riel Xin, a bold student who happened to be friends with Sila called out, gaining a few interested glances from the rest of the class, as well as a couple of chuckles.

When Sila had walked in that first day, Bay had wondered if he'd joined for Riel. Knowing that he was interested in men was torturous. Now every time Bay saw him so much as talking with another male, the spot at the center of his chest ached with even more longing than before.

It was sick, because he liked it. Bay enjoyed the way it irritated him, how he could ruminate on the subject for hours. At least then he was focused on something, even if it was something impossible and taboo.

Maybe the fact that it was forbidden also helped. The fact it was forbidden and never going to happen allowed him to sneak in dirty fantasies of himself and Sila whenever he got the chance. Those types of daydreams made his skin feel too tight and caused his body to heat in arousal.

The kinds where he tortured himself with imaginings of Sila kissing someone else, fucking someone else…His hands clenched around the edge of the wooden podium he was standing in front of.

Were Sila and Riel having sex? Bay only followed him on campus, and occasionally around main street, where it would be easy enough for him to claim he was out shopping if he were caught. It was difficult, but he'd controlled himself from ever taking things further—had only even stalked the guy home to his apartment building the once, just so he'd know what the place looked like. Unless Sila made a move on someone on campus, where Bay could see, he had no idea who he was hanging out with or getting steamy with in his free time.

It still pissed him off thinking about how August had been allowed to touch him.

He pursed his lips and dashed those thoughts away. These were his students. It was none of his business, no matter how he felt about one of them.

Five years wasn't that much older, but it was still old enough, especially when the fact he was a teacher got brought into the mix. He and Sila were miles apart and only something extreme would be able to change that.

"Or fear," Bay replied, forcing himself out of his head. "Could be they're after a relationship with the other person but don't know how to properly express their feelings, or perhaps they were already in one, got dumped, and now want an apology. The point is there are many reasons for someone to act this way. Like most other things in the universe, no two events are exactly alike, it's all circumstantial. What I can teach you is how to navigate through these events to help you potentially spot the red flags that can tip you off."

Sila raised his hand and Bay hesitated for only a split second before nodding at him to proceed. "Are you talking about antisocial personality disorder? Is that one of the reasons?"

"It can be. Though I urge everyone here to remember not to vilify an entire group of people. Many who are diagnosed with APD get the help they need and are upstanding members of society."

"And the ones that aren't?" Sila held his gaze. "What about psychopaths? Do you believe most of them get the help they're required as well? What if they don't want it?"

That was an odd turn to take the conversation and, before he could help it, Bay's brow was furrowing slightly. "I'm afraid that's another topic for a different class. For now, let's keep focused on stalking, shall we?"

"Of course." Sila twirled the stylus in his left hand. "I read that stalking can come from an illusion of love. I understand you've just pointed out there are many different reasons, but would you say that's the most common case?"

"Yes." Bay was good at keeping his composure, so even though inside he felt a tingle of concern, he was confident he gave nothing away. "Oftentimes, a person can become obsessed with someone to the extent they can even make themselves believe there's more to the relationship than there really is. This is known as erotomania." He clicked a button and a new slide with the name appeared on the projection screen. "This is also a subtype of a delusional disorder, wherein a person believes wholeheartedly that they're in a romantic relationship with someone whom they've typically not had very much interaction with."

He'd planned on going more in-depth on that one in the next class and, though he'd allowed things to deviate, he pointedly returned to the first slide. "More on that later though. For now, we'll be discussing intimacy seekers."

Sila nodded and then went back to taking notes, his attention leaving Bay as quickly as he'd given it. But that was because he'd merely been curious about the topic and, now that his questions had been answered, that was that.

Stalking was an interesting and relatable subject, after all. Everyone was obsessed with something.

"Intimacy seeking stalkers tend to experience intense bouts of loneliness. They latch onto a person and attempt to establish some sort of intimate relationship with them in the hopes to finally have a connection. Some believe their victims either do, or will eventually, love them back. These types of stalkers tend to live alone and don't have any close relatives or friends. They turn to stalking in a poor attempt to heal themselves."

"What about specific behavioral management techniques?" Sila asked then, catching Bay momentarily off guard. He'd thought for sure Sila was done engaging. He didn't typically. Usually quiet throughout the entire class, only making a sound once it was over and he could leave laughing with his friends.

"Those differ from person to person, case to case, as well, don't they?" Sila continued when Bay hadn't spoken fast enough for his liking.

"Well, yes. For some, those help to curb the urges. They can subdue the offender's habits and prevent them from acting on any of their untoward thoughts."

"But they don't always last, do they?" Sila tipped his head. "It's sort of like putting a Band-Aid on a bullet wound, don't you think, Professor? Eventually, whatever avoidance tactic they're using is going to stop working and they'll be pushed into a corner where the only option left to them is to act."

"I..." He swallowed the sudden lump in his throat and shook his head. "They aren't avoidance tactics, Mr. Varun. They're tools, just like anything else."

Bay's were his visits to the Seaside Cinema. He glanced away, pretending to sweep his gaze over the class. "It differs on a planet-to-planet basis, of course, but what matters to the law here on Vitality is that a person is at least seeking help."

"Even if it won't last?" Sila asked.

He hadn't expected this portion of the course load to go without a hitch when he'd written up the syllabus, but Bay hadn't anticipated this level of interest from his object of desire either. He'd thought he would be the one making things uncomfortable for himself, too in his head as he explained stalking and the various reasons a person turned to that extreme.

But...

"You don't think people who suffer from obsessive love disorder can be fixed?" It was out before he could stop himself.

"Is that what it is?" Sila's curious expression never altered, but there was a strange note in his tone that couldn't be placed. "I was thinking predatory stalking, but now that you mention it, that's far too intense, isn't it?"

Bay frowned. "I'm not sure what you're referring to."

"Yo," Riel slapped Sila on the side of the arm, "dude, are you being stalked?"

Sila laughed. "Of course not. This is all hypothetical," he returned his gaze to Bay, "Isn't it, Professor?"

"Yes," he nodded. "Yes, as I've said it's all case by case, so anything we discuss here on the subject —on any subjects throughout the semester—will involve many hypothetical situations to better explain the nuances of these issues."

"You keep saying things like that." Sila propped his elbows on his desk and leaned forward. "Do you think these people are broken, Professor?"

"Don't be absurd," Bay gave an awkward chuckle. "People with conditions like the one I just mentioned—"

"Obsessive love disorder," Sila provided.

"Yes, exactly, like that one." Would this conversation never end? "People with conditions like that have been medically diagnosed. It's improper to use words like broken. They have—"

"Conditions and disorders," a thread of distaste entered Sila's voice, causing Bay's eyes to widen slightly. "What you're really telling us is some people are different from the majority. Their brain chemistry is different—they think differently, and thus their actions and reactions are different from the average persons. But different doesn't necessarily mean bad."

"We were discussing stalking specifically," Bay reminded, but even he knew he was losing his grip now, his words coming out nervous. "Most stalkers end up harming their victims. You're misunderstanding me, Sila. I'm not saying people with mental disorders are all bad by nature, I'm merely suggesting that anyone who poses a danger to another living being would be considered a criminal. We're all responsible for our actions. Some choose to seek help the second they receive a diagnosis, while others—"

"Opt not to be fixed?" Sila interrupted.

"One step at a time," he said, making sure

to keep his posture straight to better establish a sense of authority. "We'll learn about stalking first and then branch out into other topics, as you've guessed."

"What's to learn?" Jol, a female student over by the window asked. "Isn't stalking pretty self-explanatory? Someone follows someone else around without consent. The end. Just a bunch of unstable creeps who throw tantrums when they don't get their way and don't understand the word no."

"Most stalkers are intelligent, actually," Sila stated before Bay had the chance. "Sure, many fall under the sociopathic or narcissistic labels, but not all stalkers are like that either. For many, a lack of decent social skills which makes communicating difficult is what causes them to lurk on the sidelines. I'm willing to bet most of us have experienced being awkward around someone or someones."

"Right, like that time you tried hitting on Feh Strong," Riel said, pointing at Jol.

Bay didn't know anything about that, but from the way other students laughed and pretended not to, it was obviously well known amongst their peers.

"Whatever. I don't know how it is on your home world, Varun, but here stalking is a crime.," Jol stated.

"Did I miss the part where he mentioned it wasn't? Are you two arguing?" Riel asked. "I can't even tell. Or, is this flirting?"

Jol rolled her eyes and closed the digital text book file. "Please. Everyone knows Sila is gay."

"Do I sense a bit of disappointment?" Riel teased.

"This is Vitality," Sila said, turning his head to catch Jol's eye with a smile. "And we're currently attending a school that literally has 'Mind the Brumal' in their official acceptance letter. How many criminals on this planet do you actually believe get punished for their actions?"

The entire class grew quiet at that, probably because none of them could say anything.

There's was a planet ruled by both an Imperial family and the Brumal Mafia. Though the Emperor was the official leader of their world, it was no secret that the head of the Brumal also had a hand in all things of great importance. They worked in tandem, the Diars and the Voids partners in, well, crime.

Sila chuckled and faced forward once more, catching Bay's gaze. "Is that why you're teaching us about the dangers of stalkers, Professor? So we know how to protect ourselves in a time of crisis?"

"You're insinuating we can't rely on our monarchy to protect us," Opal, another female student sitting directly behind Sila said, though by the way she spoke softly, it was clear she was merely trying to look out for him. "That could be considered treason."

"She's right," Riel agreed. "Remember, it's

not just the Brumal you have to watch out for on campus. A couple members of the Imperial Prince's Retinue also attend Vail. None of those guys need an excuse to pick on someone—"

Opal cleared her throat loudly and glared at him.

Riel held up his hands and left it at that.

"Thanks," Sila told them. "I'll be careful."

The bell rang then, putting an end to what had to have been the most uncomfortable class Bay had ever had the misfortune of teaching.

He'd loved every second of it for that very reason.

Sick.

But being twisted was better than being empty.

"Everyone is required to complete the homework assignment," he announced as they started gathering their things. "Just because we didn't get around to going through the official list of stalkers doesn't mean you're off the hook. There are several types and I expect you all to list each and every one with a brief description."

Some of the students gave him verbal confirmation they'd heard while others merely nodded and left as quickly as they could.

Sila lingered a little longer, taking his time to put his things in his bag while Riel and Jol waited for him.

"What the hell was that, J?" Riel asked, shoving his hands into the pockets of his black jeans and rocking on his heels. Riel always seemed to have too much energy for his body to contain.

"Just keeping things interesting." She winked at Sila who offered her a friendly smile that had Bay's heart pattering in his chest.

He'd seen the three of them hanging out around campus all semester, but their little display just now was odd by Bay's standards. Did friends tease each other like that nowadays? Was causing a scene in class the cool thing to do?

"Speaking of," she rested a hand on Sila's shoulder. "Please tell me you ditched the jerk last night."

"You swore up and down you would," Riel pointed at him and reminded sternly.

Sila winced and swung the strap of his bag over his left shoulder. "I did. He didn't take it well but that was to be expected, right?"

"Lan Avel is an asshole," Jol practically snarled.

"Plus he's the cousin of Haroon, the guy who leads the Shepards?" Riel gave a mock shiver. "Hell no."

"They're all Brumal wannabes," Jol said. "I can't believe you gave him a chance in the first place. Like, how dare he try to drug you?"

Bay's ears perked and he went still.

"Hey," Riel whisper-scolded, motioning over to where Bay was standing at the front of the class, as though to remind her there was an authority figure in the room with them.

"Someone tried to take advantage of you?" Bay asked, harsh tone cutting across the now empty classroom. They were the only four left in it, but he didn't pay the other two any mind, all his attention locked on Sila, trying to read his reactions. He'd gathered from all his observation that while Sila liked to come off as open and friendly to the rest of the world, he was actually rather reserved when it came to any true emotion he may or may not be feeling.

Bay guessed he'd been hurt by someone in the past, which would also explain why he seemed drawn to these incompetent jerks. And another Shepard at that?

If he was going to be with a bad person, he may as well be with Bay, right?

He shouldn't be thinking things like that, but the ship had sailed, so to speak, and there was nothing left to do but go with the flow.

"It's no big deal, Professor." Sila shrugged. "He wasn't successful, and anyway, I ended things with him."

"With Lan Avel?" Bay repeated, mentally noting down the name. Coincidentally, Bay taught him as well. He had class with him tomorrow, in fact. That gave him enough time to contact Lan and let him know he wanted to see him in his office bright and early.

Looked like that vial he'd gotten from Berga was going to come in handy sooner rather than later.

"Do you know him, Professor?" Jol asked.

"Don't ask him that," Sila said before Bay could reply. "Ignore her, Professor. And don't worry about me. I can take care of myself."

"Of course." Bay forced himself to nod. "But if you ever need help—"

"Thanks," he cut him off and made his way toward the exit. "I'll take you up on that offer eventually."

"Bye, Professor Delmar." Jol bowed and then took off after him, Riel following suit.

They passed Castle Stin, another professor, on their way out. The man held the door for them and then entered with a smile.

"What can I do for you, Professor?" Bay kept his voice clipped and collected his things. He was done with classes for the day and though he'd considered hanging around to grade papers, now that Castle was here, he was going to have to make a quick getaway.

"I was hoping you'd have time to grab drinks after work," Castle said brightly. "I know this great place nearby, perfect for unwinding after an arduous week teaching these spoiled monsters—oh, sorry," he laughed at his own comment, "I forgot that you're close in age to them."

Which was why Bay had no interest in whatever Castle kept trying to sell him. Castle wasn't necessarily old, only in his mid-fifties, but compared to Bay's twenty-five...

Prior to meeting Sila, it'd mostly been a mild

annoyance. Bay would sometimes feel it when Castle tried hitting on him, but more often than not, it did nothing for him at all. The older man may as well be a wall for all the effect he'd had on Bay. After Sila though, it seemed like he was more in tune with his emotional self, feeling things he hadn't in a long time.

He'd like it if someone took care of Castle the same way Bay planned on dealing with the Shepard who'd taken advantage of Sila.

If only there was a way to make that happen.

"Sorry, I already have plans." Like planning what excuse he was going to give to Lan for calling him in for a meeting. He couldn't exactly tell the student he'd merely wanted to serve him poisoned tea.

"You said that last time," he pouted. Actually pouted. Gross. "Come on, it'll be fun."

Bay inhaled slowly and straightened his shoulders, ready to use the no-nonsense tone he used on his class, but fortunately his multi-slate chimed then, indicating he was receiving a call. "Excuse me I have to take this." He answered as quickly as possible. "Hello?"

"You've been requested," his friend Nate cut straight to the chase. "Odds are in your favor tonight, Pandeveer. You in?"

The official races weren't meant to take place for another two weeks, but he'd been getting called to weekly events more and more frequently. Even though he'd gotten a good enough burst of sensation from his back and forth with Sila during class, one look at Castle had Bay instantly accepting the offer.

"I'm on my way." He hung up and then grabbed his briefcase, bowing lightly to Castle as he headed for the door. "That was my friend asking if I've left yet. Enjoy your drinks, Professor."

With any luck, the older man would choke on them and spare Bay any further tediousness.

CHAPTER 4:

"Hey, have you heard from August?" a girl asked her friend as the two of them passed Sila over the bridge that led from the East Quad.

"No," her friend replied. "He hasn't been in class all week and when I try and call it goes straight to voicemail."

"I heard his parents filed a missing person's report this morning."

"Seriously?!"

The two moved out of Sila's earshot so he wasn't able to catch the rest of their conversation, but he hummed to himself as he moved across the wooden planks, entering the quad they'd just vacated. Unlike the girls, he wasn't curious about what had happened to August, but that was because he'd bugged Bay's office.

After he'd tossed the bait about August mistreating him, he'd overheard a conversation between Bay and the other student which had taken place the next day. The talk itself had been innocent enough, with Bay even going so far as to ask if August wanted to become his TA for the semester. It was the offer of tea that had tipped Sila off to what was really going on.

Berga had been in there the day before and he and Bay had also had a rather interesting discussion. Apparently, the Brumal member was working on perfecting a more potent batch of Abundance, a strong drug that made someone act aggressive before they eventually passed out.

Bay had made sure to shoo August out of his office before that part of the effects could set in, but August had stumbled out into the hallway shaking his head as though to wake himself from a stupor, a clear indicator he'd consumed the stuff.

Their stalker was crafty and a bit obsessive.

Sila kind of liked that.

Though, he'd gone after the Shepards for a reason, and this was proof he'd been correct when choosing his targets. Bay used to live in a nice house, but that home was currently occupied by the highest-ranking gang members. Apparently, Idle Delmar had a gambling problem which had led to her losing everything.

A little extra digging had uncovered that, at least initially, Bay hadn't believed that and had tried to fight with Haroon Caddel, the leader of the Shepards, but the legal battle had gone nowhere.

It wouldn't have. Haroon may be a member of an unimportant group, but the Caddel's still had a small hand in the proverbial cookie jar. His uncle was a judge and had paid off the lawyer Bay had hired. Guess there was a reason Haroon had turned to forming a gang and becoming a criminal instead of doing something upright with his life.

Being a shitty person must run in the family.

Sila passed beneath a row of lightning oaks, tall trees with neon yellow leaves that rattled in the breeze, and caught sight of Rabbit sitting alone at one of the tables within the gazebos that made up the East Quad.

Rabbit was too busy typing away on his tablet to notice Sila's approach and he read a few lines of the report over the older guy's shoulders quickly.

"You're still doing this?" He slipped onto the empty bench seat across from Rabbit. He'd heard about the group assignment his friend had been given in one of his classes and from the looks of things—i.e., him here alone—the rest of his team had ditched early.

Last year, this had been a frequent occurrence and Sila found himself uncharacteristically annoyed on someone else's behalf.

Rabbit was popular, but friendless, and while he was cold and aloof, there was a hidden softness to him that called to Sila's darker nature. Only, not in the way it should. In the grand scheme of things, Rabbit Trace was obsolete, but that didn't mean Sila didn't enjoy his company now and again.

"I'm bored," Sila said. "Let's get out of here and find something fun to do." It was an empty suggestion. Their definitions of fun were no doubt vastly different from one another and something told him Rabbit wouldn't be up for the sorts of things Sila was into.

"I have practice after this." Rabbit went back to typing on his holopad and Sila sighed.

"Again?"

"Of course."

"Don't you find it draining?" Sila understood what it was like to be tied to something, it was why he couldn't go longer than three days without getting in the water. But Rabbit didn't need to know about the things they had in common and, unlike Sila, Trace wasn't good at managing his time or compartmentalizing.

Would Sila like to jump into a pool and stay there forever? Yes. Would he? Absolutely fucking not. What a waste of life.

"No," Rabbit lied without blinking.

To keep himself from smirking at that, Sila rolled his eyes. "You've got to get out more, Rabbit. Live a little. Oh." He propped his elbows on the table. "How'd last night go? You had your redo date, right?"

His suggestion to Arlet had gone as expected and she'd spoken with her father to arrange a meeting for her. Apparently, their first date hadn't gone very well, but they'd given it another shot and Sila was a bit curious to know how things had gone for them.

That spark of interest died a swift death,

however, when he caught sight of Bay watching from afar.

The professor was standing on one of the wooden walkways closer to the entrance of the quad, pretending to scroll through something on his multi-slate. It was clear he was actually sneaking glimpses of Sila though.

He'd tested his theory out again the other day by mentioning Lan Avel and, sure enough, this morning he'd caught sight of the other student leaving Bay's office in much the same state August had. Now there was only one question left, and that was to find out whether Sila's involvement with these particular Shepards was what had Bay acting up.

There was always the chance it was purely coincidence, since clearly Bay hated anyone that had anything to do with the gang. That was going to be a little more difficult to figure out, so he needed to switch things up a bit and instead of claim he was dating losers, target someone timid instead.

A freshman walked past then, someone Sila had spoken to a handful of times with little conviction. Good enough.

"Hold that thought," he told Rabbit before he stood and headed after the freshman. He made it to the table the black-haired kid had selected a moment after him, plastering a flirtatious smile onto his face as he eased into the seat across from him. "Hey, Noah, what's up?"

"Oh," Noah batted his long lashes at him and nervously tucked a strand of that long curly hair behind an ear, "Hi. Are you having lunch?"

"I haven't yet," Sila tipped his head suggestively, "Why? Want to get some with me?"

From the corner of his eye checked to make sure Bay was still standing there, internally preening when he saw that he was. This whole show was for the professor, after all. It'd be tediously annoying if the man had left before Sila could get to the good parts.

He'd flirt with the freshman and see if it made Bay jealous, then give it a couple of days, maybe a week. Bay taught two freshmen classes, and Sila knew for a fact that Noah was in one of them. If Noah wasn't called into his office in that timeframe, then it would seem most likely that Bay only targeted the Shepards that Sila claimed harmed him.

If this part of the experiment went without a hitch, then Sila would complain about something Noah had done in front of Bay. Ideally, the professor would summon Noah then and slip him Abundance like he had both August and Lan.

Aside from the single attempt to prove his grandmother's innocence, Bay hadn't done anything else against the Shepards. It seemed like he'd either lost faith in his grandmother or given up. His attraction to Sila was enough to spur him back into action, however, fan those flames back to life within him. That was good. That's what Sila needed.

When he was ready to finally strike, he wanted to be sure the hidden ace up his sleeve would do what it was supposed to.

"I actually ate already," Noah said, sounding disappointed before quickly adding, "But I could go with you to the cafeteria!"

"No, it's fine," Sila waved him off, keeping the friendly smile in place. "I'm not even hungry. What are you working on?"

"We were assigned a paper on pandaveers in zoology." Noah frowned when that made Sila laugh. "What?"

"No, nothing." He shook his head. "I just happen to like those. If you want help—" Before he could finish his sentence, someone was hoisting him out of the bench and shoving him back against the thick wooden beam that held up the roof of the gazebo.

Since Bay would never handle him that way, Sila already knew it wasn't the professor losing to his secret jealous nature before he even lifted his head to rest his gaze on his accoster.

A man practically as tall as he was held him by the collar. He wasn't dressed in a school uniform, sporting a crimson corset vest beneath his suit.

Fancy.

Though they'd never interacted before, Kelevra Diar was recognizable, not only because he was the Imperial Prince of Vitality, but because he also happened to be a senior at the Academy. It was rare to find him on this side of town, and on campus no less.

Sila didn't bother trying to pull away, resting back against the beam as he waited patiently for things to play out. He'd spotted Baikal Void with Rabbit earlier and knew the Brumal Prince wouldn't stand still if Kelevra tried anything funny in his territory, so there was no real worry there.

Not that Sila was opposed to trying his hand against an Imperial like Diar. It could be fun even. Maybe—

Kelevra blinked, as if seeing him for the first time and stated plainly, "You're not my flower."

He'd mistaken Sila for his brother. Which meant he'd come here with the intention of attacking him like he'd just done…It was one thing to mess around with him, but no one touched his twin.

He was in the process of considering the best way to disarm Kelevra in front of all these witnesses when suddenly his brother arrived, shoving the Imperial away before taking the spot between them.

"What the actual fuck do you think you're doing?" Rin asked.

For a split second, Sila thought the growled words were aimed at him, despite the fact his brother kept his back toward him, but then he realized he was speaking to the Imperial.

That was...Interesting. And bold. Typically, people tiptoed around Kelevra and his Retinue. He'd just heard about their situation, but he wouldn't have guessed the chemistry was real between them. Observing them now, it was impossible to miss.

Kelevra slipped his hands into the front pockets of his crimson dress pants and glanced between the two of them, gaze lingering a little longer than Sila would have liked, though he was careful to keep his expression impassive.

This wasn't his problem, it was his brother's, and as per the rules, he would only involve himself if absolutely necessary.

Actually, the fact Kelevra had thrown him around thinking he was his brother was kind of funny when he thought about it again. Sila may be the more destructive of the two, but Rin was the most volatile.

He smirked behind his brother's back, thinking of how pissed off he probably was and how that was going to bite the Imperial in the ass.

"He's not you," Kelevra said then.

Like a fucking genius.

Real observant this one.

"Who's to say," Sila couldn't help but taunt, schooling his features the second his brother started to turn so the expression was gone before he could get caught. "I was minding my business, I swear."

"Really?" Rin lifted a brow. "Is that why I

showed up to find you about to—"

"I kept my manners." In the distance, he saw Bay was still watching and internally bristled. For a second, he'd forgotten all about the professor and his intentions with this little scene. While he wanted to stir things up for Bay, involving him with an Imperial Prince wasn't on the to-do list.

That wasn't even what bothered him the most though. For some reason he wasn't too fond of the idea of Bay looking at both he and his brother together.

Would the professor compare them? Try to search for tells that didn't exist?

Well, obviously there were some since Kelevra-Fucking-Observant-Diar had caught on, but still. Up until now, no one had ever been able to tell them apart. Getting his hopes up that Bay somehow could would not only be a waste of energy, it'd be pathetic on top of it.

The two of them had continued talking during his distraction, but Sila caught onto the end of an innuendo spoken by Kelevra. Maybe if he pushed his brother past his breaking point, they'd leave and he could get back to work.

The Imperial Prince had suggested he and Rin had shared a lot.

Sila leaned forward. "Do body fluids count now?"

"No," his brother stated, leaving little room for argument.

When it came to sexual relations, the two of

them were complete opposites. He'd never admit it to anyone else, but his brother got off on the idea of losing control in the bedroom, which was something that made Sila's skin crawl just thinking about.

To his brother, control was a necessary part of their existence.

To Sila, it *was* their existence. Without control, life would be tedious and dull—more so than it already was. There were very few things that kept his interest, no spark that urged him to get out of bed in the morning. There was only the notion that he was better than everyone else and the way he secretly messed with them to prove it.

Sometimes, when the boredom struck particularly hard, he did wish there was an opponent out there capable of keeping his interest in the long term, but experience had mostly dashed that hope. When it came to selecting prey, the requirements were minimal. Anyone he could momentarily fixate on would do. Choosing a competitor was different, more complex. They'd need to be someone who could challenge him, for one. Someone with above average intelligence. Someone observant.

Someone depraved enough not to fear the shadows Sila lived in.

Most importantly, it had to be someone who could give him a run for his money. Considering he was perfect and that was rare?

He wasn't holding his breath, although…

the Devils of Vitality could provide some entertainment and may meet his conditions. Too bad his brother was so against Sila testing them out.

Baikal Void joined their little ragtag gang then and Sila kept his expression blank, even though on the inside he felt his irritation yawn dangerously.

Though he'd been eager for an opportunity to try his hand against them, he wasn't in the mood to play with the Devils of Vitality at the moment.

Sila understood better than most that just because Bay secretly spied on him, it didn't mean he was the most important thing in the guy's orbit. That was why he'd needed to delve deeper into Bay's life, pick it apart to find a better angle he could use if the professor's physical attraction to him wasn't enough to have him lapping from the palm of his hand.

Baikal and Kelevra exchanged mild pleasantries, but Sila didn't bother paying attention until his brother raised his voice. Whatever they'd been saying, it'd bothered him.

The last thing they needed was for Rin to openly pick a fight with the Devils.

"I'm here," Sila placed a comforting hand on his brother's shoulder and leaned in to whisper low enough their company wouldn't be able to catch the words. "But you and I in the same place is drawing notice."

The two of them shared an apartment in the city close to campus, though it was technically under Sila Varun's name, since Rin had a dorm at the Academy like most other cadets. Though they didn't hide the fact they were identical twins from anyone, they also tried their best not to hang out together on Vail or Academy grounds. It was much easier to establish their own personalities and lives that way, easier for others to see them as separate beings as well.

Their survival depended on that.

Although, since his brother had attracted the Imperial Prince, things might be changing for them soon. One of the rules was they avoided the Devils, which was why Sila had been forced to keep his distance despite the fact they'd make such fun playmates. Since his brother was the one who broke the rule...They should use this to their advantage.

"Does sex on this planet constitute as a claim?" he asked. It was obvious Kelevra thought so, since he'd come all the way here to hunt Rin down. Subtly reminding his brother of the now broken rule was a good way to push him in the right direction—aka, leaving and taking the Devils with him so Sila could get back to plotting.

"No, it does not." His brother glared at him in warning, knowing exactly what he was up to.

The problem with having lived in each other's skin for so long was there was no way to pull a fast one on the other.

Suddenly, Kelevra's hand was on Rin's arm, and without thinking Sila reacted to the threat, grabbing onto him in turn. Allowing them to figure their shit out and air their dirty laundry was one thing, but if the Imperial Prince posed any true threat to them, Sila wouldn't stand still.

"I know you're secretly into this sort of thing," Sila said in a low voice, opting to use the language only the two of them knew so no one else would be able to understand him, "but tell me now if you'd like for me to end it for you. Do you have this, brother, or is he a threat to us? If so—"

"No," Rin cut him off, but didn't use their personal language to do so, further proving to Sila that his words were true and he believed them. He carefully removed Sila's hand off of Kelevra's sleeve, but didn't shake the Imperial loose, another silent indicator he wanted his brother to listen. "No, I'll handle it."

The language was something they'd come up with one summer out of sheer boredom more than anything. A way they could talk openly about the people around them without worry about accidentally letting their real identities slip if they happened to have switched places that day. Now that they were so far from home, they didn't resort to it often, but not bothering with it now was also a veiled message in and of itself.

Rin really believed he could handle this.

So Sila would stand down and not stomp on his toes.

"Are you sure?" The need to protect them was gone now and Sila stepped back and leaned against the wooden beam, giving his brother the space he wanted despite his teasing words. "Shouldn't I play the part of big brother?"

Sila Varun had been born only a few minutes before Rin Varun, something that hadn't mattered on their home planet. But here on Vitality, where age helped determine hierarchy, it was an ongoing joke they liked to torment each other with. Only, this time his brother didn't seem amused.

Interesting.

"You should jump off this pathway, stick your face in the water, and not come back up," Rin snapped.

If he was thinking about murder so openly, the Imperial Prince must be affecting him more than he wanted to admit.

His brother sighed. "I'm fine. I can handle this."

Kelevra laughed.

Out of the corner of his eye, Sila caught sight of Bay turning on his heel and disappearing down the walkway. He was contemplating challenging the Devils after all, since they'd so rudely chased off his prey, but his brother left with the Imperial before he got the chance.

"You should warn him against getting involved with someone like Kelevra," Baikal said, watching as Rin dragged Kel down the wooden planks of the pathway leading to the library.

"We can take care of ourselves," Sila stated, keeping his expression blank when that earned him a look from the Brumal Prince. They stared each other down for a tense moment and he was the one to finally break it, forcing a friendly smile to stretch across his face. "Actually, it's good you're here. I was just trying to get Rabbit to go out for some fun."

The spot above Baikal's let eye twitched. "I'll be handling all of his fun from now on."

"Jealous?" Sila threw up his hands in mock surrender, still keeping that fake smile in place. "We're just friends."

It seemed like there was something else Baikal wanted to say, but at the last minute he changed his mind. Giving a single curt nod—like a prince certain his decree would be met without fail—he turned and headed back toward the far end of the quad where a nervous Rabbit was closely watching and waiting.

Sila only barely resisted the urge to roll his eyes at the display of alpha-bullshit.

Yes, one day he was going to have to test himself against the other Devils, just for the hell of it. If they were lucky, he might even let them see him coming first.

Depended on his mood, really.

CHAPTER 5:

Bay was several minutes late to his coffee meeting with Nate because that grimy Castle had tried stopping him from leaving the school. It was starting to fray his last nerve that the older guy couldn't take no for an answer and, after today's little stunt, he was seriously considering escalating things to the headmaster.

But first.

"One large vanilla, butterscotch latte, please," Bay said as soon as he was up at the counter. He turned his multi-slate to scan the screen across the pay-pad and then glanced around the shop, catching sight of Nate at the corner table by the windows.

Nate was his contact with those in charge of the races, but Bay hadn't ever asked him how he'd gotten himself involved with that sort of crowd. The two of them had attended Vail University at the same time, though Nate was three years his junior. He'd been the one to introduce Bay to the racing scene in the first place, and had helped convince his grandmother to up his monthly allowance when he'd been secretly saving to purchase his first hoverbike.

The two of them were closer than Bay was with Berga and Flix, but that wasn't saying much when this was the first hangout they were having outside of the races in...probably all year, actually.

In the beginning, when Bay had cut himself off from the world and gone numb, Nate had tried his best to first be supportive and then to drag him out of that empty abyss. He hadn't been successful, obviously, and eventually their friendship had altered to fit the new, emotionless, robotic Bay. The only time he was like his old self was when he was riding, which was probably why Nate had put so much effort into boosting his reputation.

It was kind and, now that some of his old emotions had been unlocked again, Bay admittedly felt a pang of guilt when he thought about it. Nate was trying to be a good friend. If only he knew the secret game Bay played with himself. If one day his luck ran out and he lost, would Nate blame himself when Bay's body was discovered floating down the river?

Bay had just taken his cup and thanked the barista a second time when his multi-slate chimed, giving him pause on his way over to the table his friend was at. His brow furrowed when he read the unknown number and then he sucked in a sharp breath when he scanned the actual message itself.

Unknown: Did you like the flowers? I picked

that trick up from someone recently, but I'll be honest, I don't really see the appeal. How does gifting a dying plant say 'I like you'?

He set his cup down on the nearest table and was already typing back before he knew it.

Bay: Who is this? How did you get this number?

It'd been over a month since the first flower had been left for him and he'd started to think that maybe that would be the extent of it, that whoever was leaving them would end it there.

Unknown: It's not hard to track you down, Kitten. Speaking of which...Doesn't seem like your date got you any flowers. Should I scold him on your behalf?

Bay's head snapped up and he searched for any sign of who was texting him, but aside from the two workers behind the counter and one girl who was busily typing away on her multi-slate, there was no one else around. He couldn't see any strange characters standing outside peering in through the large wall of windows that made up the front of the shop either.

Bay: Are you stalking me?

Unknown: Let's not be boring. Don't waste energy asking questions like that. You've known I've been watching for a while now.

Bay: I knew you were leaving me flowers. That doesn't mean I thought you were following me around like a freak!

Unknown: Takes one to know one, baby.

He stiffened, unable to tear his eyes off that last message.

His blood ran cold and he stiffened, unable to tear his eyes off that last message.

Unknown: What's wrong? Think you're the only one allowed to stalk people, Kitten? You can dish it out but can't handle being served?

This person knew about Sila. They knew that Bay had a crush on a student and that he— He forced himself to breathe and carefully picked up his coffee, sipping at it to give himself another moment to collect himself. When the hot liquid burned his tongue, he actually welcomed it, that sting of pain helping to clear his head. He was careful, however, not to allow that to show.

Bay had never been averse to pain, but that was another secret, and one he wanted to keep from whomever it was currently watching him. It was creepier knowing that someone out there had their eyes on him right now and yet, he couldn't find any clue of their whereabouts. It should have made his skin crawl.

But it didn't.

A zip raced down his spine, the familiar rush of adrenaline, something he typically only experienced during a race. Having that reaction now shocked him.

Bay: What do you want?

Unknown: I'm doing what I want right now.

Bay frowned and let out a sigh of exasperation.

Bay: Which is?
Unknown: Hunting.

He shuddered, unable to catch himself in time.

Unknown: Oh, do you like that idea, Kitten? Like the thought of me hunting you down and forcing you to be mine for a night?

"Bay?" Nate's voice cut through the tension swirling around Bay and he startled.

Glancing up, he found his friend had come over and was giving him a look of concern. Nate Narek was a lithe twenty-two-year-old with chestnut hair and dark brown eyes. He'd graduated a year ago and had already found work at a company but hated it. Nate was the middle child of three, with his older brother still living on their home planet, Ignite. His sister, Neve, had just graduated from Vail a semester early so wasn't attending this year, but Bay had only met her on a couple of occasions.

He didn't know where their parents were, but he assumed they were no longer in the picture. As someone who lacked parents himself, Bay knew better than to ask and had just left well enough alone.

"You all good?" Nate was still frowning at him.

"Yes." Bay tapped his multi-slate so the screen would turn black and then forced himself to smile. "Work."

"Gods, tell me about it."

As he'd hoped, it distracted Nate, who launched into an in-depth complaint about a new employee at his company who was driving him nuts as they made their way to the table he'd selected.

"The owners are selling too." Nate dropped down into his plastic chair with more oomph than necessary. "They claim our jobs are all safe and we'll be transferred over along with everything else, but would you trust that?"

Bay shook his head.

"Exactly." He crossed his arms and made an expression that could only be described as a pout. "Maybe this is a sign, you know? Maybe the universe is telling us to finally ditch our shitty jobs and do what we actually enjoy."

"How did I get pulled into this?" Bay took another sip of his latte, but it'd cooled enough there was no burn this time. He tried not to feel disappointed by that fact, or the fact that he hadn't received any more messages from Unknown, despite not having answered his last text.

"Come on, all throughout school you kept saying how you didn't want to be a professor," Nate motioned to his pressed white button up and black slacks, "Look at you now."

"It's not all bad."

"You hate it."

"I'd have to care enough for that." And he didn't.

"Be honest with me," Nate said, growing

serious, "If you didn't have racing, would there be anything left that you do care about?"

"Can we not do this again?" He appreciated how much Nate tried to look out for him, but he'd liked the reprieve from his nagging. "What made you bring this up, anyway?"

"You know how I was dating that Academy student?"

"Mercer Blakely," Bay nodded. "Yeah. You were together for like two years."

"He graduated but opted to stick around instead of sign the oath to give up loyalties to his home world," Nate said. "He works at the Inner City precinct."

"I'm not sure why you're telling me this?"

"We're still close, broke up amicably. When we graduated, I asked if he could do me a favor and keep his eye on your grandmother's case. Since it was a closed case no one cared about, he wouldn't get in trouble for it so he agreed. Well, apparently someone checked on the file."

Bay straightened in his seat. "Who?"

"Don't know. They never entered the building."

"Someone hacked the system?" That type of criminal behavior could only come from someone confident enough they'd be able to get away with it. Someone who either was or had Brumal or Imperial backing. Or…

"The Shepards might have," Nate suggested. "I can't think of a reason why, but word on the street is their members have been turning up dead. It's been kept out of the media because some of the deaths have been linked to Baikal Void—allegedly—but, what if something shook Haroon up and the guy got spooked?"

Nate and Berga were the only two people who'd believed Bay when he'd said his grandmother would never gamble. They'd known her, had come over for study sessions and stayed for dinner most nights. Idle was a warm and welcoming host, always opening her door for Bay's classmates without question.

"I know you gave up after the lawyers told you it was a lost cause, but if something is going on, I wanted to let you know. Just in case."

Bay'd gone to bed the night he'd discovered there was literally nothing more he could do and he'd have to vacate his home. And woken the next day a different person.

He'd needed sleeping pills to fall asleep due to the level of anxiety he'd been feeling, but upon waking…Nothing. That'd been the start of the desensitized version of himself that he still was today. It'd been as though the part of his brain that controlled emotions had simply flicked off like a light switch.

For a while, that had been a blessing, but pretty soon he'd realized it meant life was dull and without the ability to feel happiness or even pain, there was nothing for him to look forward to or stick around for.

Racing, Sila, and videos from the Seaside Cinema lit that spark for him, but it never lasted, always fading back until he was left in that emptiness all over again.

That was why his choice in porn had gotten more and more twisted and dramatic over the past couple of months. It seemed like in order to achieve peak pleasure, Bay needed more than simply a photograph of Sila and mildly aggressive fucking playing on a big screen. The darker the movie the better and he kept choosing worse and worse ones, things that would send his grandmother screaming into the night if she were alive and found out.

Her grandson was a freak who liked to fantasize about being tied up and beaten until red and raw and bloody.

He dreamed of being owned, because then whether he lived or died, the choice would be out of his hands. Someone else could make that decision for him, and the thought of that was such a huge relief that it actually made him hard sometimes just thinking about it.

Which made him feel like a monster.

He was too busy to advocate for his grandmother and her innocence, but not too busy to stroke his dick to photographs of one of his students while male strangers hunted each other in the woods on screen.

If Idle Delmar hadn't been cremated, she'd be rolling in her grave.

The lawyer he'd hired right after learning that his grandmother's belongings had been given away had come back not a day later and told him in no uncertain terms that everything the other party had was legitimate. Apparently, Bay's grandma had gotten into gambling while he'd been at school and had lost her small fortune as well as the three story house she'd raised him in.

Setting aside the fact she wasn't that type of person, the money at least Bay might be able to believe, but the house? That house had been in the Delmar family for generations. Even though there'd been no blood between them, Idle had taken great pains to ensure Bay knew about how every nick and scuff mark in that place had been created and exactly what family member had done the deed.

She would have rather sold her soul to the devil himself than sign away a single doily in that house.

But her thumb print had been on the digital paperwork and her signature had been right there in black and white next to it. Even though he'd been officially adopted and was considered her heir, legally there'd been nothing Bay could do to stop from being booted from his home with nothing to his name but a few thousand coin and the bike he'd left at Nate's. He'd used the money on the only place he could afford, a rundown single story unwanted house on the bad side of town.

The first year he'd been busy trying to build

up his bank account enough to be stable, as well as learning the ropes as a professor. There was a big difference between being a student at Vail University and being a teacher there.

He'd bought the new hoverbike before anything, thinking he'd need it to keep racing, to keep chasing that high, the one thing keeping him breathing even though everything else sucked ass. Finally, last year he'd saved enough to purchase an old model hovercar. It'd taken a while, but considering where he'd been left back then, his grandmother would be impressed with how quickly he'd, sort of, bounced back.

There was a roof over his head, he was making good money, and his reputation at the school had been solidified.

Which meant it was time he put in more effort to avenge the one and only person who'd ever truly given a damn about him. And if that meant he could no longer afford those indulgent trips to the Seaside Cinema? So be it.

Sila was the one who deserved thanks for waking him up in that regard as well. The anger Bay had felt learning that he was dating Shepards had rekindled that initial rage when he'd first been told by Haroon his grandmother hadn't cared enough about him not to take shitty risks.

He hadn't yet figured out how he was going to approach things, but taking the Shepards down a peg certainly felt like a good start. It was satisfying, if nothing else. But he couldn't let Nate know about the poisoned tea, which meant they needed to change the topic fast.

"Is this why you asked to meet me?" He tilted his head. "I thought you said you needed my help with something?"

"Oh." Nate leaned back in his chair and ran his fingers through the short hairs at the base of his skull boyishly. Whenever his younger sister was around, he turned into this super intense, serious guy, but if Neve wasn't in viewing range, he came off more like a giant puppy than anything. A comparison he certainly wouldn't appreciate if Bay ever slipped and voiced it out loud. "I forgot. I'm always setting up races for you. Time to return the favor. I've got one scheduled for the end of this week but my opponent pulled out at the last second. No one else is free."

"You want me to race against you?" Bay quirked a brow. "Absolutely not. Have you forgotten what happened the last time?"

"You beat me last time," Nate said. "This time will be different."

"No," Bay shook his head, "it won't."

Nate may have started before him, but Bay had surpassed him in skill and they both knew it. The last time they'd gone up against one another they'd still been juniors in college and, after losing, Nate had thrown a literal fit and ignored Bay for an entire week.

"So I used to be a poor loser," Nate rested his elbows on the edge of the round table, "It's not like you're Mr. Perfect."

Bay was interested in one of his students so, yeah.

"Come on, please. I'll owe you one," Nate pushed.

Bay sighed. "I've got a staff dinner that night I can't miss, it's mandatory."

"Race isn't scheduled till ten," Nate told him expectantly.

"Can I think about it?" He wasn't going to, but there was no way his friend was going to take no for an answer right now. The thing was, Bay couldn't do it. He couldn't do that to Nate. While he was confident he'd beat him a second time, that wasn't a guarantee, and if he lost and followed through with his personal game, Nate really wouldn't ever forgive himself.

That wouldn't be fair. None of this was Nate's fault.

But Bay also wasn't willing to change the rules of his game for him. That risk, the adrenaline he got from knowing if he lost, he'd die, it was too addicting for him to give up. Logically, he understood it'd turned into a fucked-up type of safety net for him, but knowing didn't matter.

"Sure," Nate said. "But you have to say yes. I'm serious. I need you."

Bay smiled and then drank from his cup, this time to help hide his expression.

Nate didn't need him.

No one did.

Hell, he didn't even need himself.

CHAPTER 6:

"Oops, sorry about that," Castle gave him a lopsided grin as his arm brushed up against Bay's chest when he reached for the salt.

For the fourth time.

The fact he'd actually said the word "oops" out loud also made Bay want to roll his eyes and book it, but he settled on adjusting his glasses and sending a responding stern look in his coworker's direction.

Not that it would make a difference. Either Castle was daft or ignoring all of the obvious signs Bay had been sending him for months that he wasn't interested.

"I didn't order this." Castle furrowed his brow at the waiter who was placing a neon blue drink in front of his spot at the table.

"Someone ordered it for you, sir," the waiter explained.

Castle grinned and let out an excited whooping sound before downing have the drink in one go.

If Bay had a say, he would have skipped

out on the annual back to school university staff dinner. It was happening a little late this year, with them already over a month into the semester, but it sadly wasn't something any of the professors at Vail were able to get out of. Even the head of the school, Oh North, was seated on the other side of the large private party room the university had reserved for them.

Star and Moon was a popular restaurant at the heart of the capital city, a bustling and popular location that boasted the best of the best when it came to alcoholic options and authentic Vitality foods.

If only Castle hadn't chosen to sit next to him, then maybe he would have been able to enjoy some of it. Although, probably not. It'd been a while since food, even his favorites, had done anything for Bay. Everything may as well be sawdust in his mouth.

All forty of the professors of the school were in attendance, with four long tables in use between them all. Bay had ended up at the one closest to the door by design, hopeful he could make an appearance, eat, and run. After the first "accidental" bump from Castle, which had resulted in the other man breathing his beer-tainted breath down Bay's neck to "apologize", the food had unfortunately become even more unappealing.

Across from him, Dieter Pax, one of the three science teachers, caught his eye and gave him a supportive smile. Though the two of them weren't close, Bay had spoken with her on occasion and knew from the grapevine that before Castle had set his sights on him, he'd notoriously harassed Dieter.

Bay had tried to figure out how she'd eventually shaken him, but all evidence seemed to point to the fact he'd merely grown tired of trying with her.

Bay hadn't really psychoanalyzed the other guy, not wanting to get any closer to him than he was already forced to be. Besides, he knew better than most that some things simply couldn't be explained or labeled. He wasn't suicidal, but he wasn't opposed to dying. He didn't think about killing himself anymore, but the knowledge that he'd get to if he lost when he was racing was always on the back of his mind when he was speeding down a dark street on his bike.

He'd developed emotional detachment, that was true, but it'd also turned him into a sort of adrenaline junkie. His grandmother's death had broken him and, even though he was aware of that fact, he didn't care enough to try and change anything. For now, chasing the highs he could achieve was all that mattered.

In that respect, wasn't he also a creep, same as Castle?

A number appeared on his multi-slate signaling a call then.

"Unknown caller?" Asa, the math teacher who was seated on Bay's right, asked.

"Yes." Bay hit ignore. "I seem to be getting more and more spam calls as the days go on."

After his coffee with Nate, he'd waited until he'd returned to his car before checking the chat with the stranger who'd contacted him. They hadn't sent anything else after their last message, and Bay hadn't been able to tell if they were waiting for his reply or not. So he'd opted not to send anything at all and delete the whole feed. Were they calling now because he'd ignored them?

"Tell me about it," Asa agreed. "I made the mistake of dropping my info in a lottery draw at Spark Gallery at the beginning of the summer and now I get spam email daily."

"You too?" Dieter made a face. "It's got to be illegal for them to share our info like that, don't you think?"

"Are you interested in art, Bay?" Castle's words slurred when he spoke and his cheeks were starting to turn a bright red. Before Bay could respond, he planted a meaty palm over one of Bay's thighs under the table. "I've got a lot of pieces back at my apartment I'd love to show you."

"No, thank you." Bay removed his hand, pulling away when Castle made a grab for his wrist. He ended up bumping into Asa in the process. "I'm sorry."

"It's fine." Asa was glaring around him at Castle, no doubt having witnessed the whole exchange. Under his breath he whispered, "Someone needs to report that asshole."

"Come on." Castle tossed an arm around Bay's shoulders. "I'll make it worth your while."

Bay's multi-slate went off a second time, the same number as a moment ago and, without thinking he sprung up from his seat. "I have to take this."

He exited the room, removing the earbud from the side of the device so he could answer the call as he did. "Hello?"

"Hey, Kitten," a rich, unfamiliar voice replied.

Bay frowned. "Who is this?"

"Who do you want me to be?"

He headed down the narrow hallway off to the right of the room they were eating in and found a small side room that was left empty just before the bathrooms. There was a small red sofa against the far wall and a mural of a goldfish in a box, but that was it.

"I don't have time for prank calls," Bay said as he entered the room. "If this is a student—"

"Ah," the voice interrupted. "You want me to be a student? That your type, Kitten?"

"Why do you—" Bay paused and considered it, figuring it out a moment later. He made a soft sound of understanding without thinking.

"I'm glad you got the reference," the voice told him. "Pandaveer is a bit too wordy. Not a great pet name. Why'd you choose it? Just because of your speed on the racetrack?"

This person knew who he was and what

he did on the side and every single one of his coworkers were right down the hall...Running a hand through his hair, he nibbled on his bottom lip momentarily as he tried to think of what to do.

"Relax," the voice ordered. "This isn't a threat. That's not why I called."

"Why did you call?" Bay wasn't sure how to proceed. He'd never really bothered planning for what he'd do if he was discovered because he'd figured that would also count as losing his personal game, but now that he was met with that very real possibility, he didn't want to go out that way.

"It looked like you could use the help."

His spine straightened. "You're here? Watching me again?"

Was this another teacher? Only professors of Vail had been in the private room with him. If one of his coworkers knew what he got up to afterhours he was screwed.

"I'm always watching. That should please you, actually. You're about to have company."

"What—" The line went dead before Bay could finish asking what he meant by that and a second later the sound of heavy footfalls had him spinning back toward the doorway. When Castle stumbled in a second later, Bay felt himself go cold.

"There you are." Castle smiled at him and shot forward, grabbing onto Bay's arms with a surprising amount of strength. In the next instant, he had him tossed up against the nearest wall, his muscular form flattening itself over Bay's chest so the scent of alcohol permeated the air he was breathing. "You're such a tease. Going to get you tonight though, I know you want it."

"I do not!" Bay tried shoving him away, but the other man was much larger than he was and his struggles weren't nearly enough to dislodge him. For a flash, he was reminded of the latest porn he'd watched. The script had been written so an older male had tied up a younger one and flogged him, then forced him to take his cock even though he kept saying no. It'd been hot to Bay when he'd been watching it, but that was because he'd been picturing Sila doing those same dirty things to him.

Not Castle.

He'd begun to think he was sick in the head, considering he was into watching people cut each other for pleasure, but guess he still had standards after all. Go figure.

"What the hell is wrong with you?!" he shoved at Castle again. "Help!"

Castle slapped a palm over Bay's mouth hard enough it stung. "Quit it."

When Bay felt something hard bump against his stomach he stilled and, in his messed-up state, Castle misinterpreted his reaction.

"There you go," he chuckled. "I knew you wanted it. Feel that?" He rubbed that bulge against Bay, somehow missing when that caused Bay to literally gag. "I'll give it to you good, baby, just you wait."

Suddenly, the light went off and the sound of a door slamming shut had Bay jumping.

Castle grunted and then his disgusting weight was gone. The sounds of a struggle filled the room, not lasting nearly long enough, before the door was yanked open and Castle's body was tossed out into the hall where it landed in a heap.

He didn't get back up again. Didn't so much as twitch.

The light remained off in the room, keeping things too dark for Bay to see who was there with him and he was too distracted staring at Castle's limp form to notice whoever it was making its way toward him until it was too late.

The person flipped him so he was facing the wall, forcing him back against that hard surface faster than he could blink.

Bay slammed his head back, knocking into the stranger's chin, but he wasn't released.

"Is this how you thank everyone who rescues you, Kitten?" the voice from the phone a minute ago asked.

The sound of it had the fight draining right out of him. Bay dropped his forehead against the cool wall and inhaled and exhaled slowly, the relief palpable. "It's you."

"Eyes closed." The man eased closer, the large palm on his lower back keeping Bay pinned in place against the wall. His heart leapt wildly in his chest, but no matter how scared he was, it was as if he'd been taken over, unable to turn his head to try and catch a glimpse of the person behind him.

Obeying for no real reason other than the feeling of gratitude he felt at having been rescued from Castle.

"Is he…" Bay took another stuttering breath and tried again. "You didn't kill him, did you?"

"Your coworker is on something," the stranger informed him. "He's still hard even unconscious."

Unconscious. So no, Castle wasn't dead.

That was good.

Wasn't it?

Although…

"What did you do to him?" Castle wasn't exactly a tiny person, but whoever was standing behind him, he'd managed to incapacitate him in less than two minutes. "The bathrooms are right next door. Someone will find us soon."

"Don't be afraid, Kitten," the man said, his warm breath fanning against the curve of Bay's right ear, sending shivers down his spine. "It's too soon for that. You'll ruin the game, and I didn't come here to hurt you."

Yet. It went unspoken, but Bay could hear the word floating on the air between them anyway.

The man chuckled. "You're clever. Too bad you're not better at slinking through the shadows as you believe. Things might have turned out differently for you if you were."

"What?" Bay licked his dry lips. "What does

that mean?"

"You'll understand eventually."

"I want to know now."

"You aren't ready."

"I am," Bay insisted.

"I'm not ready."

"Why?"

There was a lengthy pause, as though the person was debating over how much they wanted to divulge before the silky voice said, "I didn't mean to come to you like this tonight. But an opportunity arose wherein I could return the favor and I don't like to keep things out of balance for longer than they have to be. Now that I've done what I came here to do, I should go."

"Wait." As far as he was aware, no one owed him any favors, especially not ones that warranted getting involved with an office scuffle. Castle was a garbage person who deserved to have his hands lopped off, but he came from old money with a hefty family name. If he took actual offense to what had transpired here, there was no telling what he'd do to Bay's rescuer. "I don't like being left in the dark."

The man at his back snorted. "Liar."

He jolted when he felt a hand drop onto his hip and frantically shook his head. "Don't."

"Why not?" He didn't remove his touch, but he didn't take things any further either, merely letting his fingers rest there over the band of Bay's dress pants.

"Because," he blurted before he could change his mind, "there's already someone I'm interested in."

"Ah," the man didn't sound surprised. "Does this person reciprocate your…interest?"

Bay kept his mouth shut.

"They don't know," the man surmised without Bay having to say. "What's the plan, Kitten? Going to make your move?"

"No." That had never been in the cards for him. He could never be the one to go to his student like that.

"Is there a reason?" he asked. "I didn't take you for a coward."

"It's not about that," Bay replied.

"What's it about then?"

Any other night, with any other person, Bay would have demanded to be released and might have even risked taking a swing at the man behind him, rescuer or not. Maybe it was combination of the drinks swirling in his system, paired with his recent lack of sleep, but he found himself actually wanting to share.

What was the worst that could happen?

"I don't want to hurt him," Bay admitted softly, bracing for more questions that never ended up coming. Instead, the man shocked him further by laughing, the sound genuine and raw, the sound a lot lighter and airier than his speaking voice was. He bristled indignantly. "What's so funny? You think because of my size I couldn't do it? I'm capable of—"

"Relax, Kitten," the man cut him off. "I know how ferocious you can be. There's no need to convince me. The thing is," he finally dropped his hands and took a single step away, "there are bigger monsters than you out on the streets of Vitality. You should take more care over who you attract."

Even though he was technically no longer being held there, Bay kept his eyes firmly locked on the blank spot of wall less than two inches before him. That dark vibe he'd gotten when the man had first entered the room and spoken to Castle was still fresh in his memory, spurring him toward caution.

He wasn't wrong. There were plenty of monsters that made this planet their home, a range of demons and devils. But the person with him now wasn't either of the Devil princes—that much Bay was positive.

"Are you one of the Satellite?" he found himself asking.

"Interesting guess," the man replied. "Why not Retinue?"

"The Imperial Prince tends to surround himself with explosive personalities."

"You don't think I fit that description?" He was amused, it was obvious in the lilt of his tone.

"I'm friends with Flix," Bay said, thinking perhaps he could get the man to admit to more by doing so.

"I'm aware. He helps you at the races."

"You saw that too?"

"I've seen more than you'd be comfortable knowing."

Bay swallowed. "If you aren't Satellite—"

"I follow no one, Kitten."

"You followed me," he reminded, biting down on his tongue as soon as it was out. "I didn't mean that."

"You did," he chuckled. "But it's all right. I like you unfiltered. And you aren't wrong, though I wouldn't call it following, per se."

"What would you call it?"

There was another pregnant pause and then that warmth breath was back at the curve of his ear. "Hunting. Castle didn't understand you enough to know what types of depravity you're into. But I do. Want to play, Kitten?"

He shivered and his eyes went wide. Before he could help it, instinct finally took control and he spun, mouth already open to reply. The words got caught in his throat when he was met with an empty room.

Either the man moved at impossible speeds or he was a ghost.

Bay slumped back against the wall and pressed a palm to his racing heart. A second later, his multi-slate dinged and he inhaled sharply at the green letters that appeared on his screen.

Unknown: Next time, I won't warn you I'm coming, Kitten. Be ready for me.

CHAPTER 7:

The Brick was a small abandoned shack the two of them had discovered randomly while exploring the woods near their apartment sometime last year. They called it that because that's pretty much all there was to it, a small building that had most likely been used as storage once upon a time, now home to a couple of wooden boxes and a rickety bench.

Sila kept his composure as his brother paced the small space before him, lost in his head like he was wont to be. It wasn't an exclusive trait. They were both experts on utilizing that type of escape. When they'd been children, more often than not, slipping into their own minds was the only way to make it through their father's disparaging comments.

Now here they were, an entire galaxy away from Crate Varun, and they were still using that trick to self soothe.

Pathetic.

"Get your act together," Sila broke the silence, irritated now that he'd associated his brother's movements with weakness. They were many things, but weak wasn't one of them and he refused to allow them to be. Ever.

His brother paused and gave him an incredulous look. "Are you seriously saying that to me right now? I've got a lot going on at the moment, in case you've forgotten."

Rin had drawn the attention of Kelevra Diar and that was…messy.

Sila rested his head back and shrugged. "Have you considered—"

"No."

"Okay." He'd been about to suggest less than legal means and his brother knew it.

The two of them understood one another in ways no one else ever could. It wasn't entirely healthy, but then, very little about either of them was, so what did it matter.

Not for the first time, he considered confessing to what he'd been doing all summer, but something held him back. A tiny voice somewhere deep inside of Sila that whispered it'd be more fun to keep Bay all to himself, if just for a little while longer.

He couldn't do so indefinitely, of course. There were no secrets between Sila and Rin. There were other things he could tell him in the interim however.

"Would you like for me to transfer funds into your personal account?" he asked.

"What are you, our dad?" His brother

scowled then rested his hands on his hips. "Also, what the hell do you even mean? Since when did you have spare coin?"

"Since about two months ago," he stated. "It's enough to keep us comfortable."

"Do I even want to know how you're acquiring this kind of money?"

"No." Sila held his gaze steadily with his own. His brother never wanted details if they weren't necessary. Not because he'd judge, but as an added layer of security.

Keep no secrets, but also don't overshare. That was one of the rules.

Rin had never paid a visit to the races and he didn't have to start now. Worrying over whether or not Sila would be caught there and arrested wasn't something he currently had time for either. Keeping him in the dark was the best for the both of them.

Besides, he'd been smart about it. Sila had slowly built up his winnings, amassing enough to easily purchase two ship tickets off planet in a hurry if the need ever arose. It still wasn't enough to cover either of their tuition costs for Vail or the Academy, but it was a comfortable nest egg at least, which was more than either of them had ever had before in their lives.

"How are classes?" his brother asked then, rolling his eyes when Sila gave him a curious look. "I just want an update."

"You're making small talk." Sila cocked his

head. "Avoiding the Imperial Prince?"

"Always." Rin rubbed a hand down his face. "What about you?"

"What reason would I have to avoid him?" That's not what Rin had meant and he knew it.

"You're a real pain in the ass, you know that?"

Sila smirked. "Yes."

"Should have drowned you at birth."

"And live without me?" he clucked his tongue. "What a boring existence that would have been, brother."

The corner of Rin's mouth twitched. "True."

"I'm here biding time," Sila answered finally before checking his multi-slate.

"Got big plans later?"

"Something like that."

"It's not murder, is it?" his brother said it causally, almost like he was asking if it was meant to rain later and not if Sila intended to end a life.

Sometimes, he wondered just how comfortable with this his brother actually was. The two of them were different in that respect. Sila couldn't feel things the same way and therefore couldn't process them like an average being might. To him, hurting someone left no feelings of remorse or distaste. There wasn't even a guarantee it would please him. Half the time he did things hoping for an emotional reaction only to be left disappointed with himself.

He hated being disappointed, mostly

because those were the only times when he looked in the mirror and felt...wrong.

Weak.

It wasn't that he *wanted* to function like every other dull creature in this drab universe, he just wanted to be able to experience things as well. This was the only instance in which he was limited.

"You're angry," his brother noted, pursing his lips. "Why?"

"Don't worry," he got to his feet, "I'll entertain myself in a moment, and no, it won't involve killing anyone."

"Good." Rin eyed him for a second and then, "Need to talk about anything?"

It was tempting to ask his brother if he'd ever experienced anything like what Bay made him feel. The other night, holding him against the wall in the restaurant, being close enough to finally touch him and smell him...It'd been...a lot. Much more than Sila had anticipated, actually.

Which had to be why he was so eager to escalate things now, when before he'd been planning on dragging things out longer. Any time something interested him, that was the best course of action. Make it hold his attention for as long as possible so he didn't inadvertently snap and make a mess he and his brother would be forced to clean up. Their move to Vitality was meant to be a fresh start for the both of them, which meant he could no longer act recklessly like he had back home.

Not that his past actions could actually be considered all that reckless, since he'd never even come close to getting caught.

"No," he ended up saying, deciding not to bother his brother with emotions today. He'd needed them all explained to him at length when they'd been younger and, while he was pretty stellar at mimicking most now, there were always one or two that slipped past his notice.

"Yeah, you always have your shit together," his brother drawled. "What could you possibly need my help with?"

Sarcasm was also something he sometimes struggled with, but he'd been making improvements there.

"You may be the one with a boner for control here—" Sila began, only to have his brother snort.

"Please."

Ah, right.

"I suppose *I'm* the one who's obsessed with control in the bedroom." He considered his words more carefully, coming up blank.

"We're both strict on ourselves," his brother reminded. "And we both sometimes lose our cool. That's not what I meant. I was referring to how you like to think of everyone as a chess piece. Whoever you're playing with right now, I bet you've already planned their next three moves for them, haven't you?"

It wasn't really a question, but Sila grinned

in response anyway.

Rin's control was internal. His was external. Managing himself was easy, so he'd long since gotten into the habit of trying to control the world around him instead. It was fun, seeing how intricately he could weave other people's stories to his liking, with them none the wiser. The only person he couldn't play was his brother and that was more than all right with him.

Sila didn't want to own Rin, that would be like owning himself, and he was a force to be reckoned with. Like a bottomless, never-ending sea.

Impossible for any one person to stake a claim on.

"One of these days," his brother said, "you're going to end up meeting your match. It's going to be fucking hilarious when that happens."

"Like how it's hilarious whenever Kelevra—"

"Finish that sentence," his brother stopped him, "and I'll drown you."

"You need new material." Sila tipped his head. "I'm thinking of adopting a stray."

"Our apartment doesn't allow pets," Rin said, but as soon as the words were out, his eyes narrowed. "Which you're well aware. What kind of stray are we talking here, brother?"

He lifted a single shoulder in a partial shrug. "You won't have to help take care of it, if that's what you're worried about. In fact, I'd prefer if you didn't."

After how Castle had put his hands on Bay, Sila was rethinking a few things. He'd kept the leash rather loose up until this point because there'd been no real reason to tighten it and make his presence known, but now...

"Is this the type of pet you'll eventually get bored with and release back into the wild?" his brother asked. "You know you shouldn't do things like that. Making someone get attached to you only for you to kick them to the curb. Especially when you know that's how things will end from the start."

"Will it?" Sila wasn't sure. It wasn't like he intended to hang onto Bay forever, but there was no set timeline as of yet either.

"Whatever," his brother gave in. "Just find somewhere else to keep it. The last thing I need is to come home to find some stranger tied up on the couch."

It was his referring to their apartment as a home that had Sila mildly concerned. His brother never called it that, because that's not what it was. They didn't have a home. Things with the Imperial Prince must be stressing him out more than he was letting on, even to Sila.

"Do you need anything?" Sila asked, gentling his tone the way he knew people found comforting. His brother would see through the act, but sometimes playing pretend, even with each other, was a sort of comfort all on its own.

Sure enough, the corner of his mouth tipped

up in appreciation, but then he gave a single shake of his head. "What I need is to get back to the Academy. I've got a shooting exam tomorrow in the early am."

The exam was merely an excuse to leave, since his brother was an impeccable shot, but Sila didn't point that out. If he wanted to go, he wouldn't hold him back. There were things he'd rather be doing right now as well, actually.

"I'll see you later." Without any more prompting, his brother turned on his heel and walked out.

Sila waited for a minute or two, just to be sure he wasn't coming back for any reason, and then he made a quick call on his multi-slate.

"What's up?" a tired voice asked after only a couple of rings.

"Nate," he greeted just to be polite, since the older guy had been nice to him these past few months and got down to business. "I'd like to set up another race."

"I'm not on speaking terms with Pandaveer at the moment. Bastard blew me off last week."

Sila grinned to himself. He'd been curious when he'd spotted Bay and Nate at the coffee shop down the street from campus. Their connection with racing had already been discovered, of course, but he hadn't realized the two were also friends until then.

Friends forgave one another minor transgressions.

"I'll throw in another thirty coin for you on the side," Sila offered.

"Again?" Nate let out a low whistle on the other end of the line. "Careful. I've seen guys get cocky when it comes to gambling. You don't want to end up like them."

He smiled. "I won't."

"Takes a lot of coin to put together one of these impromptu races, man," Nate reminded, but when Sila remained silent, a clear indicator he wasn't going to budge, he sighed. "All right. You're in luck. I'm with Bauble now. He can do tomorrow at six."

Bauble Heart, another prominent racer on the scene. Nate was friends with many of the mid-tier racers, which was how he was always able to get someone to participate whenever Sila gave him a call. He must know that Sila played the game, that he set these things up and then placed bets with a third party in order to rack in the dough. Nate wasn't stupid, and he would have caught on that every friend of his he set against Bay ended up losing, but he'd never brought it up and never turned Sila down. Whatever his reasoning, it was his own and Sila had no interest in prying.

"Do me another favor," he said before Nate could end the call. "When you contact Pandaveer to let him know, include a message from me."

Nate hesitated but then asked absently, "Sure, whatever. What do you want me to say?"

"Tell him I'm looking forward to watching

my kitten ride."

There was a slight choking sound but he managed to collect himself quickly enough. Nate cleared his throat. "You got it, man."

"Thanks." Sila hung up and then exited the Brick, making his way through the forest toward his apartment building while he waited. He didn't have to wait long.

His multi-slate beeped and he was already grinning when he lifted to check the new message.

Kitten: What is this?

Humming to himself, Sila made the professor wait, taking his time as he made it to the parking lot and then up to his apartment. It wasn't until he was comfortably seated in front of his desk in his room, his tablet open before him, that he finally replied. The program he'd used to create the fake number helped to keep his identity hidden from Bay, not that he thought the guy would bother going to the authorities to ask for a trace.

Though, he may end up getting his friend Flix involved if Sila pushed things too far. That wouldn't do.

Hunter: Hello, Kitten.

Bay responded fast, giving away that he'd been waiting.

Kitten: Don't hello me. I want answers. How do you know Nate?

Hunter: You asked him that already, didn't you? What'd he tell you, Kitten?"

There was a brief pause this time. He'd hit a

nerve.

Kitten: Where are you?

He thought Sila was there watching him again, probably expected that he'd overheard whatever conversation had taken place between him and Nate and wasn't serious in asking. Obviously Sila hadn't been anywhere near the campus where Bay no doubt was, but he didn't need to be to guess what Nate would have told him.

Nate had never seen Sila's face. He couldn't give Bay any details even if he wanted to and, considering the guy was nice, he probably wanted to.

Hunter: I'm right behind you, baby. I'm always right behind you.

Sila gave it a moment and then sent off another text before Bay could freak out for too long.

Hunter: Kidding. I'm at home. But I'll be there tomorrow. Going to impress me with your skills, Kitten?

Kitten: Whatever this is, stop it.

Hunter: No.

Kitten: I'm not interested.

Sila's tablet dinged, indicating the spyware he'd placed on Bay's work computer had picked up on something, but he didn't look just yet, focused on the conversation at hand for now.

Hunter: How do you know he's better for you than I am?

Kitten: I know what he looks like, for one.

Hunter: Is that it? I didn't take you for the shallow type, Professor. Looks matter that much to you?

Kitten: His do.

Sila grinned. If only Bay knew. Perhaps he should have done this sooner, reached out anonymously and reeled him in through light conversation first. Sila had no interest in rushing things, but he'd been making them both wait for a while already and maybe that hadn't been entirely necessary.

His tablet emitted another sound and he pulled his eyes off his multi-slate to check the screen. He'd set the program to alert him if Bay ever pulled up photos of him or wrote anything with his name on it, this way he could also spy on his grades. Since he already knew about Bay's collection, he'd expected for there to be photos eventually.

But not this one.

While Bay was talking to him, he'd opened an image on his computer and left it in the center, which meant he was probably staring at it right now.

The picture wasn't one of Sila's Inspire posts and had been taken sometime last year, a student dressed in white with his head tipped down. He was reading something, probably class notes, and there was a deep furrow between his brow giving away that he wasn't pleased with whatever he found there. The slight snarl to his full lips implied he was also a little ticked off.

His brother was always like that though. Always a bit angry even when there was nothing to be mad about.

Sila's good mood vanished in a puff of smoke and, ironically, he had no doubt he probably mirrored the image of his brother a lot better now. Unlike him, it was rare for him to lose his temper, but the tight way his chest was cinching was a clear indicator he was getting there now.

Logically, he knew Bay couldn't tell them apart. He'd always known that. Few people ever could, and that'd always worked in their favor. But for some reason, Sila wasn't pleased that Bay was currently talking to him yet drooling over a photo he'd snuck of his brother.

In the past, all of Sila's actions against people had been driven by curiosity and boredom. Even his plans involving his father, the one man he truly hated, were completely devoid of petty things such as revenge. He didn't react with anger. Negative emotions like that led to impulsivity and he didn't operate that way.

Which was why it was so strange when he found himself immediately typing out a message on his multi-slate without first stopping to think things through. It was the closest he'd ever come to an out of body experience, but even aware of that, he couldn't stop himself from bitterly hitting send.

Hunter: You, me, tomorrow. It's going to be

a rough ride, Kitten. And this time? I give you permission to be afraid.

CHAPTER 8:

"Aren't you going to get that?" Flix closed the back of the truck and gave Bay a curious glance.

The race had ended fifteen minutes or so ago and Bay had made his way to the parking lot a lot faster than usual, which was saying something since he always came quickly after crossing the finish line. If Flix noticed his haste—or the way he kept sending sideways glances at their surroundings—the Brumal member didn't point it out.

He did however mention the constant ringing of Bay's multi-slate.

Bay pressed the button to ignore the call and shrugged like it was no big deal, even though on the inside he was admittedly a bit spooked. Not by much, but just enough to make him want to get into his hovercar and head home.

Just because this stranger had saved him from Castle didn't mean he wasn't still a dangerous person. If his last message to Bay was any indicator, he was exactly that even.

Flix's multi-slate went off and unlike Bay, he

answered after only two rings. Within seconds he was swearing. "I'm ten minutes away. Be there in a second." He ended the call and then waved toward the driver's side of the truck. "I have to go, Berga set off the smoke alarms on campus again."

Bay barely got a wave in before his friend was hopping into the vehicle and speeding away. As a teacher at the school, he should be more concerned over the possible damage Berga may have caused, but before he could sum up the appropriate response, his multi-slate rang again. He was keen to ignore it, only instead of a call it was a message, so with a sigh he opened it.

The sound on his device was turned up and immediately the sound of grunts and groans poured from it. He cursed and hit the volume button, glancing around to see if anyone was near enough to have noticed. Fortunately, there was another race after his, so the lot was still pretty much empty aside from a single couple making out in the corner diagonally across from him. They were definitely too distracted and too far to have heard.

Still, he wasn't as relieved as he should be, because when he looked back at his screen, his worst fears were confirmed.

The video he'd just been sent was of himself. He was kneeling on one of the leather seats at the Seaside Cinema, ass up in the air and facing whatever hidden camera had captured what was meant to have been a private moment. The thick pastel green dildo he'd brought with him gave away the footage was of his trip to the cinema two weeks ago. He'd buried it to the hilt in his hole and left it there, rocking against the armrest of the chair.

His dick had been so hard, and the smooth leather against his lube coated skin had felt so good…Bay had bitten into his arm, drawn blood, and had actually gotten off that way that night, with some rough porn playing on the big screen next to him.

He always selected the most aggressive videos he could when he went to the cinema, even on the occasions where he paid more attention to pictures he had stored on his multi-slate of the object of his desire. Bay got off on the rough sounds, the whimpers and the cries. The sharp whacking of flesh and, frankly, abuse given to one partner from the other.

Bay had only ever had one sexual partner so far, an upperclassman when he'd been in college. It'd been a one-night stand after the two of them had gone to a party and had too much to drink, and the next day the guy had pretended like Bay didn't exist anymore. He hadn't taken it personally only because it was so obvious it was because the other kid was embarrassed.

He'd slapped Bay around a bit and when Bay had expressed he wasn't into that sort of thing but that he was up for other types of experimenting, they'd both gotten noticeably more excited. And creative.

Apparently, they'd taken things too far for the other guy to be comfortable around him and, while Bay hadn't blamed him, he couldn't ignore the disappointment that still lingered whenever he thought back on it. He'd tried to soothe that curiosity about himself with porn but he'd never dared speak of it to anyone else. Especially since it was proof that part of him had already been there prior to his grandmother's death.

Now, staring at the video as the clip ended and looped back to the beginning, his cheeks stained a deep red as mortification set in.

He jumped when his device started to ring, but this time he answered, too afraid of the repercussions otherwise.

"How did you get this?" the question burst out of him frantically, even though logically he knew he should be trying to play his cards closer to his chest. "What do you want?"

"You to pick up when I call, for one," the reply came low and unhurried, but it was impossible to tell what sort of mood the speaker was in. Was he angry or annoyed? Despite his words, he didn't sound like it.

"All right." Bay licked his lips nervously. "I've done that. What now?"

"Now?" the stranger chuckled. "Now you turn on those heels of yours and start walking."

He frowned and glanced over his head. The forest was behind him, a thick wood that went on for a few miles. They didn't contain anything. There weren't even any trails leading in or out of it.

"Coming or not?"

Bay swallowed. "Do I have a choice?"

"Always," the stranger said with no hesitation. He sounded genuine too. "This wouldn't be any fun if you didn't. Just remember, Kitten, actions have consequences. Don't do anything you aren't willing to pay the price for later. So, what'll it be? Coming or going?"

He would be absolutely certifiable if he walked into the forest at the behest of a stranger.

Wouldn't he?

Bay nibbled on his bottom lip and turned to face the trees. In the darkness of the night, it was hard to see much of anything outside of the ring of gold cast down from the nearby street lamp at the center of the lot.

"What'll you do with the video if I leave?" he asked, opting to gather all the information before making a set decision.

"What do you think I should do with it?" the stranger asked casually, as though they were discussing their drink order at a coffee shop before their first date, instead of some wild sex video illegally filmed behind Bay's back. "Tell you what. I'll let you decide."

"If I were you, I'd threaten to turn it into the university," Bay said without thinking, shoulders pulling back when that earned him another dark chuckle.

"But you aren't me, Kitten."

"Who *are* you?" There were a million questions he wanted to get answers to, but he'd settle for that one for now. He needed to know exactly who he was dealing with in order to approach this situation the appropriate way. Bay had a reputation to uphold—laughable, considering the contents of the video, but still. If he didn't cling to something logical, he'd give in to the twisted voice inside of him that urged him to stop overthinking and just follow the stranger's commands.

What exactly did he have to lose after all? His life? He'd stopped caring about that a long time ago. A tedious existence and interactions that consisted of talking to students and coworkers about mundane and boring, *safe,* topics?

"Why don't you come find out for yourself, Professor?" the voice said, and the switch in names had Bay bristling.

"Are you…You're not a student, are you?" Bay asked again. Many of the people who came to the races were in their late teens and early twenties. Since they'd arrived at the staff dinner the other night, it was already apparent they were aware he taught.

"Trying to figure out how to handle me? I think we're past decorum."

"Are you one of mine?" Bay was almost certain now this was in fact a student he was speaking with. That had to give him the upper hand in some sense. He was well known for taking no crap on campus. If he approached this situation the same way he would a kid who stepped out of line in his class—

"I'm not yours yet," the stranger drawled suggestively. "Come find me so we change that. If you don't, I'll take it to mean you're not interested."

"...And then?"

"Then I cut contact."

Bay frowned, hating the flash of disappointment. "That's it?"

"Should there be something more?"

"I'm just supposed to believe you aren't going to use that video against me?"

"The one where you're being a really bad kitty?" the stranger hummed like he hadn't even considered that possibility before. "I only ever share my things with one other person, and he won't be interested in watching you fucking yourself. Come or don't come, Professor. That's the choice tonight."

Bay opened his mouth to further argue, but the line went dead, leaving him standing there in mild surprise.

With a choice to make.

Before he could think better of it, Bay found himself switching the light function on his multi-slate on and heading straight into the woods. The trees were towering here, their branches high enough the he didn't have to worry about getting slapped in the face as he made his way over the packed dirt, the light shone in front of him. He had no clue how far he was meant to go, but opted to stick to a straight line, that way once he was tired of this—or came to his senses—it'd be simple enough for him to turn back around and find his way back to the parking lot.

"This is insane," he muttered to himself as he carefully avoiding tripping over a rather large stone set in his path. The way he saw it, this could go one of two ways. The first was he gets horribly murdered on the spot, his body left to rot until some poor hiker stumbles upon it months from now. In that case, he'd be free from his emotional detachment issues.

The second way was the most likely, and also the reason he should wise up and run back toward the parking lot while he still stood a chance of getting away. An optimistic person would probably assume since the stranger had rescued them from Castle, they had only good intentions, but as a Criminal Psychologist, Bay knew better.

Predators rarely liked sharing their prey with others.

He could have been freed from one shitty situation with his coworker—who apparently called out sick all week since the incident at the restaurant—only to end up in an even worse nightmare. Watching people take advantage of someone else in porn was one thing, because that was acting. Bay hadn't liked it when Castle had tried things with him against his will. What was to say he'd be into it if this stranger on the phone did the same?

He should turn around and run before it was too late.

Curiosity drove him deeper and deeper into the forest instead, his skin practically humming with sick anticipation.

It was impossibly dark in the woods, the wide canopy above blocking out all sight of the stars, so there was only the light provided from his multi-slate to help guide him and keep him from walking head first into a tree or a prickly bush. After several minutes, he started to wonder if this hadn't been an elaborate hoax.

Maybe no one else was out here.

Maybe—The distinct sound of rustling leaves behind him cut that thought short and Bay stiffened, dread skittering up his spine a second before the sensation of being watched settled over him.

"Curiosity killed the cat," a familiar voice said and Bay twisted around, eyes going wide just as a tall figure stepped out from behind a thick tree trunk. "Or, in your case, Professor, curiosity got the cat fucked."

Being called that helped pierce through some of his fear and he straightened and cleared his throat, slipping into teacher-mode despite the fact he was dressed in racing leathers and a baseball cap. He didn't allow himself time to consider why that last part didn't scare him, but instead a small thrill coursed through him. "I don't take kindly to that sort of talk. Who are you and what do you want, really?"

Bay tried to angle his light up toward him, but the stranger clucked his tongue, and somehow the sound came off threatening enough his hand froze with the light hovering by his waist.

"Straight to the point," the stranger said, and then he reached for something and tore it off the side of his neck. He tossed the item onto the ground at Bay's feet, waiting for him to get a good look and process what it was.

Voice modulator. Expensive tech that was produced by Void Technologies. It had adhesive that allowed it to comfortably seal over a person's neck. Vibrations altered the sound of their voice whenever they spoke, changing it just enough for it not to be recognizable if someone wasn't anticipating it.

"How's it feel to be watched without knowing? My brother wasn't really a fan when you did it to him," the stranger said, only this time the voice was slightly different.

And entirely familiar.

"Sila?" Bay would have recognized that voice anywhere and it was like being hit with an ice bath a second before his words really registered. He'd mentioned his brother… "Rin."

"Are you asking, Kitten? Kind of sounds like you're asking."

"What—" The arm holding the flashlight dropped to his side, his mind struggling to come to terms with what was going on. *Rin* had followed him? "What are you doing out here? How...You knew?"

"That you're a creepy stalker?" he hummed. "Oh yes, we knew."

Bay had never spoken with Rin before, but he'd seen him a couple of times with Sila on campus when he was visiting. Unlike his twin, he attended the Academy on the other side of the city, a school training cadets how to solve crimes and deal with criminals. Something Bay fell under both categories for in this particular instance.

"Let's talk about this," he said, because even though he'd done something wrong first by spying on Sila, there could be no good reason for Rin to want to confront him all the way out here. In the dark. Alone. "I'll apologize to him, of course."

"You will not speak to him or of him," Rin stated, his tone dropping an octave, as though the very idea made him angry.

"Of course," Bay found himself agreeing out of self-preservation alone.

Rin was quiet for a moment before tilting his head. The darkness prevented Bay from getting a good look at his expression, but the beam from the flashlight managed to capture a vague outline of his general form at least. "You're lying."

"I'm not," Bay insisted, only...He might be. He wasn't entirely sure, to be honest. The problem with having an unhealthy obsession was it made it difficult to control those impulses, even if he was well intentioned.

"You suffer from hyper fixation," Rin accused, only it didn't so much as sound like an accusation as a matter of fact. Like it was no great hardship for him to have so clearly figured Bay out. "If your obsessiveness was easy to shake, you would have done so on your own long before now."

Bay didn't bother replying, choking up when Rin took a frightening step closer, his larger form practically looming in the darkness even from the ten-foot distance between them.

A distance that was slowly getting shorter and shorter with each passing breath.

His right foot slid backward in the dirt, but he froze all over again when that had Rin chiding him like a child.

"Not yet," Rin said. "We've got to establish a few things before."

"Before what?" Was he about to have to fight a cadet out in the middle of a dark forest? He'd been up for this going a lot of ways, but that hadn't really been one of them. Hand to hand combat wasn't really his forte. "How about we go somewhere and talk this out? I'm sure you're upset —"

"I'm not," he disagreed.

Bay frowned because that sounded sincere. "Then….why…?"

"I'm helping you," Rin told him and, when

that only had Bay's frown deepening, he added, "We're going to get it out of your system."

He threw up a hand when the cadet was less than five feet away, blowing a shaky breath when Rin actually stopped his advance. "Please, you're frightening me. This is inappropriate. I'm your brother's teacher and—"

Rin laughed viciously, causing Bay to bristle. "We're both of legal age here," he said once he was done. "What's the problem? Are you upset that, unlike my brother, I'm willing? Does that not do it for you, *Professor*?"

"You can't be serious?" His earlier comment came back to Bay then and his eyes went wide. "You can't honestly mean…"

"I can, and I do."

Bay might not be able to see him very well, but all of his instincts were screaming that he was currently facing a predator. The skin on his arms was prickling and his breathing had turned into short, low intakes of breath, almost as though his body was trying to make as little sound or movement as it could to avoid drawing more attention.

It was futile, that much was apparent and, if Bay didn't think of some way to defuse the situation soon, he had no doubt Rin would follow through on his threats, vague as they'd been.

Did he intend for them to have sex, or was he merely messing with Bay to get a rise of out him as revenge for his brother?

"Since you like stalking games so much, how about we play one now?" Rin said then, and it was obvious he wasn't actually asking.

"No, thank you," Bay replied anyway.

"We're going to," he stated and took another step forward. "Only, this time I'm the hunter, and you're the prey."

"And then what?" he inhaled deeply, stalling. "What happens if you catch me?"

"*When* I catch you," Rin corrected. "Isn't it obvious?"

"Perhaps you should put it to me plainly," Bay said, doing his absolute best to maintain an air of authority even though he understood that too was useless.

Rin didn't care that he was older and technically a figure of authority. If he did, he wouldn't be taking things this far, even if he intended to call it all off and laugh and say it'd only been one big joke.

It didn't feel like a joke, but that made less sense than Sila's brother luring Bay out here to force sexual relations on him. He may not have spoken with Rin personally, but everything he'd heard about the twins indicated they were friendly and charming.

No one had mentioned the fact Rin was also capable of putting the fear of the devil in a person with his mere presence.

"I'm going to fulfill all those filthy fantasies of yours," Rin told him. "When I catch you, I'll strip you down and pump you so full of my cock your voice will be hoarse come morning from all the screaming you'll do for me."

What. The. Fuck?!

"Now, see here—" Bay's dick had not just reacted to that crass threat. Not at all. Not even a little.

Traitor.

"That's the thing," Rin drawled, stopping him. "I can see, Kitten." He grinned, the light from the flashlight only just catching the lift of his full lips.

There was a pause and somehow Bay knew without being able to track his gaze that Rin was staring at the spot between his legs. He covered it with both hands, letting out an indignant sound in the back of his throat. He was only semi-hard, but there was little hope that the cadet hadn't noticed.

"Can you?" Rin asked then.

No, no Bay couldn't see in the dark. He hadn't been aware that was something Rin was capable of either. From what he knew of the man's home world, it was a sunshiny place. What use would his species have for night vision? Since he'd arrived without a flashlight or light source of his own, however, Bay was forced to believe him.

"I don't want to have sex with you." Bay figured getting it out there couldn't hurt.

"Because I'm not my brother?" he asked. "We're identical."

"You aren't. You may look alike, but that

doesn't make you the same person."

"Think you could tell us apart?" he snorted. "You can't."

Had Bay hit a nerve?

"All right, well, either way, this isn't really my thing." Bay took a step to the side, but Rin mirrored it.

"This?"

"Consensual non-consent." That wasn't exactly what was going on here, but Bay felt like if he put a label on it, he may feel a bit better about the way his body was readying for the very thing he kept claiming he didn't want. He refused to admit that his shivering was due to anticipation. It was the cold. It was chilly!

"Consent," Rin played with the sound on his tongue. "That's an interesting word choice."

"Rin—"

"It's even more interesting coming from those pretty lips of yours. Tell me, did my brother consent to you following him around? Did he consent to you jacking off to pictures of him you took when he wasn't looking? Should I send him the clip of you stuffing yourself with that silicone cock and tell him you were imagining him while you did it?"

"No!" He covered his face, mortified all over again.

"Admit it," Rin said. "Every time I brought it up before and hinted at the things I'd do to you, you got excited, didn't you?"

"No!" Yes, yes he had, but there was no way he was going to confess to something like that. Especially when there was still a good chance Rin was merely messing with him. If he was doing this out of spite to get back at him...Bay shifted backward another couple of inches, painfully aware of how hard he still was. At least he wasn't at full mast, the fear, doubt, and ever creeping darkness keeping him from being full blown turned on.

Having studied psychology for years already, he knew there was no logical reason for him to feel embarrassed about his physical reaction, and yet...

Wrong was the only right word to use to describe him getting turned on by the brother of one of his students. Period.

"You walked into these woods on your own two feet," Rin reminded.

He had. He'd come even knowing what might be in store if he did.

"You'll run on them too." The cadet grinned at him wickedly, the flash from the light catching on teeth. "No more discussing. This is the game, Kitten. You run. The main road is about a mile straight ahead. If you reach it before I catch you, you'll agree to leave my brother alone and I'll delete the video."

That didn't sound so bad. Bay was in good enough shape he was confident he could run for eight or ten minutes straight without problem. Rin

had clearly thought this through, which meant...
"You're being serious."

"Like a knife to the juggler," he agreed even though it hadn't been a question.

"What happens if I don't make it?" Bay's heart skipped a beat and the spot between his legs seemed to pulse, causing him to clench his jaw. He did not want to be caught. Getting out of here and putting an end to this was the smartest option for him.

Rin slipped something out of his front pocket, fiddling with it for a bit before he pressed a button and a blade appeared.

Bay gasped and retreated, almost tripping on an upturned root. He caught himself and went still as a statue when he heard Rin click his tongue disapprovingly.

"You said we weren't the same people," he told Bay absently, "my brother and I. If you're caught, you're going to be introduced to the real me. Fair warning, Kitten. I'm the type of hunter who never misses its prey."

"Don't," he shook his head and risked another step, "Don't hurt me."

"Save your pleas for when you're on your back," Rin said. "Tell you what, I'll give you a head start. I'll count to ten before I come after you." When Bay didn't move, he sighed. "That's you're cue to turn tail and run. One."

Bay opened his mouth and slammed it shut again, realizing there was no way to talk Rin out of this.

"Two."

He hesitated one second longer and then before Rin could finish saying the word three, he did as he was told.

Bay turned on his heel and ran for his life.

If the knife in Rin's hand was any indicator, possibly even literally.

CHAPTER 9:

It didn't matter what Bay called him. Rin, Sila, Devil. It was all the same. A name didn't define him any more than the clothes he was about to be out of did. Who he was, what he was, all of that was on the inside where no light shone and it certainly wasn't going to be affected by something as unimportant as a name.

True to his word, Sila gave him to the count of ten before he took off after him, easily navigating through the familiar forest. He didn't have night vision per se, but he was able to see more than most other species in the dark since his kind had evolved to be able to make out objects deep under water. Even without that added benefit though, all he had to do now was follow the chaotic flicker of Bay's multi-slate light as he raced away from him.

Even after catching the professor's naughty antics at the Seaside Cinema, Sila had been surprised when he'd noticed the man getting hard for him. It'd been a bit strange, a bit thrilling, and a major ego stroke which, if he were being honest, he didn't need.

Sila knew his worth. He was a god among men, with a gorgeous face and a personality capable of charming anyone and everyone. Since he'd been young, if there was something he wanted he got it and, typically, with very minimal effort. He'd always been good at setting the scene and planning ahead. Getting Bay here was just another chess game in a never-ending run of them up until Sila kicked the bucket and died.

And now, after months of preparation, the game was finally coming to a close.

There was little to no chance of Bay making his way out of here unscathed. He may have a flashlight, but it was obvious from the jerky movements ahead that he was stumbling over fallen debris. Sila was going to catch him—in half the time he'd figured too—and when that happened, he'd finally teach the professor a lesson for daring to think he had the rights to spy on a Varun.

He was going to twist the blue haired man up so thoroughly Bay would be licking his wounds for days to come. Once he'd been acquainted with the devil, there was little doubt in Sila's mind that Bay would be a good little kitten and scurry far, far away from both him and his brother.

Bay's earlier plea not to hurt him echoed in Sila's ears and he almost laughed. Of course he was going to hurt him. Not just because this wouldn't be a real punishment if he didn't, but also because he wanted to.

One of the recurring themes in Bay's movies had been primal play. Curious, Sila had looked up more about it, as he had with most of the themes that seemed to turn Bay on. Out of them all, this was the one he was most interested in exploring. Sex had always been a means to an end to Sila. It was the mental fucking that made him hard, not the physical act itself. He enjoyed sex, of course, but he'd never cared enough about sticking his cock in a hole to research all the various ways it could be done.

In the past, if he felt like cutting someone in the moment, he cut them. If he felt like tying them up, he did. Choke them to death with his dick? Did it once, it wasn't as satisfying as he'd hoped, so probably not something he'd bother repeating. But primal play...He'd never done that before. It seemed risky to try it out now, but...

According to everything he'd read on the subject, for some, primal play wasn't a form of play at all, but a chance at freedom. It was a rare opportunity to drop the roles and the masks and act on all of the impulses brewing within a person. All those instincts they shoved down and forced into the dark due to societies expectations and rules.

The closest Sila had come to something like that had been back in high school. But there'd been a layer of deceit needed still since if word got out that Crate Varun's son had hunted someone down like an animal and fucked them raw in the sand, he would have been counter fucked—and in the unpleasant way. Sila had spent the better part of a year coaxing his on and off again lover, Timon, into agreeing to be chased, planting the seed in his mind that it was something he'd be interested in and Sila was merely a willing partner helping him explore those taboo longings.

The scratches and bruises all over the two of them the day after had been explained away by an overly rambunctious sparing match, and their idiot high school teachers had believed them without batting an eye.

Timon stopped speaking to him after, but no matter. Sila and his brother had already set their sights on the Dual Galaxy as their true escape. Besides, he'd gotten what he'd wanted from Timon already, so there'd been no reason he could see to try and keep the timid guy around.

It'd actually been a while since Sila had last thought of him even.

Interesting.

Bay was stirring up all sorts of things within him and that only made him all the more curious. Back then, things with Timon had been tame despite the chasing factor. Most of the bruises had been caused from tumbling down a sand dune, the scratches the usual result from a rough, yet consensual, rutting. Basically, Sila hadn't been all that interested in giving it another go.

Until now.

Done drawing things out, Sila picked up the pace and really gave chase. He was quiet as he pushed his body forward, deftly slipping between the thick trunks of the trees as he kept Bay's light in sight. He hadn't even broken out in a sweat yet, but there was time for that once he had the professor pinned beneath him, ideally fighting for control.

Bay's pornographic preferences were dark and perverted, rough. But there was a big difference between watching something on screen and experiencing it in real life. There was a chance it was all fantasy for him, and the real deal would end up squashing the appeal instead of bolstering the flames. There was only one way to tell.

Sila wouldn't stop or let him free either way.

He controlled his breathing and pushed on, drawing ever nearer to that flickering light and the man carrying it. It was odd that Bay wasn't attempting to conceal it, since he had to know Sila was following the trail more easily thanks to that literal beacon, but Sila didn't overthink it. Now wasn't the time for using his brain.

It was the time for instincts.

Sila relished the chase. The way his thighs burned and the pressure of his lungs expanding in his chest with each deep inhale. Above them, the night sky coupled with the thick canopy kept them bathed in an eerie darkness, the only sounds their harried breaths, the snapping of twigs, and crickets. Little fuckers didn't give a damn about what was happening right now and he took a sick kind of pleasure in knowing that the only witnesses to Bay's utter undoing were a couple of dozen bugs.

He'd been dreaming of this moment for so long, he almost didn't want the fun to stop, actually considered letting Bay go, if only so Sila could mess with him some more tomorrow. There was a different kind of pleasure to be had when taking apart someone's hope. Breaking it down bit by bit after allowing someone to experience that rush of relief? After making them believe they were finally safe? Hell, that might even be better than getting his cock wet.

But then Bay slipped ahead of him, a startled yelp emitting from his throat that had Sila's dick twitching in his pants, demanding he put an end to all thoughts of letting Bay go. No, tonight he'd get answers to all of those questions that had shuffled through his head whenever he was watching Bay touch himself at the Seaside Cinema.

Sila was going to know exactly how to make him scream and cry. And he was going to know how those tears tasted.

Using Bay's momentary delay to his advantage, Sila shot forward, grabbing a fistful of the man's leather jacket. He used it to haul Bay back, pulling him off his feet with ease. When he tossed him to the ground, he followed, planting his knees at either side of Bay's hips to keep him in place as he made quick work of the jacket. It'd grown on him and he was loathe to destroy it. Everything else though...

Carelessly, he bunched the leather material and tossed it into the darkness, barely listening to the sound of it crashing into what was most likely a bush. His attention was already back on Bay, who seemed to have snapped out of whatever shocked state he'd entered when he'd been thrown about.

Bay let out an animalistic growl and then blindly lashed out, his arms swinging, fingers bent to form claws. It was an interesting choice—most other people would have gone with fists, but Bay was smarter than most other people. That was one of the things Sila liked about him. He managed to scratch just beneath Sila's jawline, all his other hits landing on his clothing.

He'd dressed for the woods, his own leather jacket thicker than the one Bay had been wearing. Sila had also ditched the school uniform, opting for an all-black ensemble that would help him blend even more in the darkness. He wanted the professor seeing only what he wanted him to see. Only what he deemed him worthy enough to.

"Get off of me!" Bay screamed, thrashing around like his life depended on it. His phone had fallen when he had, now off a few feet to the side, casting its light upward.

"Boring," Sila clipped, slapping his hands away whenever they came near his face again. One scratch was already going to get him an earful from his brother. He didn't need to make the scolding worse. "Do better, Kitten."

"I am your brother's professor!"

"So you're aware?" he hummed. "Do you fantasize about fucking all of your students, or just him?"

His bottom lip trembled. "It's not what you think."

Sila lifted a single brow, unimpressed.

"Even if it is," Bay back peddled, "that doesn't make *this* okay! You can't do this to me."

He caught Bay's wrists with one hand and shoved them into the dirt over his head, pinning them there with his superior strength. The move had his upper body leaning over the professor's, bringing his face closer, and he caught sight of the tears already spilling freely from his eyes.

"You came to the woods when I called," he reminded. "Don't pretend you didn't know what was in store for you. You're smarter than that, *Professor.*"

"I assumed we would have a discussion," Bay lied through his teeth, "Like adults!"

Sila watched a particularly large drop slip free from the corner and roll its way down the rise of Bay's cheek, trailing over toward the bottom of his right earlobe. He licked his lips and leaned in to lap at it and, for whatever reason, that seemed to set Bay off all over again.

He bucked beneath him, desperately trying to free himself, even attempting to roll to the side, but there was very little room for him to do so. His heels kicked at the ground, and he tugged on his arms, clearly with everything he had in him.

Sila merely waited, watching as his prey tired himself out. Every uptick of Bay's chest as he panicked, all the little desperate sounds he was making…It all called to him, spurred him on. He rewrote the plan as he pressed down harder into the professor, excitement returning full force.

It didn't dissipate when Bay finally went limp beneath him, on the contrary, it grew and drew up inside of him instead.

"Please," Bay's voice was low, husky from his struggles. "Please, let me go. I promise I won't touch him."

"You weren't going to touch him to begin with," Sila stated matter-of-factly. "But since you've asked so sweetly, how about this. I'll allow you one last fantasy. If you do as instructed, I'll let you go. If you don't, I'll satisfy a different curiosity of mine. I've been wondering since I came to this planet if Vitals hearts are the same size as a Tiberans."

Bay's eyes went wide.

"What do you say?" Sila asked.

"A54."

He stilled over him. "What?"

"A54," Bay repeated. "At the library on campus. That's where you'll find medical books on Vital anatomy."

Sila Varun spent three hours two days a week in that library, but then, Bay thought he was

Rin from the Academy.

"You're telling me to go research?" Sila asked. "Now? In this situation?"

"The best way to learn something and have it stick is by seeking the answer out yourself," Bay said, and then seemed to realize the way those words could be taken. He shook his head vehemently, sending sticky tendrils of his powder blue hair flying around his flushed face. "That's not what I meant! You can't just murder someone out of curiosity, Rin."

"Can't I?"

"No," he insisted. "For one it's illegal. It also happens to be morally—"

"Ah," Sila clicked his tongue. "Allow me to stop you there. It seems you haven't yet caught on. I wonder how much of that is due to your blind devotion to my brother. Could it be the shock instead? Is it making it hard for you to think clearly, Kitten?"

When Bay merely frowned up at him, he sighed.

"How exasperating. You teach this for a living and you live on a planet where you can find someone like me around nearly every corner—Not exactly like me, to be clear. I'm above the rest of course, know how to keep my mask firmly in place no matter who may or may not be around to try and check beneath it. Unlike that wild prince of yours. If my brother didn't like playing with him so much, maybe it'd be Kelevra Diar lying beneath me right now instead of you. Of course, he'd already have a knife through his gut, but I've been taking it easy on you for a while now. Treating you better than I've ever treated anyone."

Sila moved his left hand, the one still gripping the knife, and used the tips of his fingers to brush strands of Bay's hair off his forehead. "Admittedly, the Imperial Prince would be giving me more fight. Look at you, already frozen with fear. Are you sure you don't want to give it another go?"

"You want me to fight you?" Bay swallowed and Sila's eyes tracked the movement of his throat.

"It's preferable," he said. "But not necessary. I can feed myself many ways. Cooperation can be fun too, so long as you commit to the part. Can you do that for me, Bay?"

"And if I don't?" He didn't wait for Sila to answer. "You'll hurt me."

"I'll cut you open and get firsthand experience what a Vital heart feels like in the palm of my hand," he explained. "It will hurt for a while." He turned the tip of the blade downward and tapped it lightly over Bay's breastbone. "Your ribcage is made out of stronger stuff than a Tiberan's. We're faster and can breathe underwater longer, but you lot are tough."

"It's star crystal," Bay told him. His voice trembled but he somehow managed to keep steady otherwise. "All of the species born on Vitality have particles of it in our bones. We've found skeletons of our ancestors that show, at one time, we were made entirely of the stuff. The extinction of our largest predators must have meant we no longer needed to be hard as crystal, since it no doubt restricted movement. Evolution slowly phased most of it out, leaving us as we are today."

Sila stared down at him for a long time, but when Bay merely stared back, he felt a laugh burst out of him. "Did you just give me a history lesson, Professor?" He tilted his head, curious. "Were you trying to distract me?"

"No," he said. "I may have been slow on the uptake, but I've caught up now."

"Have you?"

"I still haven't decided if you lean more toward sociopath or psychopath, but it's obvious you have some form of antisocial personality disorder. Can I ask you a question?"

The surprises never stopped coming it seemed.

"All right." Sila nodded.

"What exactly can't you feel? And what is it like?" Bay pursed his lips and Sila waited for him to find the right phrasing. "Is it, more like the absence of something? Like an emptiness? Do you…get upset?"

"I can," he revealed. "I can experience anger."

"Sadness?"

He considered. "No."

"But you feel wronged, and you don't like it when your brother is sad."

Sila stiffened. He'd let his guard down and fallen for the innocent act. How very unlike him. "Is that what this is really about? You're not curious about me, you're trying to get me to tell you whether or not my brother is the same way. What? Scared you've fallen for a monster, Kitten?"

"No," Bay said. "That's not—"

"I wouldn't worry about that," Sila cut him off. "Not when you've already got the attention of the Devil." He moved fast, wanting to catch Bay off guard and cause him to panic all over again. With a flick of his wrist, Sila cut through the thin material of Bay's black t-shirt, tearing it off of his body with ease. He'd used the tip of the blade to snap the button off the top of his jeans before Bay started to fight back, but one hard shove to the center of his chest had him stilling all over again.

Even though he knew Bay couldn't see him that well in the murky darkness, the fallen flashlight and the full moon peeking through the trees directly overhead barely providing enough visibility, Sila set his expression in a steely look.

Bay remained tense a moment longer and then, little by little, he forced his muscles to go lax, until he was lying flat on the ground once more.

Sila made a sound of approval, then tugged on the waistband of Bay's jeans to pull the material half an inch away from his flesh. He turned the knife and sheered through the clothing, all the way down to the thigh, then he repeated the motion on the other side. Grabbing onto Bay's arm, he flipped him onto his stomach, pausing to see what he'd do.

Bay kept still, his palms flat in the dirt on either side of his head.

Hooking his finger in the center loop at the back of the jeans, Sila tugged them down, tossing them over his shoulder. Then he rolled Bay over once more and slowly rose to his feet so he could peer down at him.

The professor was all lean muscle and creamy skin. Aside from a thin blue trail of hairs leading down from his navel, and small tufts over his armpits, he wasn't hairy.

"Do you groom yourself, Kitten?" Sila asked. He'd wanted to know for a while now, but hadn't allowed himself to break into the professor's home. There'd been no need for it, since he could keep tabs on Bay easily enough through his tablet. Now he was starting to wonder if he shouldn't have added cameras there like he'd done to the man's office.

How much had he missed by restricting himself from bugging the man's home bathroom?

Bay glanced away, embarrassed.

He tutted at him. "Don't fret. I like it. I like how soft you are."

The professor lifted his chin as though offended and it was an obvious struggle for him when he made himself meet Sila's gaze again.

For a while, they stayed like that, Sila standing over his naked body, one leg at either side.

Tonight was meant to be the grand finale, the end to their sordid tale. And yet...The longer Bay waited silently for him, stayed still and quiet like commendable little prey, the more Sila realized he wasn't ready for this to be over.

After all of his effort, was getting to play with the man lying in the dirt at his feet a single time really worth it? Was it fair to himself? Didn't Sila deserve more than a one hit wonder?

Bay deserved it to, after how good he'd been the past half hour.

"Sweet or sour?" Sila found himself asking. They'd start again, return to the beginning and replay by the same set of rules. The best way to trap someone was by offering them a choice and allowing those choices to tangle around them.

Any sign of Bay's earlier arousal was gone now, his dick flaccid at the apex of his thighs. But Sila remembered the glimmer of excitement he'd been unable to hide.

"Going off the types of porn you get off to," Sila continued when Bay didn't answer, "I'm guessing sour."

The professor squeezed his eyes shut.

"For the record, I would have been so good to you, Kitten. Taken things nice and slow, gotten you loose and open and ready for me. But since that's not the way you want it..."

"Wait!" His eyes snapped open and his hands landed on Sila's ankles, though he didn't try to push him away. He merely left his fingers resting there.

"Changing your mind already?" Sila tipped his head. "Come on. We both know you're not the indecisive sort. You commit." He grinned, making sure not to hold back so there was no way Bay could miss it even in the dark. "I like that about you. I'll give you another chance though, since this is our first time, and I get it. You want me to take all the power so you can tell yourself later that you didn't want any of this."

"I don't!"

"Should I replay you the video?" He clucked his tongue. "My brother and I are identical. If you were thinking about him fucking you, you were basically thinking about me too."

"No!" The tears started up again, but Sila couldn't tell if it was due to renewed fear or embarrassment. "I wasn't! I wanted the good twin!"

"Should I let you in on a little secret?" Sila lowered his voice into a hushed whisper, liking the way that made Bay shudder all over again. He reached down and hauled Bay up into a seated position before crouching down before him. Leaning in, he pressed his lips close to the curve of Bay's left ear. "There is no good twin."

He didn't hold back when he bit him. A burst of copper exploding on his tongue. He was careful not to tear or make any marks that wouldn't be healed by the next day, but he wanted it to sting.

When he shoved Bay back to the ground, the professor instantly cupped his ear protectively, glaring up at Sila with watery eyes.

He laughed and ran his hand over his mouth, checking the spots of red that smeared over his knuckles. "Okay, Kitten. You've convinced me. I'll go easy on you. Two choices. Option one I gut you like an animal, play with your organs until I lose interest, and leave your body here to rot for however long it might take someone to stumble upon your corpse."

Bay flinched.

"Option two." Sila took a large step back and tossed the knife at Bay's feet. "You put on a private show for me."

The professor gave him a look like he'd just grown a second head. "What?"

"It's like I said earlier. I'll allow you one final fantasy of my brother. You're going to take that," he pointed to the weapon, "and use it to get off the same way you use those toys of yours at the Seaside."

Bay sucked in a sharp breath and Sila rolled his eyes.

"I'm not telling you to sit on the blade. Your ass is no good to me shredded to ribbons. When you're cut, I'll be the one doing the carving, thank you very much. Insert the handle, Kitten. I want to see you riding that thing like it's the pretty purple silicon cock you like so much."

He'd used the green one in the video Sila

had sent earlier, but Bay typically chose a larger toy, one with a suction cup base he attached to either the side of the snack table or the wall at the Seaside.

The knife Sila had selected for the night was roughly six inches long, three for the blade and three for the handle. It wasn't nearly enough to satisfy the professor, but since this was more about Sila getting off than him...He figured what the hell. It was hotter than handing the guy a broken tree branch or something else equally crass.

If anything, Bay should be grateful Sila felt that way.

He clapped his hands once, the sound echoing around them, and Bay startled. "I won't be generous forever. Make a choice."

"Please I..." Bay's gaze lingered on the knife, staring at it like it was a snake about to bite him. "I can't do it. I've never...In front of someone else..."

"Is that why you're hesitating?" Sila smiled softly, knowing it would momentarily give the professor a false sense of ease. "Now seems like a good time to tell you that's not the only video I've taken, Professor. I have many."

The sheer horror that washed over Bay's face was so hot, Sila wished he was filming so he could keep it forever.

Actually...

"Just because you didn't know someone was watching," he began as he activated his multi-slate and undid the device from the strap so he could hold it up in his hands, "doesn't mean you were actually alone. I've been watching you for months now, the only difference is this time I'm letting you know I'm here."

The device beeped once when he turned on the camera function and he flipped the screen. He switched on night mode, grinning when Bay's image filled the rectangular box.

"What are you doing?" Bay's voice came out breathy and terrified.

"Adding to the collection, which one depends on you. Either this is going in the hidden folder with all the other home movies of you, or it's added to the other one."

"Other one?"

"Hmm," Sila nodded. "What? Did you think come was the only bodily fluid I filmed? It isn't." That was a lie. He wasn't stupid enough to film himself taking someone apart, but Bay didn't need to know that.

The fib seemed to do the trick, because Bay turned back to the knife, this time with a different kind of hesitancy.

He was contemplating it.

"I do this and you promise you'll let me out of this forest," Bay asked, "alive?"

"Nice touch," he commended. "Yes. You put on a show for me and I'll let you leave here breathing—with," he added when Bay opened his mouth to argue, "all of your insides still there."

There was another charged moment where nothing happened, but then Bay reached for the knife, and Sila internally purred in satisfaction.

CHAPTER 10:

Was he seriously about to do this?

Bay wrapped his fingers around the wooden handle of the knife and picked it up. He inspected the blade once he had it closer, his eyes partially adjusted to the darkness now. It wasn't great, he still couldn't see well enough to make out all of Rin's expressions, but it was better than it had been earlier when he'd stumbled around even with the light from the flashlight.

His multi-slate was lying in a pile of fallen leaves a few feet away and he tilted his head, staring at it for a second. He was the one with the weapon now. Could he maybe make it to his device and fend Rin off before the younger man got to him?

"You could try," Rin's modulated tone cut through the chilly night. He kept changing it to match Bay's reactions, something he'd caught onto as soon as Kelevra Diar had been mentioned.

Rin was trying to emulate emotional responses to either soothe or get a rise out of Bay. Basically, whatever reaction he wanted Bay to give, he adjusted his speech to make it so. A moment ago, he'd come off conversational, his tone light and welcoming. Now it was somewhat smoky, deeper and with an edge of challenge.

He was letting Bay know, without so many words, that he was fine no matter which way he chose for things to go. He'd told Bay he'd let him decide and he'd meant it.

Bay turned his head to face forward again, tearing his gaze off of his multi-slate. He was immediately greeted by Rin's.

The man was holding it up with two hands, watching Bay from the screen. Filming.

He was going to film his humiliation.

"Decided against it?" Rin asked. "Probably for the best. Believe it or not, cutting you open is becoming less and less appealing as the time goes on." He noticed where Bay was looking now and shook the device a little. "This? Don't worry about this, Kitten. I'll be the only one who ever sees it."

"How do I know you're telling the truth?" If that video got leaked, his entire life would be over.

"Afraid of being fired?"

"Screw my job," Bay snapped. "If people see that, they'll—" He clamped his mouth shut.

"There's the fear again," Rin murmured, but it was as if he was speaking to himself. "It's different. When you're afraid of pain and afraid of social ruin, you look different. I noticed, however, during all of your trips to the Seaside, that none of those videos you put on ever had exhibitionism in them. Why do you think I kept the fact that I was watching to myself, even though we've been texting for weeks?"

He hadn't sent Bay that video until he'd been ready to confront him in the flesh.

"You wouldn't care about me," Bay said anyway. "My feelings don't matter to you."

"Fair," he agreed. "But my own do. I play well with others, but only on my own terms. Sharing isn't exactly one of my past times. There's only one person in this entire universe who could ask me to pass you around, and he's not interested in either one of your personas, Kitten. Stuffy professor and edgy street racer aren't his preferred flavors. How do you think you ended up with me?"

Bay dropped down, his bare ass hitting the ground, twigs poking at his skin, though he hardly noticed.

"Is that heartbreak?" Rin asked, and this time, there was an honesty in his voice that had only come through once or twice this entire night. He genuinely wanted to know. "I don't think I've seen it before. Is it because my brother doesn't care about you?"

Something clicked for Bay then, and his spine stiffened. "You're doing this on purpose."

"What's that?"

"You're trying to capture my emotions on film, aren't you." It wasn't a question because he was positive he'd hit the nail on the head. So far, Rin had scared him, shaken him, and now he'd gotten him to feel sad.

"So smart, professor," Rin praised. "That's another thing I like about you, however, the fact that sexy brain of yours is working properly again means we've wasted far too much time. You've cooled off and we need to get your body temperature back up before you catch a cold. It's not exactly the middle of summer, in case you don't recall."

The adrenaline and constant fluctuating of his emotions had kept Bay from noticing the goosebumps all over him. He shivered as soon as it was brought to his attention and Rin laughed.

"If you want me to stop leading you around," Rin began, "then you should start the show."

"You said you didn't want to kill me."

"I never said I wouldn't though."

Bay was seriously going to have to do it. He was going to have to perform for this psycho in order to make it out of here alive. How had he ended up in the middle of the woods in the dead of night in the first place? Was this seriously just because he'd fallen for Sila Varun?

"I kept my distance," Bay reminded.

"Perhaps if you'd tried things my way," Rin replied, "you would have gotten the chance to touch him. As it is...You chose not to get too close. You don't get a medal for that. Reining in our demons is sort of par for the course. It's what comes with being a sentient creature."

"You stalked me too. Can't we call it

even?" he gave it one final attempt out of sheer desperation.

"It's not my fault you targeted the wrong person. Accountability. Isn't that something you should be teaching your students? You mistook my brother for prey and ended up in the clutches of a true predator. Shit happens. I'm starting to get bored. Are you going to fuck yourself for me or am I going to have to get my hands bloody? Either way, we aren't leaving here until you give me one of your bodily fluids."

Bay rolled the handle of the knife in his palm.

"Need help? I can, if you ask me," Rin said.

He pursed his lips. Earlier, at the start of this, he'd admittedly been a bit turned on. When he'd run, his dick had still been hard in his pants. It wasn't until Rin had shoved him to the floor and he'd realized how much bigger and stronger the younger guy actually was that he'd lost the hard-on.

It'd been mostly out of sheer instinct. Fight or flight and the fear of death fast approaching. Only now it was apparent that Rin wasn't going to kill him—at least, not so long as he did as he was told.

"You may not be a fan of exhibitionism," Rin's silky tone cut through his thoughts, "but we both know there's a running theme to those movies you like so much. There's always an aggressor in the mix."

"It's called BDSM," Bay stated, only to have Rin snort at him.

"No it's not. I didn't say dom for a reason. I got the impression even that would be too vanilla for you. Too controlled. Is it the unknown that does it for you? You always stop touching yourself and watch when the videos get to that part. When things become uncertain and one of them is begging the other not to hurt them. How'd you start things off with me again?"

Bay had asked him not to hurt him.

Shit.

He'd walked right into that without even knowing, but the fact that he'd had someone's full undivided attention? That he'd filled their mind in a similar fashion to how Sila kept him lying awake at night…That was kind of hot.

Bay's dick twitched and he gasped.

"There we go," Rin coaxed. "Want to know what the original plan for tonight was? I was going to hunt you down and fuck you raw and bloody in the dirt. You would have liked it."

"No." Bay shook his head and closed his eyes when his body betrayed him, dick lengthening even more as those filthy words pierced through his resolve. "I'm not like that."

"Like what, Kitten?" Rin asked. "Messed up? It's okay to be. Isn't that what you tell your students? Being different doesn't make you a monster. There's no shame in wanting to be kept, baby. Should I tear you apart and put you back together?"

"No," he repeated, but even as he said it, he planted his knees onto the packed earth and parted them, his free hand making its way to the throbbing member between his legs. He was almost fully hard now, his dick bobbing with every movement, the cool air licking across his heated flesh and the wet tip where a drop of precome had already started to leak free.

He choked on a sob and lifted his arm to cover his face, even as he cupped his balls.

"You don't hide when you're alone," Rin chided. "No hiding when you're with me either."

Bay didn't listen.

"Drop your arm, Kitten," an edge entered his tone. "Don't make me come over there and break it."

Threats to his person didn't do it for him the same way, at least not when they were on their own. Sexual pain…That was different. Still, his dick twitched again but didn't soften. Maybe that was because on some level, he understood all he had to do was obey in order to avoid any of that actually happening.

"Is humiliating me doing it for you?" he snapped, removing his arm and resting a glare on Rin.

"What about you?" Rin countered. "We both know you're secretly a masochist."

"I'm—" the denial was instinctive, but he caught himself, remembering how annoyed Rin had gotten when he'd lied before. If he'd really spied on him at the Seaside as often as he claimed, there was no point to it anyway.

"Good choice," he said, clearly pleased Bay had stopped on his own. "I've seen you claw at your own thighs and shove toys in without preparation. I'm sure I've yet to uncover one or two, but for the most part? I know your secrets. I'll reiterate, before you freak out, I've no interest in destroying your social standing. No one has to know the types of things that turn you on but me."

"Why?"

"Because I don't need other people to do my dirty work." He grinned. "And you don't need help to do yours. Enough stalling. Start stroking, Kitten. I'll talk you through it. It'll be easier."

"Please don't." This was already embarrassing enough as it was, especially since his arousal was on full display now despite his verbal protests. His emotional state had always confused him, even after he'd gone to school and developed a professional level understanding of how the psyche worked.

There was no childhood trauma, no feeling of rejection growing up. Even having spent the first ten years of his life at the orphanage, Bay had been okay. His birth parents must have had a reason to give him up, and that was never something he'd carried with him. Until two years ago when his grandmother hid died suddenly, Bay's life had been relatively easy. Aside from becoming unhealthily obsessed with a show or a book series, Bay hadn't experienced that all-consuming drive directed at another person until he'd spotted Sila.

He'd always leaned toward the dark and murky, morally black kind of sexual fantasies, but there'd never been any particular individual who'd starred in them when he masturbated. Then Sila had come along, all sunshine and gleaming gold and...perhaps Bay's subconscious had associated that vibrancy with warmth, a thing he'd had torn away from him.

For over a year now, it'd been Sila's face, Sila's hands, Sila's cock, that Bay had pictured whenever he'd touched himself and if Rin broke one of his bones with no payoff after...He feared the fantasy would forever be shattered.

If he deflated and couldn't get it back up, there was little doubt in his mind Rin would follow through on his other threats.

Bay may like pain in the bedroom, but he didn't like it on its own. When he crashed his hover bike, that shit hurt. He didn't instantly spring a boner or anything.

"I'm going to," Rin said, completely ignoring his plea. "You always jump right in, Kitten. Let's do things a little differently this time."

Bay frowned. "Why?"

"Because that's what I want, and you're going to give me what I want, isn't that right?"

His silence was answer enough.

"Stroke yourself," Rin ordered. "Slowly."

Bay's hand shifted from where he was still holding his balls loosely, circling around his shaft. They tightened a bit as he trailed them up toward the wet tip and he shuddered at the feel of electricity that pinged through him.

"Play with the crown," Rin commanded just when he'd been about to go back down.

He rolled the pad of his thumb over the silky head a bit roughly.

"Slower."

Bay ground his teeth but obliged, shifting to widen his stance even more, the light touches making him throb with want.

"What are you thinking, Kitten?"

"Is this a punishment?" he blurted before he could help it, but even though he was mortified that he asked, his hand didn't stop its ministrations, thumb still swirling around the sticky precome on his tip. He dug his nail against his slit and groaned at the pinch.

"Doesn't sound like it," Rin chuckled. "Why? Do you want it to be? Would that make it better?"

Bay's brow furrowed as he struggled to think past the agonizing zips of pleasure. They weren't anywhere near as strong as he needed them to be and it was starting to cloud his judgment. Hell, clearly since he was here, on his knees, his judgment was already shot to shit but whatever.

He could spend an entire lifetime psychoanalyzing himself. He did that to other people for a living, after all. But Bay had long since come to the realization that he didn't want to. Who cared why he was the way he was and he liked the things he liked? He just did, simple as that. The only reason he hid it was because he knew other people wouldn't view it the same way.

Just because he didn't like his job didn't mean he didn't need it.

Just because he wasn't overly fond of his coworkers didn't mean being alone with no one to talk to would be better.

And just because he got off on the idea of being tossed to the ground like some animal and fucked like one too…

Bay forgot where he'd been going with that thought process.

Oh, right.

He'd been trying to figure out how to respond to Rin's question. One way would get him what he wanted and the other would surely have his tormenter refusing to give it to him. But which way to go?

"You read me so well earlier," Rin said. "I'll forgive you for faltering now. You can just answer honestly. I won't force you to needlessly suffer, not while you're being so good for me. So, what'll it be, Bay? Should I punish you? Do you need that to take this all the way?"

He actually did, because as turned on as he currently was, there was still the edge of uncertainty creeping at the corners of his mind, keeping him from slipping into that chaotic headspace. Bay loved that state of being, where the only thing that mattered was granting his body erotic release.

Whenever that happened, he wasn't an empty husk of a person. He was full. Buzzing and bright. It was like the high he got when he was speeding at impossible speeds on his hover bike, but kicked up twelve notches.

If Bay was going to make it through this, force himself to come in front of a student, he was going to have to enter that place.

"Yes," the single word sounded like a gunshot to his ears, but at the same time, the second it was out there, his shoulders lost some of their tension. His hand worked its way down his length and slicked back up again and, without having to be reminded, he took his time teasing his crown before repeating the motion.

"Would you like another choice, Kitten?"

Bay froze.

That tone had been different from all the rest. Raw and unfiltered.

He tried to make out Rin's gaze but couldn't see more than the outline of his face and a flash of teeth, curtesy of the light from the guy's multi-slate.

It hadn't sounded like a threat, and yet...It hadn't not sounded like one either. There was so much dark, delicious promise in it, in fact, that Bay was left confused all over again. He couldn't guess the trap. Didn't know which was the safest way forward. It was clear in the way Rin remained silent, waiting for him to come to a decision, that he wasn't going to give him any hints this time either.

It was sick, he was sick, but Bay was suddenly reminded how this was it for him. This was all he was going to get. There was no doubt in his mind if he didn't keep his word and leave Sila alone from here on out, his brother was going to gut him and scatter his entrails all over the city. This was the one and only chance he would ever have at being with a Varun and, sure, they weren't the same, but at this point? He'd take what he could get.

Or, more accurately, he'd take the way that left him still breathing at the end of it.

"Yes please," he said, still idly stroking himself.

"You come and you leave here alive," Rin reiterated, and Bay nodded. "Fast or slow?"

"Fast!" He didn't even have to consider that one. As it were, if they kept up like this he'd never get there.

"Turn around and put in the knife, Kitten."

Bay shifted on his knees until his back was to Rin, bringing the handle to his mouth. His tongue swirled around the wood, trying his best to wet it in a short time. Then he bent forward and awkwardly turned the knife around in his hand. He had no clue whether or not he was successfully giving the other man a good enough view, but all of his focus went to trying to finagle the tip of the handle to his hole. The second he felt it bump against him there, he paused.

"You chose fast," Rin reminded. "No prep."

And there was the hidden caveat Bay hadn't been able to locate. It should enrage him, but instead he felt his insides twist.

Rin hadn't been making things up. Bay did sometimes force his body to take things without properly stretching himself open. That sharp burst of pain, receding to intense pleasure, created a high for him unlike anything else.

He began to slowly ease the handle in, biting down on his tongue at the rough feel, but holding the blade was awkward, and he'd barely managed a few centimeters before he felt a different kind of sting.

Bay cursed and dropped the knife, pulling his hand back to inspect the fresh wound he'd just stupidly given himself. The blade had sliced through the side of his palm, right between his forefinger and thumb. Fortunately, it wasn't deep and there was no fear he'd done any real damage.

Unfortunately, his relief was short lived.

He registered the sound of boots crunching in the debris a second too late. One second, he was checking his injury, and the next Rin was grabbing him by the scruff of the neck and folding him over. His forehead was pressed into the dirt and held there and, even though he tried to push himself back up, it was no use against the other man's strength.

"All that talk about punishment must have really gotten to you," Rin growled over him. "What did I say before? If you were going to be cut by someone, it was going to be me."

Fear built up and Bay floundered. "I didn't mean it!"

Rin had kept him on his knees, his ass lifted high in the air. When his hand came down on his left cheek, it was with enough force that Bay's entire body vibrated.

He cried out at the sudden assault, tears pricking his eyes as he waited for another strike that didn't come. In his current position, Bay could make out his fully erect cock swinging between his legs and knew Rin had to have a good view of it too.

"Since I'm not convinced you didn't just cut yourself on purpose," Rin stated. "I'll take things from here."

"What—" Bay's sentence died on a strangled sound when suddenly something solid was shoved inside of him. He felt it pull the tender flesh of his unprepared hole, his muscles fighting against the intrusion, only causing it to burn more. A sob escaped him and he clawed at the dirt, not in an attempt to get away, but just because he had to do *something*.

Once the hilt was inside of him, Rin was surprisingly careful not to allow the blade too close. He did, however, wiggle it around, causing that straight object to batter back and forth against Bay's inner walls in a foreign way that left him squirming.

After a bit of that, Rin pulled the knife free and hummed. "You're bleeding, Kitten. And after I tried so hard to avoid it. My kindness was wasted on you, it seems. I'll remember that moving forward."

Bay whimpered and Rin hushed him.

"I was talking about your hand. Your ass is fine. Considering how much worse you've treated this hole of yours, it's not really surprising, is it." He shoved the handle back in and without any further warning, began thoroughly fucking him with it.

The object was only a few inches in length, but it was enough to hit the spots that mattered, and before long Bay was shamelessly rocking back into it, urging it deeper despite the promised agony that would come if the blade accidently slipped inside.

It never did though. Despite all his threats to harm him, Rin was meticulous with his movements, sure to never allow it to get too close no matter how Bay begged for it.

And he was begging.

He'd started mindlessly pleading, the words half muffled by the dirt he kept sucking into his lungs with every deep inhale. His dick slapped against his stomach, leaving wet trail marks behind, the sound lewd and inviting. The pain had long since dissipated, chased successfully away by an intense need the likes of which he'd never experienced before.

It was like his entire body was on fire, and yet lifesaving water was just out of reach.

Rin pulled the knife out all the way, chuckling when Bay's hole fluttered imploringly, instead of obliging, however, he switched things up.

Bay was pulled from the ground and then yanked back against the hard surface of Rin's chest. Rin's knees beneath him kept his thighs spread and he carelessly tossed away the knife to free his other hand. He kept one on Bay's throat, the other capturing his weeping cock to stroke him in the same frenzy Bay typically preferred.

Only it was nothing like how he touched himself. Not even a little.

He gasped, back bowing, cock jutting up into that hot palm now coated in his own juices. Bay watched as Rin's hand pumped him, practically choking him in such a firm grip it should have hurt a little but miraculously didn't.

On one particular stroke, Rin lifted his own hips, grinding himself against Bay's plush ass.

The knowledge that he was turned on right now, that Bay was turning him on, was what finally pushed him over the edge.

Bay screamed until his throat was hoarse, come spurting out of him in thick ropes. Even after his moans had turned to whines, Rin didn't stop milking him, his fist keeping up that erratic pace until Bay started to worry he was going to strip his dick raw.

"Stop!" He grabbed onto his wrist and tried to still his movements, but that earned him a squeeze from the hand still around his throat and Bay stilled.

Rin's hand stroked him one last time then collected rivulets of come from his shaft until his whole palm was sticky. Suddenly, he shoved Bay forward.

He was so exhausted, he didn't even have the strength to catch himself, dropping onto his chest. A small stone poked at his cheek bone and he groaned, but he didn't even have the energy to move.

The sound of a zipper somehow pierced through the fog in his head and Bay frowned. That definitely wasn't—

His eyes went wide when his hips were lifted and it dawned on him what was about to happen. The scorching thing that prodded at his entrance next felt four times wider than the knife handle had been and he became distressed, instinctively trying to crawl away.

Behind him Rin growled, and that was all the warning he gave before he was wrenching Bay back to meet him.

In one forceful thrust, he impaled Bay on his cock.

Pain exploded through him and Bay howled,

his body flattened a second later beneath the firm length of Rin's. His thighs were forced further apart to accommodate that weight and as soon as Rin was satisfied with the new angle, he pushed in even deeper, not stopping until he was fully seated.

Bay cried and buried his face in his arms, tears wetting the ground beneath him. It felt like he was being sheared in half by a molten rod of steel, his insides churning. The come collected on Rin's palm wouldn't have been nearly enough to slick his entrance and ready him, though if he were being honest, he wasn't sure an entire bottle of lube and an hour with his fingers would have either.

Sure, he'd forced himself to take rubber cocks a time or two. But none of them had even come close to Rin's size. He didn't even have to see it to know it was larger than anything he was used to playing with. And since Rin had spied on him so thoroughly, that had to mean he was well aware of that fact too.

He'd known it would hurt, but he'd shoved himself inside of Bay anyway.

He sniffled as the first rush of heat licked at his lower region. The pain, as excruciating as it was, was turning him on again.

When was the last time Bay had felt *this* alive? That pain forced him to acknowledge he was, proved to him there was still something beating within his chest, clawing to make its way out of that empty abyss that had swallowed all of his emotions. Little by little they'd been returning, and now, split by Rin's cock, they poured into him all at once, a mixture of suffering and anger and arousal and fear and elation. A confusing concoction of both negative and positive.

Wordlessly, Rin began to pump into him, pulling out almost all the way to the tip and driving back in deep. Each time he entered, Bay cried out, but that sound only seemed to spur him on, until his tempo had picked up to such a rough pace Bay could no longer track the movements of his hips as he drove into him like a piston.

It wasn't nearly as horrifying to him as it should have been when shortly Bay's dick hardened a second time, even considering it was being rubbed between his stomach and small pebbles and twigs. Rin had him pinned completely, but his nipples were forced to take a similar torture, chafing against the ground.

There were spikes of discomfort followed swiftly by the all-consuming hits of euphoria and his cries took on a different note as he was worked back up to that place where everything hovered between those two intense sensations, pain and pleasure.

Bay's favorite place.

That cock battered into him again and again, practically tearing through him and everything was a buzzing, swirling mess around him, making it impossible for Bay to concentrate on anything but what his body was being forced to feel.

Which was probably why Rin had to repeat himself enough times he lost patience with him. His teeth pierced through the skin between Bay's neck and shoulder, and he growled against the fresh wound, only letting go once he was certain he had his attention. "Call my name," he demanded, voice promising more pain if he didn't obey.

Not that Bay had the ability to deny him anything right now, with his head so muddled and his body singing the way that it was. He felt simultaneously like he was being ripped in half and sewn back together again, an altogether discombobulating experience he, up until this point, hadn't been fully acquainted with.

The second orgasm snuck up on him, exploding like a rocket launch, blinding him in an instant.

"Varun!" he somehow managed to follow the order, even as he came completely and totally undone. Like before, Rin didn't stop just because he'd reached his limit, continuing to fuck into Bay just as wildly.

As the last pings of pleasure started to fade, Bay felt his consciousness slip with it. The darkness loomed closer and closer and the last thing he was aware of was Rin burying himself as deep as he could. Warmth bathed his insides and, as it filled him, Bay's overstimulated body succumbed to the black.

CHAPTER 11:

Light dragged him from comforting darkness and Bay groaned and slapped mindlessly at it. The movement only served to pull him the rest of the way out of sleep and he blinked, allowing his eyes to adjust. He'd left the blinds open last night and sunlight was pouring in, blanketing the entire bed.

He eased up into a sitting position and winced.

That sharp burst of pain, quickly receding already, was the hard reminder that he needed. It forced his mind to kick into overdrive and he gasped.

Last night.

He'd—

With—

Bay clutched at the heavy gray comforter resting over the top of him. The shitty thing was falling apart at the seams, but he'd yet to buy a new one. It held no sentimental value, he just rarely made it to the store for anything other than food and, even then, most of his meals were either at the school cafeteria or takeout.

What struck him so much about it, however, was the fact that it was his.

He was in his bed, in his room, in his house, but he had absolutely no recollection of how he'd come to be there. The last thing he remembered was taking a sledge hammer up the ass in the middle of the dank forest and then...

"I promised you'd make it out alive," a knowing voice drawled, and Bay's head shot toward his bedroom door which was located at the far-left corner of the room. Rin was standing there, partially cast in the shadows of the hallway, almost as though he were sticking to them on purpose for dramatic effect. "You're heavier than you look, Professor."

"Get out." His hand immediately went up to his throat at the sound of his own voice. It was shredded to the point it was nearly unrecognizable even to his own ears. That concern got pushed down the ever-growing list of them, however, when his hand met something foreign around his neck.

It felt like a braid of leather, less than half an inch thick, and short, practically a choker though with a little extra give. Something metal was dangling from the front of it, and he explored it with his fingers, frown deepening. It was a tiny loop.

What. The. Fuck?

"You know, I've discovered I'm into primal

play, Kitten," Rin told him casually, like Bay hadn't just woken up to the scene of a literal horror movie. "It's honest once you get into the right headspace. That sweet spot where all you do is react and feel instead of think and plot?" He let out a low whistle that had Bay jumping slightly to attention. "That's when your true nature gets revealed. Want to know what I learned about your nature last night, Bay Delmar?"

He shook his head, too afraid to speak.

"You came alive the second I tore into you," he continued anyway. "Be it with my teeth or my cock. You hated it, but because you hated it, you also loved it. I knew you had interesting preferences, but I didn't realize they ran that deep."

Bay held up his hand, silently begging him to stop, but Rin didn't listen.

"Knife play," he checked things off with his fingers as he spoke, "Fear play—that one surprised me. In a good way. Primal play...Although, we should give that one another attempt. Do it properly."

"No," Bay did his best to make the rejection come off firm, leaving no room for argument.

"Don't fret. I'll give you a choice, same as before."

"I said no." Last night had been...He'd need at least several more days to process all that it had been and how he truly felt about it. But first, he needed to get this man out of his house so he could either scream or cry or...He didn't know what other options there were but he was sure he'd think of something as soon as he regained the ability to think at all.

"Too late," Rin motioned to his own neck. "Already collared you." Then he slipped a hand into his front pocket and held up a tiny black key for Bay to see. "If you want to remove it, you're going to have to do so yourself."

Bay held out his hand, but Rin clucked his tongue.

"No," he motioned with his chin. "Come get it."

"After what you did to me, we both know that's not possible." Bay wasn't sure he'd be able to stand, let alone walk the seven feet it would take to reach the doorway.

"Won't know until you try." When Bay merely glared at him, Rin sighed and slid the key back into his pocket. "Choices, Kitten."

"This is insanity!" Bay dropped his head into his hands and inhaled to try and calm his racing heart. "You got what you wanted. I promised you I would stop, didn't I? Why are you still doing this to me?"

"Isn't it obvious?"

"No!"

Rin was quiet for a moment and then, "Interesting."

"No, it is not!" Bay slapped at the mattress, hissing when he ended up hitting the cut on his hand. There was a bandage wrapped around it he hadn't noticed before and he stared at it.

"If you reopen your wound, it's up to you to patch it back up yourself," Rin warned. "I've done my part in taking care of you."

"What does that even mean?" Bay asked in exasperation.

"I brought you home, cleaned you off, tended to your wounds…Oh. There's water on your nightstand. Have you had any yet? You probably should. You left a lot of fluids behind in the forest."

At first he thought Rin was messing with him again, but it became apparent he meant everything he was saying.

Bay's fingers went back to the metal loop hanging from the leather around his neck. "Are you…Treating me like a pet right now?"

Rin cocked his head.

"I'm not some animal."

"Of course not," he said, and there was a very real thread of disgust in his tone then. "I wouldn't harm a helpless creature like that."

"But you'd hurt me?" Bay demanded.

"You like it."

"What if I didn't?"

"Then I like it." He shrugged, like that was answer enough. "If it helps, there's only one person I think of as anything other than an annoyance. The fact that I even wanted to tuck you in and bandage your wounds already sets you above the rest."

"Why?" Bay asked. "Why didn't you just put me in my car and leave me there?"

"I don't know," Rin admitted. "That's why I've extended our playtime. So I can find out."

"I don't want that."

"You could change your mind."

"I won't."

"Are you sure? Hear me out first."

"No, now please just leave. And," he tugged at the leather, "take this thing with you!"

"That stays on," Rin said.

"Damn it! This isn't funny!" Bay shot off the bed, momentarily forgetting all about his aching behind. The second his feet hit the ground, his legs gave out, and he toppled forward.

Rin shot from the doorway at a sped that made him look little more than a blur. His arms came around Bay, hoisting him back up. There was a crease between his brow as he took in Bay's face. "Be careful. That was careless."

Bay only partially heard him.

"What?" Rin asked when he did nothing but stare up at him. "Professor?"

He sucked in a breath. "Good Light. You!"

Last night it'd been too dark for him to get a good look, but now in the light of day, less than five inches apart, Bay could see him for who he really was. How could he not? He'd only been obsessed with the man's face.

"You're bluffing," his aggressor didn't sound so sure. For the first time, there was uncertainty in his mismatched gaze.

"Sila," Bay forced himself to say it, dropping his arms to hang at his sides. "You're Sila."

He inspected him. "What does that even mean to you?"

"You're my student. Last night, that was *you*?!"

"It's not my fault you mistook me for my brother." He lifted a single shoulder, shrugging it off like it was nothing.

"Please let me go," Bay said.

"Not yet."

"No, I mean," he motioned behind him, "I need to sit down."

Sila—the man who'd fucked him like a demonic hell beast who also was decidedly not Rin—eased Bay onto the edge of the mattress, remaining close as though afraid Bay might fall again.

As if he actually *cared*.

Bay rubbed at his temple. "Please explain to me what's going on."

"Sure. But first." Sila picked up the half-filled glass from the end table nearby and held it out to Bay.

Seeing there was no other option, and since he was parched anyway, he took it and drained the whole thing before handing it back. It wasn't until he did that his taste buds picked up on the somewhat sweetness to what he'd assumed was just water.

"What else was in that?" he demanded.

"Pearl flowers," Sila said. "It'll help with healing. Your throat should start feeling better soon." His gaze dropped low. "I already applied sun cream to your—"

Bay let out a startled yelp, only then realizing he was completely naked, and desperately tugged the comforter over his lap to cover himself. Sila's expression was blank when he looked back up at him.

"You do recall me saying I carried you here and applied ointment, right?" He blinked at him. "Which implies I've already seen you in the light. All of you. Extensively."

Not to mention all the times he'd watched Bay at the Seaside...Something he nicely didn't bring up again.

Bay couldn't believe he'd just thought the words Sila and nice in the same sentence after last night.

"I need answers." He needed to remember how fucked up last night had been.

Even if it'd also felt amazing.

Even if the fact that it'd made him feel at all was amazing in and of itself.

"How did you...find out?" Bay asked.

"About your cute little attempts at spying?" Sila chuckled. "My brother told me."

"So Rin does know."

"I am Rin."

Bay's head snapped up. "What?" He scowled.

"No, you aren't. You can't fool me. I know it's you. You've been sitting in my class for over a month, driving me half mad with your presence. How could I not recognize you?"

"Yeah, I'm the one who's been taking your class this semester, Professor Delmar."

"Exactly. You're not—"

"But I'm not always the one you saw on campus," he continued.

"What do you mean?" Bay wasn't following.

"I am Rin," he repeated. "Sometimes. And sometimes I'm Sila."

"That doesn't make any sense." He'd seen the brothers together before. He knew there were two of them.

"Sure it does. Sometimes he's Rin, and sometimes he's Sila. Are you catching on now?"

Bay gave a tentative shake of his head even though, yeah, he sort of was. "You swap places."

"Not always. Less frequently since we came to this planet."

"Then why...?"

"My brother didn't want to deal with your leering, so he asked me to handle it. That's why I'm always the one who shows up for your class. We don't interact anywhere else on campus since you fear getting exposed and having to explain your inappropriate behavior to your colleagues, so it's a simple enough setup."

Bay opened his mouth and then snapped it shut again, then repeated the process before he was finally able to formulate another question. "Then...Which of you is the one I've actually been obsessing over?"

"I can't answer that," Sila said. His gaze suddenly turned dark and the energy in the room altered, growing heavy and almost stifling. When he leaned over to put them at eye level, there was a flicker of something dangerous in his gaze. "What I can tell you is that from here on out, the one you're obsessed with is me. Understand, Kitten?"

"That's not how attraction works."

The corner of his mouth tipped up, but the look was far from kind or boyish like Bay had always thought of him in the past. "We both know how your attraction works. It's better for you to accept the things you can't change. For now, I'm your man."

Something a lot like excitement skittered its slimy fingers down Bay's spine. Had Sila seen it? If so, he didn't give a reaction. Which was good, since Bay was embarrassed enough as it was.

He'd always known he was messed up, but this? This was on a whole different level.

How could he be turned on by the note of ownership in Sila's tone just now?

"Which leads me to choices." Sila straightened.

"Please." Bay didn't even know what he was begging for anymore.

"You'll want to hear me out," he said, "I promise. Option one, I turn around now and we can pretend like this whole thing never happened. So long as you keep away from my brother, as agreed upon."

"That's it? You'll just…," Bay motioned toward the door, "go?"

Sila hummed in the affirmative. "Don't get me wrong, I'm keeping the videos, but yeah. The population of the capital city is over ten thousand, Professor."

He pulled back slightly. "You're telling me you'll just go find someone else."

"Why does it sound like you're not a fan of that idea?"

Bay dropped his gaze and then clenched his fists around the comforter when Sila laughed at him.

"Watching you struggle to figure out what you want is amusing," he told him. "But, onto option two."

"There's no need." Bay lifted his head and glared. "Option one. Please vacate my home immediately."

"You sure?"

"Yes."

"Even though that means I'll be chasing someone else through the woods and filling them with my cock instead?"

His dick twitched and he was more grateful for the comforter than before. "Good, then they can report you to the proper authorities."

He grinned and did something Bay couldn't

quite put his finger on, something that morphed his face from that of a deviant college student to a complete and total monster.

No, not monster.

The man standing less than two feet away from him was a devil, possibly even the Devil. Malice and wicked glee practically radiated off of him and there was a slightly manic gleam to his eyes, like the idea of chaos had gotten him going.

Before he knew it, Bay was crawling backward on the mattress, trying to put distance between them, only Sila wasn't having any of that.

He followed, prowling forward to drop his hands on either side of Bay's hips, climbing up onto the twin-sized mattress so he could stalk him all the way to the center.

Bay froze on his elbows, instinct telling him to freeze up in the face of danger, that if he just stayed as still as possible, Sila wouldn't swallow him whole.

Amazingly enough, it seemed to work, some of that dark energy drifting away.

It wasn't completely gone when he tipped his head down at Bay, but it wasn't nearly as intense as it had been a moment ago.

"It's bold of you to assume I'd let it get that far," Sila said silkily. "Admittedly, that was my first time playing in a forest, but it was a night of firsts all around. I don't let prey slip through my fingers, Bay. It'd be a waste of energy if I did. So, no. If you reject me now, and I go off and find another playmate to do what we just did, you should know they won't make it long enough to even consider going to the authorities. In fact," he leaned down and pressed a closed mouth kiss to the bottom of Bay's jaw, ignoring the way that caused his breath to hitch, "They'll probably only be seen again when their separated parts are fished out of Lake Cerulean."

"Is that," he licked his dry lips and focused on making his voice steady, "supposed to make me feel bad?"

"Of course not." Just like that, Sila was off of him and standing at the side of the bed again.

Bay still couldn't move.

"Why would I assume you'd feel bad for a stranger?" He waved at him.

"Then," Bay took in the relaxed way Sila was standing, noting the casual expression on his face and recognized it for the mask it was, "What's option two?"

Sila had said it over and over again to him. He'd been incredibly forthright about it in fact.

He'd told Bay he'd made the mistake of attracting a devil.

Being taken against his will in the dirt hadn't been enough to really hammer that point through Bay's thick head.

But this? Apparently this was enough to get the message across loud and clear.

Fear gripped him and when he sat up, he moved as slowly as possible, eyes glued to Sila, ready for any sudden movements.

Nothing happened though, his student merely stood there watching and waiting. As soon as Bay was sitting once more, he spoke.

"From here until I say otherwise, you agree to play with me, wherever and however I want. No rules. No safe words. And this is the important one," Sila said. "No pretend. We're playing, but this is the real deal, Kitten, and you act accordingly or I pull out—and I don't mean in the fun you get to lick come off of your face way."

Bay's mouth twisted in displeasure before he could help it and he quickly smoothed the expression away.

Sila's eyes narrowed. "That," he pointed, "That looked a lot like pretend. You're free to express yourself. I don't want lies or masks. These aren't roles. I'm me. You're you. You're mine. It's as simple as that."

"I haven't agreed," Bay reminded, if only so he'd stop looking at him like he wanted to bite him again.

His face settled back into that relaxed expression, and it was so tempting for Bay to point out Sila was being a hypocrite, only…He liked breathing. A lot.

"And?" he ended up saying instead. "What do I get in return for basically signing my soul to the devil?"

Sila smirked at that, quick and bright, and Bay's traitorous idiotic heart skipped a beat.

"How eloquently put, Professor. I wouldn't expect anything less from you. What will you get? Your greatest desire, of course. Isn't that always how deals with the devil go?"

"Yes, well, I've fucked you already so…"

Sila laughed. "Oh. No. I didn't mean me. Oh wow. That's…" He kept laughing through it and had to pause to wait for the fit to end on its own. Then brushed what appeared to be very real tears from the corner of his eyes and grinned at Bay. "My ego definitely didn't need that heavy petting you just gave it, but points anyway. I'll remember that."

Bay wished his bed would turn into a portal to another dimension and engulf him immediately.

"While my cock is phenomenal and I'm certain you already want more of it," Sila continued, "that's not the desire I was referring to. You like me, sure, but up until fifteen minutes ago you didn't even realize I *was* me. So, doesn't really seem like your biggest yearning, know what I mean?"

"I—"

"Your grandmother," Sila sobered instantly. "I'm talking about your grandmother. The reason you live in this rundown monstrosity that wouldn't pass housing regulations, and work a job you hate, that's all because of her, right? You think she was wronged."

"She *was* wronged," Bay hissed, not because he was angry at Sila, but because he could experience fury again and he welcomed it when it came now.

"Sure she didn't just gamble everything away like the Shepards claim?"

"Yes. I may not know who you are, Varun, but I knew her better than I know myself. She would never have done that. Not in a million years."

"All of the Shepards are shithead kids, most of which attend Vail," Sila nodded in understanding. "That's why you've kept your job instead of turning to racing full time. You stay in this house so as not to draw suspicion, since everyone knows you wouldn't be able to afford more on your salary alone in a city like this."

Sila hadn't been joking.

He really did know all of Bay's secrets.

And he was stripping them away from him and laying them bare.

Only…

"You're thinking too highly of me." Bay deflated back against the bed. More than anything, he wanted to agree because of how much better those reasons made him seem, but it wouldn't be true.

"Oh?" Sila asked.

"I wanted to know if you felt things," Bay reminded. "That's because more often than not, I don't. Not anymore. Not since she died."

He frowned at him. "You were emoting just fine last night. You do whenever we interact, in fact."

"Yeah," he wasn't going to correct him for considering all the times he'd spied on Sila from afar as interactions, "because I can feel things when it comes to you or racing. But aside from that…" Bay shrugged. "Everything is dull. It's like I've gone numb."

"I'm not numb," Sila said.

"I mean, I don't have antisocial personality disorder, so it makes sense we aren't the same."

He snorted at that. "We aren't the same at all, Kitten. This, however, is useful information."

Bay's heart skipped a beat, and not because it'd sounded like a threat and scared him. The exact opposite. "Useful how?"

"That's why you're so obsessed with me, isn't it. It makes sense. I enjoyed last night so much for similar reasons. Emotional responses, especially when you don't typically get them, can be addicting. That's more of a reason to agree to my offer. You're more messed up by your grandmother's death and I knew. If you could handle this on your own, you would have done it by now. Two years is a long time to carry a grudge and drown yourself in grief. Let me unburden you."

Bay felt like he was losing his mind all over again. "What can you do?"

"What can't I do," he corrected. "Don't you trust me?"

"No."

"Fair." Sila smiled. "Don't you trust I can get anything I want?"

Bay considered it, but not for long. "Yes."

Sila had figured out Bay was Pandaveer, had managed to plant hidden cameras at a place like the Seaside, and uncovered the fact that Bay's grandmother had been wrongfully accused. He'd had to have done some serious digging for that last one, since all of the official documents said she'd had a sudden stroke due to her anxiety over having gambled away all of her possessions.

"If there's something to be found, I'll find it," Sila promised. "And if there isn't, if they covered their tracks, then I'll help you make them pay for it the way they should have two years ago."

Was he offering to be Bay's personal judge, jury, and executioner? That shouldn't be so tempting, so attractive.

"I don't just want revenge," Bay said. "I want everyone else on this stupid planet to know. Even if that means we get a verbal confession before slitting their throats, I want it."

"Does this mean you're going for option two?" Sila asked.

This was a mistake, a dangerous and foolish mistake and yet...His life might no longer be important to him, but he needed to know. Once and for all. He needed proof that Idle Delmar hadn't left him homeless on purpose.

If he had to sell his soul?

He hadn't had a use for that in years anyway.

"You swear you'll help me find evidence?" he wanted to hear it again, just to be sure.

"In exchange for your complete and unwavering obedience," Sila nodded. "Yes."

He'd said there'd be no rules and no safe words, which implied there was going to be pain. Maybe even a dash of humiliation.

It was a good thing Bay wasn't averse to either of those things.

"All right," he sounded far more excited than he should and he knew it. "Option two. I pick that one."

Sila grinned and the devil seemed to be gleaming behind his eyes.

CHAPTER 12:

Something was wrong.

Bay could sense it, or more aptly, feel it. Literally. That spot of dread that he'd felt last night lingered still, and with it there was something else, something an awful lot like contentment.

It was the latter that was worrying him the most, and that in and of itself was yet another issue.

Bay shouldn't be able to feel anything this deeply or strongly, hadn't been capable of it in years, but there was no denying it as he stood in front of his bathroom mirror. His murky reflection, due to the clouded glass from the shower he'd just taken, peered back, only instead of the blank expression he'd grown used to, there was a spark in his eyes and a flush to his cheeks that had little to do with the hot water he'd just attempted to drown his sorrows in.

Sila had left abruptly yesterday and ever since Bay's body had yet to calm. He was still heightened, as though subconsciously a part of him thought perhaps the younger man would return for round two.

The fact that didn't terrify him like it should...

"There is no way I can be that fucked up," he murmured to himself. As far as he could see it, there was only one explanation for what was happening to him, and he didn't like it.

Could Sila have...cured him?

It was too soon to tell for certain, of course, but Bay was used to the feelings dissipating shortly after whatever adrenaline inducing activity he'd partaken in had ended. The longest he'd been able to keep his emotions after had been about fifteen minutes and that was only because the rush from the race itself and the stimulation from winning was intense enough to.

The other night...and then yesterday morning...

He swore and covered his face, wishing the floor would open and swallow him whole so he wouldn't have to face this situation or what it most likely said about him as a person. It was one thing, liking kink in the bedroom and being an adrenaline junkie of a sort. Getting a high from racing or watching porn was actually pretty normal. Wanting to be hunted down in the middle of a dark forest and tossed to the ground and brutalized...

Had he always been like this, or was this a change that had come after the death of his grandmother? Was it a side effect of emotional detachment? One he just hadn't read up on before? He didn't think it was possible for that to change who he was at a primal level, which meant, like it or not, he was someone who found it arousing to be taken advantage of.

Sila had made it sound like it was a no brainer when he'd tossed the word masochism around, but for Bay that had been another shocking discovery. Yes, he'd caused himself a bit of minor harm during his private play—shoving in a dildo when unprepared to see if he could take it, digging his own nails into the flesh of his thighs or palm, stuff like that—but he'd been careful to never take things *too* far.

Considering the amount of sun cream Sila had used on him, he would guess he'd been pretty beat up down there.

Only…He remembered the pain, of course, but it hadn't been all that bad. Excruciating for a blip of time and then gone in a flash, swept away by the most intense pleasure Bay had ever experienced in his entire life. Not only had he felt alive when he'd been pinned beneath Sila's hard body, he'd actually felt like he was being dragged back from the pits of hell.

Rebirths weren't meant to be easy or painless.

Was that what had happened to him? After trying for so long to "fix" himself and return to the person he once was, only to fail over and over again, had this done the trick?

His multi-slate went off, Nate's name flashing in neon lettering, and he made a sound of relief. His friend was always good at comforting others and Bay needed someone to help ground him. "Hey."

"…Hi," Nate's voice came through the other end, hesitant. "Are you all right?"

No.

Yes.

Maybe?

"I'm not sure," he ended up replying, licking his lips as he leaned an arm against the stained marble countertop. He had no idea what the stains were from. They'd been there when he'd bought the place. They'd never bothered him before, but now he frowned at them, wondering if Sila had noticed.

"You sound…" Nate cleared his throat. "Don't take this the wrong way, but you sounded happy just now when you picked up."

"It's just nice to hear from you."

"Have you changed your mind about restarting your sessions with Dr. Orion? Is that it?"

Bay winced at Nate's hopeful tone, feeling bad about disappointing him—Guilt. He felt guilty, and not that miniscule brush of it he could sometimes get tiny bursts of, but the real deal. In full, uncomfortable, brightness.

"I'm sorry I've been such a shitty friend," he said. "These past years, I know it couldn't have been easy putting up with me."

"It's okay."

"It isn't," he disagreed.

"Pace yourself," Nate urged. "From the way you sound, whatever you're doing it's working. Can I come over? Or do you want to go out and do anything?"

Bay chuckled. "Why do you sound more excited than I am?" When he was met with silence he was forced to add, "That was a joke."

"I'm coming over." The sound of a hoverbike engine revving came through the speaker. "I'll be there in ten."

"Okay." The line went dead almost before he'd gotten the response out and he rolled his eyes and tossed his device back onto the counter. Planting both palms against the smooth surface, he leaned in, practically until the tip of his nose met the glass.

He wasn't just imagining it, there was something in his eyes, an awareness in his gaze that he'd been lacking. At school, they referred to him as the Statue Professor. He'd heard the rumors, many of which hadn't been whispered all that quietly in his presence. They said he was cold and unmoving, yet beautiful, like an ancient sculpture. Like with everything else, before he'd been ambivalent about those comments, but now...

Surely this couldn't last. What were the odds that he'd been shocked awake by Sila's abusive cock of all things?

That wasn't even why Bay had been interested in him in the past. He'd liked the younger man because he'd given off this sense of light and kindness. He'd reminded Bay of the person he used to be before his grandmother's death, the kind of person who could make friends anywhere and could always find the silver lining even on the stormiest of days.

Now, that person he used to be seemed like a stranger to him, a recollection of a different person entirely separate from Bay. He held all those memories, but he couldn't figure out how to get back to being that way, or even muster the amount of care needed to truly give it an attempt.

He'd become a stone statue. The undead.

But the man staring back at him in the mirror was *alive*.

Knowing Nate was close, Bay left the bathroom and the confusing reflection behind, quickly getting ready for the day. He pulled on the first shirt he could find, a black t-shirt he probably hadn't washed, and a pair of faded jeans, then paused to stare at the unmade bed.

The sheets were a twisted mess and the comforter was rolled up in a heap at the center where he'd left it. He'd gone after Sila when the younger man had suddenly told him he would see him later, locking the door behind him. As if that would make some sort of difference.

Bay had already let the devil in. It was going to take a lot more than a shitty metal lock to keep him out. Hell, this house didn't even have an electronic keypad like most places in the universe. It was so old, the only thing keeping Bay from being murdered by an intruder in the middle of the night was a partially rusted lock.

That hadn't mattered to him before either, but now he frowned. If anyone was going to kill him, it sure as hell wasn't going to be some random junkie high off his ass breaking into the wrong home looking for drugs or coin—neither of which Bay had.

He'd lined his pockets fairly well with the races, but he'd been sitting on it all this time, all of that in the bank. Now, standing in the tiny box of room, he was looking around as though just seeing it.

There was only the twin sized bed set in the center, with one end table that was missing a front leg and had scratch marks all over the surface. There was a bookshelf in the far corner, but he hadn't touched any of the items layered in random piles there since moving in, and they'd collected so much dust it was impossible to make out any of the titles on the spines. A greenish-purple mold was growing in the opposite corner and there was water damage to the ceiling Bay hadn't noticed up until now.

He felt a twist of disgust and disappointment, but even though those were negative emotions aimed at himself every bit as much as his environment, he clung to them greedily. His brief bursts of feeling while riding or watching Sila from afar had been great, but they were nothing compared to the actual wave of emotion that he was experiencing now.

It was as though he'd been asleep for a century and was now finally rousing from slumber. The progression was slow, the lazy blink of his eyes, the stretch of his arms and then his legs. No one jumped straight out of bed when they woke, especially not from a long sleep. They took their time, waited to adjust to having their senses open up and their body unlock.

"It's me!" The sound of the front door opening caught his attention. Nate had Bay's emergency key, something he'd insisted on when Bay had first moved here. His steps were loud as he traveled through the small home, clearly on the search, and he appeared in the doorway a moment later, eyes instantly sweeping Bay from head to toe.

Bay turned to better face him, the corner of his mouth lifting when Nate blinked at him in surprise.

Nate came forward and pressed the back of his hand over Bay's forehead, frowning slightly. "You don't have a fever. Are you feeling okay? You look—"

"Good?" Bay supplied for him, laughing when that gave Nate pause all over again. "Yeah. I know. I feel good too. Isn't that interesting?"

Interesting.

Sila's favorite word.

He scowled and Nate grabbed onto his arm.

"What?" Nate asked. "What's wrong?"

"No," he shook his hold off, both thankful for and annoyed by his friend's concern, "It's nothing. I was just thinking about something, that's all."

"Something upsetting." Nate ran both of his hands through his hair and backed up, giving Bay space now that he was satisfied nothing was wrong. "Dude, what happened to you after the race last night? When you left your bike with me you seemed the same as always. You were happy you'd won, but otherwise unmoved."

Bay couldn't exactly tell him he'd been sexually assaulted by a student. Not only because Nate would freak out—rightfully so—but because there was no way in hell he'd ever understand how Bay currently felt about it.

Bay couldn't even understand it himself really.

He'd suffered from a crime, a horrendous one, and yet…He didn't want justice or revenge. Didn't want to go to the authorities and file a report. Even the thought of kicking Sila from his class made his heart seize up.

No, what Bay wanted, what he truly wanted, was for Sila to do it again.

He was ashamed to admit that, now that he had time to sit with it, he was more than a little bit relieved that Sila had offered him a chance to explore this fucked up situation further.

It was a good thing the devil wasn't done with him, because Bay wasn't through with Sila either. Especially not when being with him could bring out this much within him.

"I didn't start going back to the doctor," Bay said, because he had to say something. "Is it really that big a difference though?"

"I could tell over the phone," Nate reminded excitedly. "You picked up and sounded the way you used to."

"How's that?"

"Pleased to hear from me."

Bay tipped his head and considered. "I was. You're a great friend. Always there for me when I need someone. And you're looking after my bike. I appreciate it."

"You've said that before," Nate told him, "Only this time I can tell you mean it. Seriously, what's going on? If it wasn't the doctor, what caused this big of a change? Will it last?"

"I don't know." Bay had never heard of emotional detachment curing itself overnight, but then again, an extreme event could cause an intense reaction. "I'm timing it to see how long it does. So far, it's been...a while."

"What's a while?"

"Since yesterday morning." He didn't want to give details but he had to say something. He *wanted* to say something. Wanted to confide in his friend and not be alone in all of this. "I... was with someone. Our being together wouldn't be considered socially acceptable, so I'll leave it at that. I trust you won't pry?"

"It's a student," Nate easily guessed, shrugging when Bay glared. "What? You made it so obvious. But don't worry. I don't care who you're with so long as you're safe about it. I should be thanking them actually."

"Let's not get ahead of ourselves."

"So, what? You think liking someone helped reset your emotions?" Nate thought it over. "You haven't had a crush in a long time and they do say love is the cure for everything."

"I wouldn't call it love," Bay stuttered then cleared his throat. He took time to collect his glasses from the end table and put them on, stalling, then took a chance by admitting, "Obsession would be a more accurate definition."

"On your side or theirs?"

Sila wasn't obsessed with Bay, he was merely looking to get even. It shouldn't bother him, considering he wasn't at all the person Bay had believed him to be, and yet he found himself a little hurt by the notion that the younger man wasn't actually interested in him. He wanted to make Bay suffer and clearly last night had been fun for him as well since he'd made the offer to do so again, but that didn't mean he wanted Bay.

It didn't mean he felt the same twisted yearning that Bay felt for him.

And how odd, that Bay even felt that at all. Even stranger still was the fact it was ten times brighter and hotter within him than it'd been before when he'd crushed on the boyish Sila Varun.

There was nothing boyish about the monster who'd cut the clothing from his body and stripped him bare last night.

Bay shivered thinking about it, unable to contain the reaction in time and Nate clicked his tongue knowingly.

"Oh, so that's how it is." Nate crossed his arms and propped a shoulder against the doorframe, much like Sila had done earlier.

"Should we go to the kitchen?" Bay asked suddenly. "I haven't had coffee yet."

Nate's eyes went pointedly to the unmade bed. "What *have* you had this morning, Pandaveer?" When Bay scoffed at him, he lifted a hand to the side of his face and made a lewd motion.

Bay tossed a pillow at him—the single pillow he owned with the stained gray pillow case—and glared. "I forgot how annoying you could be."

"I haven't changed," Nate argued, picking up the pillow when it hit his chest and dropped to the ground. He tossed it back on the bed. "If anything, I kicked it up a notch whenever I was around you, you just never reacted until now."

"Really?" Bay hadn't noticed.

"Yeah, really." Nate laughed and then turned, heading down the small hallway to the main room which doubled as the kitchen and living area. Aside from that, one closet, and the bathroom, there weren't any other rooms in the house.

Bay was halfway to him when he came to an abrupt halt.

If Sila had been standing in the doorway, that meant he'd come from the rest of the house. He'd cleaned Bay up and brought him water, but… What else had he gotten up to while Bay had been asleep?

"All good?" Nate called from the kitchen, the sound of the cupboards opening following quickly after.

"Yeah, do me a favor and get the coffee started," Bay said.

"Sure."

Bay ran his sweaty palms over his jean-clad thighs as he slowly walked toward the single door in the hallway. It led to the closet, which was where…He never had anyone over—even Nate and Berga rarely showed now since they saw him at the races—and he hadn't cared enough about discovery before to rethink the location of his stash. Now however, the thought of Sila having seen it…He forced himself to grab the door handle and whip the thin wood open as fast as he could.

At first, he sighed when he saw the row of coats he kept hanging there seemingly untouched. It was a small barrier between what lay beyond, but he doubted Sila would have any reason to inspect a closet once discovering that's all it was.

He glanced to the right, checking down

the hall to be sure Nate wasn't heading back for any reason. When it was clear he wasn't, Bay shifted some of the hangers down the metal rod. Most things were digital now, but he still had a fondness for tangible things, probably because his grandmother had raised him on paper photographs of her adventures and physical textbooks filled with information and pictures that would always be there within reach.

His emotions had been cut off, but he'd still acted on instinct when it came to stuff like this, things he wanted to hold on to. That was why he'd mindlessly printed the photos, some he'd taken himself in secret on campus, others copied from Inspire.

He'd taped them at the back of the closet, a sick shrine of sorts for the student he could never have. The fact that it'd been gross and wrong had only made him want to do it more, since he'd been able to feel a small ember of emotion with each glossy image he'd placed.

Bay frowned when the first couple came into view, and then he gasped and shoved the rest of the coats out of the way so he could get a better look at the entire back of the closet.

Some of the photos had been torn down. There were empty patches where they'd once been, but it probably amounted to only seven of the three dozen or so Bay had collected. It was only then that he noticed the floor of the closet was littered with shreds of paper.

Sila had torn some of the photos down and then ripped them apart. But not all of them.

Why?

Bay moved in closer, staring for a bit at one particular image of Sila laughing at something Rabbit had said in the East Quad. He'd snapped the shot at the beginning of the semester, the same day he'd discovered that Sila was a student in his class. He'd felt dirty doing it, knowing the picture was there in his multi-slate as he taught the rest of his classes for that day.

Ironic, that Bay had violated Sila's rights long before the younger man had violated his body.

"Hey," Nate popped his head around the end of the closet and Bay startled. "You coming or what?"

"Yeah." Shoving the coats back into place, Bay shut the closet with a definitive click and smiled reassuringly. "Please tell me you made a full a pot."

"Did you one better," Nate said as the two of them moved into the kitchen. "I pulled out your espresso maker."

"You're the best."

Nate held up an already filled mug for him. "You have no idea how great it is to hear that and know you actually mean it."

Bay made a sound of agreement and took the offering, the rich smell of coffee causing him to sigh in contentment before taking a sip.

"Here's to you hopefully being on the way to a full recovery." Nate held up his own mug in toast.

He clicked them together and grinned. "Fingers crossed."

A tiny voice in the back of his head wondered if Nate would still think that if he'd known how Bay had gotten his emotions back in the first place.

CHAPTER 13:

Routine was the best mask of them all. Predictable people were easy targets and people equated easy with safe.

Three times a week, Sila could be found swimming for exactly one hour in the Vail University pool. His rotation between it and his trips to the library were all part of the camouflage he'd carefully concocted. Knowing exactly where to find him at a certain time on any given day gave those around him a sense of comfort. It made them believe they knew him and his character.

Hard working, dedicated, friendly…He'd crafted the perfect disguise to protect not only himself, but his brother as well. The best lies were the ones most heavily rooted in truth. Hiding worked in a similar fashion.

Since he didn't want anyone to ever get too close to him, he allowed them the illusion that they already were.

Sila rolled and kicked off the wall, cutting through the water with ease. He was coming to the end of his hour and wanted to get a few more laps in before then. His home planet, Tibera, was a world made almost entirely of ocean. The land, all golden sand and tall rocky cliffs, wasn't the only populated part due to this fact. Every Tiberan learned how to swim before they knew how to walk. Were taught how to manage their emotions by syncing their breaths to the motion of the waves.

Their people's emotions were heightened compared to most other species, but they filtered through them quickly so as not to allow themselves to become prey to erratic emotional states of being. Processing information, as well as feeling, and thinking critically were all important aspects to Tiberans.

It'd been simple enough for Sila to act the part growing up—at least once he'd realized he wasn't normal. Because they sorted through and compartmentalized their feelings so thoroughly, Tiberans were actually known for being levelheaded. All the times Sila showed no emotion, everyone simply assumed it was because he was properly regulating his feelings.

The never would have guessed he actually didn't have any.

That wasn't entirely true. He could feel certain things, as he'd explained to Bay two nights ago. But things like empathy, regret, remorse... Those things alluded him. Thank Light too. Sila couldn't even begin to imagine how tedious existing would be if he had to be concerned over others as well as himself.

It sounded like nothing more than an epic waste of time.

His brother was different though. He felt too much instead of not enough. It'd been harder for him to manage and stay hidden when they'd been on Tibera. It was mostly for him, and to escape their overbearing father and the predetermined fates he'd set for them, that Sila had agreed to run.

He never would have done so otherwise. He didn't run. He chased.

If it'd been solely up to him, he would have found a way to murder their father. They would have been free of him and gotten his fortune to keep them comfortable. Instead, they'd come all the way to Vitality, with a meager allowance and an agreement with Crate Varun that they would study and then return to fill the roles he'd assigned them.

If he had his way, Sila would be forced to work at the hospital for the rest of his days and Rin would be turned into the next member at the High Council table.

That would never happen.

Their plan was to escape as soon as they'd completed their time at Vail and the Academy. They'd flee and start over somewhere fresh, where they could be whoever and whatever they wanted to be. Thanks to Bay, Sila had built a hefty enough nest egg it was possible for them to go early, something his brother wasn't yet aware of.

Sila prided himself on his ability to plan ahead, but he hadn't seen the events of this past month coming. Now he had Bay and his brother was involved with Kelevra Diar. Their plans might be in the process of changing.

He was in the process of changing.

Bay Delmar should have been dealt with in the forest and left there. Sila hadn't planned on killing him, only because that would draw too much unwanted attention, but the events that had taken place hadn't been on his to-do list either. At the time, it hadn't seemed like a big deal. He was acting on instinct in a contained setting where it was safe for him to do so. But afterward…

He'd taken Bay home because the thought of leaving him unprotected, unconscious in his car in the parking lot hadn't sat right with him. Once inside, Sila had brought him to bed and cleaned him off, applied ointment to his injuries. That should have been enough, but he'd sat on the edge of the bed, watching Bay sleep until the sun had risen.

Then, instead of leaving like he should have, he'd snooped around. Since Bay's home was one of the few places he hadn't bothered with, there'd been a lot to see. Sila had already discovered that Bay used to live comfortably when his grandmother was still alive.

The house Bay had grown up in now belonged to the Shepards, a group of useless idiots who couldn't even decide how to spell the name of their gang—some wrote it as Shepherds, others as Shepards, and that had led to the city divided on the proper way of it.

Haroon Caddel, their leader, was clearly the biggest fool of them all, since he'd allowed something like that to happen.

Sila had already been looking into them, but he hadn't taken the search seriously. When he'd first arrived on planet and had been eager to learn who was important and who wasn't, the Shepards had decidedly fallen in the latter category. He'd never had any interest in playing with them, since it was apparent games with them would be child's play.

Yet for some reason, when he'd heard Bay stir awake and gone to find him sitting up in bed, Sila had changed his plans for the man. Again.

He slapped at the end of the pool and then came up, inhaling deeply as water ran down his face. Even before he opened his eyes, he could sense the presence nearby and knew he was being watched. Taking his time, he lifted himself up onto the ledge and twisted so he could sit, leaning back on his palms.

"Hello to you, too," Aneski, the only member from that pathetic group Sila didn't look down on, drawled. The sound of his combat books moving closer came a second later. "Did I get the meeting time wrong?"

"You got it right," Sila said, though he didn't turn to greet him. Yesterday, after Bay had agreed to further games, Rin had called. He'd left to go deal with his brother and, on his way to the Brick, had contacted Aneski to call in a few favors that were owed.

"Is this a safe place to talk?"

Though the Shepards were nothing in comparison to the Brumal Mafia, they still took part in illegal dealings and were typically looked down upon by the rest of society. Unlike the Voids, who'd garnered wealth and prestige out in the open, carefully conducting their shadier business ventures under the table or in the protection of night.

Aneski's brother was a founding member when the gang had first been formed three years ago. Sila had learned the guy had been murdered, most likely during a scuffle with the Brumal. He didn't know all the details and he didn't care to find them out.

A dead person could do nothing for him.

"Everyone knows I reserve the pool room during this time," Sila replied. Though it was open to every student, his dedication to swimming had spread around campus and there was rarely —if ever—anyone else here to disturb him during his scheduled sessions. Another reason why being known as a nice guy could be more beneficial than being considered a loner.

Aneski knew a little more than the rest, but only because Sila had allowed him a glimpse in order to lure him into his clutches. That was why the Shepard owed him a favor to begin with, because Sila had helped him track down the truth about his brother's death.

"You make uncovering secrets a habit?" Aneski asked then, though his tone was indifferent. "Who's this one for? Don't tell me Professor Delmar actually asked you to look into it for him."

Something twisted at the center of Sila's chest and he paused, taking a moment to inspect the foreign sensation. It felt an awful lot like anger, but there was no reason for Aneski's words to have triggered that type of emotional response in him.

"Do you know him?" Sila asked, tipping his head to the side as he waited for the answer.

"The professor? Half the school swoons over him because that face of his, so I know of him. But I've never taken one of his classes before."

There. It happened again.

Sila pressed his palms against the gray tile and lifted his legs out of the water until he was standing, then he slowly turned to face the Shepard.

Aneski wasn't ugly himself, with ginger colored hair and sharp jade green eyes. He had an eyebrow piercing, a small golden bar at his left brow, and his nails were painted. The pattern switched back and forth between mint green and burnt orange. He was wearing all black, the color indicating he was a senior, and the school's pin winked under the fluorescent lighting from where it was secured on his belt.

"What?" Aneski frowned under the scrutiny and rested his hands on his hips. "What's up?"

Sila debated whether or not to order the other man to stay the hell away from Bay, but it was illogical and his anger was misplaced. Not only because there'd been no indication in Aneski's tone that he held any interest in Bay as a man, but also because, as they'd established yesterday, Sila already owned him.

Bay was smart, smart enough to know that when Sila had told him they wouldn't be pretend, he'd meant Bay wasn't allowed to fool around with anyone else.

"Nothing." He shoved strands of sopping hair off his forehead and tugged lightly at the golden star huggie earring in his left lobe, allowing his body to relax so he presented the picture of someone with casual interest. Aneski didn't know how important this information actually was to him. "What did you find?"

"Nothing really," he said, blowing out a breath.

"The gang is young," Sila reminded. "Most of your members are still in college. There's barely even a paper trail to follow." Three years' worth wasn't much and typically people hung on to their important documents at least that long.

"Yeah," he nodded, "that's the kicker. The group was slapped together by a handful of university students who were more concerned over who they'd get to stick their dick into next and less concerned with keeping things like records. And it's not like we file taxes. Everything that was signed over to the group was actually signed over to Haroon personally."

Sila had already figured that much out. When he'd looked, all he'd been able to find was rumor that the Shepards had cleaned out the Delmar bank account. Idle's three story home had been converted into their clubhouse of sorts, with a few top tier members taking residence on the property. Haroon was one of them.

"I went through Russ's stuff," Aneski continued. His older brother had died not long after the Shepards had gotten control of Idle's assets. "There wasn't much there about it either. Just old emails sent to other group members about moving and how Haroon had come into some money and was using that for renovations."

Haroon Caddel, Russ Onus, and Bowser Kita were the three founding members of the Shepards. Russ had disappeared after a fight with the Brumal and Bowser had supposedly graduated last year and moved to the other side of the planet for a tech position in a large firm. That left only Haroon to head the group.

"Look," Aneski said, "I remember when that all went down. It was sad that a little old lady kicked the bucket, and even worse when it was discovered she'd gambled away everything to her name and left her grandson penniless, but that shit goes down all the time. The Shepards roll in dirty money."

They had several small gambling dens cropped around the outskirts of the city. Sila wasn't sure if the Brumal were aware and merely turning the other cheek because they made petty coin in comparison to what the officially run casinos the Voids owned did, or if they hadn't yet sniffed them out.

If it was the latter, there was a chance Sila could use that information to his advantage and approach Baikal for a deal. He chuckled at the ridiculousness of his own thoughts, waving that it was unimportant when that had Aneski giving him an odd look.

Aside from it keeping him entertained, there was no reason for Sila to be this invested in whatever may or may not have gone down between Idle and Haroon. He'd felt nothing when he'd taken in all the framed photos of Bay and his grandmother hanging on the aged, yellowing walls. It'd been clear he'd found the missing piece, the thing needed to force Bay's hand, but he hadn't cared about a dead woman or how she'd come to be that way.

Then Bay's eyes had lit up like tiny infernos and he'd glared down his nose at Sila—not meekly, like those other times before when he'd been trying to hide how turned on he was. A real, full-on glare filled with derision and rage.

Bay felt wronged.

By *someone else.*

Sila didn't like it. He didn't understand why it bothered him, but it did, and that was enough to make him want to remedy the situation. So, he'd figure this out for Bay and get him the answers he needed to finally move on and get to play with him a few more times in the process.

Afterward, when he was bored and over it, he'd toss Bay back like he did every other used plaything and move on.

That odd sensation in his chest returned and he frowned at himself.

"All I'm saying," Aneski said, "is you might want to consider that Haroon was telling the truth. The lawyers all sided with him when Professor Delmar tried to fight it."

Bay had used up what meager savings he'd had left to hire the best lawyer he could for that case too. He'd lost miserably and now he was living in a dilapidated monstrosity, sharing space with countless vermin.

Sila wasn't a neat freak by any definition, but after the third black blobby creature scurried across the warped floorboards in his peripheral vision, he'd had more than enough of that death trap waiting to happen.

He'd need to relocate Bay. There was no way Sila was going to be comfortable playing with him there.

"Are you listening to me?" Aneski huffed.

"It's impossible to find any traces of Idle

gambling because three years ago the Shepards didn't even have the small pop-up dens they have now. Everything was run from tents. Meaning no security footage to hack into and absolutely no records stored on any hard drives," Sila stated. "Of course I considered looking into whether or not she was actually gambling. It's an impossible task, hence why I needed you in the first place."

"All right." He held up both hands in the sign of surrender. "Fair."

"Bay has copies of the official documents at his place," that disgusting hell hole of a place, "but I need to see the ones Haroon has as well."

"You think he kept them?" Aneski asked. "If he did, the only place I can think to look is his private office. No one is allowed in there and it requires a key code to even get the door open."

Sila had originally told Aneski to look for receipts on how the money was spent, but since that was a dead-end, he'd start at the beginning and work his way through it all on his own. "You don't need to enter to get what we need."

He lifted a brow in silent question.

"You wear contacts, correct?" Sila asked even though she already knew the answer.

Corrective surgery was common, but like most of the members of the Shepards, Aneski didn't come from money. The surgery was more expensive than simply wearing contacts and few people in the lower or middle classes on Vitality bothered getting it.

"Do you ever wear glasses?" he added before he could get a reply.

"Yeah, sometimes," Aneski said. "Why?"

Kelevra Diar had a computer eye in place of his real one which allowed him to access any tech within a ten-foot radius. Obviously Sila couldn't ask the guy for his eye, but it'd been created off the blueprints of a similar product that was more accessible.

"Insight 2.0." Baikal Void frequently wore a pair of the glasses and his family's company manufactured and sold them throughout the galaxy.

"Good idea," Aneski shook his head, "but you can't use those to illegally hack into any system. They're programmed to sync only with approved devices from those devices' owners. There's no way Haroon will let me near enough his tablet to hit the accept button."

"He won't have to. I know someone who can reprogram a pair so it has the master key."

"The ones the Devils of Vitality notoriously use to breech everyone's privacy and get whatever they want?"

"Yeah," Sila said, "that one."

"Who the hell do you know who can get you something like that?"

The corner of Sila's mouth tipped up. "Kelevra Diar."

"And why would the Imperial Prince do something like that for you? If the Emperor or the

Heir Imperial found out, he'd be in big trouble."

Kelevra's sisters would give him a slap on the wrist at most, but Sila didn't bother arguing about that.

"Haven't you heard? He's involved with my brother." Sila was pretty sure everyone knew. It was practically all anyone in the capital was discussing nowadays.

"I don't know, man...That's a big ask."

"Which is why you're leaving it to me to ask it." Done with this conversation, Sila walked over to the bench and grabbed his towel, lightly drying off while checking his multi-slate. There weren't any missed communications.

Bay hadn't come to school today, but Sila's class wasn't held until tomorrow, so it wasn't like he could automatically assume he was avoiding him personally.

Was it good or bad that he'd called out sick? It was so hard to tell with the professor. Sila had already figured Bay would get off on pain and mild humiliation—nothing too serious in that last regard, since he wasn't a fan of exhibitionism—and their time together in the forest had cleared any lingering doubts he may have had. But that didn't mean Bay would give in just because Sila had made him come. Twice.

A person like his kitten, someone willing to live in a crappy house and work a job they hated, wouldn't give into temptation easily. Racing and his trips to the Seaside were already the two things

Bay allowed himself to indulge in. There was a good chance in the twenty-four hours they'd been apart, he'd started pushing Sila into that same category.

Sila wouldn't let him change his mind. He'd chosen option two, which meant he was his to do with as he pleased, and Sila would use him for as long as he wanted to. Until that odd feeling at the center of his chest stopped occurring every time the professor's name was so much as mentioned.

"Wait for my call," Sila absently said to Aneski on his way past him toward the locker room. He'd change first and then he'd find out why Bay had skipped school. If it was because he'd come to his senses and wanted his freedom, Sila's mood was going to darken.

And then no one would be happy.

CHAPTER 14:

"Let me know if you need anything," Nate said as he stepped out onto Bay's crumbling front porch. The metal railing that led down the three steps to the busted sidewalk was askew and had been for ages, so he avoided touching it. "I'll see you later."

Bay waved his friend off, watching until Nate had gotten onto his bike and started away before he began to close the door. He'd taken the day off, but there were several quizzes from last week that were sitting in his inbox waiting to be graded.

Though he didn't enjoy what he did, having his emotions locked up meant he hadn't really minded all the time spent on grading and class prep either. But now he felt annoyance at having to bother with it when all he really wanted to do was curl up on the couch and research the many things that could potentially be wrong with him.

Because clearly something was, since all he'd been able to think about during Nate's visit was how he could best lure Sila—

The door was yanked out of his hold by a strong enough force that Bay stumbled forward and almost fell out onto the porch. A solid body shoved him back before he could and he knocked into the small table he'd set up by the entranceway instead, hissing when the hard end of it dug into his side.

His curse died on his tongue when he lifted his head and processed that Sila was entering his home, his larger-than-life presence filling not only the doorway, but somehow sweeping through the entire house in less time than it took for Bay to blink.

All at once, the younger man was everywhere and everything, as though there was nothing left on the entire planet Bay could possibly focus on.

"Sila," the name came off his lips as a mere whisper, but if the intruder heard it, he gave no sign.

The younger man slammed the door at his back and flicked the lock before moving forward in a blur of motion. He had Bay spun around and bent over the table, his front flattened against the smooth wooden surface in seconds, pinned by the scruff of his neck.

Bay struggled as soon as he felt a hand slip beneath the waistband of the shorts he was wearing, but he was no match for Sila.

He tore the pants down so they dropped at Bay's ankles and then a single finger sought out his entrance, breaching his hole with no more warning than that. Sila didn't push it in far, only past the tight ring of muscle, then he made a pleased sound and released Bay as quickly as he'd snatched him up.

The small table shook as Bay grappled with it, trying to right himself as the younger man moved away. He almost fell over reaching for his pants, tugging them back on before he spun around to keep Sila in his line of sight.

Sila walked over to the small circular table that acted as both the kitchen and dining room table and stared down at the two coffee cups that had been left there. "Which one is his?"

Bay blinked and shook his head, still too shocked by what had just happened to comprehend.

"Nate Narek," Sila sneered the name and when he looked to Bay next there was a darkness swirling in his mismatched eyes that promised punishment if he didn't get an answer. "Which cup did he use?"

He pointed to the one furthest from him, confusion only growing when Sila immediately snatched it up and downed the remaining sip.

Bay bristled when Sila stormed over to him a second time, sucking in a sharp breath when his jaw was captured and his head was forced back. In one swift move, Sila sealed their lips together, that mouthful of coffee forced down Bays throat. He coughed as he was shoved away yet again, swallowing on the bitter brew.

When he went to right himself, Sila leaned in, forcing Bay to bend back over the small table in order to avoid whacking his forehead into his chest.

"I thought perhaps you were ill," Sila said, voice teetering between irritated and yet somehow still charming. "I came all this way just to check on you, in fact, and what do I find? Turns out you were here having alone time with another man."

"Are you..." Bay was almost in too much disbelieve to even ask it but... "Are you jealous?"

"That depends," Sila dropped his palms to either side of his hips, caging him in, "I just checked to make sure you didn't get up to anything you shouldn't, however, there's no way to confirm whether or not you were touched elsewhere."

That's why he'd stuck a finger up his ass just now?!

Bay blushed before he could help it and Sila grunted at him mockingly.

"I was inside there just the other day. There's nothing I haven't seen, or felt, of you already. Nate Narek on the other hand..."

"He didn't." Bay shook his head vehemently. "We would never."

"No?"

"No! We're just friends. He came by because —" He stopped abruptly, scoffing. "Why am I telling you this? I don't owe you an explanation."

"Want to rethink that, Kitten?" Sila's hands slid in a little closer, until his thumbs brushed up against the edge of Bay's thighs. "You chose Option Two, need I remind you?"

Bay bit his tongue when Sila lifted a finger to slip it through the metal loop at the collar around his neck, though he only tugged at it lightly.

"I own you," he said seductively, as though he were trying to coax Bay into admitting it. "No one gets to touch what's mine."

"We didn't…" Bay felt like he was hovering over a precipice and one single gust of wind would blow him over. All of his senses were honed in on the man in front of him, the man surrounding him with his sea salt scent with just a hint of chlorine.

Oh right. It was Monday. Sila would have been at the pool.

Upon closer inspection, Bay noted that his golden hair was still slightly damp. He must have left the university and come straight here, but why? There was no way he'd known Nate was visiting. He'd been too angry when he'd shoved his way into the house to have had time to prepare, which meant he'd arrived in time to see Nate leave and that had set him off.

A pleased thrill uncoiled within Bay's gut and he only barely resisted the urge to smile. He was insane, certifiably so, if he was actually happy about any of this. He shouldn't find Sila's pushy, overbearing demeanor attractive and yet he could already feel his dick twitching in his pants and his hole clenching in greedy need.

His hole which had yet to fully recover from the other days beating.

Yeah, he was crazy. He needed help.

"Why'd you call out, Kitten?" Sila asked.

"I…" He dropped his gaze and tightened his grip on the edge of the table he was practically sitting on, the rough wood digging into his palm.

"Still sore?" he threw him a bone and said, allowing Bay to merely nod his head and not have to say it himself. "Let me help you with that." He moved away and returned to the entrance where he'd apparently dropped a plastic bag earlier.

Sila pulled out the contents, placing them on the kitchen table and then moved over to the stove with one of them in his hands.

"What are you doing?" Bay tried to see around him, but with how broad his shoulders were it was impossible.

"Making soup," Sila replied. "Don't worry, I won't make a mess, it's premade. Just have to heat it up. It's got snow flower root and coal blossoms. My brother says it'll help with your throat."

"You told you brother about us?" Bay hated that idea.

Sila snorted. "Of course not. I asked him what would help an irritated throat, that's all. This was his suggestion."

"Does your throat hurt?"

He sent Bay a look over his shoulder. "Let's not with the stupid questions, shall we, Professor?

I wouldn't want to start thinking less of you so early in the game. I don't think you would like that either, if the semi you're currently sporting is any indicator."

Bay glanced down and then quickly covered himself. The gym shorts he was in were made of a pretty thin material and the outline of his hardening cock had been on full display.

Sila laughed at him and went back to making soup, pulling out a small metal pot after searching the three cupboards in the tiny place. He'd also brought another tube of sun cream and a packet of pills, but Bay couldn't identify them.

"Do you want to talk about it?" Sila asked cryptically and Bay frowned all over again. "You seem out of sorts."

"Oh." He was, but considering he still didn't fully understand it himself, the last thing he wanted to do was have a conversation with his student. Besides, all of this was strange enough as it was. One minute, he was accosting him and checking to be sure he hadn't just had sex with someone else and the next, Sila was making him soup? What the fuck? "No."

"Because you already discussed it with Nate?" Sila didn't sound pleased by that prospect.

"Because I don't think we have that type of relationship," he countered.

"Our *relationship*," Sila said, "is whatever I say it is. And I say you're going to open up and tell me what's going on with you today."

"While you cook me dinner?"

"Is this the usual amount you'd consume for dinner?" Sila took in the small pot. "No wonder you're so small."

"I'm not small," he huffed. "I'm average height for a Vital, I'll have you know."

"Ah, that explains why Berga is around the same size as you."

Bay didn't like the way that caused his heart to still. "You've paid attention to Berga?"

Sila turned and quirked a brow. "Now who sounds jealous?"

"That's different."

"How so?"

"If I tried to hook up with someone else, it's pretty clear what would happen."

"Murder," Sila confirmed.

"Yes," he adjusted his glasses, "exactly. But what about you? What happens if you sleep with another person? Am I supposed to just be fine with it?"

"Do you think I'd care if you weren't?" Sila asked, and when Bay's mood noticeably soured, he clucked his tongue. "I'm teasing you, Kitten. Don't worry. I only have one main playmate at a time and you're the most interesting thing on this planet anyway. Not to mention, why would I turn elsewhere when you've already said you'd willingly be at my leisure?"

"That does it. I'm insane."

"You're empty," Sila corrected, but then he

tilted his head and seemed to look at him more closely. "Or, at least you were. Something's changed. Is that what it is then? Why you really called out of work and why Nate was here?"

"I..." He blew out a breath and crossed his arms over his chest protectively, unable to meet Sila's gaze when he admitted, "I can feel again."

"Is that so?" He hummed. "Interesting."

"Insteresting?" Bay glared. "Is that all you have to say?"

"You're welcome?" he suggested. "Is that better?"

"You're serious?"

"It's because of me, isn't it." Sila stepped up to the kitchen table and leaned on the back of one of the chairs. "That's ahead of schedule."

"You predicted this would happen?"

"Hoped for, is more accurate," Sila told him. "It was obvious you hadn't picked up on the slight changes over the course of the summer, but I noticed them. We were easing you into this the whole time, Professor. Only, I assumed you'd need more time. I certainly never imagined you'd return to the living after a single rough fucking."

"That wasn't sex," he snapped. "It was—"

Sila waved him off before he could finish, clearly bored. "Does it matter what it was? No matter what label you give it, it worked. So, tell me, how do you feel? Is it everything you hoped for and remembered?"

Bay considered the question, since there was

no other choice but to answer it. Knowing Sila, the younger man wouldn't just drop the subject simply because it made Bay uncomfortable, the exact opposite in fact. The problem was, he wasn't entirely sure how or if he could give a satisfactory answer, because he hadn't yet figured it out himself.

"I feel," he began, leaving it at that for so long that Sila's eyes eventually narrowed in warning. "That's it," he sighed. "I feel. Before, I could barely do that at all, but I woke up this morning achy and frustrated. And when I found what you'd done to my collection in—" he slapped a hand over his mouth but it was too late.

Sila grinned at him. "Is that what you call it? That ridiculous shrine of us hidden in your coat closet? How childish. I wouldn't have guessed that of you, Professor. But see, this why I like you. You're forever finding new ways to amuse and surprise me."

He hadn't done it for Sila's sake, but laughter was definitely better than the alternative.

"Most people would be freaked out and disgusted if they found their teacher hoarded photos of them," Bay pointed out.

Sila lifted a single shoulder in an absent half shrug. "I'm not like most people."

Or anyone. Sila Varun was original.

The universe should rejoice for that, because Bay didn't think it could handle having more than one of him out there on the loose.

"Why did you tear some of them down?" Bay found the courage to ask just as the soup began to boil and Sila turned to take care of it.

"You don't need the ones of my brother," he gave him another dark look over his shoulder, "Isn't that right?"

"Right," he agreed wholeheartedly. Rin couldn't give him what he craved, not like Sila could. It'd been his mistake that he couldn't tell them apart before, but he'd do better from here on out. He didn't even think he'd have to try all that hard at it, in fact. When he'd been watching the twins in the East Quad the other week, their differences had been blindingly obvious, he'd actually been surprised by it.

The air around them was different for one. Rin gave off this electricity, waves of snapping energy. He demanded attention. Sila, however, gave off a calm balm edged in darkness. There was the false sense of softness tinged with the promise of pain. Like the sharp thorns on one of the bay roses Sila had left him before he'd revealed his identity.

"You shouldn't look at me like that, Kitten." Sila had placed a bowl of soup in front of the chair closest to where Bay still stood pressed against the small table. His spine had straightened and his head was tipped slightly downward, his eyes steady and unblinking.

Bay licked his lips. "Like what?"

"Like you want me to eat you up." His

expression was enigmatic and his words were spoken plainly, making it impossible to tell what he was feeling. "Like you're already playing out in your mind how the rest of this evening goes."

"How does it go?"

The corner of Sila's mouth tipped up and just like that the spell was broken. He held a hand out to the empty chair. "Eat your soup and let's find out, shall we?"

"What if I—"

"Eat," Sila commanded.

Almost without thinking, Bay dropped down into the chair and reached for the spoon. The flavor was rich with a hint of sweetness and umami that had him sighing and instantly relaxing into his seat. The water concoction Sila had given him yesterday had done wonders, but his throat was still sore, and the soup helped ease the discomfort.

"I've asked my contact to start looking into things with your grandmother," Sila announced a few minutes later after he'd taken the chair across from him.

Bay paused with the spoon halfway to his mouth again. "Already?"

"I keep my promises."

"Thank you."

"You don't sound surprised," Sila said.

"I believed you when you made your offer," Bay explained. "That's why I accepted."

"Is that why?" Sila stated knowingly, but he

didn't push the issue when Bay dropped his gaze and continued eating. "How's the soup?"

"It's good. Thank you."

"Thank my brother. He's the one who taught me the importance of taking care of things that have meaning to us. Or," he changed his mind, "actually, don't. Don't speak to him if I'm not around."

"I don't have any interest in him anyway," Bay replied.

Sila snorted. "You couldn't even tell us apart up until the other day, the proof is in your closet."

"Pictures don't count," he argued. "They're easier to fake."

"How so?"

"The feel of a person when they're standing right in front of you, when they're looking back at you…it's unique. You can't get that from a photograph." Bay finished the last spoonful and stared into the empty bowl, his disappointment palpable.

Wordlessly, Sila stood and picked it up, going back to ladle in more from the pot on the stove. When he set it back in front of Bay, he continued their conversation as though they'd never paused it.

As though he hadn't just done something sweet and caring.

If Bay wasn't careful, he'd fall into this, into this false image of the perfect, attentive lover. Things were already bad enough as they were with how obsessed with the younger guy he was.

"How do I feel?" Sila asked.

"Dangerous," he said without hesitation.

"What does danger feel like?"

Bay swallowed another mouthful and said honestly, "Enticing."

He'd expected Sila to grin again, and was a little discouraged when he continued to stare stoically at him instead.

"You were close with your grandmother?" Sila leaned back in the chair and slid the tube of sun cream toward himself, fiddling with it as they spoke. "She adopted you, correct?"

"Yes," he nodded. "She was already past her prime so she insisted I call her grandma instead of mom, but that's what she was to me more than anything. She was my parent. I only had the one, but one was more than enough."

"I only have one parent as well," Sila confided. "My father."

"You don't like him," it wasn't hard to surmise by the way his mouth twisted in displeasure.

"He's a coward and a disgrace to the Varun name. Because he isn't intelligent enough to figure out how to achieve the things he wants, he opted to have children to pass the burden onto us. My brother has taught me more than Crate Varun ever has. He's the only family I acknowledge. The only family I need."

"Sounds a lot like how it was with my

grandmother," Bay said. He could picture her bright smile whenever he walked in the door after school and hear the way she greeted him, like she meant it and was happy to see him even though it'd only been a few hours. "No one's ever taken care of me like she did."

"Come here."

Bay blinked, torn from his memories. He'd finished the second bowl without realizing and when he glanced over at Sila, he found him waiting. A swell of anticipation mixed with fear swept through him as he slowly eased to his feet and rounded the table, stopping a good two feet away.

Sila made a sound of annoyance and grabbed his wrist, pulling him forward until Bay was falling over into his lap. Then he resituated him, moving Bay around so he was straddling Sila's thighs, chest to chest.

"Stay standing," he ordered, and then he tugged Bay's pants down for the second time that day.

Bay tried to move away but Sila slapped him on the ass, the whack lighter than it'd been the other night but still enough to sting. He paused, not wanting to tempt the devil into taking things any further, especially when he already didn't know what was to come.

He'd liked the pain coupled with sex, and wouldn't be opposed if that was the direction they were heading, but Bay wasn't a fan of being hurt for no reason, with no endgame in sight. If Sila beat him or cut him, he hoped he'd earn a reward for taking it and being good. If he didn't...Bay scowled.

"What's wrong, Kitten?" Sila noticed his expression. "Not liking being exposed?"

"That's not it."

"What is it then?" He tapped on one of Bay's wrists. "Put your hands on my shoulders."

Bay obeyed. From this position, he could see the top of Sila's head, the light from the window over the sink behind him casting a golden halo there. There were no angels in Vital folklore or religion, but if there were, there was little doubt in Bay's mind that Sila would be a fallen one.

"What are you planning on doing—" Bay let out a strangled sound when suddenly Sila's fingers were spreading his ass cheeks and poking at his entrance. They were warm and wet, and it took a him a second longer than it should have to process that Sila had covered them in sun cream.

He wiggled one finger all the way in and then pushed it in deep, feeling around Bay's inner walls. "I'm taking care of you," he said, voice low and sultry. "Isn't that what you wanted?"

Was that how he'd interpreted it? Bay had been referring to his grandmother, not asking for Sila—His head dropped forward on a silent moan when another finger was inserted alongside the first.

"If you're good for me," Sila promised, "I

might even take care of this for you too." His other hand poked at the head of Bay's now swollen dick.

He cried out and rocked forward, shamelessly bumping his crown against Sila's chest.

In retaliation, Sila slapped at his member, hard, jostling his dick and wringing out another cry from Bay, this one tinged with pain.

"Don't smear your come on my shirt," Sila cautioned, the threat of another painful whack to Bay's dick needing no elaboration.

Those fingers slipped in deep and pressed against his prostate and, despite the warning—or, hell, probably because of it, who was he kidding—Bay thrust forward, rubbing himself more firmly against Sila's front. The soft material of Sila's shirt coupled with the hard plains of his abs beneath had Bay moaning in pleasure.

Pleasure that didn't last.

In the next instant, Sila had Bay flipped and planted over the kitchen table in a move that mirrored their earlier situation when he'd first arrived. Only this time he'd grabbed onto Bay's dick in the process, and now he pulled on it, tugging it back between Bay's legs. It wasn't hard enough to risk injury, but he felt it and the wave of pleasure/pain had Bay gritting his teeth.

"I came all this way to heal you, Kitten," Sila told him. "Not hurt you."

Bay emitted a sound of protest, unable to hold it in. He was spiraling, the rush of sensation taking over, driving him to want more and set all embarrassment aside. How long had it been since he'd last felt anything, least of all something as potent as this? As the things Sila could drag out of him, kicking and screaming and writhing in pure agonizing bliss?

"Please." Bay lifted his ass and brushed against Sila, not even sure what he was trying to tempt the younger man into doing. Spank him? Continue finger fucking him? Either? Both? He moaned, the sound drawn out and pleading.

"I could give you want you want," Sila said, "give you what you need. No one can play you like I can, Bay. No one knows the right formula to get you keening for them. I could have you screaming my name, begging to give me more of your blood and come…" His fingers danced down Bay's spine and he arched into the touch.

And then it was gone.

"But I won't." Sila stepped away from him, leaving Bay bent over the table and half naked, his dick dripping between his thighs. "You haven't earned it today, baby."

"Sila."

"The next time you think it's a good idea to be alone in your house with another man," Sila told him, "Remember this feeling. I can give you so much pleasure and so much pain." His lips kissed lightly at Bay's right shoulder, there and gone so fast he wondered if he'd imagined it. "Or I can give you nothing at all."

The sound of the front door slamming shut snapped Bay out of his stunned stupor and he straightened, head whipping in that direction.

Sure enough, he was alone.

And so turned on he thought his dick might fall off.

CHAPTER 15:

Bay adjusted the collar of his dress shirt for the millionth time that afternoon and scowled. The knot of the silver tie he'd chosen helped hide the small bump caused by the metal ring of the necklace he was still wearing, but knowing what was under there had kept him fidgeting all day.

A few students had definitely taken notice.

He'd escaped to his office where he'd spent the better part of an hour mindlessly grading papers, but it'd all gotten to be too much twenty or so minutes ago and he'd caved and called the number Sila had been using to anonymously contact him these past few weeks. It'd gone straight to voicemail and Bay had felt like an idiot.

Today, Sila had been the one who played hooky, not arriving for class so that Bay had spent the entire period wondering where he could be and what he could be doing. He'd thought for sure he'd come see him after, maybe at his office even, but time was ticking and there were no signs of that happening.

The last thing he should be doing is pining

over his student—who also happened to be a psychopathic stalker. What they'd done in the woods—no, what had *been done to him*—was close enough to rape to call it that.

The facts remained, Sila had accosted him, both physically and sexually, and that wasn't all right. Bay shouldn't have spent the better part of the last couple of days dreaming of it happening again. He shouldn't have touched himself to thoughts of Sila shoving his thick cock back into Bay's unprepared hole the way that he had yesterday when the object of his fantasies had walked out on him.

The waiting was honestly worse than the hunt had been and Bay just wanted to get their next encounter over with. He wanted to meet with Sila, stand in front of him and look into his eyes and get a sense of what was really going on here.

What he really wanted was to urge Sila into shocking his system back into overdrive again. He wanted him to bring him back to life like he had in the forest. The taste in his kitchen hadn't been nearly enough. Bay wanted more.

He *needed* more.

Bay hadn't returned to that numb state, but they'd started to get murky again, the emotions not as crisp or intense as they'd been that first day, but he still *felt* them. And the fear that they would stop? That he'd slip back into that numbness entirely?

That rocked him to the core.

He didn't care what it said about him, Bay had come to the very clear realization that he would do anything and everything in his power to avoid going back to that place. He didn't want to be undead anymore, not now that he'd gotten a taste of what it felt like to be alive.

His multi-slate rang and he jumped a little in his chair, forcing himself to let it ring a couple of times before he answered. "Hello?"

"Was there something you needed, Kitten?" Sila's silky tone, the one he used when he was trying to coax someone into a sense of ease, tickled at Bay's ear. "I was in the library. But you should have known that already."

He had. He'd memorized Sila's schedule that first day of the semester, but in his haste it'd slipped his mind.

"You weren't in class. Where are you now?" Bay asked.

"I just left campus."

He pursed his lips. That wouldn't do. "Come back."

There was a pause and then, "I don't think I will."

Bay should have known he was going to make things difficult. "I wasn't asking, Mr. Varun. I need to see you in my office."

"Going to slip me some spiked tea, Professor?"

Of course he'd discovered the drugged tea leaves Flix and Berga had given Bay. Taping his fingers on the surface of his desk, Bay considered what that meant.

"Have you bugged my office, Sila?" It was the most logical explanation.

"Wondering if I know you did the same to Lan? Of course, Professor," he replied, tone sweet as candy.

Bay hummed. It was easier like this, separated and only connected through the phone line. Here, seated behind his desk, surrounding by textbooks and his house plants, Bay felt more like himself and therefore more in control. He was the teacher and Sila was his student. There was a level of command in place between them.

They both needed to remember that.

"What else have you gotten your hands on?" Bay asked.

"Recently?" It was obvious when he paused he was doing it purely for affect. "That firm, round ass of yours, for one."

He inhaled sharply, freezing so he could listen more closely to the sounds on the other end of the line, hopeful that Sila hadn't picked up on his reaction.

"Have you been thinking about it, Kitten?" Sila drawled, and it was clear by the way his voice turned husky and deep that he had in fact heard Bay's gasp just now. "Remembering the way my cock tore through your tight hole? I didn't get a chance to show you, but you coated my cock in both your come and your blood and it was such a lovely sight."

Bay's legs shifted under the desk as his dick began to lengthen against his will.

"Why so quiet all of a sudden?" A horn honked in the background. Sila must be driving. "Going to try and lie and say you didn't enjoy yourself?"

"Yes," Bay said, knowing it was a mistake even before he'd finished. "I have no recollection of enjoying it." He leaned back in his chair and spread his thighs wider. "Maybe you should remind me."

There was silence for a long time, the only indicator that he'd caught Sila off guard. Bay smiled triumphantly at himself while he waited, though the smarter part of him knew it was foolish to relish playing with fire.

Taunting the devil never ended well for anyone.

"Are you sure?" Sila asked then, in a rare show of caring. It was true he posed everything as though Bay had a choice, but they both knew the truth of the matter was it was merely an illusion. He manipulated people like pawns, giving them the impression they were making moves on their own volition even when they weren't.

Bay knew this. He'd combed over dozens of research papers and reviewed countless cases about psychopaths. Sila ticked off all the boxes.

"I almost jumped off Sickle bridge," Bay said softly. "Did you know about that? It was three months after my grandmother's death and I'd just lost the case and been told I had to vacate the only home I'd ever known immediately or face imprisonment. Something like that would have affected my record and the university would have fired me before I'd even officially started."

"At a job you've never wanted," Sila filled in.

Bay dropped his head back against the top of his chair. "It felt so…pointless."

"What stopped you?" Sila asked. "Why didn't you jump?"

"Would you have cared if I did?"

"I wouldn't have known you," Sila replied without skipping a beat. "So it wouldn't of mattered."

"Would you care if I did it today?"

Tires squealed and Bay sat upright, momentarily worried that Sila had just gotten into an accident.

"Is this a threat?" All the easy playfulness that had been in his tone before was gone. "I don't react well to those, Professor. Proceed with caution."

"Answer the question."

"No," he stated.

"Is that your answer?"

"I've sent you an address," Sila told him a second before Bay's device dinged. "You have twenty minutes to meet me there. No stops on the way. If someone tries to talk to you in the hall when you leave, you shoot them down. If I find out you kept me waiting, there won't be any sun cream the next time I tear through that ass of yours."

Bay shivered, but the call ended before he could come up with anything to say to that. He shifted on his seat and glanced at the message Sila had sent him. The location was nineteen minutes from campus. The bastard had left him a single minute to collect himself.

His inner muscles clenched at the dark promise of being abused. Aside from the initial sting he'd experienced when he'd woken in his bed, the sun cream had done wonders and he'd been completely healed by this morning. He was good as new and, instead of thinking about how that meant he was ready to go another round, he should be trying to come up with a way out of this whole mess.

Only, Bay didn't want out.

People like Sila didn't make it a habit to stick around for the long-haul. Bay wasn't delusional—a freak who liked being hurt during sex, sure, but delusional? No. He knew it was only a matter of time before Sila got what he wanted out of this and threw Bay aside like used garbage. Even though the younger man had been tender toward him after the fact, he needed to remind himself it'd all been part of the show.

Part of the game.

A charismatic person like Sila understood it was easier to catch flies with honey than it was with vinegar. So no matter what he said or how sweet the words sounded, Bay needed to keep in mind that it was all an act. That was the only way he was going to survive this detour with the devil.

But he wouldn't deny himself the chance. Where else was he going to find someone like Sila, someone who wouldn't be disgusted by his sexual preferences or threaten to out him to the world. If word got around that Professor Delmar liked the idea of being whipped and cut and brutally fucked no one would ever look at him the same way. He'd go right back to that low place where nothing had felt worth it.

That was why he'd always kept his preferences to himself, only getting pleasure from the videos he rented at the Seaside. His attention had shifted once he'd met Sila, of course, his fantasies acquiring a face to the body he'd always imagined ravaging him in the dark, but the basic concept of the scenes hadn't.

In his mind, Sila had already fucked him and hurt him a dozen times over. The fact that none of those fantasies had even come close to the explosive sensations he'd experienced the other night was yet another reason Bay couldn't give this up.

He'd agreed to keep playing in part because he believed Sila when he'd promised to help him get answers. His grandmother deserved justice.

But he'd be lying if he didn't admit, if only in the deepest recesses of his rotten heart, that he'd also wanted to agree. That he'd almost been grateful at the opportunity of having Sila pin him down a second time.

That he was already praying there would be a third. And maybe even a fourth.

He wouldn't get greedy and hope any further than that, but...

Bay wanted to be punished.

What better punisher than the Devil?

* * *

There were far too many people here.

Bay stood just within the entrance of the crowded noodle restaurant, glancing around at the patrons. It was a busy evening with few empty seats available, and for a moment he was certain he'd gotten the wrong location. He couldn't be seen even talking with Sila here, not when there were too many eyes that could recognize who they were.

Technically, there was no rule about student/teacher relationships at Vail, mostly because at one point twenty or so years ago, apparently a Brumal member fell for her science professor and the school didn't dare try to keep them apart.

Still. It pretty much went without saying it was taboo and frowned upon. He might not lose his job the same way he would if it were discovered he was Pandaveer, but he'd be ostracized all the same. There was no need to make things more difficult for himself than they needed to be.

He checked the message for the third time, still convinced he had the wrong place.

"Excuse me," a waitress possibly around the same age as him approached with a friendly smile. "Are you Bay Delmar?"

"Yes." He closed his multi-slate and forced his pressed lips to curve slightly. "I am."

"Perfect." She held an arm out to the side, indicating a tight pathway between two of the four rows of square tables. All of the tables either had two or four seats, the color scheme a mixture of warm tones, like bright reds and rusty oranges. The door was located on one side, with the kitchen on the opposite. "Your table is ready for you."

"I didn't make a reservation." He hadn't even been aware places like this took reservations.

"Your friend did it for you," she explained as she led him to the back corner where a lone table rested. "He already placed your order as well. It'll be right out, but please let me know if you need anything else."

Answers would be nice. Since she clearly wasn't the one who'd be able to supply them, Bay merely smiled politely and took his seat.

The wall was to his back—a large mural of a waterbridge bird scarfing down noodles painted over the entire expanse of it—the floor to ceiling window that overlooked the street to his left and filled tables at his front and side. There was only one other chair at his table, and he was expecting Sila to arrive to fill it when the devil called him again.

"Where are you?" Bay demanded, skipping

over the pleasantries this time.

"You sound miffed, Professor."

"I'm not—" He pinched the bridge of his nose, just above his glasses. "This is not at all how I pictured spending my night."

"Oh," Sila let out a knowing chuckle, his deep timbre sending shivers skittering up Bay's spine. "I get it. You're disappointed about the venue. Are you sulking, Kitten?"

"Try to remember that I am older than you," Bay stated, only to have Sila snort.

"I'm not the one with a bad memory. Whenever and however I want, that's what you agreed to. The food is coming."

The waitress from earlier returned with a steaming bowl of dumplings and placed it carefully in front of him. "Can I get you anything else?"

"No, thank you." Bay just wanted her to leave so he could continue his conversation with Sila. He tapped the earbud in his right ear so she'd catch on he was on a call, and she nodded and then left him alone. "Why dumplings?"

"You like them," Sila said matter-of-factly. "They also take less work than noodles and, in a moment, you're going to find it difficult to use a pair of chopsticks. I was thinking ahead for you. You're welcome."

Bay latched on that middle part like a dog with a bone. "Why?"

"Getting ahead of yourself there," he chided.

"Try one first. Make sure they didn't give you the wrong kind before we proceed. I don't want any interruptions once we start, and trust me, neither do you."

Even knowing it was ridiculous taking orders from his student, Bay dutifully picked up the set of metal chopsticks and selected a round dumpling from the bowl. It was warm and flavorful, with a hint of spices and a bit of sweetness at the end.

"Roast ternog," Bay said, knowing Sila would want to know.

"Good." That was the only indicator that they'd given him the right order.

Bay took another bite and waited, mentally reminding himself not to let his guard slip. This was a dangerous game, even more since he had no clue what was actually going on. There was no way Sila had called him out here just to feed him, especially when the younger man was nowhere in sight.

He'd done a thorough check when he'd first arrived. The restaurant may be packed, but there was no way Sila could have blended in with the crowd enough for Bay to have missed him. After months of watching the guy from afar, Bay could pick him out of a mass of a hundred, let alone the thirty currently filling the medium sized space.

His multi-slate lit up with an incoming message and he was in the process of twisting his wrist to check when the voice in his ear stopped him.

"Remove it," Sila commanded. "You'll want to hold it closer so no one can catch a glimpse. We wouldn't want tonight to end with you in the back of a police cruiser, now would we?"

"Why…" His sentence trailed off as he removed the device and hit accept on the message. Thankfully he had the earpiece in, so sound was automatically directed to it instead of playing out load. At the first sharp wail, he jumped and dropped the device face down. It just missed the food, hitting the yellow tabletop instead.

"Careful, Kitten," Sila drawled. "You're already drawing unwanted attention."

Bay bowed his head slightly at the couple of people seated nearby who'd turned at the clattering noise, then he took a deep breath before picking the device up once more.

The image was displayed in mixtures of black and green, somewhere in the middle of the woods. A man was bent forward on his hands and knees, naked and shaking. There was the barest hint of an outline of a handprint across his left ass cheek.

"Recognize yourself from behind?" Sila asked, his voice spoken dangerously low.

"What is this?" Bay swallowed and glanced around uncomfortably. Everyone had gone back to eating and talking with their friends.

"Don't ask stupid questions," he said. "It'll only annoy me. Enough stalling. Hit the play button again. You're going to watch and eat at the same time. I edited the clip so it'll loop back to the beginning as soon as it's done. You'll sit there and watch it as many times as it takes until you've licked your bowl clean. Understood, Kitten?"

He gave a slight shake of his head and tore his eyes off of the screen to search for signs of Sila out the window.

The restaurant was located on Main Street and since it was getting late and the sky was darkening, the whole street was already lit up with strings of lights and the neon glow from shopfronts. Some of the buildings were taller than others and Bay paid extra attention to those that had darkened windows, though there was no chance he'd be able to make out anyone concealed behind the paned glass.

He'd already figured that Sila was watching him from somewhere.

"Not knowing where I am adds to the intrigue," the younger man said then, and there was a hint of excitement in his tone to add proof to his words. He was getting off on hiding.

"Creeping in the shadows seems beneath you," Bay stated, trying to get a rise out of him. He should have learned by now that Sila rarely reacted the way that he hoped.

"It isn't creeping," he corrected, "it's hunting. I can wait here all night. Neither of us are going anywhere until you finish. It occurred to me after I got off the phone with you what you were doing, by the way."

Bay didn't need him to elaborate to know what he was referring to. It wasn't like he'd done a good job of hiding the fact he'd wanted to see him. Bay had shown his cards the moment he'd tried to get Sila to come to his office.

"What's wrong? Only interested in playing if you're not the plaything?" Bay had been testing the waters, trying to get a feel for this new version of the guy he'd inaccurately believed he'd had a grasp on all this time.

Sila Varun wasn't anything like he'd imagined however, the image that had been built up in Bay's mind of him faker than they came. He'd hoped by pushing his buttons he'd get him to show up, but instead they were here.

"You didn't play me, Professor," Sila said.

Bay motioned to the restaurant with a small flick of his wrist, conscious of the video that was still paused on the screen in front of him. He was holding the device closer to his chest to avoid anyone nearby standing up and catching a peek, but part of him wanted to hit the play button just so the frozen frame would change to something other than an image of his ass front and center. "Didn't I?"

"No," he chuckled darkly. "This could only be considered a success if I never caught on, but I did, and now you're going to have to pay the price for attempting to manage me. Now, begin, or I promise you won't like the consequences."

He considered disobeying just for the heck of it, but it would be a lie to say he wasn't already thrumming with anticipation and a thread of excitement. He'd never done anything inappropriate out in public before, his only experiences with it at the safe, contained space at the Seaside Cinema and their time in the woods.

The time that Sila had filmed.

Bay swallowed and then reached for the chopsticks once more, his hand only slightly shaking as he took them up and then hit the play button.

CHAPTER 16:

Bay choked when Sila's massive cock filled the screen, coughing as a bit of dumpling went down the wrong way. He almost knocked over the tall glass of water that had been left by the waitress earlier, catching it at the last second so only some of it spilled over the top of his hand.

He guzzled down half the contents, clutching the multi-slate to his chest in a death grip.

"I haven't given you permission to die, Kitten," Sila said, his voice coming out over the sounds of the audio from the still playing video.

Bay wasn't watching it, still too stunned. *That* had been inside him?! There was no way. No way only half a tube of sun cream—because Sila had left it on the counter in his bathroom and Bay had seen how much was used—had been enough to heal his insides after taking *that*.

Forget that it was the biggest cock he'd ever seen, that wasn't even half the reason he felt like he was about to spontaneously combust.

"It's *pierced*!" he whisper-hissed, unable to

withhold the hint of accusation from his tone.

"It's called a magic cross," Sila told him, and Bay got the distinct feeling he was laughing at him from wherever he was lurking. "Now, watch the movie like a good boy. Your food is getting cold and you're wasting both of our time."

"I'm older than you," he grumbled. Bay shook his head frantically even though a small part of him was curious. All of that had been inside him...

"Do it," the warning was delivered in a growl that had Bay's spine snapping straight, "Now."

Inhaling, he lowered the phone, eyes widening to find the scene that had kept going had changed. There was no glimpse of the four metal balls that decorated the flushed head of Sila's dick, because said appendage was currently buried so deeply in Bay's ass, all he could see was the stretch of his hole forced around the thick root of that shaft.

In the video, Sila pulled out and, though it'd been filmed with night vision mode and therefore there weren't colors other than shades of green, the way his cock glistened made it obvious Sila hadn't been lying when he'd said he'd been slicked with Bay's come and blood.

He must have used Bay's release to coat himself before entering, even though that had provided very little relief for Bay. Still, seeing it now, watching the way Sila worked himself back in, he had to admit even a little lubrication was better than none at all.

"Eat," Sila ordered.

Almost robotically, Bay lifted a dumpling to his mouth and chewed, his eyes glued on the screen. The sounds of his own sobbing filled his ears, coupled with Sila's low growls and heavy panting. He sucked in a sharp breath when the angle of the video changed again.

Sila lowered himself overtop Bay, pinning him to the dirt, and brought the camera around to where their heads rested. Bay had his face pressed against the ground, tears streaming down his cheeks, but Sila was grinning from ear to ear, his head hovering just over Bay's shoulder. The camera captured the rise and fall of his ass as he ruthlessly continued fucking into the man beneath him.

It was aggressive and primal and wrong. There was no mistaking what was taking place in the video. No mistaking that Bay was being forced to take Sila's body into his own, whether he wanted to or not.

Experiencing it had been one thing, but through the shock, pain, and then euphoria, much of it had been blacked out in his mind. The sensations were all there, but the exact events, the way he'd begged and clawed at the dirt...those details were muddied. Watching them, seeing how unapologetically brutal Sila had been with him that night...

"I've never made the mistake of filming my

face before," Sila confessed and, if the husky note in his voice was any indicator, he was just as turned on as Bay was.

And he *was.*

Knowing that was his blood smeared all over Sila's cock, that the guy had used it as lube and screwed him raw until he was completely and utterly destroyed…It should make him queasy. He should feel abused, taken advantage of, and disgusted.

But he wasn't. Instead, Bay's dick pressed painfully against the seam of his dress pants, hard enough the button threatened to pop at any given second. There was already a wet spot forming, the dark material only somewhat hiding that fact.

"What is wrong with me?" he breathed out, the words meant for himself.

"Nothing's wrong with you," Sila answered anyway. "You're a masochist. Surely you knew before?"

He'd had some notion. Regular people didn't watch the types of porn Bay did, after all. But he'd never realized it ran to this extent. He understood the mind was far too complex for anyone to ever be able to fully pick it apart or label it, and that there were no indicators in his childhood to provide clarity over why he may get off on this type of thing.

Bay might just be built this way.

Just how Sila was built the way that he was.

Sila continued to stare back at him from the

scene, his teeth white and harsh, his expression wolfish. Then Bay made a strangled sound from beneath him and suddenly Sila was dropping the camera. The noises continued even though all Bay could see now was black. He listened intently as he orgasmed, then held his breath at the sounds of Sila chasing after his own release.

The clip ended and restarted before he did and Bay blinked when his ass filled the screen once more, that damn handprint seemingly leering at him.

"It'll keep playing until—" Sila abruptly stopped talking when Bay slammed the multi-slate down and reached for the bowl with both hands.

He practically inhaled the remaining four dumplings, only chewing them enough to get them down before he chased them with the remaining water. He was about to stand when the clicking of a tongue gave him pause.

For a moment, Bay didn't understand, brow furrowing as frustration built up at the center of his chest. He was so hard, he wanted to move on to the part where Sila came out from wherever he was watching and *did* something.

Then he recalled the exact wording and after a quick glance from beneath his lashes to see if anyone was paying attention—they weren't—he lifted the bowl a second time and stroked his tongue against the porcelain. He lapped at it until he was certain there wasn't a single drop of broth left and then he set it back down.

His cheeks were flaming red from embarrassment when he caught the eyes of a girl sitting at the table diagonal from his, but her laughter at his antics seemed in good nature, and she lifted her shot glass in a salute before downing the alcoholic contents. With any luck, she'd be too drunk to tell her friends about this come morning.

"That's better," Sila sounded pleased. "I already paid the bill."

"Where are you?"

"Patience."

Bay fisted his hands and rested them on his upper thighs. "What do you want me to do?"

"I wonder what the rest of your students would say if they knew how good at following commands you are," Sila said. "That the stern, cold as ice Professor Delmar they all know and touch themselves to at night gets hard and dripping when someone else takes control."

"That's not..." Bay glowered.

"Please. Don't pretend you haven't heard the rumors about yourself. You know half the student body wants you. But," something shifted in the background, but it wasn't enough to clue Bay into where Sila may be, "you're leaking for *me* right now, aren't you, Kitten?"

"Varun." He wasn't sure if he was scolding him or not.

"Have you soaked through your pants yet?" Sila asked. "If you're as horny as you should be, you're going to want to rush out of there as fast as you can so you don't give people the chance to notice."

"What?" Bay's eyes went wide.

"Oh, did you think I would be coming to you?" He grunted. "I might have gone easier on you earlier, but you had to go and piss me off."

Was he talking about Bay's comments about the bridge?

"That was a long time ago," Bay said just in case. "I wasn't trying to imply—"

"Get up and get moving," Sila cut him off. "The second you step out that door the hunt is on."

His dick twitched painfully at the promise. "Hunt?"

"You'll run, just like in the forest."

"But…" The streets were still packed with nightlife. "That'll draw attention."

"Exactly."

"What if someone—"

"No one will come to your rescue," Sila told him. "This is Vitality, remember? They'll assume you're running from the Brumal and won't risk getting involved. How do you think they're able to get away with so many crimes? Didn't you hear about the two bodies that were found dumped?"

Bay had. It'd been all over the news.

"Even Kelevra knows better than to bother looking into things. Baikal and he are clever. They run this city through fear and promises. So long as no one sticks their nose where it doesn't belong, they won't have to worry about suffering the wrath of the Devils of Vitality. That's how the worst of the worst get away with things in the bright of day. Willful negligence is what makes it all possible."

It was bleak, but true. Idle Delmar had been a respected member of society. Most of her friends had already died of old age or other illnesses, but she'd had a few still living when she'd passed. After the funeral, they'd all turned their backs on Bay, unwilling to get involved when he'd contacted them asking for help with the case. They'd known his grandmother the same as he, had to know the accusations about her were bullshit and yet none of them had been willing to speak in her defense.

And that had been against a low-level gang like the Shepards.

Sila was right. If there was even a slight chance someone had angered the Brumal, no one in their right mind would dare get involved.

"Where am I running to?"

"Anywhere," Sila said. "Just run far and run fast. I'll catch you, baby."

Bay grabbed his multi-slate, not bothering to reattach it to his wrist. He could use it to help shield the view of his straining dick, hopefully that would be enough. Once he was running he wouldn't have to worry, but walking out of here it would be more obvious.

Nervousness ate away at him as he got to his feet and started for the exit, keeping his eyes on the door as though that would somehow help to keep all others off him. The waitress who'd helped him was standing nearby it and she smiled and gave a small bow as he approached, but her gaze never wandered down his body.

As soon as he was outside, he took a deep inhale of the chilled night air, still holding the multi-slate in front of him.

"Run," Sila's order came clipped, and that was all it took.

He was a respectable member of society, a professor at the most elite school in the Dual Galaxy.

And he was currently racing through the streets with a boner while a twenty-year-old hunted him down like an animal.

The crowd had thinned somewhat, but it was a small reprieve since there were still far too many people wandering Main Street for Bay's comfort. Many of them turned their heads to watch as he darted past, some pointing and whispering to their friends. But Sila had been right. No one reached for their multi-slates to contact the authorities and no one attempted to stop him and ask if he needed any help.

Bay had grown up on these streets, the home he'd lived in only a fifteen-minute hovercar ride away, so he was familiar with all the hidden nooks and back alleys. Knew which places would be his best bet at staying hidden.

"Are you hoping I don't catch you?" Sila

asked.

"Yes," it was a lie, but Bay said it anyway, the word cracking past his lips as he finally came up to the turn he'd been waiting for. It led between the bakery and a sticker shop, narrowing out toward the end before the opening would deposit him on Igor Road, directly behind Main Street. It was still part of the general area, filled with shops and restaurants, so he wouldn't get away from prying eyes for long, but it was better than sticking to the most popular street.

He shouldn't, because it was wrong on so many levels, but Bay wanted to be caught. He wanted Sila to find him and give him a repeat of the other night. He wanted that so badly, a needy moan escaped him.

"Weren't you the one who told me consensual non-consent wasn't your thing?" Sila taunted from the earbud still secured in Bay's right ear. He didn't sound nearly as out of breath as Bay was.

Was he even chasing after him like he'd promised? Bay twisted around another building and halted, sucking in as much air as he could.

"Why'd you stop, Kitten?"

Oh. He was chasing him. Good.

Bay started running again without giving a response.

"You won't get far," Sila told him.

"Shut up," Bay didn't want him to. He liked the sound of his voice too much. That was the problem. Even as his heart thumped wildly in his chest and his thighs burned, his dick didn't seem to care that the rest of his body was aching. He was still stiff and hard as a rock, and running like that wasn't easy by any means.

As badly as he wanted to be consumed by Sila, Bay understood the assignment. Just because they were both willing didn't mean things had to be boring between them. Hadn't that always been his secret desire anyway? In all the inappropriate fantasies he'd had of his student, not a single one of them had been of the missionary position. Bay didn't want soft or sweet.

He wanted to feel alive.

He wanted something, anything, to breathe this dead thing in his chest back to life, if only for a moment.

Maybe he hadn't been bluffing when he'd brought up the bridge earlier. Maybe a part of him had finally been voicing the truth that he'd kept buried within himself since he'd chickened out while peering over that edge the first time.

Bay had been very close to giving up last year when he'd heard Sila's laughter and had spotted him standing across the courtyard. It didn't matter if it'd actually been Rin, if the twins had swapped places that day and Bay had gotten it wrong. Because in that moment something within him had shifted, had brightened and yawned and stretched for the first time in a long time and Bay didn't give a damn which Varun was responsible.

Back then, he'd been close to giving up, and now here he was, racing through the streets as though his life depended on it. As though his life was important enough for him to even want to hold on to.

With a start, he realized he'd been unconsciously heading in the direction of Sickle bridge. It was a large bridge that stood over the Kefa river. Many people crossed it to make it into the heart of the city for work, so there were two hovercar lanes and a bike lane and walkways on either side.

Jumpers sadly weren't unheard of.

The lights from the bridge winked almost viciously at him in the distance and Bay slid to a stop, almost slipping in the dirt. At the last second, he changed directions, a small needle of fear piecing through him as he deviated and moved off to the left.

Somehow, despite the fact they hadn't actually known one another very long, Bay knew without a shadow of a doubt that heading this way had been the wrong move. Sila was probably thinking he'd done it on purpose, that he'd headed toward the bridge to—

The large body came out of nowhere. One second Bay was running down the narrow passage between two buildings, circling back around to Main Street, and the next he was being shoved roughly against the brick wall.

His head whacked against the stone and he

cried out, momentarily seeing stars. He was forced against it. His chest connecting with the wall, his palms coming up in a poor attempt to press back against that force.

Sila was too strong though, and he kicked Bay's feet apart and then forced one of his legs between his thighs. When his knee bumped against Bay's hard-on, he chuckled darkly, a gust of hot breath fanning across Bay's ear and the side of his neck.

The click of a knife blade springing free had Bay's eyes going wide and he stilled.

"Always so easy with you in the end," Sila said, shifting so that he could bring the blade up to the side of Bay's face, allowing him a good view of it as he tilted it in the lighting provided from the street at the end of the alley. "Just a little promise of real pain and your freeze up like a deer in headlights."

"Hold on." Bay's eyes went to the opening of the alley. They were somewhere in the center, with a turn at the opposite end, but the one in front of them was busy enough people walked by every now and again.

"They won't be able to see us," Sila promised, knowing exactly what he was fearing without him having to articulate it. "If you aren't careful, however…Sound travels. So," he leaned in and pressed his mouth to the curve of Bay's ear before dropping lower to nibble on his lobe, "you have to be really, really quiet."

He startled when Sila suddenly bit down, and made the mistake of jerking his head away, which only made the pain worse.

"Too loud," he chided and then licked the wound, though he hadn't broken skin. "You'll have to do better than that, Kitten." He dropped the hand with the knife, his hard front keeping Bay caught against the wall so he couldn't follow where the weapon went.

"Wait," Bay took a shaky breath, recalling what had happened the last time they'd done this. "Not my clothes. I need them."

"Do you?"

"You can't carry me out of here without us being seen the same way," Bay said.

"Want to bet?"

"Sila, please."

"You don't get to make demands, Professor. That was the agreement."

"We both know this was never really an agreement," he shot back before he could help it. "That I never really had a choice but to accept your offer."

Sila thought it over. "Didn't you?"

Bay winced when he felt the blunt edge of the blade drag up the side of his right leg. It wasn't the possibility of getting hurt that had him struggling—he'd welcome the pain—it was the idea of having to figure out how to leave here without getting arrested for public indecency that bothered him.

"I gave you the chance to make me go," Sila argued. "You decided to keep me around."

"I did that because at least this way I get something out of it." Bay felt the mood darken and trembled. "I didn't mean that how it sounded."

"Oh?" Sila rolled his hips and the full length of his cock rubbed against Bay's ass suggestively. "It sounded a lot like you were saying letting you experience world shattering orgasms wasn't enough."

"No," Bay shook his head, his cheek scrapping lightly against the brick from his efforts, "No, I only meant this way I can also get justice for my grandmother."

"Justice," Sila sneered. "Don't make me laugh. You don't give a damn about justice, Bay. If you did, you wouldn't have poisoned August or Lan and you wouldn't have been up on that bridge that day, ready to end your life while the people who'd driven her to death were still breathing."

"I poisoned them for you."

"Don't make me laugh. You did it for you. Sure, I provided an excuse and gave you an opportunity, but that was your revenge. Don't fret. I don't mind. I wanted you to do it. The only thing that annoys me is that you didn't take things all the way and kill them."

This was not the direction Bay wanted them to go. This felt too scary, cut him too open. He was still hard, but if they kept going, he wouldn't be for long. That familiar grief would take hold, followed swiftly by the numb state he'd been stuck in for the past two years.

The state he was only able to escape whenever he thought of Sila pinning him down and ravishing him like a demonic monster.

Like a Devil.

Bay needed the Devil right now. Needed to taunt and coax him out to play before the night was ruined for the both of them.

"Please," he asked, making his voice meek, "not my clothes. It's not a demand, it's a request."

Sila paused, and if he knew what Bay was really doing, he didn't call him on it. "Requests can be ignored."

"I know." He held his breath while he waited for a verdict. Humiliation between himself and his bedpartner was one thing, letting others in on it… He couldn't.

It felt like a million years later when the knife clicked back into its sheath and Sila tucked it into his front pocket. "All right, Kitten. But in return, you're going to have to purr for me, long and hard."

Sila's hands wrapped around Bay's front before he could reply. He unbuttoned his pants and slid the zipper down, slowly easing the charcoal material down until they were stuck around Bay's knees.

Cool air licked at Bay's skin and he squeezed his eyes shut, waiting for whatever the younger man planned next.

"Anyone could walk by and see, Professor," Sila said quietly as he slipped his hand down the front of Bay's black boxer briefs and cupped him.

He hissed and jerked, pressing back against Sila's bulge, that large palm chasing after him, keeping its grip on his balls.

"All they'll have to do is get curious about what the noise is and turn on their flashlight to check. Then they'll see you and know," he continued.

"I don't want that," Bay insisted, gasping when Sila's other hand trailed past his waistband from behind, his fingers slipping between his crease to play lightly at his hole. The touches were barely even, mere grazes against that ring of muscle, teasing but never entering.

The hand on his balls rolled them in his palm, and then Sila readjusted his hold and gave one solid pump of Bay's dick from root to tip.

"Why not?" Sila asked, and it took Bay far longer than it should have to follow. "Who cares if people know what a dirty freak you are? You don't want to keep living anyway. Right?"

He sucked in a breath and opened his mouth to argue that fact, only for Sila to let go of him all at once. Bay ended up making a sound of disappointment instead, his body already on fire and eager for more.

"Isn't that what you were saying to me earlier?" The sound of Sila working his own zipper free was the only thing keeping Bay from losing his mind and all out begging already. He'd stopped touching him, but this wasn't over.

All Bay had to do was give him the right answers and those hands would be back on him.

"I've thought about it before," he admitted, opting not to lie.

"Why?"

"Because I didn't have anything to live for." Bay sighed contentedly when he felt Sila draw his boxers down. His dick sprung free and slapped against the wall uncomfortably, but he didn't complain. "There was nothing interesting left."

"Racing?" Sila was doing something behind him, something that required both hands.

Bay hated it.

He pressed back, angling his hips so he was presenting his ass, but all that did was earn him a hard spank. "Racing stopped being enough a while ago," he dutifully replied.

"That when you started going to the Seaside?" Sila dropped something at their feet, but Bay couldn't turn to look at it because in the next instant Sila had a finger at his neglected entrance. He didn't go slow this time, forcing the digit in all the way past the second knuckle. Almost as soon as he'd driven it in, he pulled out and repeated the process, practically hammering into him.

Bay cried out and moaned, nails trying and failing to dig into the solid brick wall keeping him upright.

"Here." Sila took his right hand and lowered

it, forcing Bay's arm down. Then he rested Bay's hand over his bare thigh. "Dig them into me, Kitten. Claw me to ribbons if you've got it in you."

Bay hadn't gotten to touch that night in the forest and, shamelessly, he felt around, feeling the bunched muscle beneath his palm, hard as steel. "Do you like pain too?"

"Hurting me won't set me off, don't fret. I won't harm you out of anger."

"Because?"

"Do you really want to die, Professor?" He'd stalled his ministrations to move Bay's hand, but now he slipped in a second finger to meet the first and wiggled them around.

The tip of the middle one found Bay's prostate and he jumped, sparks of intense sensation bursting through him. "Right now?" He shook his head. "Not even a little."

Sila hummed. "But you did before?"

"I thought you'd figured out all my secrets already, Varun?"

"It's impossible to know every single secret a person keeps," he said. "There are things you keep even from yourself. If you aren't aware of them, how could I possibly be? I can follow an electronic trail, can track your movements without being seen. But I can't read your mind. I can't know what you were thinking yesterday, or the day before, or the day before that."

"Yes," Bay confessed, "I wanted to die. Before."

That earned him another finger and, now with three inside of him, it was getting harder to keep quiet. Sila worked him open, stretching and stroking his insides, taking his time with it as though this was a class assignment and he hadn't just hunted him through the streets.

"But not anymore?"

"Not since I met you." Bay didn't understand when Sila went still at that. He tried to turn to see, but then his face was shoved against the brick and held there, making it impossible for him to move.

Sila pulled his fingers free. "I was wrong."

Bay shivered at the odd hint malice in the younger man's tone. "About what?"

"Harming you out of anger."

It was the only warning he gave before the entire mood shifted.

CHAPTER 17:

Sila regretted having lubed him up and stretched him out, which was dangerous, because regret wasn't typically an emotion he was capable of.

And yet here they were.

He notched the head of his cock into Bay's hole and then thrust, not bothering to hold back. The force of it shoved Bay's front against the wall and his next cry was a mixture of pleasure and pain that only served to spur Sila on.

If they really did draw attention and were discovered, it wouldn't be good for either of them, and yet for the first time in his life, Sila didn't give a shit about playing things smart. Logic could go fuck itself for all he cared. Brutally and unapologetically. The way he was currently fucking his infuriatingly complex professor.

He slammed in as deep as he could go and then pushed in even though there was nothing left to give, the motion forcing Bay onto his tiptoes.

"Wait!" Bay dug his nails into Sila's thigh, slicing through skin to draw blood, but while he didn't seem to notice he was doing it, he'd been careful not to raise his voice too high.

Sila pulled all the way out to the tip and paused, just long enough to give Bay's body time to start closing, before he pumped in with the same level of drive. In order to get that deep, his movements couldn't be as quick and chaotic as he'd like, but that wasn't enough to keep him from doing it. Every time he filled Bay up, he knew he caused his dick to grind against the rough texture of the brick wall. When he pulled out, Bay's ass followed despite his verbal protests.

That wasn't right.

He wanted to hurt him. Sila wanted to expel some of this strange, pent-up emotion swirling within him and the only way he could think of to do that was by taking it out on Bay's flesh.

Why'd he have to remind Sila of how this had started? They'd been having fun, enjoying things, but then Bay had to go and bring up the fact that his interest in the Varuns was what had kicked this off.

Why did it even *matter*?

Sila and Rin were the same.

There wasn't one without the other.

Them being identical was their greatest asset.

There was no reason he should be angry that Bay couldn't tell them apart.

"Varun," Bay sobbed, "please! You're killing me!"

"Not yet," he growled back, but he did give in. Grabbing onto Bay by the hips, he pulled him partially off the wall and then began to mercilessly fuck him. His balls slapped loudly against Bay's inner thighs and he didn't even care that he was the one breaking the rule and putting them at risk.

He was relentless with his cock, moving at the fast speed his people were known for, but that he was always careful to control when in the bedroom. Bay was blubbering and crying and when the braided leather caught Sila's eye, he reached for it.

Twisting it around so he could slip his middle finger through the metal loop, Sila allowed Bay one last deep inhale before he pulled. He yanked Bay away from the wall by the throat, his other hand flattening over his hip to keep him in place as he continued to pummel his hole.

Bay's back bowed and he let go of Sila's thigh to claw at his forearms instead, desperately trying to get him to loosen his hold on the collar that was now cutting off his supply of oxygen.

Breath play had been a prominent feature in the videos Bay had selected at the Seaside, so Sila wasn't all that concerned over his reaction.

He shouldn't have been concerned even if he didn't know Bay was into it.

Damn it.

The hand on Bay's hip moved to find his dick, taking the heavy member in a firm hold. He worked him in time with his thrusts, easing up slightly on the collar so Bay wouldn't actually pass out.

"Come, Kitten," Sila growled against the curve of his neck. "Or you really might get your wish and die tonight."

He was bluffing.

Sila wouldn't kill him.

Not tonight.

And maybe not ever.

Dangerous. Dangerous. Dangerous.

Bay gurgled and his whole body went taught. His dick in Sila's palm twitched and gushed, shooting thick ropes of come against the wall. He jerked as he was pumped through it, until every last drop had been wrung free.

Sila let go of the metal loop and shoved Bay forward until he was sandwiched between him and the brick all over again. Then he buried himself in that silky heat and unloaded, filling Bay up.

"My cock," he growled the words against Bay's nape, teeth grazing the delicate skin there. "My come." When he licked a strip of that flesh from the back to the side of his throat, it was salty. Sila grabbed a fistful of that blue hair and yanked, giving himself access to Bay's face and the tear tracks there.

Even in the darkness, Bay's expression shone brightly. His pupils were blown and his mouth was hanging open, breaths coming in and out at a harried tempo. He was completely and totally blissed out despite how rough things had gotten, how quickly they'd gone from gentle to intense.

Sila bent down and his tongue darted out over the rise of his cheek, tasting those tears finally. They were salty, but not much more so than Bay's sweat soaked skin. His cock finally started to soften, but he kept his hips pressed forward so he didn't slip free, not ready to leave that warm, gripping hole.

Wanting to stay locked together with Bay a moment longer.

"Sila," Bay said his name reverently.

It snapped Sila out of it like being doused by a bucket of ice water. He sprung back, not bothering to catch Bay as he immediately lost control of his legs and slid to the dirty, trash littered ground. Instead, he tucked himself back in his pants and turned to go.

Bay's strangled sound of panic stopped him short.

Sila closed his eyes and gave himself a second to collect himself and get his head on straight, then he turned and hauled Bay unceremoniously off the floor. He had the professor's clothing sorted and his messy hair finger-combed back into place—close enough anyway—within minutes. Once that was done and there was no other reason to touch him, he dropped his arms.

They stood there and stared at one another.

"Are you going to kill me?" Bay broke the silence first. He didn't sound all that put out by the prospect, almost as though he'd expected as much from the beginning.

Smart guy like him, he probably had.

Too bad one of them seemed to have had their brains fucked out of their skull, and it wasn't the professor.

"I should," Sila concluded, voice monotone and empty. The way he typically was on the inside when there was nothing interesting going on to keep him from falling into that abyss where the devil demanded destruction to alleviate their boredom.

This was meant to be a game, a problem he solved so he and his brother could go back to their regularly scheduled program and switch whenever they felt like it without being leered at. Bay had posed a risk and it was Sila's job to handle any and all major risks.

He'd gotten too invested, spent too much energy and time fixating on Bay and the things that made him tick. What had started as a mild fascination had turned into something different, something foreign and consuming.

Yearning.

There were very few things Sila had ever coveted. To learn what it felt like to take a life with a blade was one. Freedom from his father was another.

That had pretty much been the extent of

it. He liked to fuck and understood desire, but he could get off with just about anyone under the right circumstances. It never had very much to do with the individual he was with. They weren't people to him; they were just holes to use and discard once the experience was over.

Sila was the collected twin. The twin who kept his shit together because he didn't have any shit to begin with. He didn't act on impulse, didn't take risks that could affect them as a whole, and he certainly didn't feel useless things like possessiveness and jealousy.

And yet...

"I should," he repeated, if only to test how he'd feel once the words were out there in the open. It didn't change anything though. The damage was already done. He took a single threatening step closer to Bay, who this time had the good sense to back away, a flash of fear entering his eyes.

"Keep this in mind the next time you think of visiting the bridge," he warned. "The only way you're allowed to die is if it's at my hand. I'm the only one who gets to kill you. Your life now belongs to me, and if you try to take something that's mine..." He eased Bay's chin up with a single finger. "I'll tear you apart for real, Bay Delmar, and I'll leave you bare, lying in a pool of your own blood for the whole world to see."

* * *

"Did you do it?"

Sila almost rolled his eyes at his brother's accusatory tone, but kept a straight face as he made his way down the hallway in building H of the Academy. He put in the earpiece a minute before his brother had called him, but he was sort of wishing he hadn't picked up.

Screening calls was a trick of his that his brother was well aware of, however.

Pity.

"Did I do what?" Sila asked, even though he knew what this was about. That was half the reason he'd expected the call in the first place.

"Did you kill him?" His brother should be in Vail, headed toward their sociology class, playing the role of Sila, while Sila was here, acting as Rin. He must have overheard the gossip that had spread through the city like wildfire the past few days.

"I didn't," Sila smiled to himself, "as far as anyone else knows."

"Seriously?"

"Relax. They'll never suspect me. I was meant to be at the library during the time of the murder." Which was exactly why keeping an open and public routine was so important.

"And when they ask around and everyone says they didn't see you?"

"Won't be a problem," he said. "I move around on purpose. Every day. If someone didn't notice me, they'll just assume it was because I was in a different section of the library that day." With any luck, people would also get confused. Since they did see him on those days he was meant to be there, they'd mix and jumble up to the point it'd be hard for anyone to be certain they hadn't seen him even if that were the case.

Last month, he'd waited for the right time before following after August, trailing behind for a while to confirm whether or not Bay meant to take things further. When it became apparent he wasn't going to add any fuel to the fire, Sila took over and did the job for him.

The only way to guarantee there was no evidence? Get rid of it. Bay and Berga believed the drug couldn't be traced, but why take the risk when it wasn't necessary? When the professor had someone like Sila there to take care of him?

He'd repeated the process with Lan, waiting for the student to stumble out of Bay's office. Lan had been a bit easier since he'd been so out of it, he'd gone straight to his car and sped off. Sila had followed and caught the guy just as he'd driven off the road and into a tree. August he'd hidden away to ensure the body had plenty of time to start decomposition before it was discovered, but that hadn't been necessary with Lan.

The official verdict for his death?

Car crash.

No one had to know he'd still been breathing when Sila had found him.

"I know you're doing something for that professor," his brother accused.

"Yes," Sila confirmed. "But the professor

didn't ask me to murder for him."

"There was no mention of it being a necessary killing."

Sila took a detour on his way to the shooting range and slipped into an empty classroom, clicking the door shut behind him. "He got in the way. I didn't just kill him for the hell of it." Mostly true. Sort of.

"Whatever you're doing with the professor, call it off."

He bristled. Usually, his brother was the only person allowed to try and give him orders and it was rare for him to react negatively to them, even if he didn't want to listen to his nagging. But in this regard… "No."

"You were supposed to fix this stalker problem and that was meant to be the end of it," his brother argued.

"We're both happy where things are and you know it," he retaliated. "What takes place between the professor and me is my business."

"Not when he spends an hour and half staring at me the way he did in class today," his brother snapped.

Sila felt his stomach clench and he lowered himself down to the surface of a nearby desk. "Explain."

After the confusion he'd experienced in the alley last week, Sila had needed a change. He'd gone to his brother and asked for them to switch places for a bit, just long enough he could contact

Kelevra and ask about Insight, and ideally, figure out these odd feelings.

The corner of his mouth turned upward smugly. He'd known Bay was bullshiting him and just gotten lucky when he'd called him by name at his house. He may have recognized him once, but that'd been a fluke. He couldn't tell them apart any better than the next useless meat sack. Now that he'd cleared that up, Sila could forget all about—

"He knows, asshole," his brother said.

Sila shot back onto his feet.

"The way he was looking at me," his brother continued, "was different. He knows. Did you tell him?"

"Yes, I begged him not to grade this week's pop quiz because my twin and I had planned to swap places and he's bad at psychology," Sila retorted, testing out the sarcastic tone his brother often used on him, though he was only mildly paying attention now.

"You're such a dick."

"I didn't tell him anything," he said.

"Obviously I know that," his brother snapped. "But something happened. Before he could never tell us apart, gave us that sappy, puppy dog love look—"

"Cat in heat," Sila corrected.

"What?" He blew out a breath. "What the fuck ever. My point is, he figured it out."

"I've got this."

"You don't have shit."

Sila's hand clenched into a fist. "Brother. I've got this."

There was a pause and then a heavy sigh. "Fine, no need to come at me with that scary tone of yours. It's in the rules anyway. I don't fuck with what's yours, you don't fuck with what's mine."

"What's mine is what's yours," Sila said, "and vice versa."

"Yeah? Well, I don't want Professor Delmar, so you keep him, and more importantly, you keep him the hell away from me. Got it?"

"Afraid your Imperial might get jealous?" Sila asked. Then he really considered it and came to the conclusion he wasn't overly fond of that idea. "If he tries anything—"

"He won't touch your precious professor," his brother cut him off, and there was a hint of sulkiness in his voice. "He's too busy playing games. You assholes, you're just alike. Always thinking you can manipulate people right into the palm of your hand."

Sila kept quiet since there was no arguing about that and he knew it. Though, he wouldn't say he and Kelevra Diar were all *that* similar.

Kelevra allowed his devilish nature to explode on the world around him.

Sila kept his more contained, homing it on the things that mattered, allowing himself to slip through the cracks unseen. But then, this was mostly due to the fact he didn't have the same luxuries as the Imperial Prince. There was no

Emperor or Heir Imperial who would clean up his messes if he screwed up and caused a blood bath.

He'd been saddled with Crate Varun as a father.

Fate must have taken pity on him, however, because in that moment, the door to the class room opened and in walked in the Devil of discussion.

Sila grinned when Kelevra paused in the doorway.

"I'll have to call you later, brother," he said, hand already lifting to the circular emblem-slate around his wrist. When he hung up, it was to the sound of being cursed in their secret language. He tipped his head at the Imperial. "Not your flower."

"No shit," Kelevra drawled. He made his way over to the front of the classroom and turned to perch against the edge of the teacher's desk. When he crossed his arms, it completed the picture he was no doubt trying to portray of the man in charge.

The corner of Sila's mouth curved upward and he dropped his gaze before it could be noticed.

Even though they were currently on Academy grounds, Kelevra wasn't in uniform like the rest of them. He'd never been held to the same rigid standards, and instead was sporting one of his famous corset vests. The colors were a mixture of bold blues and swirling patterns of gold, the suit jacket and pants matching so it all came together. He looked like he was about to head to a ball or a party, not whatever the hell this class was called.

Sila glanced over the Imperial's shoulder at the projection board. Ah. Nano Tech 101.

"I assume there's a reason for your visit, Imposter," Kelevra broke the silence then. "If it's about—"

"My brother doesn't know we're having this discussion," he interrupted and held his gaze. "I'm expecting it to stay that way."

Kel quirked a brow. His hazel eyes tracked Sila's movements and, though it was subtle, it was obvious he was using his computerized eye to check on his physical health. He could lock onto people's bodies and use that information to determine if they were lying to him or even what kind of mood they were in.

"You don't work the same way normal people do," Kelevra said then, sounding interested in that fact. "It's similar to what I see when I look in the mirror and try to get a reading on myself."

"What about Baikal Void?"

Kelevra was the one grinning this time. "Curious about him, are you? I don't blame you. With the way he acts, it would make sense if he was like us. Alas, unlike you and me, the guy was actually bred to be a monster."

"We aren't monsters."

"Right," Kel snapped his fingers, "We're Devils."

Sila tipped his head, trying to sense if this were a trap. "And I'm included in that now?"

"Void is the one who called you out on it first," he told him.

It couldn't have been right away. If Baikal had, he would have done everything in his power to separate Sila from Rabbit. He must have realized Sila's true nature later on, once he was already secure in his relationship with the musician.

"Interesting," Sila said.

"I thought so too. But you didn't come here to make chitchat with me."

"I don't really like you," Sila confirmed, "So no. I did not."

"I'm going to have to ask Rin how he keeps you in check. I get the feeling it'll come in handy."

"Ask," he dared. "It'll only piss him off."

Kelevra tutted and dropped his hands back on the desk, leaning on them. "Everything pisses him off."

"True."

"It's cute."

He didn't come here to talk about how the Imperial Prince was obsessed with his brother either.

"You owe me a favor," Sila reminded, and a look passed between them, letting him know he didn't need to spell out the details of when that had transpired. "I'm calling it in."

"All right."

"I need a pair of Insight glasses," he said. "They need to be jailbroken."

"That's incredibly illegal." Kelevra lifted his

multi-slate and started typing out a message to someone. "I like it." Not a minute later, his device dinged. "You're in luck. Madden has a pair. He'll meet you in the south parking lot in twenty."

"I'll be there."

Kelevra got to his feet and adjusted his clothing. "If that's all?" He'd posed it as a question, but he didn't wait for Sila's reply, exiting the room as quickly as he'd come.

Perhaps he wasn't taking Nano Tech 101 after all.

CHAPTER 18:

Was he looking at him?

Bay turned from the projection screen and sent a subtle glance over toward the back where Sila Varun was seated with his friends.

Only, it wasn't Sila at all, at least, not *his* Sila.

After not hearing from him since he'd left Bay standing there alone in the middle of that dank alley after experiencing the most intense orgasm of his life, his stalker had gone quiet. Bay had actually been looking forward to class two days ago, because at least then he'd get to see him.

Wrong.

He'd sent his brother in his place.

Bay had been watching the way other people interacted with him and it'd become painfully clear that Sila had been right. He hadn't made it up when he'd said the twins made it a habit of switching and no one was the wiser. Not a single person seemed to notice that there was a replica in the usual Sila's place. Even his friends laughed and joked with him the same as always.

But Bay could tell. Now that he knew what

to look for it almost seemed comical that he'd been tricked by them before. It was all in the eyes. While this Sila, the one currently listening intently to something Riel was whispering to him, had the same overall composure, there was a flash of something in his mismatched gaze. He contained it well, but two days ago when he'd walked in and caught Bay's eye, it'd been impossible to miss.

Admittedly, aside from that their likeness was uncanny. They moved the same, lounged the same, even smiled and made the same types of comments. It wasn't until no one else was looking that the Sila seated in his class room dropped any bit of the mask and, even then, it was fleeting. If Bay hadn't been looking, he would have missed it.

Even if they always appeared the exact same, however, Bay would have known. It was the feel in the air that did it. There was no thick tension that made his insides swirl, or his skin prickle with awareness. The Sila talking with Riel was every bit as physically attractive as the one who'd pinned Bay to that brick wall and fucked him madly.

And yet Bay's body gave no reaction to seeing him. His dick remained flaccid in his pants and his heart completely unaffected in his chest.

He'd tried to contact Sila several times since that night but all messages had gone unanswered. After that first class with his brother in his place, he'd sent another text, only the device on the replica's arm had beeped.

So they exchanged everything when they

swapped places, even their multi-slates. Made sense if they wanted to stay in character. Still, the disappointment Bay had felt in that moment had been impossible to hide, and Sila's brother had looked at him and tipped his head in clear observation.

It made Bay wonder how much he knew. Had Sila told him all the sordid details of their time together? Had he shared the videos of Bay touching himself in the Seaside or taking it up the ass in the woods? He'd wanted to ask, wanted to demand an answer, actually, but fear kept him silent.

There weren't many things Bay was afraid of, but the idea that Sila had given his brother insight to their private moments…that frightened him. For a couple of reasons, but most of which because it would be a betrayal, and even though their time together had thus far been brief in the grand scheme of things, Bay was already attached. He already wanted to rely on Sila, at least to keep his word about his grandmother.

He taught Varun's class twice a week, with a day between, and he'd been hopeful today his Sila would arrive, but no such luck.

"Read the case provided to you all," Bay announced when class finally ended. "You each need to write a profile of the criminal spoken about. It'll be due next week."

"You coming to lunch," Jol asked the fake Sila as the three friends stood and collected their things.

Riel scowled at her. "And put up with all the rumors about Rin that keep going around?"

The Sila replica's mouth twitched but that was all the reaction he gave. If only they knew they were talking about *him* right now.

"How about we check out that restaurant nearby? They have private room seating," Riel offered.

"I'm going to the pool," the replica replied and his friends both frowned.

"Without eating?" Jol clicked her tongue. "That's not healthy."

"I'll be fine." He winked at her. "Thanks for worrying about me."

She snorted and tossed her backpack strap over her shoulder with more gusto than necessary, then linked her arm through Riel's to tug him toward the exit. "Whatever." She stuck her tongue out on the way and then the two of them were spilling out of the room with the rest of the class.

Bay held his breath when the replica didn't immediately leave with them, instead heading up toward the front where he still stood behind the podium with the controls for the projector at his back. He pressed against his glasses over the bridge of his nose and cleared his throat uncomfortably. "Is there something I can help you with, Mr. Varun?"

The replica tipped his head toward the still open door and listened, almost as if he was making sure everyone else had truly left. Then he turned back and it was like his entire demeanor changed at the snap of a finger.

His shoulders pulled back and his hand tightened on the strap of his black backpack, the other slipping into the front pocket of his black dress pants. He cocked his head and there was something in his eyes, nothing dark or empty like the real Sila, but something wild and angry. Almost like there was an entire volcano hibernating within him that was at risk of blowing at any moment.

"You knew I wasn't him," he asked, and even the voice had altered slightly, an accusatory edge there that Bay had never heard come from the real Sila before. "How?"

Bay blinked at him and then gripped the podium, taking a second to remind himself that they were currently on Vail, in his classroom, and he was the professor here. Even if that weren't the case, this wasn't his Sila. His brother, the replica, wasn't in charge.

"I'm not sure what he's said to you—" Bay began, only to have the replica grunt at him.

"He's told me jackshit, Professor, that's why I'm standing here asking you. He'll be pissed if he finds out, so give it to me straight already so we can both go on our ways."

"I'll remind you that I'm your teacher, Mr. Varun."

"Ah," he hummed, "so I suppose that means

you scold my brother whenever he's rude to you, huh?" He rolled his eyes, the golden star huggie earring in his ear swinging and catching the light.

They switched down to even the minute details.

"You don't seem interesting enough to have caught his attention. My brother doesn't bother with anyone. But now he's investigating murders for a stranger. I don't like it."

"I'm not a stranger," Bay said. Sure, they hadn't really known one another for long, but Sila had been *inside* of him. That had to count for something.

"Everyone who isn't me is a stranger to him," the replica corrected. "Everyone who isn't him is a stranger to me."

"Oh?" Bay quirked a brow. "Is the Imperial Prince aware of this detail?"

His eyes narrowed. "You've heard the rumors."

"Everyone's heard the rumors."

"Figured you'd be above all that garbage, seeing as how you're a professor and all."

"Is teaching here the only thing you know about me?" Bay gave in and forced himself to ask. "He hasn't told you anything else?"

"Like what?" He shook his head. "I already said he hasn't filled me in about anything. I'm in the dark here."

"You're taking a risk by exposing yourself to me right now, aren't you?" It was a rhetorical question; it was obvious by the way the replica's gaze hardened in suspicion he'd caught on. "Why is that? Are you worried about your brother? I understand things started off…poorly, but I assure you didn't mean either of you any harm."

"You were just infatuated," he said. "Yeah, I figured that out already. Let's get one thing straight here. It isn't him I'm worried about. It's you."

Bay pulled back slightly. "Me?"

"Cut the act. He's obviously already shown you who he really is, at least to some extent, otherwise you wouldn't have been able to differentiate between the two of us so easily. You're a criminal psych professor, you better than anyone should know the type of person you're getting involved with."

"We're…" Bay wasn't really sure how to put whatever they were into words. "He's helping me with something and I'm spending time with him in the process."

"Spending time with him?" He set his hands on his hips in clear exasperation. "He's toying with you, and you're letting him. It's a dangerous game, Bay Delmar."

"I'm okay with losing." If it was to Sila? Yeah, maybe it made him pathetic, but Bay was fine with that. As long as Sila kept his promise and Bay learned what exactly transpired between his grandmother and the Shepards, then it didn't matter what happened to him at the end of all of this.

"Something important you should know about my brother," he said, hesitant, almost as though he felt like he was about to betray Sila by speaking, but his conscience—which he clearly had even if his twin didn't—wouldn't allow him to remain quiet. "It's not about winning for him. He's fine with losing so long as he's entertained in the process. It might seem black and white to you, but it isn't. Nothing with him ever is."

"I'm not sure I'm following," Bay admitted.

"I'm saying," he hissed, "he might let you win. He might let you lose. You won't have a choice in the matter either way. And by the end? You may even come to realize you've lost when you hoped to win, or won when you'd hoped to lose."

If he wasn't already used to Sila talking to him in weird tongue twisters, this conversation might be more off-putting. Bay was struggling to follow still, but at least he could keep his composure throughout.

"We have an agreement." And for some strange reason, he trusted that Sila would keep his end of it.

"Did you set rules?" the replica, the one who usually went by Rin, asked.

Bay frowned.

"Don't tell me the two of you shook hands and that was that?"

He thought of it more like they'd sealed the deal with a kiss, but he so wasn't about to tell Sila's brother that.

"Just because he's a college student and five years younger than you," the replica's tone eased then, dropping low in warning, "don't underestimate him. The only reason he hasn't ended up in one of your case files is because he's smart and in control. The second he slips up..."

"Are you saying your brother is a murderer?" That seemed extreme, and also not something his twin should be sharing, especially not with a figure of authority like his teacher. Even if the guy clearly didn't consider Bay as much of an authority figure. Bay was the one checking the doorway this time to be sure they were alone. "You shouldn't say things like that."

"Guess he hasn't mentioned he's killed in the past."

Bay blinked at him. "What are you trying to do here, Rin?"

The replica huffed. "Don't call me that. And I'm not trying to do anything. I just can't be bothered to clean up my brother's mess if he makes one."

"He isn't going to kill me." Bay wasn't actually convinced that was true, but he'd say it now to put an end to this conversation anyway.

It was obvious from the look Sila's brother sent him, he wasn't falling for his poorly veiled act.

The multi-slate Sila typically wore, the one strapped to his brother's wrist, went off then, and without skipping a beat he tapped the button and accepted the call.

"Where are you?" Sila's voice trickled through.

"Talking with Professor Delmar. Want to say hi? You're on speaker." He sent Bay a taunting look.

Bay held his breath, waiting for Sila's reaction, but he wasn't expecting the flippant response that came through the speakers on the side of the device.

"Touché, brother."

Rin grinned. "That's what you get for sharing shit with Kelevra."

"So you mentioned the pill then?"

He shared a confused look with Bay. "What pill?"

"The one I got off of your Imperial," Sila said. "The one I slipped to Castle that night the staff met for their back-to-school celebration."

"You what?!" both Rin and Bay exclaimed at the same time.

"I assumed you were doing your best big brother impression and attempting to warn Kitten off of me," Sila continued. "Turns out you didn't even have anything real in your arsenal to work with."

Bay felt a bit light headed and braced himself against the podium as he considered that admission. That night, Castle had taken it up a notch when he'd cornered Bay, but he'd assumed it was due to alcohol consumption. Now Sila was saying it'd actually been because he'd drugged the man?

To what end? Surely the goal hadn't been so he could swoop in and play hero? Although... Bay had accepted the messages but ignored all attempts at phone calls up until that point, hadn't he? Sila had successfully gotten him to answer his call, and then he'd won him over with his act of kindness when he'd torn Castle off of him before things could go too far.

"You...Set me up?" Bay shouldn't be surprised. It was everything Rin had literally just warned him about, after all. He waited for the anger to come, for the disgust and the humiliation over having fallen for it but none of those feelings came. He was upset, sure, but not livid.

Even knowing that Sila had put him at risk that night by drugging Castle, Bay didn't regret anything that had transpired between them since.

Probably because a stupid part of himself was convinced that he'd never really been in any danger to begin with. That Sila had been there the whole time to ensure Castle never got the chance to do anything more than fondle him a little and—

"I must be certifiably insane," Bay said to himself, running a hand down his face, partially knocking his glasses askew in the process so he needed to correct them.

"Still want to play with me, Kitten?" Sila asked, all buttery soft words spoken through the device attached to his twin, like he couldn't care less about their audience or how shameless he was being.

"Hey," Rin's voice dropped lower but he didn't switch the device off of speaker even though it was obvious he wanted to, "you do realize you're outing yourself right now, right?"

"I know you'd never do anything to hurt me," Sila told him. "Which means all you really wanted to do was test the waters and see if the professor could be trusted with our secret. But since we're already in the process of tossing it all out there, why not go all in? You should tell him about Ally Orld."

Rin glanced at Bay, but spoke to his brother. "This is risky."

"You're currently standing in a room alone with the guy who's responsible for August Bril's death."

"What?" Bay shook his head, staring at the multi-slate as though he could see Sila through it even though that wasn't the case. "I am not!"

"You slipped him poisoned tea," Sila reminded.

"Yes, but it wouldn't have killed him!" He held up a hand to Rin. "Honestly, all it did was make him a little delirious. He would have acted like a fool and eventually passed out somewhere, that's all. He wouldn't have died!"

"He would if you made him vulnerable to attack," Sila corrected.

"Attack from who?"

"Come on, Kitten, you aren't that naïve.

Admit it, part of you suspected as much when you heard August's body had been found the other day. And what about Lan?"

With Lan, Bay had thought it was his fault, since he'd been the one to drug the guy just before he'd supposedly crashed his car into a tree. Hearing that it'd actually been Sila? That was a relief. Not because it got him off the hook—Lan took advantage of people, Bay doing the same had merely been karmic justice—but because in his own fucked up way, that was Sila showing Bay he cared.

"This," Rin shook his head, "sounds very much like a you two problem to me."

If his brother was bothered by the discovery Sila had recently killed a couple of people, Bay couldn't tell.

"You won't be needed," Sila agreed.

"Good, because I have my own shit to deal with."

"I've got everything under control."

"Drugging teachers," Rin glared at Bay, "*and* students is under control now, is it? I take it back. I'm starting to understand what my brother finds attractive about you and I really wish I hadn't. The last thing I need is more chaos in my life. I'm hanging up. Finish this conversation on your own." Without waiting even a second, he did exactly that. Then he pointed a finger at Bay. "If anything happens to my brother while he's helping you with whatever the fuck he's helping you with, I'll catch you on your way home from campus and drown you in Cerulean Lake."

Bay opened his mouth to reply, but Rin didn't wait for him either, twisting on his heels and practically storming out of the room.

He replayed their entire conversation over in his head, but it was a spontaneous cluster fuck of odd interactions and hidden double meanings. At least he'd unearthed another interesting difference between the twins that could maybe come in handy one day.

Sila was calculative and unsympathetic, like a glacier in the middle of a still ocean.

Rin was the opposite. He had a conscience, but he was hotheaded and impulsive.

As someone who'd extensively studied criminology, Bay was admittedly fascinated by the two of them and their differences. He also knew to take the fact that they'd both now threatened his life, openly, without hesitation, to be the very real threat that it was.

In that moment, Bay decided to try and avoid interactions with Rin as much as possible. He'd take the devil he knew—the one who *knew* how to make him scream and pant—any day.

Dropping from a bridge was one thing.

Drowning?

Big no.

Which, he cocked his head, must mean he was no longer as open to dying as he'd once been, right?

CHAPTER 19:

Bay stirred awake, coming to bit by bit, the darkness of his bedroom greeting him. For a long moment, it took his brain time to catch up and process there was something off, his gaze stuck on the luminescent lines cast from the street light outside on the wall. The clock on his end table read that it was only three in the morning. He should still be asleep.

It was the odd heat radiating from behind him that finally slipped through the fog and a second later an arm reached around his middle, tugging him flush against a solid body.

He let out a startled sound and tried to pull himself away but the person at his back held firm, clicking their tongue chidingly at him. Bay had gone to bed alone and he'd been sure to lock the front door, so there was no reason anyone should be lying under the covers with him.

"It's me," Sila's voice cut through the panic like a swift blade, his words kept low and unhurried, as though Bay's fear didn't matter to him in the slightest. He was simply annoyed about all the struggling.

"Sila?" He deflated, head dropping back down to the pillow as he exhaled in relief. "Where have you been?"

Bay's bed was small, a mere twin sized mattress with squeaky springs and a lumpy surface. There were some nights he barely fit on the thing alone, which explained why Sila was pressed in so close, his knees bumping against the backs of Bay's. He'd gotten beneath the gray comforter as well and Bay jumped when the tips of Sila's fingers traced the waistband of his boxer briefs.

"Shouldn't you be more curious about why I'm here?" Sila said. "Didn't you ask me in the alley if I was going to kill you? Maybe I'm here to do that now."

"You won't," Bay replied, shivering when those fingers continued to lazily trace over the edge of the band, back and forth, so that he barely brushed against the exposed flesh of Bay's lower stomach. He'd gone to sleep in nothing but an old Vail t-shirt and his underwear, but even with so few clothes on, he couldn't tell by feel what Sila was wearing.

The idea of him waking Bay already fully naked...He licked his lips.

"So certain?" Sila asked.

"Yeah." Bay lifted his ass, bumping back against the hard bulge that'd been nudging him since he'd woken. "I'd say my odds are good here."

Sila hummed. "What if my intention is to fuck you then kill you?"

It very well could be.

"This is a shitty neighborhood. Even if you screamed for help as loud as you can, I doubt anyone would call the cops. I could strangle you," Sila's other hand tugged lightly at the leather chord still secured around Bay's throat, "and leave you here. No one would come looking. When your body is eventually discovered, it'll be because the mailman complains about the smell."

"We don't get physical mail delivery here," Bay said.

Sila's hot mouth ghosted over the curve of his right ear. "Guess no one will ever find you then, huh?"

"You won't do that either."

"No?" The hand at his waistband paused. "What gave you that impression?"

"This." Bay pulled his head forward slightly, knowing Sila's finger was still looped through the back. It caused the leather to press uncomfortably against his neck for a second before he eased off. "You collared me."

"They did it a few times in the porn you seemed most fond of," Sila explained.

"You were curious to try it out," Bay nodded in understanding. "So, this is all new to you?"

"What is?"

"BDSM. Stuff like—"

"You're misunderstanding something here,

Kitten," Sila stopped him. "That's dangerous. I left you alone for a few days and it seems you've concocted a fairytale in my absence. That won't do. Play like that comes with guidelines, safety precautions, and rules. I told you this wouldn't be pretend."

Play *like that* wasn't pretend, it was an understanding. A mutual trust. But Bay didn't point any of that out.

"I don't think this is pretend."

"If that were true, you would be terrified right now."

"I am," Bay admitted.

Sila paused and he felt his gaze on him, but didn't risk turning to try and catch a glimpse of the younger man's face. With Sila's back to the window, he probably wouldn't get to see it anyway. "You don't seem afraid."

"It's because I'm dead inside," he said. "I *can* feel it, but it's muted at the moment. Since you've done so in the past, I know you'll bring it out of me eventually. I don't think you're here to kill me, but I recognize the promise of pain when I see it."

"You haven't seen me yet."

The corner of his mouth twitched. "Figure of speech."

There wasn't any reason Bay could think of for Sila to visit him like this in the early AM without warning. If it was about his grandmother and the Shepards, surely that could have waited. Plus, it'd been over three days since they'd last met, their conversation on the phone shared with Rin this afternoon the first contact they'd had in all that time.

"To me, the collar means we're in a relationship of sorts. It means ownership. I swore I'd do whatever you told me to? That's total power exchange. You're in control," Bay tentatively explained, not sure how much he should reveal or how much Sila might actually care.

"Ownership," he seemed to be testing the feel of the word on his tongue, his fingers starting back up with their slow back and forth over Bay's waistband. "That seems so easy. Was that really all it took to win you over?"

"You didn't *win* me," Bay reminded.

"That's right." He shifted and then ground his hard-on against Bay's ass, flattening his palm over his stomach to keep in him place as he did. "I took you. But, Professor, shouldn't you be more opposed? More indignant? Is it because you spent all that time fantasizing of having me this way? Did all that daydreaming mess with your ability to think critically? I raped you in the forest, on the ground, with the dirt and the leaves sticking to your sweaty skin. Have you sugarcoated that fact in this pretty head of yours, the same way you've romanticized my reasoning for locking this twist of leather around your neck?"

"No." Bay knew exactly what had been done to him. Their time in the alley could be considered consensual by some, but there was no mistaking what'd been done in the forest had been a crime of the worst sort. He'd been sexually assaulted and brutalized against his will. He'd been humiliated, overpowered, and hurt physically.

But mentally...

"Do you want to know the last time I felt anything as vividly as I did that night?" Bay asked. "It was when that lawyer told me there was nothing I could do to save my home from being stolen by the Shepards. I was so angry that day that I took my bike out and ended up crashing it. I broke an arm, but otherwise was unharmed."

"Is that when you went to the bridge?" Sila asked, and Bay shook his head in the negative.

"That came later, once I'd gone numb. It's like I sunk to the bottom of a deep, dark pool and not only could I not find my way back up, but I lacked interest in even trying. My grandmother was gone and life felt like it had no meaning, no joy."

Sila snorted. "Making you bleed on my cock did not bring you joy."

"No," he agreed, "it didn't. It hurt like hell. I even felt like I might be dying for a brief moment there. Society likes to look down on people who enjoy pain, but our bodies are built in such a way it's more common than anyone wants to admit. Our central nervous system's natural response to pain is to release endorphins to help counteract it. You brought me to the lowest low, which in turn brought me to the highest high...And when I fell...

Euphoria."

"You're sounding a bit insane, Professor," Sila said, though it was impossible to tell what he was feeling from his tone.

"I never claimed to be right in the head."

"I would never be attracted to someone who was normal."

"Are you?" Bay risked asking. "Attracted to me? Or is this all part of it? Are you hard right now because of what you plan to do next, or are you hard because—"

"Your hair looks as pale as moonlight right now," Sila cut him off. "It's practically silver in this lighting. When I came in, you were huddled beneath this trashy comforter, already close to the edge of the mattress, as though you were waiting for me. If I'd tormented anyone else the way I have you, they would have gone to the police or tried for revenge. Do you know what you did when you woke up here the morning after?"

"What?"

"You looked at me and held my gaze."

"Yeah, because instinct told me to keep the predator in sight."

Sila chuckled. "You wanted me back inside of you. I could tell. It was in those golden eyes of yours. They remind me of the beaches back home, by the way. When I first saw them, I wanted to gouge them out."

Bay sucked in a sharp breath.

"That wasn't a threat," he reassured him. "I

have no intention of ever doing that now. I like the way you look at me too much. Maybe that's the problem."

"Problem?"

"I haven't been able to stop thinking about you," Sila told him flatly. It was clear it wasn't meant to be a confession. "That's new for me. I put space between us, but then you had to go and differentiate between myself and my brother. I wonder, Bay Delmar, if you know what you're doing, or if it's merely luck on your part."

Considering Bay was finding it difficult to follow the flow of the conversation, he was going to have to go with the latter. If only he knew what that meant.

"You claim you've lost the ability to feel?" Sila's fingers finally slipped beneath his waistband, easing their way down through the curly blue hairs until he could wrap them around the root of Bay's swollen and eager dick. He gave him a leisurely pump, clicking his tongue again when that instantly had Bay's back bowing. "I find that hard to believe. Every time I saw you, what you were feeling was written in technicolor across your face."

Bay's hand went to Sila's wrist but he didn't stop him or attempt to pull him away, merely leaving it there while Sila continued to pump him in measured, torturous strokes. "That's because you were there. That's why I liked looking at you so much. Why I like looking at you. You make me feel

—" His sentence died on a strangled yelp when that hand dropped lower and gave a tight squeeze to his balls.

"Open yourself up for me," Sila demanded, still gripping him. "Do it."

Bay started to turn but a low growl stopped him.

"I put that collar on you because I want my brother to stay away," Sila said. "Have you looked at it properly?"

He'd checked it out in the bathroom mirror, of course. It was good craftsmanship, probably expensive, with just enough give around his neck that it could be turned so the loop could settle at any direction. The loop itself was gold, heavy and polished, with a tiny pale blue stone at the center.

"Do you want to know a secret?" he continued without waiting for Bay to answer. "For the longest time, that was the only way we differentiated between the two of us. He was Green and I was Blue."

"Your eyes." They both had the same pair of pastel, two-toned eyes.

"It was a game," he said. "We'd refer to each other as such out loud to see if anyone would catch on. This was just before we realized we could escape our home world and come here. We'd grown bored with hiding and that boredom drove us to taking risks. No one noticed anyway. I could be Sila or Rin, and my brother would call me Blue in front of the same people. They didn't catch on. It isn't that big of a stretch to assume identical twins might swap places now and again, not nearly as much as imagining a professor stuffing himself with silicone cock to pictures of his student, in any case, yet no one caught on—You aren't following my order, Kitten."

Bay hesitated but then he moved his arm and reached back. It was awkward due to their positioning, but he managed to wiggle his hand down the back of his underwear and shifted so he could locate his hole. "I don't have any lubrication."

"You should probably be gentle then," Sila told him.

He clenched his jaw and then worked a finger in, wincing over the mild discomfort that caused. It wasn't too bad, but it definitely lacked the pleasure he'd get if he'd been given some type of lube to ease his passage. The back of his hand grazed Sila's cock when he tried for a better angle and he froze.

A flash memory of what it'd felt like having that thing literally split him open had him clenching up and tensing all over. The pain had led to a phenomenal experience overall, but that didn't mean he wasn't still afraid of going through it again.

And, if his pulsating dick was any indicator, also extremely turned on by the prospect.

He was naturally associating that type of pain with pleasure now, and when he gathered enough courage to press in a second finger, he wasn't as easy with it. A sharp breath escaped him at the slight burning sensation and he paused with the two digits only buried past the first knuckle.

Sila thrust his hips forward with little warning, his cock bumping against Bay's hand. His fingers pushed in further and he gasped.

"It doesn't matter what I make you feel so long as I make you feel something, is that it?" he asked, and Bay found himself wildly shaking his head. "No? Isn't that what you were trying to convey earlier? You said you liked it when I made you bleed."

"I liked it because the pain turned to pleasure," Bay corrected.

"You liked it because you were dormant and the pain forced you to wake up. You cried and begged to get away after the first orgasm though."

"What—"

Sila went back to working him with his hand, his thumb collecting droplets of precome from Bay's crown so he could glide easily up and down his shaft. He was quicker about it this time, rubbing at the head whenever he reached it and cinching his fingers around the base when he went down.

It wasn't long before Bay was thrusting into his fist, his fingers held still buried in his tight hole. He forgot all about them until Sila started gyrating behind him, his hard length rubbing against his hand so that those fingers slid just a little bit and bumped against his prostate.

Suddenly, Sila was pulling him up so he was kneeling on the bed, still facing the wall. He tore Bay's shirt over his head and tossed it into the corner, then forced him to bend forward so his head was hanging over the side of the mattress.

Bay sucked in a breath when his boxer briefs were yanked down to his knees and his thighs were forced apart as far as they could go with the material restricting them. He was positioned with his ass held high up in the air.

"Choice," Sila offered. "You still want that lube, Kitten?"

Bay considered. He needed some type of painful stimulation to get off. Sila had been right in his assumption that it'd taken that explosive, super charged event to revive that dead part inside of him, but it was roused now, maybe not fully in working order, but close enough. He could feel things, in any case, even when the younger man wasn't around, something he'd realized these past three days apart.

"Yes," he settled on. There needed to be pain, but not always to that degree.

Not only that, but he didn't think it would ever work out the same. At the time, he'd been hopped up on adrenaline and fear because he hadn't yet slept with Sila and he hadn't known what the other guy intended. Now? He was certain he wasn't going to die here tonight. Knowing killed some of the appeal their time in the woods had held.

That was so twisted and fucked, but it was what it was.

"Hold yourself open for me," Sila ordered.

"What?"

He grabbed onto Bay's wrists and pulled them back, placing his hands on either ass cheek before letting go. "Open."

A rush of embarrassment twisted in Bay's gut and he blushed and hung his head further off the edge, as though there was a chance Sila could catch a glance of his face from where he was kneeling behind him. Curving his fingers, he gripped himself and then pulled the flesh apart, grimacing when he imagined what he must look like.

Naked and presenting himself to his student, his dick hanging heavy between his thighs. The tip brushed against the sheets beneath him and he groaned at the minor sensation.

The sound of Sila's zipper going caught his attention and Bay homed in on it like a beacon. There was the shifting of clothing, and then the sound of foil tearing, and he braced himself for the feel of cold lube only for it to never come.

"What are you doing?" he dared to ask after the waiting become too much for him to handle. He tried to lift his head to see over his shoulder, but all he could make out was Sila's looming form in the dark. Like some shadow devil come to claim his prize.

"I'm giving you what you want," Sila said cryptically.

And then he started to jerk off behind Bay.

CHAPTER 20:

Sila groaned as he masturbated to the sight of Bay's puckered hole. He'd slicked himself up with the packet of lube he'd brought but his Kitten wasn't going to be getting any of that tonight. No, the only thing allowed inside of him was Sila.

He'd been thinking about it, and there was a very real chance he'd gotten off the other two times on the way Bay had cried all pretty and clenched around his cock.

So they were going to do things differently this time. Experimentation was a part of the game that Sila always enjoyed. Though, while testing limits had always been a part of that, it'd never been about his own before.

Bay wasn't crying now, wasn't bleeding anywhere or trying to get away. On the contrary, he was ever so subtly rubbing his dick against the mattress while he listened to the sound of Sila screwing his own fist.

Sila whacked him across the left ass cheek, using all his strength to do so.

That had Bay falling forward, crying out.

The opposite of what he was supposed to be doing.

"Get back into position," he demanded, but any irritation he'd felt instantly vanished when Bay immediately struggled back onto his knees, his hands spreading his cheeks a second time.

"Sila," Bay said his name with a pleading note to it.

"What's that, Kitten?"

"I feel like I'm on fire."

Sila had never been the jerking off type of guy. Once in a while, sure, but for the most part, Sila didn't derive much pleasure when he was doing things on his own. It was the feel of the person he was with, their hot skin, the sharp intakes of their breath, the way they screamed and writhed and sometimes tried to get away...that's what made him hard. That's what made electricity zip through his cock and draw up his balls.

It had little to do with the physical stuff at all, and everything to do with what that told him about the person he was screwing mentally. He liked knowing he was making them lose their minds—be that from fear or something else. Moving them around like pieces on a chess board so they ended up exactly where he wanted them, that was the hottest thing ever.

Only, here Bay was, folded over his bed, ass high in the air, presenting himself without a single complaint...and Sila wasn't entirely convinced it was his doing.

"You want this, Professor?" he asked, the springs beneath his knees squeaking as he worked himself harder. "Did you fantasize about me like this? Abusing you? Taking advantage?"

"Please."

"You're going to wait until I finish. You wanted lube, remember?"

"I don't—" He paused and if his gravely moan was any indicator, finally caught on.

"Beg for it." Sila wanted to see how far the older man would let this go. Right now, there was nothing but his verbal commands keeping Bay from climbing off this bed right now and making a run for it. There was no doubt in his mind that he wanted it—their past two encounters, Bay had been hunted. Sila was curious to see if he was going to initiate another chase, or if he was truly going to leave it in Sila's hands.

Total power exchange he'd said?

They'd see about that.

"I'm coming tonight," Sila told him. "You're just here for the view."

Bay made a strangled sound. "Please."

"Please what?"

"I want to come too."

"No."

"Sila." His grip on his cheeks changed, his fingers splaying out so he could get a better hold of himself and spread them even further apart, as though trying to tempt him to slip inside.

"You begged better before."

"You were fucking me before."

"What if I cut you?" He hadn't brought his knife, but Bay didn't know that. "What if instead of giving you want you want, I slashed a line across those round cheeks of yours and came on your open wounds?"

Bay shivered. "Do it."

"I still wouldn't let you come."

"My arms are starting to hurt from holding this position."

"So?"

"I'm *feeling*."

Sila's hand on his cock slowed. "What if I—"

"Do whatever you want to me," Bay interrupted, voice breathy and low. "Anything. Just don't do *that* again."

"What?" Sila tilted his head.

"Don't leave," Bay said. "You didn't even post on Inspire."

"I think you have enough of me saved on both your multi-slate and in your spank-bank, Professor."

He shook his head. "Not the same."

"How so?"

"It's not the real you." He sucked in a shaky breath, his muscles straining and his body beginning to shake slightly from it. "Nothing's better than the real you."

"Acquaint yourself with my cock a couple of times and suddenly you think you know me?"

"I *do* know you," he argued. "I know you

twist the tops off your soda cans and pocket the tab. You don't really like Jol, you just keep her around for appearances, but Riel can entertain you. It's his humor, right? You're trying to learn how to utilize sarcasm from him. You pay closer attention whenever he makes a sarcastic remark in class. And I know that even though you're really good at mimicking your brother, there's one thing that will always give you away to me."

"What's that?" Sila almost didn't recognize the sound of his own voice. There was a strange feeling gripping him and he took it out on his cock as he waited for a response, twisting his palm around his thick shaft.

"Your eyes."

He snorted. "We have the same eyes. You said it yourself."

"Not the color," Bay clarified. "What's behind them. Have you heard the expression the eyes are the window to the soul?"

"I don't have a soul." But his brother did. Was that what he meant?

"You have a soul, Sila. It's just warped and debauched. Whenever you stare back at me, I can see either one of two things. There's either the vast, empty sea, or there's the storm promising to drag me under until my lungs are on fire and my only hope for reprieve is your mercy. Rin doesn't look at people like that. He can't. He doesn't have it in him."

Whether it was a mixture of the words or

the fact he'd been at it a while, the orgasm snuck up on Sila, his balls tightening a second before come shot out of his slit. He aimed and squirted all over Bay's ass, groaning when the professor jerked at the first hit against his skin.

As soon as he'd emptied, Sila leaned forward and ran his fingers through a thick glob, smearing it up and down the seam of Bay's crack before he pushed into his hole. Bay held still for him as he collected his come and forced it inside, rubbing the stuff around his inner walls until the man was a writhing moaning mess.

Watching his spunk disappear inside of Bay had Sila's cock coming back to life in no time at all.

Acting on impulse, Sila flipped Bay around and tossed him onto the bed on his back. He followed, plastering himself over the smaller guy as his mouth captured his, tongue forcing its way past those full lips to taste him. There was a hint of toothpaste but nothing else, and he found himself dissatisfied.

He grabbed Bay's dick, pumping him a few times until a large drop of precome leaked from his tip. Collecting it with his thumb, he brought it up and shoved it into Bay's mouth, rubbing it on Bay's tongue despite the way the other man gagged.

When Sila kissed him again the mint was accompanied by a hint of salt that had him moaning and rolling his hips, dragging his heavy cock over Bay's stomach.

He'd never been all that interested in

kissing, but there was something about the way Bay opened for him, the way their tongues danced and the sounds that he emitted when Sila nipped at him hard enough to almost draw blood. His heart was racing in an unfamiliar way that felt both uncomfortable and comfortable at the same time.

That inner voice whispered possessively that he could get used to this.

If he hadn't already.

Dangerous.

"Me." Sila reared up slightly so he could wrap a hand around Bay's throat. "That's what you have in you, Bay. Me, just me. Nothing is permitted to touch you, not even those dildos you have an obscene collection of. You want something, baby?" He used his knees to spread Bay's legs. "I'm it. I'm all you're allowed to have."

"Yes." Bay kept his arms at his sides, palms flat on the bed, giving Sila all the control.

He didn't have to look to find his entrance, instead holding the professor's gaze steadily with his own as he lined himself up and then pushed past that ring of muscle.

They both cried out at the first burst of sensation as he entered.

Sila held him down and fucked in deep, groaning once he was completely buried in that silky heat. He stilled for a brief moment, one hand still pressing lightly down on Bay's throat in warning to stay put, the other gripping the smaller man beneath his left knee to hold him at the perfect angle. His gaze dropped to the place where they met and he tilted his head, curious over the electric spark of something hot and possessive that went off in his chest at the sight of them coupled.

Sex was an exchange he was familiar with, a transactional means to an end where both parties left satisfied and went their separate ways. During the act, he'd play the role of dominant lover, sure, but it was mostly a rouse. When he had his cock inside of someone, that person belonged to him, were his to do with what he pleased, but the second he released them it was over. His interest fled as quickly as it came. Half the time he couldn't even recall their faces.

But right now…

"You're in trouble, Kitten," Sila lifted his gaze just in time to catch the slight widening of Bay's eyes, "Or maybe this is what you wanted." He undulated. "No, that can't be right, can it. You were after the good twin."

That idea pissed him off.

"You said," Bay had to pause and swallow when Sila pulled out and snapped his hips forward suddenly before stilling all over again, "there is no good twin."

"That's true," he hummed. "But you didn't know that previously. All those times you touched yourself at the Seaside, bet you pictured my brother taking you nice and sweet, didn't you?

Instead, here you are, on your back for a devil."

They both knew he was full of shit. Sila had watched him. Bay hadn't touched himself gently in any sense of the word during any of his jaunts at the cinema.

"Sila?" Bay used his no nonsense teaching voice for the first time since the start of this. "Stop talking and mess me up already."

His brow lifted in a mixture of surprise and arousal at the bold statement. It was ballsy, something a person might say to him if he was still acting the part of boyish and charming Sila Varun and hadn't shed that identity so wholly like he had in front of Bay already.

It was kind of hot.

"The only one who dares talk to me like that is my brother," he mused, the hand around Bay's throat tightening for a heartbeat before he forced his grip to loosen again.

"I'm not afraid of you," Bay said.

"Is that so?" He didn't entirely buy it. "You're shaking like a leaf."

"It's called trembling," Bay corrected tersely, and there was little doubt in Sila's mind that had he been wearing his glasses, he would have adjusted them in that pretentious way he often did when he was trying to make a point to someone he viewed as less intelligent than himself. "And it's because your cock is huge and currently splitting me open."

"Does it hurt?" Sila glanced back to where

they were still joined, but there weren't any signs of bleeding. Vaguely, he wondered if he'd pull out if there was. That wasn't something he would have even checked on if this had been someone else on their back for him, but he was starting to accept that Bay elicited a different set of responses where he was concerned.

"Don't stop." He grabbed onto Sila's wrists, clinging.

"Is that an order, Professor?" His eyes narrowed. "I'm in charge here, remember?"

"How could I forget?"

Sila lowered himself over Bay, chest to chest. "Put your arms around me."

He did, settling his palms over the backs of Sila's shoulders.

"Now," he bit at Bay's bottom lip, working it between his teeth until the other man made a pained sound, "claw me up, Kitten."

He started pounding into him with a vigor, fucking him into the mattress with enough force it was an actual wonder he didn't snap the other man in half. The bed shook and rattled, the metal headboard clacking against the wall hard enough it dented through the plaster. That only spurred Sila on more, and he rammed into Bay and nipped and sucked on his neck as that last thread of control on himself he'd had snapped.

To his credit, Bay dug in his nails and held on for the ride, hissing beneath Sila with every stroke against his prostate. His eyes rolled and his mouth was permanently open on a gasp and, though his dick was trapped between them, he did his darndest to try and wiggle and rub it against Sila for friction.

Sila moved lower and licked at his right nipple. When that caused Bay to arch, he switched tactics, sucking the rosy bud into his mouth before running his teeth over the sensitive flesh. Then he pulled up so he was kneeling between Bay's thighs, careful not to lose the rhythm of his thrusts as he did.

Bay's dick was hot enough to sear flesh when Sila finally wrapped his hand around it. For a moment, he merely held on, using it for leverage as he fucked him.

Bay whined, his hands finding Sila's knees, fingernails scraping at him, and that was enough to get Sila to give him what he wanted.

Even though Sila had told him this wasn't going to happen, he found himself working Bay toward climax. He pounded his hole and pumped his dick in a frenzy and in no time at all Bay exploded.

He came all over himself and Sila's hand, body going taught as he hit that peak.

Sila wasn't far behind, giving one final thrust before he plugged him up and filled him.

Nothing had ever been like this for him and he watched as Bay whimpered and took it, his dick going limp. Leaning back, he dropped his gaze lower to where his hole stretched around his cock, clinging to him even though it had to have started to be uncomfortable now that Bay had already come.

Sila gave an experimental twist and Bay gasped and twitched on the bed as though he'd been hit by a bolt of electricity.

The professor's skin was covered in a sheen of sweet and smeared in already drying spunk. His blue hair was a mess—sort of like this entire place. He looked too pretty, too perfect, right now to be lying on stained bedding surrounded by water damaged walls.

This wouldn't do.

Sila hooked a finger through the loop of the collar and hauled Bay up into a seated position despite his protests and the way that shoved him down further onto his still semi-hard cock.

Bay grabbed onto his wrists for purchase and searched his gaze, brow furrowing. There was a hint of fear in his eyes, that fear that Sila had been asking for earlier but hadn't been sure of.

Seeing it now didn't do for him what he'd hoped, however, so Sila pulled him closer and kissed him. He kept it gentle this time, lapping at Bay's tongue, sucking lightly at his bottom lip. With the promise of soft, safe touches, he was able to coax his kitten down from that confused state, despite still being stuffed with cock and, once he was certain he had Bay right where he wanted him, he slid his hands beneath his ass and lifted.

"What are you doing?!" Bay wrapped his

arms around Sila's neck as he was carried from the room to the only bathroom.

Sila sneered at the stained tub, but it wasn't enough to deter him. The only good thing about this awful house was the size of the bathtub, large enough to easily fit a man of Bay's size.

It'd be a little more difficult for Sila, but at this point, there weren't any other options.

"Hey!" Bay clung to him when Sila leaned over to turn on the tap. "Put me down first!"

"No." He held him as they waited for it to fill, catching Bay's gaze with his own once the professor finally eased his hold and risked lifted his head from the crook of Sila's neck.

"Aren't I heavy?" Bay asked.

"No."

"Are you," he licked his lips and there was worry in his eyes, "going to fuck me again?"

Sila shook his head. It didn't take a genius—which he was, but still—to tell that his kitten was exhausted. Considering he'd been woken in the middle of the night and then forced to endure a hard-on for a while, that was fair.

The tub finished filling and Sila repeated the process of bending while still holding Bay to turn the faucet off. Then he stepped over the rim and lowered, carefully keeping the professor in his hold and his cock still firmly buried in place. Once they were down in the water he rested back against the off-white tiles and adjusted Bay over him.

He sucked in a sharp breath and winced as his thighs were spread over Sila's lap. "Aren't you going to—"

"No," Sila cut him off.

Bay blinked. "But you said you weren't—"

Sila hushed him and sat forward to press his lips to the rise of Bay's cheek. "I'm not going to do anything, I just want us to stay like this for a little bit longer. I like being inside of you, it feels—" He stopped himself from saying what had almost slipped out.

Home.

He'd been about to say like home.

Bay waited expectantly, but Sila turned his head and reached for the bottle of body wash that'd been set on the floor nearby. There weren't any shelves in the tub for them, so Bay kept them lined up on the other side instead.

There was no sponge or washcloth, so Sila squirted some of the green goo into his palm and then lathered his hands before running them over Bay's arms.

"What are you doing?" Bay asked.

"What did I say about asking boring questions?"

"Do you typically end your play sessions like this?"

Sila paused with one hand at the center of Bay's chest. "I also told you this isn't that type of game. Forget all about BDSM and scenes and anything else like that. This doesn't stop just because we came. There is no *end*."

Bay touched the back of Sila's hand on its way down the slope of his stomach. "That sounds…"

"Like I'm keeping you?" He dared him to protest with a dark look, but the professor remained silent either due to shock or something Sila couldn't interpret. "I am. I don't know for how long, but I call the shots here."

"What about a choice?" Bay asked quietly, and it was still hard to tell what he was feeling, if he were upset or not. "I agreed to do whatever you said until you helped me prove my grandmother's innocence."

"You need a better memory, baby," Sila smirked. "That was never one of the terms. We put no time limit on it. It doesn't matter if I bring you proof tomorrow, you'll still have to sit on my cock, just like this, if I tell you to."

Bay shifted as though reminded and then winced.

"Does it hurt?"

"It's…uncomfortable," Bay said. "Will you take it out?"

"No."

"Please?"

Sila grabbed onto his hips and thrust up sharply, relishing the way Bay cursed and instinctively reached for Sila's shoulders to steady himself.

Between them, Bay's dick started to thicken

despite his protests.

"Stay still so I can clean you and get you back to bed," Sila ordered, ignoring that rising member, even when it grew large enough to poke its head just above the waterline. "We have somewhere to be early and I don't like listening to grumbling from sleep deprived people—What are you doing?"

Bay had snatched the bottle off the edge of the tub and was lathering up his hands.

"I just said I would—" Sila frowned when Bay started to wash him.

Bay gave him a coy smile as he soaped up the rise of his shoulders. For a long while, he concentrated on his task, taking extra care around Sila's nipples and at the spots behind his ears. Then his hand dipped beneath the water and trailed lower, and before he could be called out on what he thought he was doing, he glanced up from beneath hooded lashes, that smile still in place.

Sila's heart stopped in his chest.

"If I'm good," Bay asked, "will you change your mind?"

At first, he thought he meant about ending the game and anger swept through him, but then Bay continued and it was gone in a flash.

"You got to come twice," he pouted. He actually *pouted* as his fingers circled Sila's navel.

"We're here to clean off."

"Exactly," he agreed. "The water is already dirty, and then I'll go straight to bed. There's no way I'll be able to sleep with this thing," he jutted with his chin at his dick, "like this."

"You're already tired," Sila pointed out.

"I know," he sounded very pleased. "I'm exhausted. I feel like I might even pass out."

"That's—" Ah. Bay *felt*. "Afraid of going back to that place, baby?"

Bay lost some of his luster and Sila actually felt bad about that. "I don't like feeling empty."

"You aren't." Sila lifted his hips again, chuckling when this time Bay's reaction was a needy moan. He hadn't planned on fucking him again so soon but... "Buy a new bed. Immediately."

Bay frowned.

"You want to come again?" Sila moved so his hand was hovering over Bay's dick. "You'll get rid of that piece of junk and buy a new bed. A king size."

"That won't possibly fit," Bay argued.

"You thought that about my cock too and look where we are. That reminds me, you haven't told me how good my piercings feel yet."

"If you—"

"No," his eyes narrowed, "this isn't a negotiation. You'll buy a new bed or you'll go back to that disgusting one hard. I'll tie your wrists to the post to keep you from pleasuring yourself as well, so don't get any bright ideas, Professor."

"Fine," he gave in. "I'll buy a new—"

Sila didn't let him finish that sentence.

More water damage to this place wasn't going to make a difference, so when it sloshed messily over the sides, he merely took that as incentive to fuck Bay harder.

CHAPTER 21:

"Do you recognize her?" Sila asked as he pulled the car into the empty lot at the side of the road. They were close to the Academy but it was early enough in the morning no one was out and about yet, aside from them and the person they were meeting.

The obscure location was by design, the place chosen by the young woman who was standing off the side of the lot near the tree line, watching as they entered.

Bay frowned and leaned forward in the passenger seat so he could get a better look as Sila drove them to a spot and parked. "I don't. Should I?"

"Her name is Nila. She was dating Haroon two years ago." He exited the car and then waited for Bay by the trunk before continuing. "The police spoke to her a few times after you tried filing that case. She was marked down as a witness. You didn't know?"

Bay shook his head. No one had told him there'd been any witnesses. He inspected her as they approached, but she looked like every other university student he'd ever seen.

Nila had a backpack strapped over both shoulders and was dressed in long pants and a windbreaker. Her auburn hair had been left down, but she'd pulled a wool cap over it as though that would help keep her inconspicuous. She seemed nervous as they drew nearer, but held her ground.

"Going somewhere?" Sila spoke first once they were within earshot, motioning to her pack.

"If I was smart?" she grunted. "I'd be taking a long vacation, but this being my final year at Guest…"

"I won't tell if you don't."

"I'm thinking you didn't tell on the others either," she said. "August and Lan? Look at them now."

Did everyone assume it'd been Haroon who'd killed them? That was odd.

"Well," Sila lifted a single shoulder, "they've already been cremated so, not much to see."

"The fact that Haroon somehow found out they'd been talking to you is bad enough in my book," she countered. "I don't want to die."

"Should have thought about that before getting involved, no?" Sila laughed to show he was only kidding, the light, friendly sound of it had the desired effect on her. "How were those two involved anyway?"

"I made the mistake of telling Lan about it," she admitted. "I don't know for sure about August, but my guess is Haroon slipped up. I'm honestly shocked he was able to keep it a secret this long. He's got such a big mouth. What did I ever even see in him?"

"Don't be too hard no yourself. We all do dumb shit when we're young."

Bay glanced between the two of them, an uncomfortable feeling piercing through his chest at the way they volleyed back and forth. So far, Sila had brought many emotions within him back from the dead, and Bay had been excited over each and every one, even the painful stuff.

But he was over the jealousy.

He cleared his throat and adjusted his glasses, giving Sila a pointed tight expression before turning his attention to the girl they'd come all this way to see. "How do you two know one another?"

"We met over the summer," Nila dropped her gaze, as though she were unable to meet his eyes. "When he called asking me about what happened two years ago, I knew I had to get this off my chest once and for all."

"What does it have to do with you?" Bay frowned. If she was still studying at Gift Fine Arts, then she was younger than him and Haroon by a couple of years. He'd never paid much attention to who Haroon was hanging around with outside of the classes they took together. The two of them hadn't been very close back then, but Bay would have considered him a friend, which was what had also made the situation worse when he'd found out about it.

Even if his grandmother really had been wasting her time and money gambling at Haroon's makeshift booth, a good friend would have given Bay a heads up. Haroon had said nothing.

"We were dating at the time," she explained. "I was at Lady Lucky a lot."

Lady Lucky had been the name they'd spray painted on the outer flap of the green tent they'd pitched between two rundown buildings on the outskirts of the city. It'd been pathetic and grungy, a joke amongst their peers at Vail. Back then, the Shepards were known as Brumal wannabes. It wasn't until after Haroon had gotten them a house—Idle Delmar's—and funding—also Idle's—that they'd become more notable to society.

Although, not by much.

"The police wanted me to tell them if I'd ever seen your grandmother there before."

"What did you say?"

"I should have told them that Idle Delmar never stepped foot on that side of town, let alone Lady Lucky," she hesitated. "But I didn't. I lied."

"To protect Haroon." Bay clenched his hands into tight fists but otherwise kept his composure. It wouldn't do to lose it now, not when he was finally getting answers. Even if he was outraged that Nila had helped someone screw over an old lady and tarnish her reputation.

"To protect herself," Sila corrected. He

crossed his arms and stared Nila down. His expression was enigmatic, but the way he held himself, loosely, as though ready to move at any moment, gave away how irritated he also was by all of this, any of the playfulness he'd shown before gone.

Bay couldn't help but wonder why that might be.

Couldn't help but hope it was because, despite all the times Sila had said or implied otherwise, maybe the younger man was developing real feelings for him and was upset on his behalf.

Could Sila experience things like love? It was hard to know for certain, though the professor in him told Bay the answer was most likely a resounding no. That didn't mean he couldn't feel other things however, things that came close enough to love he'd react the same way, treat Bay the same as he would if he did love him...

This was not the time for his mind to be spinning down that rabbit hole and he forced himself to slam a lid on that and concentrate. This was what he'd wanted for years. He couldn't allow his messed-up obsession with Sila Varun to distract him.

"Tell him," Sila demanded in a cool, even tone that still managed to have Nila jump as though he'd yelled it.

"I didn't know why we were going there, I swear," she began, only to have Sila click his tongue.

"Skip over the part where you make excuses."

"Right." She nodded like that was fair. "That day, Haroon asked me to go somewhere with him before we went out for dinner. It was our anniversary, so I thought it was a surprise for me and went happily. Only, we ended up at this house I'd never been to, and when he knocked on the door, a woman I didn't know answered."

"You went to see my grandmother?" No one had told Bay anything about her having had visitors that day, but then again, it wasn't like it was the neighbors' job to spy on what the others were doing. "When?"

"The day she was found," Nila admitted, clutching the straps of her backpack so hard her knuckles turned white. "He said he was a friend of yours from class and he was there to pick up notes. I...We both believed him, me and your grandma. There wasn't really a reason not to."

No, there wouldn't have been. Bay hadn't had many, but the few friends he did have he'd brought over a time or two to study. Of course Idle would have believed he'd sent a friend to pick up notes he'd left there.

"I never even talked to him about where I lived," Bay said. They hadn't been close enough for that.

"He knew," she told him. "He called your grandmother Ms. Delmar when she answered the door. I remember thinking he seemed so charming and kind. She welcomed us inside and then went to the kitchen to get us drinks. Haroon was given directions upstairs to your room and she said he could go on up and find what he was looking for."

"Then what happened?"

"He got a message on his multi-slate and kicked me out."

He blinked at her, certain he'd misheard. "He what?"

"Yeah," she nodded frantically. "On our anniversary he kicked me out of someone else's house. He'd texted Russ to come and get me and bring me to the restaurant to wait for him. I left and had Russ take me home instead, because screw Haroon, but Russ seemed just as confused over why he was there as I was."

So Haroon had gotten Bay's grandmother alone in her house that day.

"When I heard about her death, I knew something was up, so I went to Haroon to ask him about it," Nila continued. "He was like a different person. He threatened me and told me I was an accessory, that he would ruin my life and make sure I went to prison instead of him if I talked. I called Russ trying to get him to back me up, but..."

"Russ disappeared," Sila supplied. He waited to see if Bay had known, and when it was clear he hadn't, added, "They still haven't found his body, but it's widely believed that he was murdered. No one understood what for, but if what Nila is saying is true, we now have a motive. And a suspect."

"Everyone assumed it was the Brumal," Nila said. "It's caused bad blood between them and some of the Shepards. There was a huge brawl at the mall that same day, but no one seemed to remember if Russ was there or not."

Bay remembered that, not only because it'd been a huge discussion in the papers for a solid hour before the Void's had the story pulled from the media, but also because Flix had been involved. He'd come out of it with a busted lip and two broken fingers and the grudge he'd held for the Shepards had lingered ever since.

He wasn't positive, but Bay was pretty sure Flix had lit one of the Shepards cars on fire later that week even.

"Haroon did it," Nila insisted. "I'm sure of it. He would have silenced me too if I didn't swear not to say anything. Since I wasn't involved in any of his other dealings, and we'd dated for so long, he left me alone after I ended things."

"Hold on." Bay rubbed at his temple, struggling with this new information and what it actually meant. "The day my grandmother died, Haroon went to go and visit her and they were alone? And? What about after? He wasn't the one who called it in so…What time was this?"

"Mid-afternoon."

Idle had been found around six pm.

Bay stared at her and for once, she actually held his gaze. "You're telling me that Haroon might have murdered my grandmother."

"Yeah," Sila said. "That's exactly what she's saying."

"But…How?" She'd suffered from a heart attack brought on by extreme emotion. That's what he'd been told. "I suppose he could have threatened her, made her sign everything over to him by holding a blaster to her head and that could have been enough to—"

"The Shepards aren't all wannabe Brumal," Nila stated. "Most of them were just kids who had shitty homelives they wanted to avoid. Haroon was the one with the weird complex. His biggest infatuation at the time was the concept of a Butcher. It'd gotten out that Baikal Void was already grooming his and that made Haroon want one even more. So he hired this really scary guy to fill the role."

"Who?"

"It doesn't matter," Sila sounded annoyed. "He was killed recently by the Brumal for unrelated reasons."

"I'm certain he had something to do with it though," Nila nibbled on her bottom lip. "I remember seeing Haroon grab something from the dash of the car before we got out. It was a small bottle of clear liquid."

"Even if this fake Butcher had created a poison for him, it does us no good. There's no way to prove it or get answers since he's dead. I had my contact in the Shepards try to dig for more information on it, but Haroon must have scrubbed his shit clean. There's no mention of him ever experimenting with anyone in any capacity, let alone someone like a Butcher." Sila slipped his hands into his front pockets. "Going to Haroon himself is the only way we're going to be able to clear any of this up."

"He won't tell you anything," Nila said, and she sounded concerned for him. "Seriously, I don't want you putting yourself at risk."

"You're unwilling to make a new statement with the police," Sila reminded, cluing Bay in to the fact the two of them must have already discussed this amongst themselves before he'd been brought on.

He didn't like that much either.

Stupid jealousy.

"He already killed someone to keep them quiet," Nila argued.

"That's a theory."

"It's a good one, you even said so yourself! And Russ isn't the only one." She turned to Bay. "I'm still close to some of the girls who've stuck with the gang. There's talk that August was taken out too because he got too close to something Haroon didn't want him knowing about."

Sila hummed. "His throat was slit, so the police assume he was killed by someone he knew. Haroon could have easily done it. Especially since August was already drugged and out of it when it happened."

Nila grabbed onto his wrist. "What?"

"Someone slipped him Abundance and wandered around town for a bit in a rage," Sila said, as though it disgusted him that someone would do that.

"The police said he must have been wasted." She frowned at them.

"Lan was drugged too."

"Is that why he picked that fight with Kazimir?!" She gaped and slapped her hands over her mouth. "Kaz almost killed him!"

According to the timeline of events, Bay didn't think Lan would have been able to confront Kazimir at all before he'd gotten into his car, so it must be another occasion she was thinking of.

"He's fine," Sila rolled his eyes. "Unfortunately."

"Who's going around drugging people?" Nila asked. "Should I be worried?"

He shook his head. "Don't think so. At least not about that. You're right to be concerned over Haroon though. Make sure you don't tell anyone that you're talking to us."

"I don't have a death wish," she said.

"If you told the police they could protect you," Bay tried. He didn't think he could convince her, but now that there was a very real thread of proof standing in front of him, he had to give it a shot.

Sila leaned in then and brought his mouth close to the curve of Bay's ear, whispering, "We can always drug her and force her to the station. Got anymore Abundance, Professor?"

He shoved him away and gave him a stern look that didn't affect the younger man in the least.

"I'm sorry," Nila said. "I know it's wrong of me, it was wrong from the start, but I can't. I won't wreck my life like that. I'm sorry."

"For being a shitty person?" Sila waved a hand like it was no big deal. "We're all selfish and terrible. Why should you be any different?"

Nila at least had the good sense to look ashamed.

* * *

"You're quiet," Sila broke the silence when they'd made it halfway to the campus. He seemed calm and relaxed as he drove them to the school, as though he didn't have a care in the world.

Meanwhile Bay felt like his entire universe was on the verge of collapse.

He rested his arm against the open window and rubbed at his temple. "For the first time, I'm wishing you didn't kick start my ability to feel again."

"Is that so?"

"Yes."

"That's a big change from what you were saying last night."

"Can you not?" Bay glared at him. "I don't want to think about your dick and my grandmother at the same time."

"Calm down."

"Don't tell me to calm down!" Bay felt like his entire being was about to explode and yet there Sila was, completely unaffected by anything. For some reason, that made Bay feel utterly and entirely alone.

Wordlessly, he pulled the car off the road, waiting until they were parked on the edge out of traffic before he turned to Bay. "If I'm not mistaken, you're experiencing emotional overload. My brother goes through that sometimes. Must be because you're no longer used to feeling such intense emotions all at once. You need to breathe through it and focus. Sort through what you're feeling and why."

"Forgive me for not taking the advice of someone who lacks the ability to feel himself," Bay snapped, freezing as soon as it left his mouth.

Sila merely tipped his head. "My brother's tossed that line at me during one of his episodes too. Further proof that's what's happening here."

"Do you talk him through them?"

"No. He handles himself."

"Oh."

"But I'll talk you through it, Kitten. You're not alone here." Sila rested a hand over Bay's thigh. "Tell me what you're going through. What do you feel?"

"Anger," he said, glancing away so he could focus and not get distracted by the intense look in Sila's mismatched eyes. "Sadness. I feel hopeless and like I failed her. I didn't even know about Nila or that there were witnesses that claimed they'd seen my grandmother gambling."

It helped explained why the police were so adamant, but it didn't make sense that they wouldn't have told him about the evidence. Unless it was because they simply didn't care.

"This is Vitality," Sila said as though having read Bay's mind. "The authorities have their hands full with a million and one other crimes on a daily basis. They saw a deceased old woman and were told the cause of death was heart failure. Clear cut, open and closed case. They didn't inform you, so of course you didn't know."

"You found out."

"I have an informant and a jailbroken pair of Insight glasses."

"How did you—" Bay held up a hand. "You know what, don't tell me."

"Probably for the best. You're already involved with all sorts of illegal activity, Professor."

"Why'd you do it? Why did you murder August and Lan?"

"They were assholes who deserved it," Sila said. "I'd mentioned your grandmother to the both of them and in each instance, they laughed."

"You would have laughed too."

"No, I wouldn't have, because I don't find death funny. That's not why I kill. Besides, it wasn't about me. It was about you. Trust Berga all you like, but I wasn't about to take the risk that some of that drug would linger and lead back to you."

"Careful," Bay warned. "That sounds awfully romantic."

He quirked a brow. "Most people would be horrified if I told them what I just told you."

"Is that why you drugged Castle?" Bay asked. "Because I went after August and Lan for you? It was for you," he added before Sila could argue. "Sure, the fact they were Shepards helped weight my decision, but up until today, I'd had no clue either of them knew anything about what happened to my grandmother. They weren't even in the gang then."

"Drugging Castle was a good way to return the favor," Sila agreed. "And it also provided me with the perfect excuse to come to you. Two birds, one stone—or, should I say one white pill."

"Are you ever going to delete those videos?"

"No."

"Even though I've already agreed to be yours?"

"You could change your mind," Sila said, and an inkling of displeasure slipped through his stony exterior then. "People have a tendency to do that. I won't leave it up to chance. Since you say you're mine anyway, what does it matter if I keep them?"

"Holding leverage over my head isn't exactly a kind thing to do," Bay pointed out, only to have him snort. "Right. You aren't kind."

"I'd have to be caring for that," Sila agreed.

Bay turned toward the window, not wanting him to see the flash of disappointment that raced through him then. He should have known nothing got past the younger man's notice though.

"Hey." Sila captured Bay's chin between his thumb and forefinger and gently eased him back so he was forced to look at him. "I can care to an extent, it's just not in the traditional way. For example, it bothers me when I see my brother upset. I don't like it. There's pretty much nothing I won't do to make him feel better."

He ran the pad of his thumb over Bay's bottom lip, then in a quieter voice divulged, "I don't like seeing you upset either."

Bay sucked in a breath before he could help it.

"You just found out your grandmother may have been murdered," Sila continued. "My guy is still looking, but I'll be honest, it doesn't seem like there's any evidence left to find. Haroon covered his tracks—mostly with dead corpses."

Bay's grandmother may have been one of them. The thing was, whether she'd really died from panic because she'd been forced to sign everything over to him, or Haroon had slipped her something, either way, as far as he saw it, it was Haroon's fault. A guy Bay had been friends with. The only reason he would have known about Idle's assets was because he'd known Bay, even if they two of them had never actually spoken about such things.

It was still hard for him to wrap his head around that and he dropped back against the inside of the door, effectively pulling away from Sila in the process.

He didn't seem pleased by the sudden separation, but he dropped his arm and remained silent while Bay thought things through.

How had he gone from walking around numb to the world to this?

"Up until a couple of months ago," Bay admitted, "I wasn't all that interested in getting justice or revenge. I wasn't interested in anything at all."

"Except for speeding and fucking," Sila corrected, smirking when Bay's eyes narrowed. "Sorry. That's right. No talk about cock and your grandmother at the same time."

"What I mean is, if we can't," he circled a finger in the air, "find evidence, it'll suck, yeah, but I'll mostly just feel bad for her. She deserved so much better than what she got in the end. And if Haroon used me as his reason for being there?"

"She didn't think you helped kill her, Bay," Sila stopped him firmly.

"How can you be sure?" He hated how weak he sounded, but he supposed experiencing self-doubt came with the territory of having his emotions restored.

"She knew you as well as you knew her," he said matter-of-factly. "You insisted she would never gamble. You were right."

"I gave up." He dropped his head in his hand. "I almost—"

"But you didn't. You're still here and breathing."

For now. Bay didn't say it, but he thought it, and he wondered if Sila thought the same thing. This tumultuous thing between them could come to a screeching halt at any given moment and if that ever happened…Sila had the videos to keep him tethered, but what about Bay? What pull did Bay have on the younger man?

He'd been trying but to no avail it seemed. What could Bay possibly do to ensure Sila never got the chance to leave him?

"We're close," Sila told him. "Do you have a preference?"

"Of?" Bay's brow furrowed.

"Now that you thought about it, you should choose. Am I getting you justice, Bay?" Something wicked flashed within Sila's eyes. "Or am I getting you revenge?"

CHAPTER 22:

Bay ended up entering Vail alone. Sila had gotten an urgent message just as they'd pulled in front of the main building and he'd dropped Bay off before quickly leaving. He hadn't even bothered saying where he was off to.

He'd spent the better part of the afternoon replaying that last question Sila had asked him over and over again, but he still couldn't settle on a definitive answer. It was obvious which way Sila wanted to go, but…

Drugging August and Lan had been the worst thing Bay had ever done to another person. Aside from that, he'd never harmed anyone. Still, even knowing it'd eventually led to them being murdered, Bay didn't feel guilty. He'd do it again if given the chance. Maybe all of Bay's emotions weren't fixed after all. Or maybe he'd just grown permanently numb in some regards, even if he was now able to access others.

He was subconsciously pressing at the spot at the center of his chest when he found Berga waiting for him in front of his office at the end of his final class.

"Something up?" Berga asked, eyeing Bay's hand over his heart.

He dropped his arm and straightened his spine, checking to be sure there weren't many other students mingling in the hall. The two of them never acknowledged one another on campus, so this visit was odd and, considering how many unsettling things Bay had experienced already that day, he was automatically on high alert.

"Can I help you with something, Mr. Obsidian?" Bay unlocked his office and then held the door open for him. "We can discuss this inside if you'd rather?"

"Thank you," Berga nodded. "I'm thinking about taking one of your classes next semester and I had a few questions."

"Of course." They kept up the act until Bay had closed the door behind them. Then he moved to his desk and sat down, waving for Berga to take the empty chair across from him. "Anything the matter?"

"I wanted to see you for myself," his friend said, eyeing him openly. Berga was a Vital like Bay, but his hair was a jet black, and he'd been born with two small crystal horns, a feature that for the most part evolution had done away with. On the outside, he appeared stoic, a little nerdy even, but the truth of the matter was he was anything but.

If Bay hadn't grown up with the guy, he

might even be afraid of him.

"Flix told me you've seemed different lately," Berga began. "I didn't believe him. I didn't see how there could be results when you've all but given up on experimenting."

"It's called therapy." Bay corrected lightly.

"A doctor gives you a set of instructions you're told to follow, and then you log the possible changes that result from following said instructions," Berga stated plainly. "I'm not sure how that's any different from conducting an experiment."

"I haven't gone back to therapy," Bay confirmed. But he was recognizing similarities between his friend and Sila that he hadn't noticed before.

"But you're no longer looking at me like I bore you." He frowned and cocked his head, clearly perplexed by this. "These past couple of years you've regarded everything with disinterest. Even after I told you, in great detail, about how I'd taken apart—"

Bay held up a hand to stop him. "I remember, thank you. I don't need to hear about it again." His stomach wasn't exactly turning inside of him but it certainly gave warning signals. Considering everything he was able to put up with from Sila, that had to mean something.

But then, Berga was a different sort of devil entirely. He was the devil other devils went to when they didn't want to get their own hands dirty, after all. It was no great secret. Bay knew what a Butcher was, as well as the types of things his friend got up to in his free time. Testing out a couple of non-lethal poisonous teas was nothing.

"Are you fully recovered then?" Berga asked, thankfully dropping the story.

"I'm not sure," Bay said. "I think so?" He'd been able to maintain a balanced emotional state ever since their second time in the alley. Even when Sila had vanished on him for three days, Bay had been able to feel just fine without him.

He knew that, because he'd been in a total and complete panic that he'd never get to see the real Sila again.

Pathetic.

"Are you logging—"

"Not an experiment," Bay cut Berga off. "Remember?"

He slumped back in the large wooden chair and made a huffing sound. "Suit yourself."

"I will be, thanks." Bay smiled. "You didn't come here just to see if I got my emotions back, right?"

Berga was too busy for something like that.

"There've been a few situations this past month," Berga began. "Many deaths. Messy."

Bay went on alert but tried to keep himself composed. "And?"

"Baikal asked me to check with you," Berga said, and the way he was looking at Bay made it clear he thought that was a good idea. "I know August was your target. He had to be. He was Shepard and now that you're no longer an unfeeling robot..."

Bay quirked a brow. "You think I killed August to get back at his gang for taking my house?"

He sort of had, hadn't he? But it hadn't been entirely for that reason and that alone wouldn't have bene enough to knock sense into him and pull him from that stupor. He'd spent the better part of two years walking around, caught in a fog. Sila was the one who'd gotten him out of it, who'd saved him from that fate, even if his means had been nightmarish and cruel.

Bay had loved every bit of that cruelty in any case. But he couldn't confess any of that to his friend now, if he did it would only lead to more questions and he wasn't ready to give answers to any of those.

"It wasn't me," he ended up telling him, dropping back in his desk chair. He crossed his legs and slowly shook his head. "I did poison him, true, but that was all. And he's not the reason I've been more myself lately."

Berga didn't appear to believe him, so Bay sighed.

"It really wasn't," he insisted. "I would tell you if I had. I know you need to stay in Baikal's good graces." The position of Butcher was important to Berga, not only because of the status it provided, but because Berga, like Sila, was a little bit...different. Off would be a better way of putting it, but for the sake of being technical, Berga also had a penchant for taking apart others to peek at what was beneath their outer layers. He and Sila just happened to come at it from different angles.

Maybe that was also why Bay wasn't as horrified by his interactions with Sila as he should have been. He'd already surrounded himself with people who didn't come with an intact moral compass. Besides, for a person who hadn't cared whether he'd lived or died up until two months ago, why should it have mattered to him? Even that first night when Sila had hunted him through the woods, Bay had been terrified, sure, but it hadn't been of death.

He'd been scared because he'd felt it. He'd felt the way his heart had pumped wildly in his chest. Felt the way the adrenaline coursed through him and spurred him on despite the way his legs cramped. He'd felt excited thinking about how someone was right behind him, growing ever nearer, and whether that person planned to kill him or not hadn't even crossed his mind.

Bay had been solely focused on the emotions of it all, the twisted, chaotic explosion of them popping off inside of him like accidentally lit fireworks on a crowded dock. Hazardous. Dangerous. Thrilling.

And once Sila had caught him...Then his attention had turned lower, to the agony and the pleasure and—

Berga snapped his fingers in front of his face, frowning at him. "What was that?"

"Sorry," he mumbled and then checked the time on his multi-slate. He was done for the day, but there were a ton of papers that still needed to be graded before the night was through, and now all he could think about was how he could convince Sila to come back over to his place and give him a repeat of last night.

"If it wasn't you, then I'm not sure who's responsible," Berga said, but at least now he seemed to believe him.

"I've heard rumor it might have been an inside job," Bay told him without thinking, mind admittedly still conjuring images of the four metal balls that protruded out of the sides of Sila's cock crown. How they'd felt when they'd stroked against his inner walls. The way electricity had shot up his spine.

How much he'd wanted more. Then, and now.

Berga's gaze homed in on him dangerously. "How do you know that?"

He didn't want to lie to his friend, but if it was a choice between Varun and literally anyone else, it was a no brainer which Bay was going to choose. He wouldn't be the one to put him on the Brumal's radar, that was for certain. Giving them somewhere else to look could only help Sila in the end. And, if Sila could figure it out, surely the Brumal would be able to, so it shouldn't be too big of a deal for him to stick to his statement now that the cat was already out of the bag.

And now he was thinking in cat terminology as well.

Damn Varun. He better pick up when he called later. Bay was very quickly becoming an addict and he didn't even care.

"You should look into Haroon," he said, before grabbing up his tablet, an indicator he needed to start getting to work. "You should be able to find answers that way."

With any luck, they'd also discover something about his grandmother for him.

"You sound confident," Berga noted. "How?"

"It doesn't matter."

"It does to me." And maybe to Baikal, though Berga didn't add that part. He was always careful to keep Bay and the Brumal as separate as possible, knowing that Bay had never held any interest in getting involved.

The Brumal needed to stay the hell away from his Varun, otherwise Bay wasn't sure what he'd do. He hadn't set out to murder August, but things had been different then. He'd only unlocked a portion of his old emotions, so that they were there but muted, just beneath the murky surface. Now?

Now Bay felt everything in vivid technicolor.

If he got jealous or angry or protective on Sila's behalf, there was no telling what he'd be capable of. And no one got away with messing with the Brumal. No one.

"Look where we are. I overheard a bunch of students discussing it. It's a fairly big topic since August was popular," he reassured. "Don't you trust me?"

"I'm part of the mafia," Berga told him. "I don't trust anyone." He sighed and rolled his eyes. "But yes, fine. I'll tell Baikal that you're overheard it from a student."

"It was from a student," Bay confirmed, only so Berga could feel confident in doing so. He didn't want his friend to think he was lying to his future Dominus. Nila *was* a student too. Just not one at Vail. "There's something else." He hadn't planned on looping any of his friends in, but now that he was confronted with it, it didn't seem right now to. "I found out more about what happened with my grandmother."

Berga's gaze turned as sharp as his horns in a flash. He'd always hated what had happened to her, had even wanted to get the Brumal involved. Bay had stopped him, at first because he'd been concerned over getting them in trouble—Berga had only just turned twenty at the time—and then later because he'd given up and hadn't wanted to deal with it.

"I'm hoping you might be able to help me actually," he continued. "Shed some light on something for me."

"Of course, tell me."

"It wasn't a heart attack. Or, even if it was, it wasn't done naturally. She might have been drugged."

"How did you learn this?" Berga rubbed at his chin in thought. "The medical report came back with no traces of any foreign substances in her blood."

"Yes," Bay drawled, "and you and I both know that means one hundred percent that she wasn't slipped anything." He gave him a pointed stare.

"Abundance doesn't cause heart attacks."

"I'm aware," he agreed. "But there's got to be something out there that does, because my grandmother had one right after being given it."

"And this person definitely wanted her dead?" Berga snorted as soon as he said it. "Right, of course they did. It was Haroon, wasn't it? That worm took everything right out from under you, it had to be him."

Bay waited for him to ask if he had any proof, but Berga didn't.

"So, we're looking for something that someone like Haroon would have been capable of getting his hands on two years ago," Berga began ticking things off with his fingers, "And something that leaves no traces in the body. There weren't any injuries or defense wounds found on her either."

"Haroon told her he was my friend from school and he needed to pick up some notes," Bay confided.

"That would have done it." Berga was well aware how kind Idle had been. "Anything else?"

"Apparently there was someone in the Shepards he'd brought on to act as a Butcher," Bay made a face at the same time as Berga, them both obviously finding that ridiculous. "I heard you recently dealt with him, so he's no longer in the picture."

"Did we?" Berga twirled a strand of black hair around his pointer and shrugged. "There've been a few things going on between us and the Shepards. I can't keep track anymore. I wonder if this person left any records."

"I can have someone look into it." Bay said, recalling Sila's contact within the gang, whoever that may be.

Actually, he made a mental note to demand Sila tell him. He didn't like not knowing. What if they were a potential love rival and—

What the actual fuck was wrong with him?

He dropped his head into his hand. "I'm losing my mind."

"Do I even want to know about who this person may be?" Berga clucked his tongue when Bay gave no reply. "All right. I'll trust you on this as well then, since you're older and all, Be'tessi."

Bay lifted his head at that. It'd been a while since Berga had last referred to him as "older brother" in the old language. Up until a hundred or so years ago, the planet had operated on a much stricter hierarchal system. There'd been important titles given to everyone from close friends to relatives. Many of the older generations still used them, but people their age tended to forgo, so it wasn't as common to hear.

Before his grandmother's death, Nate, Berga, and Flix had all called him that, especially in front of her.

Berga didn't seem to notice however, and he stood with a flourish, clapping his hands together. "I'll get right on this, let me know if you come across any new findings that could be of any help. And do try to see if you can uncover any notes from this wannabe Butcher."

"Sure." Bay nodded, but his friend was already halfway to the door.

Almost as an afterthought, he turned and gave a partial bow. "Thank you for your time, Professor."

Bay blinked as Berga slipped out into the hall and the door shut behind him. Things were always odd with that one though, so he should be used to it. Since he'd had coffee with Nate at his house that morning weeks ago, Bay wondered again over all the subtle things he'd missed out on with his friends while he'd been shut off.

A robot, Berga had called it.

He chuckled, but his good mood soured shortly after.

The Brumal were getting too close to this, and there was little doubt that Baikal would eventually find out what Berga was looking into for Bay as well. When that happened, Sila couldn't be anywhere near it.

Baikal Void didn't suffer from anti-social personality disorder as far as Bay could tell, but that didn't mean he didn't have certain attributes in common with Sila. They both liked being in charge, for one.

And they were both deadly.

Bay wasn't sure which of them would survive in a head-to-head fight, but Baikal had an entire mafia army at his beck and call, whereas Sila was alone. If for any reason the Brumal looked unfavorably upon Sila, Varun wouldn't just stand there and take it. He'd fight back, probably for the fun of it.

His multi-slate went off then and the devil in question's name flashed over the screen.

Varun: Nila is dead.

Bay shot upright, his fingers swiftly clicking over the screen faster than his mind could process moving.

Professor Delmar: What?! Tell me everything.

He wanted to ask if Sila had done it, but knew better than to leave any physical evidence. When he tried to call, however, he was sent to voice mail.

Varun: Can't talk now. Busy. Trying to figure out who's behind it with my Shepard contact. That's who told me about it. Then I've got something to do for my brother. Don't worry about it. It won't link back to you.

The Brumal were already looking into things and now there was *another* Shepard murder? If they heard about this while Sila was out actively investigating, they'd surely cross paths. Bay couldn't allow that to happen. He needed to get the name of Sila's contact and then take over himself. Berga could vouch for him, but his friend could say nothing in Sila's defense that would appease Baikal. From the sounds of it, things were heating up between them and the gang, which meant tensions would be higher than usual. The Brumal had made more than one person disappear in the past, innocent or otherwise.

Sila already done everything he'd promised Bay he would do. He'd gotten him the answers he'd been wanting, and even if they didn't have any physical evidence to back it, it was looking like that would never happen anyway. Which meant it was fine to tell him to stop searching and leave well enough alone.

He thought about the question Sila had asked him earlier again, about whether he wanted revenge or justice. He still couldn't answer it, but what he did know was he wanted Sila to be safe.

He wanted him to be his.

The last time he'd gotten his grandmother involved with a dangerous person, it'd been accidental. If he'd known there was ever even the slightest chance Haroon would target her, he never would have befriended the guy. This was different.

If Bay allowed Sila to get involved with the Brumal, that would be entirely on him.

He couldn't lose Sila, and not just because there was a very real chance he'd die inside all over again, but because…Well. He just didn't want to.

Before he could change his mind, he entered a reply and hit send.

Professor Delmar: Let's stop here. I've got what I needed, so there's no reason to continue.

CHAPTER 23:

Hadn't he promised Bay he wouldn't pull the disappearing act again?

He tried not to scowl as the class Sila should have been in came to an end with the younger man nowhere in sight. His friends stood quickly, as though in a rush, the two of them already deep in discussion the second the clock had struck the hour.

They seemed nervous.

Yesterday, Bay had waited for a reply from Sila but it had never come. He'd resisted the urge to call again, not wanting to turn into a clingy lover. He didn't have the right to demand Sila's location, and what's more, he worried bringing something like that up would push him away.

Sila only did things he wanted to do and the second Bay was no longer interesting to him he'd leave. Maybe he'd kill Bay on his way out, maybe he wouldn't, either way the ending would be the same.

Bay alone.
Again.

Bay didn't want to be alone anymore.

Since he'd studied psychology so extensively, he was aware of what was happening to him, what must have been happening for some time now without his notice.

He'd started becoming reliant on Sila, on the things he could force Bay to feel. That rush, after so long dormant, was like a potent drug, and Bay wanted more of it. Before, he'd thought of the student fondly whenever he was alone, but now he was constantly on Bay's mind. It was hard to focus on anything else in fact.

Logically, he understood he should put an end to whatever was between them before it was too late. He was already addicted, in no time at all it could become a permanent change and then what would he do once Sila left?

He knew what he'd do. He just didn't want to admit it, mostly because over the course of the past couple of weeks his mindset had finally deviated away from that line of thinking. He hadn't sought out death frequently, but he'd welcomed it with open arms. Now…Shamefully, his sudden will to live had little to do with what he'd learned about his grandmother and everything to do with what had been unlocked within himself.

Bay liked pain during sex, liked to feel small and taken advantage of. It wasn't about power or control, but about being forced to endure something, something others might—or probably would—find horrifying. His desires were dark and deeply ingrained on his psyche in such a way he hadn't even realized how etched into him they'd been, even with all the dark porn he'd watched at the Seaside. Since he'd barely managed to get a small thrill out of viewing those scenes on the big screen, he'd assumed it was more the violence of it that was tugging him out of that fog.

Seeing someone brutalized, even knowing it was in a controlled setting since those movies had been staged and scripted, had called to his inner self. He'd thought it was shock, since prior to turning into an undead, Bay hadn't explored many kinks and certainly nothing as graphic or extreme as primal play or rape fantasy.

Even when his fantasizing had begun to star Sila as the male antagonist, Bay had still assumed he was upping the ante in order to keep that small ember that had finally been lit inside of him alive.

He'd been so wrong it was almost laughable.

Bay hadn't started to feel again due to shock or horror at seeing other people tied up and cut and chased. He'd started to feel out of longing. Subconsciously, he must have known experiencing those things himself would save him from drowning in the empty black abyss. He just hadn't been capable of admitting it.

And now he was screwed, because there was only one person on this planet he could trust with a secret like that, and that person was ignoring his messages.

"Mr. Xin," Bay stopped Riel and Jol before they could leave, acting on impulse. He couldn't wait another moment to find out what was going on with Sila. He had to know right now. "Do either of you know why Mr. Varun wasn't present for class today?"

"It's bad," Riel said, stepping up to the podium Bay was still standing behind. "Someone said they heard that Sila's dad showed up on planet."

"Hey," Jol glanced between the two of them and pursed her lips in obvious displeasure.

"It's fine," Bay reassured her. "If there's something going on with a student and their family, eventually the school will be notified. Telling me now just allows me to prepare ahead of time. Continue, Mr. Xin."

Bay didn't know much about Sila's father, only that neither of the twins were very fond of him and he lived on their home world, Tibera. That planet was in another galaxy a good distance from their own, so the fact he'd taken the time to make a personal trip instead of simply calling them was unnerving.

"No one really knows what's true or not," Riel explained, "but it sounds like his dad is here to take him back home."

"That's absurd," Bay stated before he could help it. "Why would he do that? Vail University is one of the top schools in the universe. People spend ages praying for an acceptance letter and his son is already in his second year."

"I'm not sure," Riel admitted. "But from what I've heard of Sila's dad, it wouldn't surprise me."

Sila couldn't leave. Especially not before talking about it with Bay.

"He'd never go willingly," Jol joined the conversation. "But his dad is the one person who could force him to leave no matter what he personally wanted."

"Do you know where they are?" Bay wasn't sure why he was asking. It wasn't like he could show up and announce he was Sila's professor. He didn't have a say, either as Sila's teacher or as the man he was currently sleeping with. Neither of those titles gave him the right to make demands.

Bay didn't have the right to do or say anything.

If Sila really did leave, could he even be mad about it? The younger guy hadn't made him any promises other than that he'd help him find out what happened with his grandmother. He'd done that and, to add insult to injury, Bay was the one who'd messaged him saying not to bother continuing with the search. He wasn't foolish enough to assume for even a second that Sila would hang around for his sake or the agreement they'd made—Sila wouldn't care enough to do that. He only did what benefited himself, after all —but even if there'd been a slim chance of it before, now that Bay had called the whole thing off…

"No," Riel shook his head, looking every bit as upset about this whole thing as Bay was starting to feel. "Right now, we're just waiting to see if he gets back to us."

"He hasn't contacted you?" So it wasn't just Bay he was ignoring? "When was the last time you heard from him?"

"This morning," Jol replied. "He messaged me saying he was going to be late to breakfast. We were supposed to meet in the school cafeteria to go over class notes but he never even made it."

Oh.

Bay had tried getting a hold of him yesterday. Clearly his multi-slate was working. What did that mean?

"When did you say his father arrived?"

"Supposedly he came in on an early shuttle," Riel said.

"And Sila had no idea he was coming?"

"Are you kidding," he snorted. "Sila hates his father. He would have talked our ears off about it if he'd known."

Bay doubted that, considering the real Sila wasn't as big of a sharer as the fake, friendly person he presented as a front to the world, but he might have mentioned it at least. He definitely would have been in a bad enough mood he would have sought Bay out, if only to take out those frustrations on Bay's flesh.

He wished that's what had happened.

Wished he'd been woken last night like he'd been before, with Sila behind him, holding him close. Threatening to cut off his air supply or slit him open with a sharp blade.

There'd been minor disappointment when he hadn't taken things further, when he'd fucked Bay and then taken him to the bath like they really were lovers. It'd been upsetting for a number of reasons, but mostly for two major ones.

Bay had craved the promised agony Sila's presence now brought him and had been downcast when it hadn't come.

He'd also enjoyed the warm bath and sitting in Sila's lap, being stretched by the thickness of his shaft. Being washed and touched lightly while Sila had held him and spoken in a low, warm tone that had sent shivers skittering up Bay's spine. The moment had felt...relaxed. Comforting. Dare he say, wholesome.

It was everything Sila Varun wasn't and, maybe because of that, Bay's sick mind had lapped it up like a kitten to cream.

He realized with a start that it wasn't just the pain he was craving. He wanted more of those soft moments too. Wanted more of Sila's care and attention. It'd made him feel special—loved probably wasn't the right word, because who knew if a psychopath like Sila was even capable of that emotion, but definitely something akin to it. Something close enough that Bay's heart skipped a beat when he thought of it.

There was no time limit on how long they played together, as his student put it, so he idiotically hadn't even considered things between them might come to an end sooner rather than later. Yet here he was now, learning from someone else that Sila might be leaving the planet with his father...

If he left, that would be it.

Bay would never see him again.

Was it illogical to believe his father might have taken his multi-slate from him? Sila was a twenty-year-old man and, what's more, he wasn't the type of person who'd allow anyone, even his father, to walk all over him. He may have fooled the rest of the universe otherwise, but Bay knew better.

If Sila really didn't want to go, there was nothing and no one powerful enough to make him. Which only meant if he did really leave, if he'd left already without any of them knowing, it was because a part of him had agreed to it.

A part of him had wanted to.

Had wanted to leave Bay.

Hell, maybe he hadn't even considered Bay at all in his contemplations.

"Three ships already launched off planet," Jol said then, twisting the knife stabbing through Bay's gut even harder with her statement. "Do you think he was on any of them?"

"He wouldn't leave without saying goodbye," Riel argued, only for her to give him a dark look.

"That's exactly what he'd do and you know it. He'd send us an email once it was too late for us to see him off in person saying he was bad at farewells or something stupid like that," she said, "but he *would* just leave."

Even she thought so and Jol didn't know Sila didn't actually even care about them. She was operating under the assumption they were all great friends and even then, she knew Sila would just go without looking back.

Bay's multi-slate dinged and he checked it so quickly it was a wonder he didn't get whiplash from the moment. It wasn't Sila though.

"Anyway," Riel gave a small bow, still upset, "we'll see you next class, Professor."

Jol nodded and the two left.

The message he'd just received was from Nate reminding him about the impromptu race Bay had agreed to the other day. He wanted to call it off now but thought better of it. There was nothing more he could do and he wasn't equipped with the proper tools to regulate his emotional response to Sila's potentially leaving. Racing was exactly what he needed right now to help take his mind off things and give him somewhere else to focus all of that pent up emotion.

Still, that didn't stop him from calling Sila on his way out of the classroom.

Or trying again when walking to his car after there'd been no answer.

Or again while he drove to the docks.

*　*　*

He'd lost.

Bay stood on Sickle bridge, staring down sightlessly at the inky water below. The night sky was dark above him, only the twinkling stars and their small pinpricks of brightness there to witness him coming apart.

The streets were quiet and still, with the last passing car on the bridge itself having been almost a half hour ago. The race hadn't ended until after midnight as per usual, and it was probably close to three am now. Bay had no idea how long he'd actually been there, standing in the chill in only a t-shirt and frayed black jeans, but he hardly felt the sting of the weather anyway.

Nate and Flix may have tried to get him to hang around after the race, but those memories were murky at best and he couldn't be sure about that either. Had he seemed off to them? That was the only reason he could think of that they'd offer to take him out for coffee instead of them all going their separate ways like they usually did.

It must have been because he'd lost. For the first time since he'd started doing this professionally, Bay had come in second. It'd been close, with him only a couple of seconds behind, but that didn't change things.

The railing of the bridge wasn't very wide, maybe only four or so inches. Just enough he could probably stand on it without tipping over the edge. He could hoist himself up onto it in no time at all and then he'd be able to see the bottom better. The water was so dark, like a yawning cavern below. It reminded him a lot of the emptiness inside of him, the fog that threatened to consume him.

He could feel those dark, familiar edges creeping in on him now, almost as though they hoped to catch him off guard and drag him back into the deep abyss before he had a chance to stop it from happening.

As if he wasn't already aware it had started.

When he'd crossed the finish line just behind his opponent and registered the disbelieving shouts from the crowd...he'd felt nothing. Not a single emotion stirred within him at the loss, he'd simply gone numb. Again. It was almost impressive how easily it had happened, how quickly and seamlessly his body had shut itself down. Like a switch being flicked in his mind, he'd gone from hopped on adrenaline and worry and doubt over Sila's whereabouts to... emptiness.

He couldn't even say it was the opposite of caring, because there wasn't even feeling enough in him for that. It was almost as though the person standing here, staring down into the ocean was someone else entirely. Like an out of body experience.

Bay hadn't even been aware he'd been driving to the bridge until he'd gotten there and parked on the side of the road at the end of it. He'd walked the rest of the way to avoid drawing attention, not that he thought for a moment anyone would really bother with him even if they did see someone had left a car running on the bridge itself. This was Vitality. No one cared about anyone else on a planet like this one, a planet that pretended it was upright and elite, but was really just the home of demons and devils the likes of which would send the rest of the universe running in fear.

One of those Devils had Bay's heart in a chokehold. It wasn't just obsession, not on Bay's end. It would be so much simpler if it were.

Sila had never called him back, hadn't replied to the dozen or so other text messages Bay had sent and, to top it all off, he'd just lost a race.

Oh, right. That's why he was here. He'd almost forgotten about the game.

What did it matter if he died tonight? Pandeveer would go out in a blaze and his friends would finally get to stop worrying about him. Maybe his identity would get out and the press would talk about him for a bit until his name faded back into obscurity. His grandmother would have been disappointed, but she was no longer around to see him fall.

Bay didn't want to live like this anymore. He couldn't. There was a black hole in his chest and it sucked the life out of everything around him, everything that should have brought him comfort and joy. Everything that should have made him want to fight and yearn to keep going.

What was the point of existence when he couldn't feel anything but unfulfilled?

His perfect record as Pandeveer was gone.

Sila was gone.

He was aimless, not even drifting but stuck in the center of a vast sea with nowhere to go and no motivation to even try.

Why bother?

A strong gust of wind blew past him and he shook on his feet. Below, the waves crashed, the sound lulling and inviting and without thinking he planted his palms on the metallic edge and prepared to lift himself as planned.

Just before he was able to hop off the ground, however, something latched around the leather braid around his neck and yanked. He gurgled as it pressed painfully against his throat, instantly cutting off his air supply. Whoever was accosting him kept out of sight, just behind him, ignoring the way Bay flailed and struggled to free himself.

He desperately tried to pull the cord forward so he could catch a breath, but the person behind him was too strong, not letting up even a centimeter. He was hauled back against a hard surface—someone's chest—an arm banding around his waist to keep him in place as he continued to flail. Even when he switched to clawing at that arm, digging his nails into his attacker's flesh as deep as he could get them, the cord remained taught.

Black spots began winking in and out in front of him, his vision becoming blurry with each passing second his body was deprived of oxygen. There was a big difference between wanting to jump off a bridge and being strangled, not that Bay would have thought as much a moment ago when he'd been so set on jumping in the first place.

The panic was raw and all consuming, forcing him to fight back despite his earlier intentions to end things himself. He kicked, landing a couple of blows against his attacker's shins, but the grip around him never loosened.

He tensed up as the burn in his lungs became too much.

"What's wrong, Kitten?" a voice cooed into his ear then, warm breath fanning across his skin.

That voice. That familiar voice.

"You're so eager to die," Sila continued, only there was a sharpness to his tone, something demonic and feral. "Allow me to help you."

The leather cord was pulled even tighter and all at once Bay's body gave out. His vision turned black and he slumped, only remaining upright due to the man holding him. Just before he passed out completely, he felt the corner of his mouth turn up in relief.

Not because he was getting his wish and finally dying.

But because Sila was there.

He hadn't abandoned him after all.

CHAPTER 24:

Sila had never felt this way before. Anger, though he was capable of feeling it, was beneath him. A useless emotion that never led anyone down the right path. Anger dulled the senses and made one stupid and rash—just look at his brother who was always a slave to his fury and his ever-changing mood swings. Always quick to lash out, only to regret it once the damage was done.

Sila was the collected twin. The calm one. The smart one. He prided himself on his ability to remain in perfect, impeccable control at all times. It's what kept him hidden from the world, what helped keep him and his brother safe. He played the pieces on the board, but he wasn't one of them.

Sila was a slave to nothing, least of all himself.

And yet here he was.

Completely and totally incensed.

It was all the fucking professor's fault.

His devilish nature was spitting mad, demanding retaliation. In the past, if he hurt someone, it was out of curiosity or boredom.

Those were the only reasons he ever did anything. He appeased his darker self, his true self, by keeping it occupied and entertained, because not doing so would be the same as signing his own death certificate. Not doing so would be dragging his brother down with him because they were one and the same.

Only...

His brother wasn't here.

His brother wasn't the one currently seething and wrathful. He may have a penchant for drowning people, but his brother had never been all that interested in drawing another person's blood. That's why he'd always preferred the blaster as his weapon of choice, unlike Sila who'd had a fondness for knives for as long as he could remember.

Usually, even with their differences it was obvious they were still the same. Sila was Rin and Rin was Sila.

But who the fuck was he right now, in this moment? Who was the person losing his control? Unraveling? He didn't recognize this role. It wasn't a part he'd played in the past and it wasn't his true self without the mask.

Or...Was it?

No. No it couldn't be because who he was, who he was straight down to his core, was calculative. He was the master of his and everyone else's fate. He didn't slip. Didn't faulter.

Sila Varun did not make mistakes.

Killing the professor on the bridge? That would have been a mistake.

It didn't even matter that he'd stopped himself. It didn't change anything, not when he was currently sitting in the dark, staring across the medium sized room at the professor's unconscious form.

It didn't matter when that he'd come to his senses back there since all he'd been able to do since bringing Bay here was picture all the ways he could take him apart.

Sila clenched his jaw and gripped the sharp blade of the knife in his hold, gritting his teeth at the sting of pain as it sliced through his skin. Blood pooled in his palm but he hardly noticed, trying to chase after that burn in the hopes it would center him. He needed grounding, fast.

Tiberans were excellent at grounding techniques and, even though he'd grown up without access to the full range of Tiberan emotion, Sila had been taught the same as everyone else. He'd rarely needed to utilize those teachings, of course, but desperate times called for desperate measures.

The fact that he was desperate only infuriated him further, however, and with a snarl he shot up from the chair and chucked the knife as hard as he could. The blade imbedded itself in the wall only inches from Bay's face.

The professor didn't so much as stir.

This wasn't supposed to happen. Sila hadn't

meant to bring Bay here like this. He'd planned to show the professor over the weekend, calmly, politely. To ease the older man into a false sense of security they both knew was a smokescreen. Sila liked that about Bay.

Bay knew exactly what Sila was, yet he never shied away. He ran when he was told, sure, cried and screamed and bled and begged. But at the end of the day, whether they wanted to admit it or not, that was all by choice.

All of Bay's actions had been done by choice. It was Sila who'd fooled himself into believing otherwise. Sila who had fallen into the other man's trap. He'd thought he'd caught Bay?

He chuckled at himself humorlessly.

Bay had been the one catching him. Well and truly.

Sila's multi-slate went off and he shoved the earbud into his right ear and hit accept hard enough it was a wonder he didn't crack the screen. "What?"

There was a pause and then, "...What's wrong?"

His brother, ever the perceptive asshole. Like his fucking Imperial Prince. Geniuses the both of them. It'd be a miracle if the entire planet didn't go up in flames with an Imperial family like the Diars in charge. And now his brother was tied to that.

And Sila had encouraged it.

Fuck.

"Brother?" there was a note of actual

concern in his voice. "Where are you? I'm coming."

"Don't," he clipped, closing his eyes in yet another attempt to focus the rage causing a tempest to rise and swirl within himself. He felt like his skin was on fire and his head was about to split open and spill out all over the polished floorboards.

He scowled at his injured hand, reminded of the mess he was already making. A trail of blood from the chair to the two feet he'd moved painted the ground in red, visible even in the low lighting of the room.

He'd left the hallway light on, but otherwise hadn't bothered operating any of the light orbs he had strewn about the ceiling. This place wasn't one he frequented too often, especially since he'd only just purchased it a week ago, so it was also pretty barren. There was a bed, a large four poster king sized monstrosity, but he'd ignored that when he'd entered, dragging Bay's body behind him.

He could have easily carried him, but his anger had gotten the best of him and he'd opted to pull him through the house by the ankle instead. If Bay woke with a couple of lumps on his head from where he'd whacked against the flooring? Served him right.

"Something happened," his brother said, waiting a moment for a reply that wasn't going to come before adding, "This is the part where you reassure me you have everything under control."

But he didn't. He didn't have it under

control. Not any of it.

"Where are you?" his brother repeated, and he could hear him moving around on the other end of the line, no doubt preparing to come find him.

"Stay away," Sila warned, and his voice actually shook slightly. He tightened his injured fist, digging his nails into the fresh wound. "If anyone comes near him right now, even you, I don't know what will happen."

Bay could wake at any moment and if there was someone else here he could call to for help… Sila would kill them. He'd do it without thinking, without stopping to see who the other person was first. If his brother walked through the front door right now, not even he would be safe from Sila's chaos and that—

"Stay away," he said a second time, almost pleadingly now. He'd never begged for anything a day in his life, but begging for his brother's safety was the same as begging for his own.

Wasn't it?

Was it still?

"We're the same," he mumbled, and though it was meant for himself his brother heard.

"We are," his brother agreed.

No, that wasn't right either.

"We aren't." Sila shook his head. "You have the Imperial now."

"Is that what this is about?"

Was it?

"That doesn't change anything for us," his brother insisted. "You and I are still the same. We'll always be the same."

Sila was not the same. Not the same him.

"I'm not myself." He snorted. "What does that even mean? Who even am I?"

There was another long stretch of silence and then, "Okay, I'm going to be honest, brother, I'm worried now. Like, full-fledged freaked the fuck out. What's going on?"

What was going on? He wished someone would tell him because then whatever it was could stop. This wasn't his usual state of being. Sila always understood exactly what he was feeling and why. It helped that he didn't have that many emotions on his personal checklist to go through.

To be fair to himself, he didn't *not* understand this time. It was just, he didn't know where it was all coming from. The professor had kept him so distracted, Sila hadn't really stopped to consider the things going on with his brother or how it would affect them as a whole. It was true he'd been supportive, if not even a little pushy, but it was also true that the two of them were unhealthily attached to one another.

Codependent, in some sense of the word.

Earlier, when his father had arrived without warning, threatening to force one of them off planet, Sila's immediate reaction had been cool detachment. He'd observed the situation from all angles and easily come to the conclusion that he, his brother, and his kitten could get off Vitality together. He had more than enough coin saved up for their tickets and, after the message Bay had sent him last night, he'd been certain Bay would be willing to leave with them.

He'd been so sure of it, so certain that Bay was right where he wanted him and would do anything he said.

Fortunately, fleeing wasn't necessary and their father was already on a one-way flight back home. They wouldn't have to worry about him ever again, and he and his brother no longer had to consider their original plan to run themselves. Vitality was going to be their home for good.

Sila had gone to the shuttleport to see for himself. He'd waited in the shadows and watched as Crate Varun was forced to board by the authorities and hadn't dared to leave until the ship was high in the sky on its way off planet.

When he'd received Bay's message last night, he'd assumed it was in reference to his grandmother's case. Sila had waited, wanting to discuss it with him in person, but then this whole mess had taken up his entire day and by the time it'd been truly over, night had already fallen.

The tracker he'd placed on Bay's car had led him to the bridge and it wasn't until Sila realized where Bay was that it hit him maybe the message had meant something else.

Had Bay been trying to end things with him? Trying to call it quits between them?

In a godsdamn text message?

A low growl rumbled past his lips before he could contain it and he heard his brother's sharp intake of breath on the other end of the line.

"I," Sila licked his lips, forcing the words out, "may be losing control. Just a little."

More like a lot, but his brother didn't need to know that.

"Tell me what to do." Sila had never listened to anyone other than his brother and, even though it annoyed him to have to ask, there was no shame in doing so. His brother suffered from emotional deregulation, something Sila had no personal experience of. He didn't think that's what was happening to him here either, but it couldn't hurt to learn what helped his brother whenever he felt like the world was slipping through his grasp.

"Are you alone?" his brother asked, then swore before Sila could reply. "No, you already said someone was there with you. A he. Is he safe?"

"He's tied up." Sila had secured Bay to the chair on the other side of the bedroom. The chair itself was bolted to the floor. When he'd done it, it'd been with locking Bay up in mind. But not like this.

Bay's body was slumped forward, his wrists and ankles tied to the arms and legs of the metal chair. He was pale, his hair a mess, but he was breathing.

For now.

"Are you a danger to him?"

"I'm a danger to everyone," Sila growled. "Just tell me what you do."

His brother clearly didn't want to, but after a moment sighed and gave in. "Sex helps."

"What?" Sila frowned.

"Yeah. Giving up control—"

"No."

He sighed again. "This is why I didn't want to tell you. We're—"

"Different?" Sila finished for him. Something in his stomach sank and he closed his eyes a second time. "Yes. We are." But not entirely. "Sex you say?"

"Brother..."

"Sex and control." That was it. That's what had gotten away from him. Sila just needed a way to regain control, then everything would be fine. He'd tuck his true nature back within the Tiberan skin he wore and everything would return to the way that it'd been.

Because this? Sila didn't like this.

And he only ever did the things that he liked.

"Thank you, brother," he said, and then he ended the call before he could say anything else. He turned the multi-slate off and tossed it onto the long desk at his back next. There was no reason to keep it active since he didn't want to be traced or disturbed. His brother wasn't yet aware of this place, so there was no way he could show up out of the blue either.

"It's just you and me," he whispered into the

darkness, easing his way across the room toward Bay's unconscious form. "Just you and the Devil you called out to play."

Sila dropped into a crouch before him and stared at him for a moment. The house he'd purchased was in an expensive part of town, a far cry from the garbage place Bay lived in. There were two large casement windows set in the same wall he'd placed the bed against, and moonlight trickled in through the blinds of one now, painting swaths of pale light across the rise of Bay's cheeks.

Reaching out, Sila traced the plump outline of Bay's full bottom lip, then moved up to do the same with the straight bridge of his nose. He'd removed the man's glasses earlier when he'd tossed him into his car and they were probably still sitting on the floor of the backseat since he hadn't even thought to grab them when he'd carried Bay inside.

When his finger ghosted over the arch of Bay's brow, the professor stirred, but that didn't deter Sila. He continued his explorations, mapping the older man's face by touch and sight, committing it all to memory.

"What...?" Bay came awake slowly, groaning and shifting in the chair. It was obvious he struggled with opening his eyes, but eventually he got there, blinking and frowning all at once. He cleared his throat and winced, no doubt at the slight pain that would have caused after how Sila had so thoroughly choked him.

He'd almost killed him actually. It was honestly a miracle he hadn't, that he'd stopped after Bay had passed out and not just tossed him over the edge of the bridge and into the sea out of sheer anger alone.

Sex and control, he reminded himself, grappling with that twist of fury now, refusing to allow it to get hold of him again.

Sila slipped a second knife from his back pocket, the flick of the blade springing free causing Bay to still. He brought it to the rope fastened around Bay's left ankle, then the right, cutting him loose with a casualness he wasn't feeling in the slightest.

Appearances were important. Presentation was just another form of control.

Sila would get it back, even if he had to fight with himself for it.

"What are you doing?" Bay asked when Sila stood and made swift work of the bindings holding down his wrists. There was obvious fear in his tone, but there was also a thread of something else.

Anticipation.

"You tried to go for a swim without me," Sila said, leaning down so his face hovered in front of Bay's. In the partial darkness of the room, he doubted his kitten could make out much of him however. "Pity you didn't make it."

"What?"

"For you," Sila elaborated. Quick as a whip,

his hand shot out and he grabbed Bay by the scruff of the neck, hauling him out of the chair. He dragged him across the room, the professor stumbling over his own feet, unable to get his footing with how fast Sila kept them moving.

The master bathroom was attached and he led them through the door and over to the massive clawed tub. It was one of the reasons Sila had chosen this place, because his affinity for water. It was twice the size of the one in Bay's home, more than big enough to comfortably fit them both. With a flick of his wrist he had it filling, but he wasn't patient enough to wait for it.

Wordlessly, he shoved Bay to his knees and then forced his head under the faucet, the heavy flow of water battering down on him as he struggled. Bay's arms flailed and he tried pushing off the edge of the tub, fighting Sila's hold.

Like he had back on the bridge.

Sila dug his nails into the sides of his neck, hard enough to draw blood, then he yanked Bay back, practically bending him backward so he was forced to stare up at him.

Bay gasped and coughed, his hands going to Sila's wrist. His eyes stared up at him wildly, the fear swirling in that golden gaze potent and raw.

"What?" Sila asked. "Wasn't this what you wanted? Didn't you plan on filling your lungs with water? I'm merely helping you out, Kitten."

"No." Bay shook his head, grimacing when that had Sila's nails digging even deeper into his flesh. "No, that's not what I want."

"Could have fooled me." He growled. "Actually, you did fool me, isn't that right?"

"I don't know what you're talking about. Sila, you're hurting me."

"I'm helping you feel," he corrected. "Or are you going to say that's not something you wanted either?"

"Sila. Please."

The tub was mostly full now and Sila shoved him back in, this time submerging him up to the shoulders. Water sloshed over the edge and splattered over Sila as Bay fought, but he hardly noticed, too focused on the feel of keeping him steady beneath the surface, of the control he had over Bay, a full-grown man in his own right.

One who'd thought to leave Sila behind.

With a roar he pulled him out and practically tossed him away, that seething sensation burning through his lungs as he turned his back on the tub to keep Bay in his sights.

Bay slammed into a small wooden shelf hard, yelping as the drawers snapped behind his weight. He shook his head, trying to clear water from his eyes and panted. When he looked up at Sila, there was a desperation in his gaze, but it was impossible to tell what for.

Sila didn't really care anyway. He didn't care whether or not the professor was getting a sick thrill out of this type of treatment or not. This wasn't for him. This was for Sila. This was so he could get back to that calm and collected place he liked being in. The place he was fucking furious he'd been taken from.

"Who the hell do you think you are?" he asked darkly. "A pathetic nobody who broke at the first sign of distress. How dare you think you have the right to take from me."

Bay shook his head wildly. "I don't. I would never."

"You were going to jump." Sila started for him. "You want to die so badly you'll die at my hands." Gripping the front of Bay's shirt, he yanked him off the floor.

Bay immediately went lax in his hold, eyes slipping closed, hands light on Sila's wrist.

"What are you doing?" Sila paused and tilted his head, taking in the blank expression that had settled over Bay's face.

"Go ahead," the professor said softly, and the fear that'd been there earlier was gone. "If you want to kill me, do it."

"What?"

"You asked who I am," Bay continued still in that empty voice. "Yours. I'm yours, Sila, to do with as you please. If you want to kill me? Okay."

"Okay?" He'd thought he'd been angry before. "Okay?!"

Sila slammed Bay against the wall, but when Bay's face remained set in that stony mask, he hesitated. Through the haze of anger, he saw things for what they were, realized that this was just another way the professor was going to try and play him.

"You don't get to do that," he said cynically. "You don't get to hide from your emotions." Because it was so obvious that's what was happening here. Somehow, Bay had shut down all over again, cutting off the part of him that felt. That was the exact opposite of what Sila wanted. He shook him by the front of the shirt until Bay's eyes popped open and he was looking at him once more. "You don't get to hide from me."

He undid the clasp of the earring he always wore, noting the way that drew Bay's attention. Good. It wasn't fair if only one of them was suffering here.

"Mine?" Sila asked. "I can do anything with you?"

A spark of delicious uncertainty flashed behind Bay's eyes.

Sila grabbed him by the jaw and forced his head back against the wall, keeping him steady as he brought the earing to Bay's left ear. "That means I can mark you, can't I? Claim you in a way everyone can see."

"Wait," Bay sucked in a breath. "I don't have —"

He tightened his grip, forcing Bay to instantly stop talking, then he brought his face in closer and grinned. "I know."

Bay howled when Sila snapped the earring into place, the post stabbing through his unpierced lobe. He kept hold of it, making sure it was locked in and not going anywhere, watching as the area around it turned bright red and crimson smeared the tips of his fingers.

"There's not enough blood," Sila complained, and he wasn't sure which of them he meant the words for, but it didn't matter, because Bay's whimper in response was like music to his ears. He actually preened, a low groan rumbling up his chest.

If Bay had successfully jumped earlier, Sila would never get to hear that pained sound again.

He tore him off the wall and dragged him back into the bedroom, discarding him onto the bed. Sila kept his gaze on Bay, who scrambled to the opposite side in a futile attempt to put distance between them. His clothing came off in a rush, the silent promise of what was to come evident with every scrap he dropped carelessly to the ground.

"Wait!" Bay held up a palm the second Sila was completely naked.

Sila paused.

"What about a choice?" Bay asked frantically, and it was evident in the way he was shaking he was well and truly scared now. For real this time.

But he wasn't crying.

Sila didn't like that.

"You always give me a choice," he added weakly.

"That's rich coming from someone who

almost took their own life less than an hour ago," Sila drawled. "Where was my choice in that, Kitten? Hmm? If I hadn't gotten there in time, they'd be fishing you out of the river and I—" He stopped himself.

He'd be a wreck. A bigger one than he was right now.

And he hated that. Hated knowing it was the truth.

"You called so many times," he switched tactics, wanting answers. "Was that why? Did you hope I'd show up and find you dead? Or did you want me to save you? What were you trying to accomplish? Tell me!"

"No!" Bay was all the way on the other side, practically hanging off the edge of the bed. "That's not why I called at all! I wasn't trying to trick you into doing anything!"

"No?"

"I mean it!"

"You're seriously going to sit there and claim it wasn't on purpose? That you didn't turn things around on me expertly like you did?"

"I—" Bay frowned. "What?"

"It was a brilliant play, Professor. I was so distracted by you I didn't even notice what was happening until it was too late. You purred and cried so pretty for me, always so receptive, of course I fell for it."

"I don't understand what you mean."

"I'm *attached*," Sila confessed, though he

was sure to make it clear he wasn't pleased by that fact. "The whole time I was focused on making you addicted to me, you were doing the same. You should have died on that bridge, but I couldn't let you. I couldn't bear to part with you. But now... Now I'm coming to my senses."

He wasn't.

Good Light, help them both. He really, really wasn't.

CHAPTER 25:

"You want a choice?" Sila opened the drawer of the end table and pulled out another knife. "Here's your choice, Professor. I can either fuck you bloody with this blade and then slit you from throat to navel and see what you look like on the inside, or you can choke on my cock. Either way, this ends tonight, Bay Delmar. Tonight, I take your life."

It's what he should have done from the start. Instead of getting wrapped up in Bay's routine and allowing himself to become enthralled by his secrets, Sila should have stuck a blade through the man's gut the second his brother had told him someone was watching. He should have dealt with the threat, washed his hands, and forgotten all about it. Instead, he'd stalked his prey for too long, long enough he'd forgotten his original intentions.

"Sila," Bay's voice shook.

"Choose," he snapped. "Or I choose for you, and we both know which way I'm leaning." He twirled the handle of the weapon pointedly.

He was always curious about what people

looked like beneath their outer layer. When he'd said he wanted to know what a Vital heart looked and felt like before, he hadn't been over exaggerating. Sila had only ever been able to cut one person open for the fun of it before and his brother's reaction—anger and disgust—had been enough to keep him from doing so again, however...

His gaze trailed down Bay's body and even though the professor was curled in on himself protectively, Sila could easily picture exactly where he'd cut if given the chance.

And if that meant he no longer got to play with Bay? So what. Why was that so important to him anyway? Playmates changed. Pieces fell off the board. That's how the game worked. Sila did away with one and then went out and found another. It wasn't that hard of a concept. Wasn't anything new.

He'd always known the two of them were going to end up like this, with Bay dying at his hands, so why was his gut twisting and his chest constricting the way that it was? Why did his skin feel too tight?

Why wasn't Sila acting like *himself*?

He might not feel in control, but whatever Bay saw when he met Sila's gaze proved otherwise. All at once, the professor slumped, the fight draining out of him as quickly as it'd come.

He was giving up.

"Your cock," he whispered, so quietly that

Sila had to strain to hear it. "I," he took a shaky breath, cheeks staining pink, "I want to know what it tastes like before I go."

What an entirely morbid and fucked up thing to admit.

He hadn't meant to say it out loud, but he must of for Bay flinched away from him after hearing it.

Sila growled in warning, then ordered, "Strip."

Bay frowned at him.

"You're going out the same way you came in," he explained. "Naked and crying. Do it. If I have to come over there and do it for you, we're going back to option one."

As Bay started to slowly undress, a small voice in the back of Sila's mind whispered to him how wrong he was. Sila had given him those options knowing full well which of the two Bay would choose. He may be into pain, but it was a no brainer he'd want to avoid being cut to ribbons with no payoff. At least while giving a blowjob, Bay could most likely become aroused himself.

The professor stepped off the edge of the bed so he could lower his pants and sure enough, his dick was semi-hard when exposed.

Sila reached over and flicked on the light switch, the seven light orbs hovering by the ceiling casting the entire room in a bright florescent glow. It highlighted everything, so no part of Bay could remain hidden from his viewing pleasure as Sila swept his gaze down the length of his chest to that bobbing member.

"Crawl to me," he demanded, breath catching in his throat as anticipation chased some of the anger away when Bay immediately did as he was told.

He climbed back onto the bed, the silky material of the dark blue comforter, so deep a shade it was almost black, dipping under the weight of his knees and palms as he slowly made his way across it toward Sila.

Sila had been soft at the apex of his thighs, the anger too much for him to handle, but now, watching the way Bay's eyes lit up with excitement and the way his kitten licked his lips with obvious eagerness, his cock lifted and swelled, until he hung painfully hard. He shifted on his feet, something in his chest stretching in satisfaction when that had Bay's gaze landing on his cock and staying there.

"Any last words?" he asked, trying to ignore the odd prick of something uncomfortable he felt when he did.

"My body," Bay glanced up at him from beneath long lashes, the picture of calm despite the fact he knew what was coming. "Make sure whatever you do with it, it can't be linked back to you."

That prickling got worse.

"I left your car at the bridge," Sila forced himself to say. "When you don't turn up for classes tomorrow, everyone will just assume you jumped."

He nodded as if that'd been incredibly wise of Sila to do.

"Anything else?" Was he drawing this out? To what end? Sila had already decided to kill him. He was done with him. This was what Bay wanted too, after all. The guy had been about leave. If Sila didn't take his life now, it'd be like admitting defeat.

If he let Bay go, Bay would just try again, and eventually he'd succeed. Then what?

Then Sila would have lost his prey and the chance for closure.

Bay wanted to die. If Sila didn't kill him first, he'd do it himself.

"Have you done this before?" Bay surprised him by asking.

"What? Murdered someone with my cock?" Sila chuckled despite the tumultuous way he felt inside, the sound forced and fake. Not his best work. "You'll be the first, Kitten."

"Can I ask for a favor then?"

Sila nodded.

"Let me also be the last."

This was insanity, and that was saying a lot coming from a person like him, but Sila only hesitated for a brief moment before he gave another nod.

Bay smiled broadly, the way someone would if they'd just walked in on a surprise birthday party held in their honor. Definitely not the look of someone who knew they were about to breathe their last breath. "Thank you."

Sila didn't get the chance to respond, which was probably for the best since he had no clue what he would have said. In the next instant, Bay opened his mouth wide and dropped down over his dick, swallowing it all the way until it hit the back of his throat in one go.

He gagged and pulled off, licking circles around Sila's crown, teeth tugging lightly over the ends of his piercings before he sucked him down again. Bay kept his palms flat on the bed, his back arched so he could lean into Sila as he buried his nose in the patch of wiry golden hairs just above his cock.

Lights burst around Sila and, before long, he was dropping the knife to the ground with a clatter so he could run both hands through Bay's soft, powder blue hair. He didn't take control just yet, content in letting the older man set the pace, rocking his hips forward ever so slightly whenever Bay's warm mouth pulled away from him.

Why hadn't he done this before? He could have spent the better part of a week making Bay do this to him, watching the way he disappeared into his mouth, the way his nostrils flared and tears leaked from the corner of Bay's golden eyes. Every time he came off his cock he sucked in a deep breath before going back for more, greedily lapping at him as though Sila were an ice cream cone.

He should have—

Sila cut those thoughts short. It was happening again. He was allowing Bay to lead him—literally—by the balls. He was the one with the power here. He was the one with the power everywhere.

Before he could change his mind, his grip tightened on Bay's head, and then he was ramming himself as deep into his mouth as he could get, watching the way that caused his kitten to panic and sputter. He slid halfway out, allowing Bay the false hope of another breath, and then fucked back in before giving him the actual chance.

Sila was hard, but he'd been harder before. Hornier. Their last time together, he'd thought he was going to blow his load after the first touch of Bay's skin on his own. It made no sense that, in the midst of the best head he'd ever received, he was struggling to reach that peak.

Maybe if he got the killing portion of the evening out of the way, it'd be different.

Maybe if he did it so that Bay could no longer look at him with that dull expression he'd had on his face earlier. That lifeless, empty, expression...

The same one he'd been wearing when Sila had found him on the bridge.

The same one he'd worn before Sila had entered his life and chased him in the forest.

Damn it. When had Sila started caring about that look and what it meant?

When had he started to miss the charged

version of Bay? The alive one. The breathing one.

Bay wasn't breathing now. He was struggling to, tears flowing down his cheeks like tiny rivers. Snot and spit covered the rest of him and his pallor was starting to take on a definitive blue tint as Sila held himself still, his cock buried so he actually felt his member blocking off Bay's airways.

At first, the struggles were minimal, instincts forcing Bay to resist despite his earlier agreement that they do this. But then they quickened, his look of panic growing until he was practically sobbing and quaking around Sila. He pushed at Sila's stomach to try and dislodge him, but Sila kept firm. When he started to slap and hit at his thighs, the movements strong enough to rock them both, Sila wondered at the way his cock pulsed simultaneously with that sharp, foreign sensation at the center of his chest.

The one telling him to stop this.

The one promising that he'd regret it if he didn't.

It made no sense, and yet...

Sila loosened his grip on Bay's head, just enough the other man could get away if he really wanted to.

Bay pulled off of him so hard he fell backwards on the mattress, heaving and coughing and gasping for air. He cried through it all, ugly tears—nothing like the pretty ones Sila was fond of seeing—his sobs strong enough to wrack his entire body as he curled into himself at the center of the bed.

Sila watched him as he wrapped his arms around himself and tucked his knees up to his chest. That feeling grew and grew until it was no longer a small prick but a full-on stabbing sensation straight to the heart. Without thinking, he lifted a palm and pressed it against his breastbone.

"Please," Bay's gravelly voice pulled Sila's attention off of himself and the weird feeling and back on him. "Please, Sila. Please."

Sila was so confused, but he wasn't angry anymore. Without the fury looming over his head like a threat, he was able to trust himself acting on instinct.

He planted a knee on the mattress and lifted himself up, then he stretched out an arm and brushed a few silky locks of hair off of Bay's face. "What, Kitten? You can tell me."

That stabbing eased a bit as he stroked Bay's hair, so he settled closer to him and kept at it. When he'd been on the phone with his brother, he should have asked about this instead. He should have asked if he'd ever felt anything like it. His brother had helped him learn and sort through every other emotion, both the ones Sila was capable of experiencing himself and the ones he couldn't. His brother would know what was happening. What he was going through.

His brother could help him.

But not right now. Right now he needed to get through this with Bay.

He shushed him when the professor continued to sob. "Tell me, Kitten. It's okay."

"It's not," Bay disagreed. "It's not."

"How so?" He cocked his head. "Why'd you stop? Isn't this what you wanted?"

Bay was up and throwing himself at him so fast Sila almost tumbled backward off the bed. He wrapped his arms around Sila's neck in a vice-like grip, settling in his lap so he could do the same with his legs around Sila's waist. His face disappeared in the crook of his neck and he felt the hot, wet press of tears.

"Please," Bay begged. "I don't want to die. I was wrong! I don't want to die! Please, Sila!"

That stabbing in his chest turned to an ache, and it made him want to hug the professor back, but he resisted. "The bridge."

"I thought you'd left!" Bay explained in a rush, digging his nails into the backs of Sila's shoulders even though it wasn't like he'd tried to shake him loose or remove him. "And then I lost a race. It doesn't matter. I don't want to die. Don't kill me. Keep me instead. Permanently."

Sila's brain fritzed out for a split second, that was the only explanation for why his entire body went still and the world seemed to freeze in place. "What?"

"Keep me," Bay repeated. "Give me that choice. Death or you. Please."

If he agreed to that, wouldn't that mean Bay was calling the shots?

Hadn't Sila sort of been letting him do that for a while now though?

He frowned at himself as the realization struck that yes, he had in fact been doing that. He'd been in denial about it, but subconsciously, ever since he'd hurt Bay in the woods, he'd been going easier on him, letting him set the tone and the pace of their interactions.

Hell, Sila had disappeared for three days straight because he'd needed space to sort through this weird thing that was happening to him and he still hadn't been able to properly deduce what it was.

But at the sound of that offer, that feeling within shifted.

"Keep you?" It'd never occurred to him that was a possibility. He figured he'd play with him until he got bored and that would be that. But keeping him…Sila had never met anyone like Bay before. Was there a chance he could entertain him for the rest of their lives? Forever was a really long time. "Do you understand what that means?"

That small voice within scolded him for asking. It whispered he shouldn't give Bay any chances to change his mind and just take him now. Take him and claim him for real.

"I don't want to die." Bay removed his face from hiding and pulled back enough to meet Sila's gaze. His eyes were puffy from crying and there was still dried spit on his chin from sucking him off. "I did before, but I don't anymore."

"Death or the Devil?" He lifted a brow. "You could have asked for anything, but those are the options you picked?"

"Without the devil," Bay dropped his gaze, embarrassed, "death is the only option anyway."

Sila stilled. "What does that mean?"

"You brought me back to life," Bay said. "You should take responsibility. Wouldn't it be a shame if all your hard work went to waste? If you just killed me and it was over? Isn't that why you stopped on the bridge? You could have choked me to death there, but you didn't. You want this too, Sila."

"Do I?" His eyes narrowed. "You're trying to manage me."

"I'm trying to stay alive," Bay disagreed.

"Oh?" Sila felt the call of his base nature and he welcomed it, basking in the familiarity. The calculations ran through his mind and it was as though that whole confusing mess of a person he'd been only a moment ago was finally washed away, replaced with his true self.

There was a way Sila could have everything he wanted, everything he needed to appease both his devilish side and the strange aching part of himself. The part that didn't want to see Bay's lifeless corpse after all.

Bay didn't want to die?

He was in luck. It turned out Sila didn't want

that either.

However, there was no way in hell he was going to roll over and allow the professor to think he was in charge here. He wasn't and he never would be.

Sila still wanted to punish him for the bridge, even if Bay had come to his senses and changed his mind. But the idea of keeping him also appealed...

"Here's the deal, Kitten," Sila said, easing Bay down onto his back on the mattress so that he was looming over him. He ran his tongue over his teeth, his full cock bumping against the side of Bay's naked thigh. "I'll let you live. If you can survive me."

Bay inhaled and Sila grinned viciously down at him.

Even if this thing in his chest was care or, dare he say, love, it would take a lot more than that for a person to be a good fit for Sila. He'd never even considered taking a life partner before, had scoffed at the idea, in fact. But now...admittedly, there was a sort of appeal to the thought of having Bay whenever and however he wanted him. From now until the end of time.

He'd have to prove he could handle it though, handle Sila's true self, because if he couldn't...Well, that wasn't the type of disappointment Sila wanted to deal with later on down the line, once he'd gotten even more attached to the older man.

Sila lowered himself, careful not to crush Bay, wanting to ease him back into a sense of security. That was also why he kept the kiss light, just a brushing of their lips before he was pulling back and smiling down at him all over again.

"Remember what you said, baby. Try to stay alive."

The doubt had only just begun to trickle into Bay's eyes when Sila let go off the last thread of control and finally introduced the real Devil of Vitality to the world.

CHAPTER 26:

It should have made him realize what an epic mistake he'd made when Sila forced his thighs apart and practically bent him in half to get to his unprepared hole.

But it didn't.

Bay didn't even fight it when that massive cock poked at his ass, seeking out his puckered entrance, even knowing the absolute hell it was about to bring him. Sure enough, that hot rod of steel tore him open in one brutal thrust, his insides screaming in agony as a fresh wave of tears flooded from his eyes.

His cry gave him away though. The sound of it, a distinct mixture of pain and pleasure, laying him barer than the man currently on top of him had.

As if to prove that fact further, Sila paused over him and stared at Bay incredulously.

Maybe it was all in his head, but Bay thought perhaps there was also a hint of approval. He couldn't be certain and, in the next instant, all rational or coherent thought fled his mind as

Sila started to fuck into him in sharp, unharried strokes.

The way he did it kept himself from ever fully pulling out, the head of his cock constantly battering against Bay's prostate. The attention ensured that it wasn't long before Bay's dick responded, his balls drawing tight as arousal swept through him. The pain from being too dry was still there, but it didn't prevent him from enjoying himself, the exact opposite actually.

The pain reminded him he was still alive.

The pleasure made him grateful for that fact.

Within a matter of minutes, Bay was shamefully close to spilling his seed and he gripped the comforter in his hands and moaned, arching his back to meet Sila's next thrust.

Only to whine when all at once that cock left him, the hot body that'd been hovering over him leaving right along with it. His eyes popped open, tracking Sila's movements as the younger man got off the bed and grabbed something else from the end table he'd left open.

"We fuck too often," Sila grumbled as he returned. "You're not as tight as that first time."

"You mean I'm not bleeding as much."

"It hurts for me when you're too dry. Don't get this twisted. This isn't for you."

"I know." Bay grew silent as he watched Sila open the bottle of lube he'd just gotten. He sucked in a breath when one of his legs was shoved back up, his knee practically at the side of his head now, lifting his hole high in the air for Sila, who aimed and squirted a generous amount all over it.

As soon as he was satisfied, he tossed the bottle somewhere off to the side and then flipped Bay onto his stomach. Instead of lifting his hips, he blanketed his body over his, slipping a knee between his thighs so they were spread. His cock found its target in a flash, and then he was back to rutting into him, his movements more primal than they'd been before.

"That's better," Sila groaned and dropped his mouth to the spot between Bay's left shoulder and his neck. "Now I can get in all the way. I couldn't before." As if to prove it, he slammed in and rotated his hips.

Bay felt himself stretch around that intruding member, felt it bump up against his lower stomach in a way that was uncomfortable and pleasurable all at once.

"You owe me blood," Sila said absently, and that was all the warning he gave before his teeth were clamping down and breaking through Bay's skin.

He screamed and grabbed at the comforter, but there was no way he could move himself from beneath Sila's heavy form. The pain in his shoulder had only just started to turn to a dull throb when suddenly Sila was lifting him onto his knees.

Sila captured both his wrists and tugged his arms behind him, forcing his cock in at the same time. He pulled hard enough the muscles in Bay's arms strained. "I want to hurt you."

"So," Bay gasped and rocked back into a particularly hard thrust, "do. Hurt me. I can take it."

Or he'd die trying.

He'd meant it when he'd said he changed his mind, but it wasn't because he'd gotten sudden clarity that the world was a beautiful place and worth living in or any such nonsense.

No, as he'd been choking on Sila's cock, his vision winking out for the second time that night, it'd really hit him that if he died, that would be it. There'd be no more Sila delivering pain or pleasure. No more of Sila's devilish grins, the ones he kept hidden from the rest of the world and only showed Bay when they were alone like this.

No more touches, rough or soft or anywhere in between. No more bleeding for him or coming for him or running from him for the thrill of it.

Everything would just be…over.

And wasn't that what had driven him to that bridge in the first place? The fear that Sila had left him, that he was now alone, that's what he'd been about to jump from. That's what scared Bay the most. Death was nothing. But losing Sila?

Bay understood what was happening here. What his student intended to do. He'd taken Bay's words as a challenge, which meant he'd do his hardest to prove Bay couldn't take it. That Bay had made a mistake and chosen wrong. He wanted to make Bay regret forcing his hand—because that's what he'd done, and they both knew it.

"You dropped the knife," Bay reminded him, the words coming out a slur delivered between gasps and grunts as that cock speared through him over and over again. The lube had provided an easier glide in, but it'd done nothing to abate the fact he hadn't been properly prepared beforehand. Taking something that large without being opened up meant it still hurt.

But not nearly enough.

"Don't tempt me," Sila replied, his voice a low growl. He shoved Bay back down and held him by the back of the neck with one hand. The other slapped him across the ass, hard enough there was no doubt he was leaving behind fingerprint shaped welts all over Bay's skin. He kept it up too, one hit followed by another, and then another.

Until Bay was a wriggling mess, his ass burning on the outside and inside, his face shoved so hard into the mattress he could only suck in short intakes of breath from one corner of his mouth.

Sila vanished from behind him a second time, and this time Bay sobbed at the sudden absence, his entire body going lax and boneless. The sound of metal clinking against metal came soon after, and then Sila was hooking something to the ring at Bay's collar.

Bay's eyes shot open as he was hauled up at the neck by the leather, his fingers just barely having enough time to slip beneath it so there was a little space keeping it from completely strangling him this time. He held on as he was lifted all the way up over the bed until he was on his tiptoes, then Sila rounded the fourposter and came into view, holding the end of the pulley he'd attached to Bay.

He coiled it around one of the wooden posts of the bed, staring at Bay triumphantly all the while. It was clear he was enjoying Bay's panic.

And he was panicking, because even though Sila had supposedly given him a chance, there was no mistaking the way he'd phrased things wasn't exactly in Bay's favor.

He could live only if he survived.

"Since this might be our last night together," Sila said, ignoring the way Bay whined at that, "I figure I should try out everything I've been wanting to, don't you agree?" He came forward and laughed when he reached for Bay's dick and Bay tried to move away. Capturing him in a firm grip, he slipped something over, pushing it all the way to the base before securing it in place and letting go.

Bay didn't have to ask to recognize the cock ring for what it was, though he'd never played with one himself before. He jerked and almost lost his footing and hold around the collar when suddenly it began to pulse, sending strong vibrations through him.

"I wore one of these when I got my

piercings," Sila said, then chuckled and stepped up onto the bed when Bay noticeably paled. "Don't worry, that's not my goal tonight." He was holding something in his other hand, but keeping it out of sight. Once he was standing in front of him, he gave a little push with a single finger at the center of Bay's chest. "How you hanging, Kitten?"

Bay made a sound of alarm as one foot came off the mattress, more pressure instantly applied to the collar around his throat.

"Steady there." Sila rested a hand on his hip as though really interested in helping him. "You're going to want to keep still for this next part." Finally, he pulled what he'd been keeping hidden into view.

Bay felt a thrill rush through him and gave a slight shake of his head in the negative that Sila promptly ignored.

"I like the way my earring looks on you so much, baby," Sila told him as he sprayed a small bottle of antiseptic over Bay's chest. He repeated the process over the long needle he also held then dropped the bottle at their feet. "But we can't exactly have you going around like that, now can we? It would be too obvious and you don't want to get in trouble for sleeping with one of your students."

"Sila," Bay managed to croak it out but even that was difficult.

"Hmm?" He pretended not to understand, and it was so obvious that was what he was doing,

Bay felt a prickle of annoyance.

Which only managed to turn him on even more.

Because if Sila was going through all this effort, that meant he wanted to keep Bay, right? He didn't want to kill him either, and this whole thing was just another way to give them both what they wanted without having to admit defeat.

He wasn't going to strangle Bay so long as Bay was good for him and accepted what came next.

He could do that.

If suffering meant winning Sila at the end? Not only could Bay endure, he'd flourish under all of that attention, torturous or otherwise.

"I can be good," he promised, even though Sila had never actually asked for that out loud.

Fortunately, hearing it seemed to please him, and he reached out and tweaked Bay's left nipple once in reward. "Yeah? Then do me a favor, Kitten, and cry pretty for me."

The needle pierced through that same nipple a moment later and Bay ground his teeth and squeezed his eyes shut. The pain was brief, the sting lingering but nowhere near as bad as the beating his ass had already taken. When he felt the cold metal from the jewelry being forced through, he risked opening his eyes to see.

It was a small golden barbell with two blue gems at either end, like the stone that was in the ring of his collar.

"Not painful enough for you?" Sila mused, a second before he leaned in and bit at the fresh wound. He was careful not to damage his work, but made sure it would hurt.

Bay jerked and lost his footing again.

Sila steadied him and then smiled, that sweet boyish smile he gave his friends.

Bay had thought it was fake all this time, but maybe there was some truth to it after all. Maybe it just took something extreme and debased to actually bring it out in him.

The second piercing hurt more than the first, possibly because this time Bay was tense and waiting for it. He cried out, shifting on his toes, his erect dick slapping lightly against Sila's stomach in the process.

That one small touch was enough to send electricity and pangs of need shooting through him, the pain in his nipples immediately forgotten.

"That's cheating," Sila scolded, though he didn't actually sound all that upset. "Look at you." He pulled back and flicked a finger over Bay's swollen cockhead. "You're dripping. Too bad you can't come with that ring as tight as it is."

The look he gave Bay next could only be considered pure, undiluted evil.

"Please," Bay wasn't above begging. Sila could cut him, whip him, pierce him all he wanted, so long as this ended with Bay finding his own release.

"Oh no," Sila promised, "the night is young. I'm only getting started with you, baby."

* * *

Bay lost track of how many times Sila had come after the fourth round.

After piercing him, he'd fucked him hard from behind, all while Bay had struggled not to slip and hang himself. When Sila had pulled out and painted Bay's inner thighs with his spunk, Bay had felt momentary relief thinking it was over and he'd get his turn.

He'd been wrong.

Sila hadn't even let him down. He'd simply walked around him, given himself a couple of strokes as he lapped at the beads of blood trickling from the piercings, and then lifted Bay and started it again from the front.

When he finally undid the chain at his neck and lowered him back to the bed, it was so Sila could lick and nip at Bay's abused balls, never once loosening the cock ring or touching his dick. He only bit him once or twice, and never hard enough for it to truly hurt, as though he preferred keeping Bay in sexual torture down there instead of causing any real damage or harm.

Then he'd fucked Bay lying down again.

On his back.

On his stomach.

Sila had lifted him and brought him over to the metal chair and shoved Bay down on his cock in a similar way he'd done in the bathroom back at his place. At some point, he'd tied Bay's wrists together, and looped them over his neck so Bay had purchase while his body was lifted and lowered.

He may have passed out, but he couldn't be sure, because when he came to again, he was still there, only he'd been turned around, his back against Sila's front, that cock still hammering his hole as if they hadn't already been at it for hours.

Bay ended up on the floor next, warm liquid dripping from his entrance, making a sticky mess of both him and the cold wood he was lying over. His eyes had just begun to drift shut, his body completely and totally spent, when he felt a sharp sting and yelped.

Sila crouched next to him holding one of the knives he'd discarded earlier. "Stay awake, Kitten. You said you'd be good, remember?" He lowered the blade to Bay's upper thigh where he'd just cut a shallow line and repeated the motion.

Bay hissed and gyrated his hips, trying to find friction for his poor neglected dick.

"How sick do you have to be to still be hard after everything I already did to you?" Sila asked, but despite the harsh words, there was no malice in his tone.

"Coming from the guy who got off inflicting it," Bay countered, his own voice filled with exhaustion, "that doesn't really mean much."

He let his head drop against the floorboards. Sila had finished and pushed him to the ground where he'd rolled onto his side. His dick was straining and he ached all over. He'd long since stopped noticing the fact he was crying, but the tears were never ending. He had to blink through them a few times to focus on what he was seeing, but then Sila's hand where he had it rested casually over his knee came into few.

"What happened?" Bay bolted upright, grimacing from the pain in his backside the sudden movement caused, before reaching for Sila's hand. He turned it over, inspecting the deep cut across his palm—far deeper than any of the surface level wounds Sila had delivered to Bay with the weapon. "How did you do this?"

"It wasn't an accident," Sila told him.

"We need to get this cleaned off before it gets infected. How long has it been like this?" Bay demanded.

"Since before you woke up."

"What?!" Bay gave him a disapproving look. "Did you at least have the foresight to spray some of that disinfectant on it earlier when you prepared me for the piercings?"

Sila gave him a blank stare, which was all the answer Bay needed.

"Come on," he tugged at him but the younger man refused to budge. "Let's go to the bathroom and run it under water. Do you have a first aid kit?"

"You want first aid?" Sila asked cryptically.

Bay sighed. "Are you even listening? Yes, of

course I want first aid. We need to bandage you up. You may even need stitches! This is too bloody for me to tell. Honestly what were you thinking?"

"Professor."

"What?" he snapped.

"Did you hit your head when I pushed you off of me just now?"

Bay frowned but thought it over. "No, I don't believe so. Why?"

"Are you serious?"

"Sila, I don't—What are you doing?!" Bay tried to move away, but his body was too exhausted to get far and Sila had him back on his back on the ground easily enough.

He yanked the cock ring off and Bay jerked and moaned as the pressure eased, his eyes momentarily rolling in the back of his head. Then Sila wrapped a hand around him and gave him one long pump and his hips lifted off the ground to chase after that sweet friction. He gave into it for a moment, relishing in the delicious snaps of electricity that brought him closer and closer, before curiosity got the best of him and he opened his eyes and glanced down.

"Stop!" Bay tried to sit up but Sila pinned him with his other hand on his shoulder. "You can't do that!"

"Afraid of a little blood?"

"I'm afraid you're going to get infected, you idiot!"

Sila's injured hand slowed at the base of

Bay's dick, squeezing once before loosening again. "Did you just call me stupid, Professor? You do recall I'm your top student, don't you?"

He did have the highest grade in all of Bay's classes, true, but that was beside the point at the moment.

"Are you really that worried about me?" Sila asked as he began pumping Bay again, this time in slow, torturous strokes. His blood and Bay's precome acted as lube, helping his palm slick up and down his velvety skin in a way that had him writhing despite his protests. "You really want me to stop?"

Bay bit his tongue but forced himself to nod. "Yes. Yes, we really need to get that treated, Sila. Please."

"Are you begging for me to not let you come?" He clicked his tongue and, even though the comment had meant to be teasing, Bay captured his gaze and made sure to push as much of the stern professor as he could into his own eyes.

"Yes, that is exactly what I am saying because you're no good to me if you get blood poisoning and die."

He tilted his head as though seeing Bay for the first time. "You're afraid I'll die? It's not that serious."

"It is," Bay disagreed.

"You should worry about your own injuries," Sila said. "There are many."

"I'll survive."

"Will you?"

"You want me to."

Sila's eyes narrowed. "That so?"

Considering it'd been hours since he'd gotten the injury and yet he was still bleeding so much, Bay was pretty certain he was in fact going to need stitches.

Sila pulled him forward an inch by the root of his dick and it smarted but felt amazing all at once and Bay moaned. "There you go, just feel, isn't that better? You don't have to care about me, Professor. This isn't the classroom and right now I'm not your student."

"That's not," he gasped as Sila rolled his thumb against his slit, "why."

"No?" he hummed, clearly not believing him. "If it's not moral responsibility then—"

"I love you." It shocked Bay every bit as much as it did Sila and they both froze. But he didn't take it back. It actually explained a lot. He'd thought it was just obsession but it was so much more than that, why else would he be lying here taking this type of abuse?

His asshole and his nipples both burned, as well as his ear where the earring had been forced through without proper attention. Fluid was spilling out of his bottom and his dick. He was covered in bruises and welts and a few fine cuts, and all the sun cream in the galaxy wasn't going to be enough for him to walk into work tomorrow on his own two feet and Bay well knew it.

A sane person would be humiliated and enraged right now.

Bay just wanted to come.

And sleep for a week.

Or seven.

But after he'd tended to Sila's nasty cut.

"You're confused," the younger man broke the silence first, but Bay was quick to disagree, knowing if he wasn't careful and he didn't convince him it'd all be over.

For real this time.

"I'm not. I know what love feels like. I know that's what this is."

"You're just saying that because up until you met me you couldn't feel at all."

"That's probably part of it, sure," he admitted, because lying would do neither of them any good. "But that doesn't mean it's not also true that I developed a stronger connection with you. I love you. You don't have to love me back, I'm not asking for that."

"What are you asking for?"

"Let's just take a break and put a bandage on your cut, okay?"

"You're crazier than I am."

"Sila—"

"Here," he held out the knife. "If you slit your own throat right now, I'll leave and go straight to the hospital. That's what you say you want, right? Because you love me."

Bay's brow furrowed. "You don't believe me."

"Of course not. You're blissed out and high on endorphins and adrenaline right now."

Bay's hand whipped out and he took the knife, but just as he was about to bring the blade to his neck he paused. Bay searched Sila's expression and, though the other man had gone unreadable again, he thought he saw a flash of something there.

"No." He lowered the knife. "You don't want me to die."

"That so?" Sila drawled.

"Be honest with yourself. You know I'm right."

"Sure you aren't just trying to get out of it? Isn't true love all about poetically throwing yourself on the proverbial sword for another person?"

Bay thought about his talk with Rin and considered all that he knew about Sila.

This was a test. He was certain of it.

"If I killed myself right now that would be the end," he said. "It'd be boring, and you would never fall for someone who was boring."

Something dark flickered behind Sila's eyes. "You're insinuating that I've fallen for you."

"You've taken a liking to me," Bay agreed. "That's why you're acting like this. Why you stopped me on the bridge and brought me here."

"Don't—"

"That's why I was on the bridge too," he added before Sila could get too angry over the reminder. "I thought you'd left me."

Sila frowned.

"You weren't answering my calls and your friends said your father had arrived demanding you leave with him," Bay confessed. "I got scared."

Sila was quiet for a long moment before, "My brother and I would never leave with Crate Varun. We had an escape plan." He hesitated and then added more quietly. "You were a part of it."

Bay's head snapped up.

"I wasn't going to leave you, Bay."

The sound of his name sent shivers through his entire, exhausted body.

"I'm not sure if that's because I'm fond of you or if I've just gotten used to having you around, but you aren't going to get rid of me that easily."

"The bridge," he shook his head, "that's not what I was trying to do."

"No?"

"No."

Sila held his gaze. "All right."

"So then—"

He shoved him back down, hand instantly returning to Bay's dick. "Come for me and then I'll let you see to my hand, Kitten."

"Sila."

"Come."

Even if he'd wanted to continue arguing, Bay didn't have it in him. After being denied for so long he couldn't last and after only a couple of hard

pumps he orgasmed.
    And promptly passed out.
    Again.

CHAPTER 27:

The room was even darker than before when Bay woke next. This time he was tucked under the silky covers on the right side of the bed, closest to the door leading to the bathroom. There was a soft golden glow spilling from the open doorway, casting the man seated in a chair next to him in silhouette.

"Sila?" his voice was croaky and raw and he winced but didn't dare move. There was something about the charged energy in the room that kept him lying still, his eyes searching through the darkness to try and make out anything that could help him gauge what the younger man was feeling.

Bay was under no illusions. He'd almost died tonight. Three times, in fact. The first attempt had been at his own hand, but the other two…

"Sila," he tried again, a bit more firmly, and he saw the set of the other man's shoulders shift slightly a second before a warm palm settled over Bay's exposed calf. He hadn't realized his legs were sticking out from under the comforter, but it was impossible to ignore when those fingers started dancing lightly from his knee to his ankle and back again.

Something was wrong. The touch wasn't caring or sweet. He didn't know how he knew it, but he did. Bay risked trying to sit up only to have the collar around his neck tug, digging into the bruises that already littered his throat. He sucked in a sharp breath and rested his head back, tipping it to see that he'd been secured to the bed post with black rope through the loop.

"Tell me what you're thinking," Bay asked, trying not to panic. Technically, the night wasn't over. Was this still all part of the test? Earlier, he'd passed out then woken in the bath with Sila. The most he'd been able to do was help clean off the wound on his palm and help bandage it, but Bay was still of a mind that it needed to be looked at by a proper doctor.

"Should I break your legs?" Sila murmured, and Bay went still as a statue beneath those trailing fingers. "It wouldn't be enough, would it. Eventually they would heal and I'd have to repeat the process, and that isn't the type of pain you're into."

"No," Bay agreed quietly, "it isn't."

"Would you be sad because you couldn't race anymore?" Sila acted like he hadn't heard him, like he was off in his own little world. "You won't need racing if you have me. I can give you all the oxygen you need."

"What?" This wasn't the same Sila from earlier. Wasn't the same person Bay had been interacting with all those other occasions either. There was something off about him, but also, there was a strange inkling in the back of Bay's mind that he was actually getting a glimpse of the true man behind the mask.

As if the Devil he'd met already was only another layer to who Sila Varun truly was.

As if he hadn't actually been the real Devil at all, but another smoke screen Sila had provided to throw him and the rest of the universe off.

It made Bay wonder...Did Sila really even know himself? Was he hiding even when he faced the mirror?

Had he stopped hiding because of Bay?

That was presumptuous and narcissistic of him to even consider, but Bay felt an altogether pleased sensation skitter through him at the notion. He'd never thought all too highly of himself—he didn't suffer from low self-esteem or anything, but he was a realist, and realistically speaking, he'd always been only slightly above average in every department.

Sure, he had good looks, but those had admittedly come later in life and, by then, he'd been too studious to attract the popular girls and guys at school. He was smart, smart enough to have completed his degree and held onto his position at the university. But he was no genius. He just happened to have developed the skill to accurately read people, and much of that was thanks to his schooling in the first place.

He'd been fun and open to new things prior to his grandmother's death, but after he'd turned into a closed off robot, going through the motions without ever really feeling or caring about any of it, people stopped coming around. No one wanted something like that. Even he didn't want himself.

But now...

"You said it felt like you were drowning in the ocean," Sila reminded, proving that he had in fact heard him, at least that last time. "I dragged you up for air once. I can keep doing it. I can breathe life back into you, baby," his hand ghosted higher, over the curve of Bay's hip, "I can make you keep going."

Bay swallowed the lump in his throat. "I don't want to die anymore."

"No?" Sila's hand paused over Bay's arm, then lowered so he was actually touching him again.

His skin felt hot in the chilly room, the pads of his fingers lighting Bay on fire instantly.

"Are you not feeling well?" Bay wondered if he had a fever. If the cut on his hand might already be infected. "We should go to the hospital."

"Go?" His hand tightened around Bay's bicep. "You aren't allowed to go anywhere."

"Sila," he kept his composure despite high hard he was being held, "you're ill. We need to get you checked out by a doctor."

"Excuses."

"It isn't."

"If I break your legs, you won't even be able to try."

Bay risked reaching forward, his hand shaking as he did. When he pressed his knuckles to Sila's forehead it was to find him clammy and hot. He almost tried sitting up again but recalled how his collar restricted him.

Had he been wrong earlier? Was the real reason Sila was acting this way because he was sick and out of it?

That was...scary. And not in the fun way. Caution. He needed to proceed with caution.

"Breaking my legs won't be necessary," he said.

Sila cocked his head. "No?"

"I already made my choice, remember? Death or the Devil. I chose you."

"People change their minds all the time," Sila argued. "That's the problem with emotions. They're fickle. They trick you into believing one thing even if logic dictates another is true. You chose me because you believe you no longer want to die. What about tomorrow? Or the day after? Or the day after that? I can't be around you twenty-four-seven. I can't be there to ensure you don't go back on your word."

"I'm not going to try and kill myself again."

"I don't believe you."

"Sila."

"You shouldn't believe yourself."

"Do you believe yourself all the time?" Bay countered, though he kept his tone soft. This was a precarious situation, he was aware. Whether Sila was acting like this due to the fever lowering his inhibitions or what, he was dangerous and volatile right now. Unpredictable. "Do you trust yourself implicitly?"

"I trust no one," he said.

"Not even your brother?"

Sila paused. "Of course I trust my brother."

"But he has feelings. How do you know he isn't a slave to them just like everyone else?"

"He is." He didn't sound all that upset by that, not like he had when they'd been referring to Bay and others.

Bay hated it because of how pathetic that made him, but he felt a stab of jealousy toward Sila's twin. He wanted all of Sila's attention. His trust. His care. He didn't want to share any of it, not even with the guy's flesh and blood.

Hell, Bay had already given over his literal flesh and blood to Sila. Couldn't that be enough?

Maybe he was also feverish because what was he even thinking right now?

Damn it.

"You have feelings, too," Bay said.

"I do."

"What are you feeling right now?"

"Anxious."

"Why?"

"Should I—"

"You don't need to break my legs," Bay snapped, losing his patience for the first time. He froze, waiting for the backlash but it didn't come.

"Okay." Sila's grip on his arm loosened.

"Okay?"

"Yeah." In one swift move, he had Bay sprawled out on his back with Sila lowering himself over top him. He was careful distributing his weight so he wouldn't crush him, however, planting his forearms at either side of Bay's head, his legs at either side, caging Bay in on all fronts. "Okay."

Bay stared up at him, but even though his eyes had partially adjusted to the dark, he could still only make out a slight glimmer where Sila's multicolored orbs peered back. "You have all of those videos of me, remember?"

Changing tactics here seemed to be the best course of action. He was starting to get really worried, and not for himself—or his legs. If Sila was this out of it, the fever had to be bad and the only cause Bay could think of was the cut on his palm. They needed to get out of here and get to a hospital before things got any worse, but that meant getting through to him.

In his current state, the only thing Sila seemed to care about was locking Bay down. If he helped him see that he'd already done that, maybe he could finally convince him to let him drive him to see a doctor.

"You have leverage," Bay said.

"It's useless if you're dead and you know that."

"I was only on that bridge because I thought you'd left."

"I didn't."

"You told me you wouldn't vanish on me again, but you did. I tried calling and you never answered," Bay reminded. He was the one who should be upset here. "I'm the one who should be scared of being tossed aside."

"You asked me not to ghost you," Sila replied, "but I never agreed."

"And what about the other part?" he persisted. "You told me this would only end when you want it to. Am I supposed to just hold my breath and wait for *you* to wake up one day and change your mind and realize you don't want me anymore?"

A dark, lethal sound rumbled up his chest. "That isn't going to happen."

"How can you believe yourself?"

Sila frowned.

He'd tossed the words back at him in the hopes it would help his see reason and trust Bay when he said he wanted to stay. But seeing his reaction now, it was clear that wasn't working.

If it wasn't just the fever causing Sila to act this way, then what else could it be? When he'd first woken and seen him sitting next to the bed, Bay had sensed the change as though it were a live thing lounging in the room with them.

What if Sila hadn't changed though?

What if this was really who he was at his core, the same way Bay's obsession with pain in the bedroom was who he really was?

"You're fracturing, aren't you?" Bay tried to reach up to touch a wave of Sila's golden hair, but his wrist was instantly captured and pinned to the bed with a warning growl. "I'm not trying anything funny. I'm not going anywhere."

"You can't," Sila stated, grinding down into him. He was getting hard again but now wasn't the time for sex.

"Are you feeling confused right now?" Bay kept trying. "You said you were anxious. Because you think I might try to leave? Or because you don't like that idea and you're not sure what to do with that emotion?"

For a long moment, it seemed like Sila wasn't going to answer, but then he took a deep breath, as though trying to steady himself, and when he spoke his voice was a little more even. "I didn't like seeing you on the bridge," he confessed. "It...hurt."

"Hurt how?"

"That's it," he said. "I saw you, it hurt, and then I got angry. I don't get angry, not like that. Anger always leads to mistakes, and I don't make those. I'm the levelheaded brother."

"You don't have to be that all the time."

"Yes," he stated firmly, "I do."

"All right." Bay nodded slowly. "I won't do it again. You don't have to worry."

"I don't get worried."

"Sila." It was so obvious to him what was going on here, that the student was having a crisis of self and that was partially to blame for his actions. Because of what he was, the way his brain worked, if they didn't get him back on track he may lose control entirely and lash out. Bay liked pain, sure, but he'd been telling the truth.

He didn't want to die.

"You're worried right now," Bay disclosed, gently. "You're worried because you don't want to lose me and you don't understand what that means. Would you like me to help you?"

"Help me how?"

"I could tell you what it mostly likely is." The same way Rin had always done. Sila had learned most of his mimicry from his twin. "Or should I call your brother?"

He stiffened overtop him. "He won't save you."

"I'm not looking to be saved," Bay reassured. "You're the one who needs help here, not me."

"You aren't that naïve, Professor."

"Sure, you could kill me—"

"I won't." Sila tipped his head and seemed to consider how quickly he'd replied just now. "I would never. You're mine, Bay Delmar. You said you were mine, back in the car, and again, earlier."

"I did," he agreed, "and I am."

"For how long?"

"Forever." Bay wanted that and he was starting to think Sila wanted that too. Why else would he have gotten this bent out of shape over Bay almost jumping? Even when he'd been hurting him earlier, it'd been in ways that would mark Bay up, permanently in some cases like with the piercings.

You wouldn't bother decorating an item you planned to immediately throw away.

"Here." Bay moved slowly, reaching for Sila's arm until the younger guy shifted and allowed him to take him by the wrist. Then he led him to his chest and pressed Sila's fingers over the tender flesh of his left nipple. It stung and he almost moaned, the thick length of Sila's cock resting against his stomach reminding him of what they could be doing, but he held it together.

His body was battered and he might not make it through another round of Sila's rough lovemaking and, even if that weren't part of the equation, the fever was still coursing through Sila.

"There's this too." He moved Sila up again so he could touch the collar. "And this." He lifted his hips, rubbing himself against Sila's cock through the comforter between them. They were both naked, but that barrier kept them separated and if they were in any other situation, Bay would have begged to have it removed.

"You already claimed me." This time when Bay went to run his fingers through Sila's hair, the younger man let him. "You punished me for the bridge, mercilessly, thoroughly, and I loved every second of it."

"That's incredibly fucked up of you," Sila told him.

"You loved every second of it, too."

"I didn't," he disagreed. "I should have, but it's mostly just a blur."

"Because you were angry."

"You said you'd tell me what I'm feeling," he reminded.

"Will you untie me from the bedpost first?" Bay risked asking. "It's uncomfortable, and not in the pleasurable way." When Sila hesitated he added, "You're lying on top of me, Varun. You don't need the rope."

He removed his hand from where it was still placed at Bay's throat and there was a click before the pressure around his neck eased. The collar was still on, but at least he was no longer attached to the bed.

"Tell me," Sila urged, and it sounded like he was open to it, like he'd decided he'd listen to whatever explanation Bay wanted to give and would roll with it.

Wasn't that a form of trust? Was he getting through to him?

"You like me." Bay had tried to broach the topic earlier, but they'd both been too caught up in the haze of sex and Sila—the non-feverish Sila—clearly hadn't been ready to hear it or fully admit it to himself. "You like me as more than a playmate or a pet. That's why you're concerned over my wellbeing."

"I've literally marked you all over," Sila pointed out.

"You applied sun cream after I passed out." Bay could tell. The aches weren't nearly as bad as they would have been otherwise. It was the same thing he'd done after their first time in the woods. "You break me and then you stitch me back together again. And I keep coming back for more."

"I like you," he rolled the words on his tongue as though they were foreign to him. "That's…" All at once, he swayed, barely catching himself. "Something's wrong."

"You're sick," Bay explained pressing at his shoulders to try and get him to move. "We need to get you—"

"No," his voice wavered and his eyes slipped closed, "No leaving."

Bay opened his mouth to argue, but then Sila dropped over him, crushing his chest with his heavy weight. The fear he felt was a thousand times more potent than when he'd been practically dangling from the ceiling.

"You only just brought me back," he grunted as he got to work shoving the younger man off of him. "You aren't allowed to leave me behind."

Death or the Devil.

Bay had been serious about that too.

He'd made his choice, and no one, not even

the Devil himself, got to break that bargain with him.

CHAPTER 28:

It'd taken Bay longer than it should have in his beat-up state to finally roll Sila off of him and onto the other side of the bed. Then he'd moved without rationality, instantly getting up to search for one of their multi-slates. His was nowhere in sight, but he located Sila's on the long table across from the bed.

He was halfway to calling for an ambulance when it hit him, he had no clue where they even where. Rin's number was the last called contact and without further hesitation, Bay selected it and hit call, rushing back to check on Sila.

The younger man was covered in a fine sheen of sweet and he was shaking. He'd never heard of anyone getting an infection this quickly. Typically, it took two to three days. Had they been here that long? Bay didn't think so.

"Asshole," Rin's grumpy voice came through. "Do you have any idea what time it is? Are you still in a mood? You better have just killed someone or —"

"It's Bay Delmar," he interrupted, turning

Sila's hand and removed the crude bandage. A gasp escaped him before he could stop it. "Do you have a way of locating us?" Too late he recalled Sila mentioning that not even his brother knew their current address. "Please tell me you do."

"What's going on?" Rin sounded more alert than he had a moment ago, then he turned to someone and said, "Run a trace on my brother's multi-slate. Just do it. Professor Delmar?" he came back on. "Tell me what's happening. I just saw him this afternoon. Why do you have his multi-slate and why do you need me to find you? Did he—"

"It's not me that's the problem," he stopped him, knowing that Rin was thinking he was going to have clean up after Sila after all. "He's sick and unresponsive. He cut himself earlier but I don't understand how it could get this infected this quickly."

Greenish-blue veins snaked beneath Sila's skin, branching out from the cut. They'd traveled partially down his wrist already, and all the way to the ends of his fingers. Bay was no medical student, but he'd never seen anything like this before…

"I'm afraid," the admission crept out of him. He didn't even have the energy to be embarrassed by it or the fact that Sila's brother was listening.

"Got him?" Rin asked whoever he was with and then the sound of him racing down a set of stairs echoed through the line. "We're on our way, Professor. Stay with him."

"I'm not going anywhere," Bay promised.

"We aren't far," Rin said. "We can be there in ten minutes, maybe seven. Describe what's wrong."

Bay told him about the veins. "He's also burning up."

"He cut himself? How?"

"No, he…"

"Oh. You mean *he cut himself*." Rin growled. "Dick. Always causing problems."

"And on our honeymoon, too," a new voice said close to Rin as a car engine roared to life.

Bay was pretty sure that was Kelevra Diar's voice.

"This isn't our honeymoon," Rin snapped. "We only just agreed to be together. That's not how honeymoons work."

"Is now really the time to argue over this, Flower?"

"You know what—"

"Are you almost here?" Bay didn't want to leave him, but he forced himself to climb back off the bed and go to the other doorway. There was a hallway that led down to a room lit by moonlight and he walked toward the pale glow, coming out into a living room. It was an open floor plan with the living area in the center and the kitchen off to the left. Next to that area, there was another door.

Bay checked it, sighing in relief when he found it was the exit. "I'm unlocking the front door so when you get here just let—"

Sila slammed into him from behind, hard enough Bay's chin whacked against the door. The multi-slate he'd been holding clattered to ground, the screen cracking. It emitted a couple of beeps before it went silent, but Sila didn't seem to notice, all of his wild attention aimed directly at Bay as he spun him around.

He was still sweating profusely and was wobbly on his feet, but he managed to hold Bay by the neck with ease, using his superior strength to keep him pinned to the hard wood.

"Sila." Bay tried to coax his hand away, but all that did was irritate him further.

He squeezed and Bay's eyes bulged. "Trying to run, Kitten?"

Bay tried to shake his head but Sila's grip was too tight. He slapped at him instead, hopping to get him to let off enough he could get a word out, but Sila merely stared at him with empty eyes.

He was definitely unwell. Sila kept losing focus on Bay's face and trying again.

When he couldn't think of any other way out of this, Bay blindly reached down, grabbing onto Sila's limp cock. He pulled, not hard enough to injure but definitely hard enough it would be felt.

Sila snarled and yanked himself free, letting Bay go in the process. Unfortunately, that also made him loose his balance, and he stumbled and fell back, hitting the floor in heap.

Bay moved off the door, about to go help him, when suddenly it was opened and slamming into his back. He cried out as he was pushed, tripping over his own feet in the process. When he fell, he landed over Sila, both of them groaning.

"Um, what the fuck?" Rin's voice came then and Bay lifted his head and glanced over his shoulder to find him and the Imperial Prince crowding up the doorway.

And that's when it finally occurred to him that both he and Sila were still completely in the nude.

And that he was sprawled out on top of him, with Sila's legs bent at either side of his waist as though they'd been—

"Good Light!" He scrambled up, yelping when Sila immediately latched onto his wrist and pulled him back down. He landed on his elbow this time and cried out, slapping at Sila in a poor attempt to get him to release him so he could cover up.

"Brother," Rin drawled, just that. One single, irritated word, and Sila went still.

"You're here." Sila's expression was still blank when he glanced over at Rin. The second their eyes met, his rolled back into his skull and he passed out all over again.

Bay untangled himself from Sila's arms and knelt at his side, tapping at his cheek. "Sila? Sila, wake up!"

"Get him to the car," Kelevra told Rin, moving around him to step into the home. He pulled something shiny from his back pocket and

Bay gasped when he registered it was a blaster. "I'll take care of this."

"Take care of what?" Rin demanded, though he did shoot forward. He crouched at his brother's other side and tugged him up, pulling an arm around his shoulder so he could hoist the unconscious Sila onto his feet. His eyes widened when he turned and saw the gun as well, then he glanced between the prince and Bay. "Hold on."

"Why?" Kelevra asked nonchalantly. "It's clear what happened here. Look at him," he motioned at Bay with the weapon. "He's covered in bruises and cuts. Considering the blotches around his throat, it's a wonder he was able to talk to you over the comms at all. Your brother was exercising his demons and took things too far. If he was conscious, he'd no doubt do this himself." He aimed at Bay's chest.

"Do it," Sila's mumbled threat gave them all pause, "and I'll skin you alive."

Kelevra cocked his head, intrigued. "Sure he isn't going to report you for torture as soon as we let him out of here?"

"Yeah," it was obviously a struggle for Sila to remain conscious long enough to have this discussion, his eyes barely open more than a slit, is head lolled against Rin's for support.

"Brother," Rin didn't sound any more certain than the Imperial Prince appeared to be.

"How certain?" Kelevra asked one final time.

"He's mine," Sila growled.

Bay moved to adjust his glasses when Kelevra turned that dark gaze his way, realizing too late that he of course wasn't wearing them. He cleared his throat instead, trying to pretend he wasn't stark naked in front of the Prince of Vitality. "What he said."

"I see." A knowing look passed over him and Kelevra tucked the blaster away with no more argument. "Kinky."

Rin shook his head. "When we get to the hospital, ask around and see if there's any pill I can take that can help erase my memory of all of this."

"Why?" Kelevra turned to hold open the door for him as he started dragging his brother forward. "An hour ago, I had you blindfolded and—"

"Not another word or I will drown you," Rin snapped.

The Imperial Prince chuckled.

"Wait," Sila said just as they made it out the door.

"Still awake?" Rin asked at the same moment that Kelevra drawled, "Still alive?"

"Give him your jacket." Sila motioned with his chin toward Bay. "And if either of you make a joke about liking the view—"

"Here." Rin practically tossed his brother into Kelevra's arms, who begrudgingly caught him. He stripped out of the long-sleeved windbreaker he'd been wearing and handed it over to Bay.

Bay quickly put it on and zipped it all the way up. It was long enough that it covered all his unmentionables, and since he hadn't even thought to look for his clothes earlier, it would have to do. "We should hurry, before he gets any worse."

Rin nodded and then took his brother back, glaring at Kelevra. "You better not have been about to make a comment about liking the view."

"Wouldn't dream of it, Consort." Kelevra smirked at him seductively.

"Whatever."

Bay followed the two of them out to where they'd parked the car in the driveway, silently envious of their obvious chemistry.

Wondering if he'd ever be lucky enough to get to that point with Sila.

* * *

Bay came out from behind the folding screen dressed in a pair of cotton pants with the hospital logo on them and hospital gown. He'd been given slippers as well, though he'd hardly noticed the bite from the cold stone of the sidewalk or the tiles when he'd rushed in through a side entrance of the hospital.

The doctor was checking on Sila who was unconscious again and lying in bed in the private room Kelevra had gotten for them. The Imperial had gone off somewhere, but Rin was there, hovering by his brother's side, listening intently as the doctor did his examination.

A nurse was currently operating a machine on the other side of room.

"We're running a test on his blood samples," the doctor, Dr. Ome, said to Rin. "For now, he's stabilized, but we won't know how to properly treat him until we figure out what's wrong."

"It's not an infection?" Bay asked, stepping forward. His chest ached when he looked at Sila's unmoving form.

He'd been given a hospital gown and pants as well, but even though they'd gotten him here and he was hooked up to three different machines, he didn't look any better. His skin was still a bright red and the veins trailing from his palm had gone higher up his arm to the crease of his elbow.

"I'm of the opinion that it is not," Ome clarified. "No. It could take some time for us to figure it out. In the meantime, you should also be looked at."

It took Bay a moment longer than it should have for him to register the doctor was talking about him. When he'd walked in, the older gentleman had spared him a mere glance before setting all his attention on Sila. Considering the two of them had come in practically naked though...

"Relax," Kelevra appeared then, entering the room with a metal tray, "this is the Royal Hospital, Professor. Anything seen or done here is strictly confidential. No one would dare speak of your injuries outside of this room. Isn't that right,

Doctor?"

"Yes," he hummed in agreed. "Quite right. If you'd please." He motioned to the empty bed next to Sila's.

Bay blinked at it, and it occurred to him that they'd gotten a two-bedroom room specifically for this reason.

"There's nothing to be embarrassed about, sweetie," the female nurse moved away from the machine and came over to help urge Bay onto the stiff mattress. "We see all kinds of things here. Rough foreplay is surprisingly common amongst our patients."

The doctor cleared his throat in warning but she merely winked at Kelevra and then switched places with Ome so he could check Bay over.

The doctor lifted the shirt to expose his chest.

"Maybe not *that* rough," the nurse winced.

Worry for Sila kept Bay from sinking into full blown humiliation, thankfully.

"If it'd been something that we were exposed to together," Bay turned to keep Sila in his sights as the doctor inspected him, "wouldn't I be affected as well?"

"Most likely," he agreed. "How do you feel?"

"Fine."

The nurse snorted.

"Rebecca, please," Ome lifted his gaze toward the ceiling as though seeking divine intervention. "I apologize on her behalf. She's—"

"Madden's sister," Kelevra provided. "Nepotism at its finest."

"Hey!" She had the common decency to appear affronted for all of five seconds.

"Does this hurt?" Ome pressed beneath Bay's jaw on either side.

"No." A little, but nothing he couldn't handle.

"Please don't pop a boner in my presence," Rin sighed and covered his face, clearly done with all of this.

"Don't listen to him, sweetie," Rebecca countered. "You do whatever you need to feel better."

"I don't—" Had he just been thinking he was too worried to be embarrassed? Wrong. "That's not how it works." He needed more than pain on its own. He needed sexual stimulation, or the promise of impending sexual stimulation.

From Sila, specifically.

"It's fine if it is," she insisted.

"It's not!" Bay inhaled slowly and tried to get a hold of himself.

"Is there anywhere else that—" Dr. Ome began to ask.

"No." There was no way Bay was letting him near his lower region. He was fine anyway.

"Are you sure? Tearing can lead to infection if left untreated."

"I've already been taken care of," Bay confessed, glancing at Sila once more. "He applied sun cream."

"He took care of you but didn't look after himself?" Kelevra seemed to find this information fascinating. He'd brought the metal tray he'd gotten over to Rin at some point and Rin was picking at the plate of fruit absently.

He kept frowning at his brother while he pretended to eat, clearly concerned even though they were in the hospital and their doctor was one of the finest on the planet.

Bay understood the feeling. He was also freaking out internally and trying his hardest to keep it all together on the outside. Panic wouldn't help anyone, least of all Sila. Right now, he should just be grateful he'd been included and no one had tried to kick him out of the room. They'd even gotten the doctor to look him over as well.

That was…nice.

It was a far cry from having a blaster aimed at his face, that was for certain.

"Do you happen to know where the patient has been all day?" Ome asked.

"He was with us earlier," Rin supplied, chucking his chin toward Kelevra.

"He made a trip to the shuttleport after," Bay said, and he could tell that this was news to Rin. "Then he came to find me. We were on Sickle Bridge for a little and then…" He pursed his lips.

"Crescent Street," Rin told the doctor, and him. "They were in a house on Crescent Street."

Rebecca let out a whistle. "Nice

neighborhood."

"Any unusual substances there?" Done with Bay, the doctor moved over to the machine the nurse had vacated a while ago and clicked a few buttons before humming to himself. "As I've thought."

"What is it?" Rin asked.

"There are signs of a foreign substance in his system," Ome explained. "He was poisoned."

"What?" Bay shot off the bed and almost fell, catching himself just in time.

"I advise against any sudden movements," Ome said. "You're running on fumes right now, Mr. Delmar. I'm going to prescribe you a sleep aid. You should try and get some rest to recover."

"I'm fine, thank you."

"It's not like there's anything you can do," Rin told him. "Unless of course you know who poisoned him?"

"And with what," Ome added. "Unfortunately, it's coming up as an unknown in our system."

Bay felt his stomach plummet. "What does that mean?"

"Can you not treat him?" Rin demanded to know.

"We'll do our best, of course." Ome didn't seem convinced.

"Can I borrow your multi-slate?" Bay held his hand out to Rin, assuming he'd agree. "I might have someone who can help."

"I can have a team of toxicologists here within a half hour," Kelevra stated. "Who could you possibly know that would be better than them?"

He set a cold stare on the Imperial Prince. "Berga Obsidian."

Rin immediately offered up his device. "Call him."

CHAPTER 29:

He felt a lot like that time he'd been acting as Rin and had been dared to jump off the Highgate Bluffs back in middle school. Sila had hit the surface of the ocean hard enough to jar his entire body and he'd needed to be fished out by his brother and some friends. The end results had been a couple of broken bones and two weeks of bedrest due to a high fever.

Everything ached and when he came to, it was slowly, as though unconsciousness was trying desperately to cling to him. His eyes were sticky and gunky and he had to pry them open, only to be met with the harsh overhead glare of a blinding white light. The curse heaved out of him, said in the private language between himself and his brother, and then hands were on his arms, helping to lift him into a sitting position.

Sila blinked and processed it was his twin, and then the rest of his surroundings came into focus.

Hospital.

He was dressed in a thin blue and cream-colored gown with a white sheet tossed over his bottom half. It was clear he needed to be there, that there was in fact something wrong with his body, but he couldn't for the life of him recall how he'd ended up lying in bed in the first place.

The last thing he remembered—

"Move." Sila shoved at Rin and tossed his legs over the side of the bed, attempting to stand. He stumbled and his brother caught him, but he still tried to free himself of his hold, stubborn as per usual. "Let go. Now."

"You're sick," Rin snapped back. "Stop it."

He grabbed onto the front of his brother's shirt and hauled him close, almost falling over a second time for his efforts. "Where *is he*?" he snarled, the achy and dark, molasses like thing sticking up his gut, causing the control on his emotions to slip. His mask cracked and the look he set on Rin was anything but caring or brotherly.

But the last thing Sila recalled was him and Kelevra showing up at the secret house Sila had purchased and a blaster and—

A wounded sound slipped past his lips and both he and Rin froze as though it'd been a gunshot instead. While the two of them were busy staring at one another, the door to the room slid open and two people stepped inside, pausing just within the entranceway.

Sila registered Bay's surprised look, scanning him to check for any serious injuries or bullet holes. As soon as he processed everything was fine with the professor, all of the energy drained out of him. He let go of Rin and dropped back down onto the bed, clutching at the sheets as a wave of dizziness swept over him.

"I believe I told you not to let him get up," a familiar voice he was pretty sure belonged to Berga scolded, followed by a grunt from his brother.

"Yeah, well, he's not exactly the type to listen to others," Rin drawled, sounding every bit annoyed as the future Butcher of the Brumal Mafia did.

"Come here." Sila didn't want to listen to the two of them squabble. He'd seen his kitten, but he needed more than that to soothe the tumultuous thing clawing at his chest. He held out a hand, palm up and waited, not bothering to open his eyes.

Sure enough, a moment later he felt the warm press of Bay's hand settling in his own and he tugged, pulling the older man into a hug. He buried his face against Bay's chest and breathed him in, that smell of bergamot and tea leaves, the smell of Bay, oddly comforting. Sila didn't even care about the audience, clinging to him while his heartrate finally started to even out and return to normal.

When he'd realized Bay wasn't there, he'd panicked. The sensation had been visceral and all consuming, foreign, yet familiar. He'd felt something similar when he'd arrived at the bridge and spotted Bay leaning over the railing.

He was decidedly not a fan of the feeling.

"Where were you?" Sila asked, voice muffled by the soft material of Bay's clothing, which he noted was also a hospital gown.

"Berga and I stepped out to grab some coffee," Bay explained, running his long fingers through the sides of Sila's hair as he spoke. "We've been here for over a day and Rin hasn't had anything either, so we were grabbing him something."

"If you leave again—"

"I'm not going anywhere," he reassured, not put off by the beginnings of what had been a threat. "You need to lay back down. The doctor said you shouldn't be moving around yet."

Sila shook his head.

"Don't be like that," Bay told him. "Behave, that way you get better soon, and we can—"

"Go home." Sila didn't like it, but it made sense. With a grumble he released Bay, keeping a hold on the material of his shirt by Bay's left hip though to ensure he couldn't go anywhere. As soon as his head hit the pillow, he had to admit there was some instant relief in his achy joints and muscles.

"Are you okay?" Berga asked, and Sila was about to reply when he turned and caught the man staring at his brother instead of him.

Rin's mouth was hanging open and his eyes were wider than Sila had ever seen them before. He was also looking back at him as though Sila had turned green and sprouted a second head or a tail.

"Are *you* okay?" he demanded. "Did you hit your head when you passed out earlier, before we got there?" He shot that incredulous gaze to Bay. "Did he?"

"I don't believe so," Bay answered, nibbling on his bottom lip in contemplation. "No."

"You're being dramatic," Sila said.

"You're being *clingy!*" his brother shot back before pointing to where Sila still held onto Bay's shirt. "What is that?!"

Berga glanced between the two of them and then leaned toward Bay and said in a voice not nearly low enough not to be heard by everyone in the room, "Isn't Sila Varun known as a flirt?"

"He's also his student," the door whooshed open and Kelevra strolled in as if he owned the place.

Probably because he did.

"Don't give me that blank look," the Imperial Prince said to Sila, coming to a stop at his brother's side, close enough that his chest grazed Rin's arm. "In fact, how about dropping the act all together, hm? We all saw what you did to the professor here. You're not the friendly, boy next door you peddle to the masses."

Sila cocked his head. "You say that as if you didn't already know as much. I'm curious, out of the two of us, which do you think—"

"That's enough of that," Bay stated tersely, slipping into the role of professor with ease, even in the presence of Kelevra. "The two of you aren't doing anyone any good by teasing one another. Let's focus on what's important, shall we?"

"Like how you're getting dicked down by your student?" Kelevra said.

Rin elbowed him in the stomach.

"There are no rules in the handbook stating it's against school policy," Bay stated, holding his ground.

That was a far cry from all the whining Bay had done with Sila about getting caught, but whatever. He certainly wasn't going to be the one to point it out, at least not in front of all these people.

People Sila really wished would vanish so he could be alone with his kitten. They were all way too close—especially Berga. Berga needed to back the hell up before Sila made it so that Baikal was going to have to find himself a new Butcher.

"Relax, Professor," Kel rolled his eyes. "I'm not going to tell on you."

"You were poisoned," Berga stepped in then, clearly wanting to put an end to all of this as well. "By noxious, actually."

Sila rested his head back against the wall and smirked. "No shit?"

"You should be dead," he agreed, picking up on the fact that's where Sila's mind had immediately gone. "Your quick Tiberan healing is the only thing that saved you. That, and the fact you were brought to the hospital so soon."

"Isn't noxious slow acting?" The drug was highly illegal and hard to get your hands on. Once it entered a person's system, it took anywhere from a few days to a couple of weeks to get to the point where their life was in peril. "I felt fine this morning."

"Yesterday morning," Bay corrected. "You've been out for a while."

"You should be out still," Rin crossed his arms over his chest and scowled. "You need to rest. They saved your life, but you're not fully functional."

"There are still traces of the poison in your system," Berga explained. "But I'm working out a way to purge it from you. The doctor is overseeing it as we speak. It should be done shortly."

"What should?" Sila asked, just for clarification.

"The antidote."

"Which you made for me…why?"

Berga frowned at him. "Because you're Bay's…" He turned to the professor. "What are the two of you, exactly?"

"I own him," Sila stated. "So back off."

"Mr. Varun—" Bay began, only to suck in a breath when Sila sent him a dark look.

"*Mr. Varun* me again and I'll finger fuck you and leave you wanting in front of everyone here."

Berga quirked a brow, but something on Bay's face stopped him from coming to his friend's defense. Instead, he nodded as though he'd just found the solution to an impossible math equation he'd been working on for months. Then he clapped his hands together to regain everyone's attention.

"The reason the poison worked through you so quickly is because it was able to enter your body through the cut on your hand. Typically, noxious is a fine powder that seeps through the victims' pores and enters the bloodstream that way."

"So it was already on me before then," Sila surmised. He tried to think of anyone he'd come into contact with prior to meeting with Bay, but aside from his brother and Kelevra at their apartment, and then being alone at the shuttleport, there'd been no one.

"It was on your car," Berga said. "I tested the handle and it was smeared all over. You wouldn't have been able to see it."

"Just the driver's side too," his brother added. "You were the target."

"We just need to figure out—"

"It was Haroon Caddel," both Sila and Bay cut Berga off.

"The leader of the Shepards?" Berga's brow furrowed. "Does this have something to do with Grandma Idle?"

"Who the hell is that?" Rin asked.

"My grandmother," Bay told him. "She's dead."

"Oh. Sorry."

"Haroon cheated her out of everything she owned," Bay filled them in, mostly talking to his friend. "We also just discovered that he more than likely caused her death."

"He might have poisoned her," Sila elaborated. "Since you seem to be the expert on such things, any thoughts, Butcher?"

"Ah, right, yes," Berga nodded. "Bay asked me to look into things."

"What about noxious?" Rin suggested. "Any chance that could have been the culprit?"

"It wouldn't have left traces in the blood," Berga said. "And she died specifically of heart failure."

"Tundra," Sila murmured, thinking to himself. "If Haroon mixed the two, tundra would have broken down the noxious partials, making them virtually undetectable."

"Noxious would have sped up her heartrate and given her a fever," Berga agreed excitedly. "Mixed with tundra, a cold killer, that would have led to shock to the system, resulting in a heart attack. By the time the medical team arrived, her body would have been cooled and any signs of either poison would have already started to dissipate." He snapped his fingers. "Oh, that's good. That's so clever. That's evil genius at its finest."

"Berga." Bay glared.

"Apologies." He dropped his gaze to his shoes.

Which Sila realized for the first time were covered in plastic.

Interesting.

"But," it seemed to occur to him that Sila shouldn't know this and Berga glanced back up at him, "how did you come to that conclusion?"

"I'm a medical student," he said, only for Kelevra to snort.

"He's a psychopath," the Imperial Prince corrected. "He's probably considered using that concoction on others before."

"My brother would never," Rin immediately came to his defense. "Killing through poison isn't hands on enough for him."

Or not.

"You're a psychopath?" Berga asked. "Fascinating."

"Who invited him again?" Rin clearly wasn't pleased about their secrets getting out.

"You did, Flower," Kelevra reminded, laughing when Rin turned the glare his way.

"Okay," Rin waved him off, "so some bastard poisoned you," he turned to his brother, "clearly with the intent to kill, and I found you in an unknown location with a man covered in bruises —" he motioned to Bay "—sorry—which means this is no longer something 'you're handling'. Tell me what's going on. Now."

"It's not that big of a deal," Sila began only to stop short when Rin obviously was about to blow his top. There were very few things he gave a shit about and not setting off his brother, when they weren't in a controlled setting at least, was one of them. A pissed off Rin on the loose never did anyone any good, and with everything they already had going on, Sila didn't have the time or the patience to have to reign him in. "I'm going to have murder the leader of the Shepards, that's all."

"Oh," Rin drawled, "is that all?"

"Sarcasm." He nodded in understanding. "I'm getting better detecting that."

Rin went to move for Sila, but Bay stepped between them before he could take more than a few angry steps. He came up short, eyes narrowed, fists tightening at his sides, but all he did was stare the professor down wordlessly.

"That's unnecessary." Sila tugged on Bay's shirt until he fell backwards, landing on the edge of the bed, then he sat up and wrapped his arms around him, one over his shoulders, the other around his narrow waist, and clung to him. "My brother poses no threat to me, Kitten."

"Kit—" Rin blew out a breath and squeezed the bridge of his nose. "This is the pet. The one you said you were considering taking in."

"You had one stipulation," Sila reminded, resting his chin on Bay's right shoulder. "You didn't want to come home and find him on the couch, remember? I took care of that issue. You should be pleased."

"Did you buy a house to keep your professor on a leash?" Kelevra tipped his head. "That's not an entirely bad idea."

"There's enough water in this pitcher for me to fill your lungs with," Rin glowered.

"This has been fun," Berga cleared his throat, eyes glued to his multi-slate, "but I'm needed by the Brumal. The doctor will contact me with any important test results, since I'm your best bet at finding an antidote, but until then, you've been ordered to remain in hospital, Sila Varun."

"No, thanks." He didn't take orders, for one, and there was far too much that needed handling for him to waste time idling here.

"Bay's already called out of work," Berga said, a knowing glint in his eyes. "He can't exactly call them back and say the emergency he reported was false and he can come in after all, now can he?"

Sila felt Bay stiffen in his hold and he felt a race of excitement that he banked down. They had an audience and now was not the time for play. He wasn't even sure his body was healthy enough to get it up at the moment which, now that he was thinking about it…

"As soon as I'm better," he promised the room, "I am going to brutally, unapologetically, murder Haroon Caddel. Just so we're all on the same page."

"Here." Kelevra clicked a few buttons on his device. "I've just sent you the direct contact to my personal Cleaners. Make sure you leave them enough time to get the job done before anyone can stumble on the body. If you're caught, you're on your own."

"Are you seriously helping him commit a crime?" Rin sighed. "This family is so fucked up."

"Who's *family*?" Sila stated. "You two aren't married yet."

"Don't make me regret helping you out," Kelevra told him. "I liked you better when you were pretending to be a nice guy."

"Most people do." Most people couldn't handle the real him. Not like Bay could. He pressed his lips against Bay's throat, just above the twist of leather. "Professor, the Imperial Prince is being mean to me."

"It's not like he's one of my students, Sila. I can't exactly dock his grades because you have hurt feelings." Bay set both of his hands over his wrists and added in a cool tone, "However, Zane Solace is one of my students at the moment. He's been a bit distracted lately as well. Has been late to several classes."

"Are you," it was hard to tell if Kelevra was upset or impressed, "threatening me right now, Delmar?"

"It's *Professor* Delmar," he corrected snidely.

"All right," Rin relaxed and said to Sila. "Keep him."

"I was planning on it." He grinned and even winked when that had his brother rolling his eyes.

"Let's leave," Rin grabbed onto Kelevra's arm and dragged him toward the door. "He's fine."

"I'll call you if anything changes," Bay reassured, and Rin paused just before going and turned to look at him.

"My warning from before still stands," he

said, "Just to be clear."

"I don't like you messing with my things, brother," Sila kept the smile firmly in place, though his gaze hardened some. "Unless you want me breaking rules, you'll keep that in mind. I'm still curious which of us is more depraved, me or your Imperial Prince."

"It's you," Kelevra answered without skipping a beat. "I'm down for a little knife play now and again, but bruising? Too noticeable."

"You'll forgive me for not taking advice from someone who's spent their entire life standing in the light, wearing their proclivities for the entire planet to see."

"You're looking down on me."

"That's not a new development."

"And we're leaving now before one or both of us do something we regret," Rin stated.

"Considering only one of us is capable of feeling remorse, brother," Sila pointed out, "it'll end up being you."

He rolled his eyes again and took Kelevra's hand. "Whatever. We're out of here."

Berga watched them go and then waved at Bay. "I'll be back soon."

"Thanks." Bay smiled at him. "And really, I'm fine. I promise."

Sila figured the two of them had discussed those markings while he'd been unconscious. He didn't blame them. Despite what he'd said to the Imperial, the types of brutal play they got up to in the bedroom wasn't meant to have been shared with anyone. He simply hadn't accounted for Haroon poisoning him or his brother having to get involved in the end.

He'd underestimated the enemy.

That wouldn't happen a second time.

CHAPTER 30:

It took another two days for Berga to develop an antidote and, by then, Sila was on the verge of going stir crazy. His mood was so sour, not even his brother wanted to hang around him, so driving Sila home from the hospital fell on Bay.

Not that he minded. If he had his way, the two of them would never be separated further than twenty feet again.

He hadn't left the hospital once in all the time Sila had been bedridden, only going so far as down the hall to use one of the vending machines when the cafeteria wasn't open and he couldn't call for meals to be delivered. Because Kelevra's family name was plastered all over the place, he'd pulled some strings and allowed Bay to bypass visitation rules, allowing him to stay indefinitely.

The Imperial Prince had also ensured no one else filled the extra bed in Sila's room, so there'd been somewhere for Bay to sleep. If only Kelevra had known not to bother, since every night Bay had curled up against Sila's side, his ear pressed over his heart.

He'd been afraid the poison would get him and he'd wake only to find the younger man gone. It'd bothered him more than it had Sila even.

"Do you want me to stop anywhere?" Bay asked as he drove them away from the looming building. Berga had cured Sila and reassured them that he was fine now, though Bay had tried insisting he stay another night. It was dark out, with no other cars on the streets as they made their way through downtown. "There might still be a fast-food restaurant open."

"Are you hungry?" Sila had his head back against the headrest, his eyes closed. His coloring had mostly returned, but the fever that had swept through him for two days straight had taken a toll.

"No," he admitted. "But—"

"Just take me home, Kitten." His brow furrowed as a thought occurred to him. "Damn it. No one was there to clean up the mess we made."

Right, all the blood and...other bodily fluids that had no doubt stained the flooring and the sheets.

Bay grimaced. "I didn't get a good look at the place, but I'm pretty sure you had a big enough couch in the living room. You can lay down there while I take care of the cleaning. Do you happen to have an extra set of sheets?"

"Is that a joke?" the corner of his mouth tipped up, but his eyes remained closed. "I bought several knowing that you were going to dirty them, Kitten."

"I'm not sure how that falls on me," he replied. "It takes two to—"

"Do not say tango, Professor. Laughing hurts."

"Chest pains still?" Bay asked worriedly. The fever had turned into a tightness in his chest, resulting in shortness of breath. The doctors had put Sila on half a dozen medications to keep him stabilized while Berga had worked. "Should I turn around?"

"I just want to go home with you," Sila sighed. "No more doctors or hospitals or *people*."

"I'm a person," Bay drawled, only pretending not to understand.

Whenever a stranger was in the room, be it Doctor Ome or one of the nurses, Sila automatically slipped into the role of Prince Charming. He'd smile even through the pain, laugh and tease the staff. Put on a show. Bay was convinced that half the time, he wasn't even aware he was doing it, so used to needing to hide behind a mask it'd become second nature for him.

"You?" Sila snorted. "You're a kitten. My kitten."

He licked his dry lips and swallowed the sudden lump in his throat. There'd been possessiveness in Sila's tone just now, but in all the time they'd spent in the hospital, neither one of them had brought up the things spoken about in that house or while the younger man had been out of it with fever.

"Should we talk about it?" Bay sounded uncertain even to his own ears. He was afraid though. Afraid it'd been the poison talking and Sila hadn't meant any of it. According to Berga, he'd been infected even before Bay had woken tied to that chair, which mean all of the younger man's actions were questionable.

What if he no longer felt or thought the same? What if Sila was annoyed that Bay was even considering that he could have been telling the truth when he'd been in that state?

The bridge came into view then and his hands tightened on the steering wheel. He'd forgotten about how they'd have to cross it in order to make it to the house Sila had purchased. When they'd driven to the hospital, he'd been too distracted to notice, clutching Sila to him in the back seat while the Imperial Prince had sped and Rin had asked a slew of never-ending questions Bay could only partially recall now.

He risked a sideways glance over, sighing in relief when he found Sila's eyes still closed. If he could just get them over the bridge without drawing attention then maybe—

Someone rammed into them from behind suddenly, cutting that thought short. In a panic, Bay struggled to control the wheel as their hovercar swerved. From the rearview mirror, he saw a black vehicle coming up on them a second time, and only just braced when it crashed into their bumper.

He lost control and they spun, the sound of metal scraping against metal as they slid against the guardrail piercing through his ears. His head whacked into the window and he saw stars, but fortunately the car came to a stop soon after.

Sila recovered before him, throwing off his seatbelt to lean over and check Bay. He cupped his cheek and tilted his head, inspected where he'd hit it, but he didn't ask Bay if he was all right. When he was certain Bay was at least functioning, his eyes whipped toward the back and he growled when the black car came to a stop only a few feet behind them.

"Wait!" Bay tried to stop him when he tossed the passenger side door open, but Sila was too quick. He sucked in a breath when headlights appeared in front of them, another car entering the bridge from the opposite side, but before he could feel relief at there being help, it came to a crawl.

And Haroon Caddel stepped out.

He adjusted the collar of his jacket as though he was a cliché mob boss in a bad movie, and Bay would have rolled his eyes at the gesture if not for the fact he was approaching Sila who was standing at the front of the car already waiting.

Bay shot out, rounding it and coming to Sila's side before Haroon could reach them.

"I wasn't aware Tiberans had nine lives," Haroon said. The sound of car doors opening and slamming shut at their backs drew his attention over their shoulders momentarily, and he smirked. "Looks like you've finally run out of luck tonight however."

"Do I know you?" Sila slipped his hands casually into his front pockets and tipped his head, eyeing Haroon down like he'd never seen the guy before. "Your friends slammed into us. If this is about money, insurance should cover it. Don't tell me you're not insured?"

"Playing dumb?" he said. "Really?"

"It was worth a shot."

"Why are you doing this, Haroon?" Bay asked. "Anyone could show up and see that you're harassing us out in the open like this."

"I wasn't going to bother," he admitted. "Especially since you never showed any interest in me or what happened with your grandmother before. Why couldn't you have just stayed indifferent, Del?"

"Don't call him that," Sila ordered.

Only a few friends from college had ever referred to Bay by that nickname. Unfortunately, Haroon had been one of them, but he wasn't going to disagree with Sila here. He didn't like the closeness calling him by that name implied either.

"You murdered my grandmother and stole all her stuff," Bay accused. "What kind of person stands by and allows that type of injustice to go unanswered??"

Haroon barked out a sharp burst of laughter. "Please. Injustice? You tried *once* to get her name cleared and then promptly gave up. Let's be real here, if anyone did that poor old lady an injustice, it was you. I actually thought you'd be a bigger issue, had planned to wait it out and deal with you later, but then you stopped talking about it and I was convinced you didn't care anymore. Is he what changed?" He jutted his chin toward Sila. "That was a mistake. He's the reason you're both going to have to die tonight."

"Interesting logic," Sila replied. "I'm curious though, if you're so well informed and know we've been digging around your closet, shouldn't you also be aware that we've found no evidence? Why so afraid? Ah," he hummed mockingly. "Afraid to face the Devil?"

It was clear by the way Haroon scoffed haughtily that only Bay understood which Devil Sila had been referring to. This only became more apparent when he spoke a second later.

"Your future brother-in-law can't help you now, Varun," Haroon declared. "And neither can Baikal Void."

Sila's brow quirked. "Are you saying the only reason you've escalated things this far is because of my connections? Allowing an emotion like fear to drive you is dangerous, Haroon. Someone in your position, someone in charge of a group of people like the Shepards, should know better than that. But then, rumors all mention you're shit at your job, so I suppose I shouldn't be all that surprised, should I?"

If Bay hadn't involved Sila, did that mean Haroon never would have attacked them in the first place? He didn't view Bay as a threat, but Sila was a different story because his brother was publicly tied to the Imperial Prince, and Sila was openly friends with Rabbit Trace, who was also well-known to be linked to Baikal Void.

He'd been aware it was his fault Sila had been targeted, of course, he wasn't an idiot. But this made things a little clearer, and not in a good way. Guilt assaulted him a second before Haroon lifted a hand and motioned to the people who'd crashed into their car.

The sound of approaching footsteps had Bay turning, gasping when he spotted four fit men who were no doubt Shepards. Two of them even smiled at him, the promise of pain in their expressions.

Not the kind of pain Bay was into, thank you.

The last guy at the back of the group caught his eye and winked. He looked familiar, enough so that Bay wondered if he was also a student at Vail.

"Sila," he tugged on his sleeve. "We should get back to the car."

"Too late for that, Kitten." Unlike Bay, he didn't sound nearly as concerned about their current predicament. In fact, he actually sounded…

"You can't seriously be excited right now?" Bay might have been comforted by that if he didn't know himself as well as he did. Fighting had never been his forte.

"Why not?" Sila cracked his neck and grinned at Haroon, who he'd yet to take his gaze off of even as the men surrounded them. "After all that time in the hospital, I could use a good workout. Here's to hoping you and your boys are worth the time. I'm already in an irritable mood. Would suck if I got bored before I could properly hack you to pieces and let the professor here listen to you beg."

Haroon blinked, clearly caught off guard by that type of threat coming out of someone with Sila's kind reputation, but his stupor didn't last nearly long enough to make much of a difference. He snapped his fingers and the Shepards moved in.

Sila shoved bay back against the hood of the car. "Stay out of the way, baby. Only one who gets to mark you up is me."

A burly man at the right dove forward, making the first move, and Sila rushed into the attack. He caught the swinging fist and twisted, his strength easily overpowering the older guy. The way he moved was almost too quick for Bay's gaze to follow, and he watched wide-eyed as Sila practically danced around their attackers.

He had one on his knees and another's skull shattering the glass of the driver's side window in a second. Then he absently reached out and tore a jagged shard of glass at least six inches long from the frame and slowly advanced on the remaining two Shepards.

"This is pathetic," he said. "No wonder you lot aren't considered in the same league as the Brumal."

The guy to his right roared and tried to kick him, but Sila caught him by the ankle and tugged.

Swiping the sharp edge of the glass across the back of his ankle, Sila dropped the now howling man and grinned wickedly. "Achilles tendon," he noted. "Vital anatomy is similar to my own."

The last standing Shepard landed a blow to the side of Sila's jaw while he was distracted, but all it did was force his head to the side sharply.

Sila's tongue poked out, licking at the droplet of blood at the corner of his mouth before setting his intense gaze on the guy who'd hit him. There was a spark of something bright and almost gleeful that was unmistakable in his mismatched eyes, and it finally seemed like the others took notice.

The Shepard retreated a few steps.

Bay watched Sila stalk him to the end of their car, but no further, because in the next instant Haroon was yanking him off the hood and tossing him over the railing. The metal guardrail separated the walkway on the side of the bridge from the road itself and Bay hit the concrete on his knees, hard. He'd only just manage to climb to his feet when he was grabbed again, this time pulled over to the edge of the bridge.

It was too high for Haroon to force him up and over it, but he tried, attempting to lift a struggling Bay.

"Your grandmother was such a sucker," Haroon told him, laughing as he fought and captured Bay's wrists. "All I had to do was smile and act like you and I were best friends and she let me right in. When I offered to make tea for her? She ate that shit up. Rich people are so stupid, thinking their money will protect them."

"You didn't have to kill her!" Bay yelled, thinking about how he'd found her that day, lifeless and lying on the floor. Like trash.

"Of course I did," he snarled. "How else was I going to get her thumbprint on the paperwork? The scanner only tests to be sure the signee is still breathing when they apply their signature and print. I drugged her with something that would have her out of it enough she'd believe me when I said it was a school form she needed to sign on your behalf. Then all I had to do was walk out of there."

Was he implying…

"You didn't even wait to make sure she died?"

"What? Mad she was alone in her final moments?" Haroon scoffed. "Enough. Why am I even telling you this?" He pulled back and slammed a fist into Bay's stomach.

He heaved and caved in on himself, the pain shooting through him—and not in a pleasurable way. Tears stung the corners of his eyes and he wobbled on his feet, forced back up when Haroon grabbed a fistful of his hair.

"You did all of that just for her money?" Bay demanded. "Why?"

"You mean why you? Why your grandmother? Your house?" Haroon shrugged. "Picked it at random honestly."

Something in Bay broke at that and he let out a wounded sound that seemed to echo into the dark night. His grandmother, the kindest person he'd ever known, had been murdered and for what? No reason other than she'd been unlucky? It shouldn't make a difference, shouldn't make it worse, and yet, knowing it'd been a pointless crime did.

It also made Bay livid, unlocking a fury within him he wasn't aware he was capable of feeling, not even before he'd suffered from emotional detachment. From over Haroon's shoulder, he registered Sila heading toward them, and without stopping to consider what he was about to do, Bay worked a leg between him and his attacker and kicked with all his might.

He cried out as strands of hair were ripped from his scalp, but couldn't take his eyes off of Haroon who stumbled backward a single step.

It was enough.

Within a flash, Sila was there, right behind Haroon, catching him with a single arm around the waist. The other lifted, the crimson covered shard of glass in his hold winking in the vibrant bridge lights a split second before he swiped it across Haroon's throat.

Red spurted, splattering over Bay's face, and the smell of copper permeated the air.

Haroon gurgled and desperately clutched at his neck, falling in a heap when Sila released him.

Bay watched as the blood pooled around him and he eventually stilled.

When he finally tore his gaze off and looked back up at Sila, what he saw took his breath away.

Sila was watching him back, arms down at his side, blood smeared up his arms and over his cheeks, hair wild and windswept.

And he was grinning.

CHAPTER 31:

"How incredibly anticlimactic," Kelevra said, watching as a group of men in bodysuits lifted the dead Shepards and cleaned blood off the street.

They'd shut down the roads leading to and from the bridge, but there was no telling how long they'd be able to keep that up before word got back to one of Kelevra's sisters. None of them wanted this getting out, and while they'd always protected him, there was no telling how they'd react if they discovered Sila had murdered five people.

"You have no idea," Sila agreed at his side. "I might even be experiencing disappointment at the moment."

"If they were going to bother you like this, they could have at least kept things entertaining. He should have brought more men if he really wanted to beat you. And blasters. Lots of blasters. Clearly Haroon didn't bother actually looking that deeply into you."

"It wouldn't have mattered," Sila said. "I

don't flaunt my darkness like some people."

Kelevra chuckled, not the least bit insulted. "How long did it even take you to beat them?"

He thought it over. "Ten minutes? Maybe twelve."

"What, not good enough to get it done in five?" his brother stated sarcastically as he walked over from one of the black vans that was being filled with bodies. He scowled at the scene. "Pretty sure I told you I didn't want to have to clean up your shit again."

"Mine?" Sila pointed to Kelevra. "Or his?"

Rin glared, but Bay ended his conversation with Madden who'd arrived with the cleaning crew, putting a stop to their teasing.

After Sila had slit Haroon's throat, Bay had gone back to the car to grab his multi-slate to call Rin. Since Sila's was still back at the house, they didn't have the contact number Kelevra had sent over back at the hospital. They'd both known they couldn't just leave this type of mess behind to be discovered, so calling for backup was the smart play.

His brother had been nonstop scolding him since their arrival, but the Imperial Prince had appeared almost impressed by the scene, asking Sila enough questions that both Rin and Bay had eventually wandered off to deal with other matters while the two of them discussed the gruesome details.

"Madden says they'll be finished soon," Bay

informed them, coming to a stop in front of Sila.

Without much thought, Sila stepped forward, closing the small distance between them so he could wrap an arm around Bay's narrow waist. As soon as they had physical contact, he sighed, a coiled knot he hadn't been aware of in his chest loosening all at once.

When he'd turned around earlier and realized Haroon had Bay and was hurting him...

"I shouldn't have killed him so quickly," he said.

"From the sounds of it," Kelevra stated, "doesn't seem like doing the job any slower would have made it anymore worth your efforts." He clapped Sila on the back, leaving his hand resting there, obviously ignoring the way that had both of the twins tensing and their eyes narrowing. "Think of it this way, now you have more time to take the professor home and get him on his back. Or his front. Actually, have you tried the G-Tester 450?"

"That's enough death for one night," Rin growled, shoving Kelevra off his brother roughly. "If they're done here, let's get going."

"Why?" the Imperial gave him a flirtatious grin. "Did my mention of—"

"Are you sure you don't want us to send some people to the Shepards to dig into things?" Rin cut him off and directed the question at Bay. "If there's evidence to find, the Retinue can be trusted to find it without leaking it to anyone else."

Bay nibbled on his bottom lip but ended up shaking his head in the negative. "There's nothing. If there was, Sila's information would have discovered it by now."

"He's right," Sila agreed, though he didn't like it. Aneski would have undoubtably found the proof they were after if Haroon had left any lying around, he was certain of it. The other day, after Bay and he had left Nila, it'd been Aneski who'd first discovered her body and called him back to the scene. They'd tried to track down Haroon, but the guy had already gotten away, so Sila had focused on other things.

He took in the mostly cleaned crime scene. "It's too bad I didn't keep one of them alive. We could have tortured them for a confession."

"People like that?" Kelevra snorted. "There's no way Haroon trusted them with details. I doubt they even knew what they were doing here. They probably just followed orders like the sheep they were."

"The next in line will make things more interesting," Sila promised.

"That so?" he let out a low whistle. "Baikal is going to be pissed when he finds out there's going to be a next in line. He's barely held himself back from destroying the Shepards on more than one occasion. The only reason he hasn't is they've never been a big enough threat to warrant how many people he'd have to bribe to look the other way."

"I wouldn't bet money on that," Sila said.

"Know something I don't, Imposter?"

The Imperial Prince's nickname for him made Sila shrug. "Guess you'll have to wait and see."

"Still," Rin crossed his arms, "there's got to be something we can do to kick them out of your house and get it back." He turned to Kelevra. "Buy it for him."

"Oh, no," Bay held up his hands. "That won't be necessary."

"No? It won't be a problem."

"I've already got a place to live, but thank you."

"That monstrosity is no place—" Sila began, only to have Bay send an innocent look his way.

"It's true I didn't get to see much of it," he said, "but there's no way that house you bought could be considered a monstrosity in any sense of the word."

Sila blinked at him.

"Ew," Rin made a gagging noise. "Did he just agree to move in with you?"

"In a very sneaky fashion too," Kelevra nodded in approval. "Impressive, Professor."

"We should clear out," Madden called to them then.

"You got everything?" Kelevra asked, and his second in command grunted.

"Is morning wood hard?"

"Lovely." Bay pinched the bridge of his nose.

"He's right," Sila told him, noticing how tired his kitten appeared to be. "We need to go."

"Take my car," Rin pulled a set of keys from his front pocket and tossed them at him. "We'll get Bay's looked at."

"No need," Bay said. "It's junk anyway. Just scrap it. It's past time I get a new one anyway."

"That's my baby." Sila linked their fingers and began to lead him away from the group and over to the other end of the bridge where his brother had parked his hovercar twenty minutes ago. "Let's get rid of all the junk that's falling apart around you and upgrade."

"I never would have taken you for a neat freak." Bay slipped into the car when Sila opened the door for him.

"I'm not," he explained. "I just don't like things that are already falling apart before I can get my hands on them."

When Bay flinched, Sila internally swore at himself, then he crouched down at the side of the car and rested a hand on the professor's thigh until he'd peeled his gaze off the floor and met his.

"That was a poorly worded attempt at a joke," he admitted. "What I meant was, I don't like thinking about you in a house that's crumbling and filled with mold, or a car that could give out and crash at any moment. I want you to be safe."

"Careful," Bay drawled, and there was a snide hint to his tone that Sila took as a challenge immediately. "That sounds an awful lot like you care about me."

"Of course I care about you," Sila stood, face hovering dangerously close to Bay's. "You're mine." They stared at one another for a couple of seconds and then Sila hit the roof of the car, chuckling when Bay jumped at the sound, and then straightened. "Come on. Let's go home so I can show you."

Murdering those Shepards had whet his appetite.

Bay Delmar was going to be his main course.

* * *

"Are you certain we can trust the Imperial Prince?" Bay asked as he came out of the bedroom, calling down the long hall before appearing at the end where it opened up into the living room.

Sila was lying on the couch, an arm thrown over his eyes, though they hadn't bothered turning on all the lights when they'd arrived an hour ago. As soon as he'd gotten behind the wheel back on the bridge, a wave of dizziness had overcome him, resulting in the professor—in a fashion that would have given Rin a run for his money—chiding him for being reckless.

The doctor had warned that he'd need to take it easy for another couple of days despite the fact he was discharging him. At Bay's accusations, Sila had merely pointed out that it wasn't like he could have said that to the Shepards and gotten them to come back another time.

Maybe it'd made Bay feel guilty, Sila wasn't sure, but after that he'd insisted on cleaning the entire bedroom on his own when they returned. He'd mentioned as much before, but Sila had sort of figured it was for their audience's sake. He should have realized the professor didn't bother with masks like that.

"Come here." He held out his free hand, not removing the arm blocking out the city lights that streamed through the large floor to ceiling windows that made up practically the entire wall behind him.

He'd chosen this location because it was located in a rich neighborhood, close enough to Main Street for them to walk to all the restaurants and stores, yet far enough not to have to worry about being recognized whenever they left the house. It was two levels, the living area on the top floor, with an entire garage/work room taking up the bottom. When he'd purchased it, he'd told himself it was so he'd have space to play if he wanted.

Since the cat was out of the bag though, Sila admitted he'd done it with Bay's hoverbike hobby in mind.

The idea of something so important to his kitten sitting at some other man's house pissed him off.

Bay's palm slipped into his and he let out a startled yelp when Sila pulled him, settling the older man's body over his. "Take it easy!"

"I'm all right," he reassured, finally moving so he could look up at him.

Bay's blue hair was messy and his cheeks were flushed. Those golden eyes searched Sila, the concern there potent. Real.

"Worried about me, baby?" Sila cooed, moving his hands to Bay's hips.

"It's your fault," Bay said. "You're the one who woke me up."

"Were you sleeping?"

"Like the dead."

Sila chuckled. "You're so funny."

"I'm really not. You just don't have a strong enough grasp on humor. I suppose that works in my favor though."

"Does it?"

"I can keep you entertained."

It was the note in his voice, the slight tremble, and the way Sila felt Bay's heart skip a beat from how closely their chests were pressed together, that gave the professor away. Most of the events of their last time here were a blur in Sila's mind, due to the fever that had raged through him. He couldn't recall much of what had happened after he'd dragged Bay through the door by the ankle, in fact.

"Did I hurt you that badly?" he asked. Eyes roaming down Bay's bare arms. In the t-shirt the man was wearing, it was impossible to tell. He couldn't see any obvious markings in any case. "Kelevra made it sound like I'd broken you."

"Nothing I couldn't handle," Bay replied. "And nothing permeant. Well." He seemed to rethink his words. "Nothing other than the piercings."

Sila frowned. "Piercings?"

"You really don't remember any of it at all?" Bay sounded disappointed.

"Berga explained that I was poisoned before I even found you on the bridge," Sila reminded. "I must have been sick long before either of us realized, and even if I wasn't, the fever knocked me out and has made it difficult to recall much of anything leading up to when I woke in the hospital."

"Yeah."

"Where are they?" Sila stroked a finger down the curve of Bay's left ear. "Was one here?"

"It was your earring," he said. "I took it out because everyone would recognize it."

"Too many people know about us now. There goes my plan of possibly locking you up." He had a vague recollection of the earring though, now that it was brought up. And…

"I pierced your nipples too, didn't I?" He placed a hand behind Bay's head to hold him steady and rubbed their chests together, feeling the small bumps through their clothing. "Yeah, I did."

"I liked it," Bay reassured.

"Of course you did, Professor," he smirked. "You're a freak. Did it hurt?"

He nodded.

"A lot?"

"Not enough." Bay bit the bottom of his lip, clearly wanted to say something but unsure. Sila waited him out, until finally he blurted, "So you don't remember anything you said to me that night either?"

"You keep asking. Why? What was said that was so important?"

Bay pushed at him lightly, sitting up and moving to the edge of the couch when Sila released him. He sighed and ran a hand through his hair, looking…sad.

Sila didn't like it.

He got up as well, moving to sit behind him and wrap his arms around the older man's body. Resting his chin on his shoulder, Sila tried to make his tone as soothing as possible, though he knew comforting people wasn't exactly his strong suit.

"You were so angry after you found me on the bridge," Bay whispered. "It seemed real."

"Oh, that *was* real." The fury was just about the only thing Sila could recall with perfect clarity. "I was, and am, mad enough about that still it's tempting to drag you into the bedroom and lock you to the bedpost so you can't try it again."

"I won't," he promised. "I don't have any interest in killing myself."

Sensing they'd most likely already had this conversation, Sila opted not to beat a dead horse. He nipped at the underside of Bay's jaw. "Want to get naked?"

"The doctor said you needed rest."

"I did rest," he told him. "While you were cleaning."

"Why don't we watch a movie instead?"

Sila quirked a brow. "One of your dirty movies, Professor?"

He lowered his head but hummed in agreement.

"Do you have one of those on hand?" Sila asked. That wasn't exactly the sort of thing he expected anyone, let alone a prestigious teacher, to carry around on their person.

"On my multi-slate," Bay replied, then untangled himself from Sila's hold to make his way over to the large holo-screen set on the wall opposite the couch.

"You know," Sila drawled, leaning back against the black leather while he watched Bay sync his device with the square gray box on the shelf next to the holo-pad the images would project from, "I bought that for this very reason. I was thinking we could watch a few together and take notes."

"This is perfect for that," Bay said.

He stretched his arms over the back of the couch and drummed his fingers. They'd been through a lot in the past week, so there was a good chance he was imagining things but... "You seem off, Kitten. Something on your mind?"

Sila had assumed when he'd woken in the hospital with Bay by his side that things were good between them. That no matter what had taken place in that lost time, he hadn't done anything overly extreme that would cause the other man to run from him. Bay had also been telling the truth just now when he'd said he didn't want to die anymore, he was sure of it.

"Is it about your grandmother?" That made the most sense. "Because we weren't able to find any physical evidence?" In Sila's mind, the fact the guy was dead would be enough, but he and Bay weren't the same. Perhaps the professor wanted more for closures sake.

"I don't care about that." Bay stepped away from the screen, but instead of returning to the couch, he stood off to the side, clicking away at his multi-slate, seemingly selecting the right file to play.

He had been on the fence before over whether revenge or justice was what he was after. Haroon having his throat slit and his body swept under the proverbial rug where no one would ever find him was pretty decent revenge in Sila's book. But if that wasn't what had his kitten twisted and sullen, what—

"*...why your grandmother?*" Footage of the scene on the bridge from earlier flickered and settled over the screen. Haroon was holding Bay against the siding, the camera picking up on the audio, though it wasn't very loud. "*Picked it at random, honestly.*"

Sila stood slowly, unable to keep the frown

from furrowing his brow. "What is this?"

"A confession," Bay said, gaze locked on him. He didn't so much as glance at the screen as the scene continued to play out.

"The dashcam," Sila guessed. Their car had been facing that direction and the windows had been left open. It could have easily recorded the entire events of the night as well as captured what they'd said. "Why didn't you turn that over to Kelevra?" Why'd he keep something like that to himself when it would easily be enough to prove his grandmother's innocence?

"You don't get it, do you?" Bay sighed and rocked on his heels, slipping his hands into his front pockets. He was trying hard to come off relaxed, but Sila could see right through him. He was nervous despite his casual tone. "You're so used to being on the other end of these types of things, it makes sense."

His eyes narrowed. "Easy, Kitten."

"This is the best part." Bay pointed to the screen, but again, he didn't look himself.

Sila did though, just in time to see a clear image of himself step into view. He caught Haroon and in a flash of motion sliced the man's throat, deep enough to cause blood to splatter. The expression on his face could only be considered pure evil. There was no hiding the fact that he'd just enjoyed slicing through Haroon's carotid artery.

"What do you think?" Bay asked then,

pausing the video so Sila's vicious grin was frozen on screen. "The only reason it was so easy for you to stop them today was because the whole planet thinks you're a nice guy. It'll be pretty hard to maintain your innocent persona if this is leaked, don't you agree?"

Something flipped in his gut and Sila barely held himself together as he stared Bay down. "You're threatening me."

"Sila Varun," he smiled, but it was bitter, "My top student. Nothing gets by you."

"Professor."

"Actually," he waged a finger, "a couple things do. Admittedly. We were *so close*, but then Haroon had to go and fuck it up by poisoning you. If you'd only remembered..." He sighed. "I guess there's no other choice now but for me to come clean."

"Come clean about what?" Sila wasn't sure he could describe what he was feeling in that moment.

He *should be* furious and maybe even a little concerned—that was legitimate leverage Bay now had against him—but if he did feel either of those things, those emotions were currently being drowned out by the bubbling dejection crashing against his insides like a raging tempest.

He'd foolishly believed...Well, everything.

"The Seaside Cinema is run and owned by the governor," Bay informed him. "He works closely with the Imperial Family. More Royals visit to tug their dicks than you'd be able to count on both hands. Do you really think it'd be that easy to bribe one of their workers to let you into a private room?" He clicked his tongue. "No, *baby*. It isn't."

Sila kept his expression blank but on the inside his mind howled, forced to acknowledge that he had a point there.

"You figured you'd stroll in and offer a wad of coin, bat those long lashes of yours, flirt a little, and that would be it, right?" Bay continued.

"You knew I was following you."

"I was *stalking you*," he reminded. "Of course I figured out when the tables had turned. Although, to be fair, it wasn't until that night, when you first followed me there after my race? I hoped you'd be back again, that you'd want to know what I got up to, so I paid the employee to give you the info if you ever came asking about it. Since I was the client using the room, he didn't have to worry about breaking any rules by giving it to you."

It had been rather easy for Sila to get the keycode to the room Bay always used and hide the cameras. No one had come looking or patrolled the floor whenever he was there, but he'd just assumed that was par for the course at a place like that. That they kept security light so they didn't run into any of the paying customers who preferred to keep their identities anonymous.

"I mixed the pictures of you and your brother in my closet, hoping you'd stumble on them," Bay said next. "It was a month into this semester. You never came by though."

"I bugged your car and your office," Sila told him. "That was enough to keep tabs on you."

"When I realized that was all you were doing, I was pretty disappointed. I had to keep my distance, but you didn't have reason to. I wasn't sure the bay roses or the text messages were from you, because you always seemed so indifferent to me on campus. It could have been Crate even. It wasn't until you saved me from him at the restaurant that I was reassured it wasn't him."

"I'm the reason he came after you in the first place though." Sila had drugged him.

"That's okay. You also took care of him. I still didn't have enough proof though, because you used that voice modulator. I figured it was someone else, even. It was disappointing."

"Whether it was me or not, you could have been murdered."

"Truthfully?" Bay shrugged. "In the beginning, I didn't really care one way or the other. Then when it turned out it was you...You have no idea. Either you killed me, you fucked me, or you warned me off. If it was the latter, I'd force the issue until you changed your mind and went for the first. Getting to sleep with you felt more like a fantasy than a real possibility."

"When you came into the woods—"

"I went there to die," he confirmed. "Imagine my utter shock when you screwed me instead and

I woke up still breathing the next morning."

Sila cocked his head, reassessing everything he thought he'd known about the older man and their interactions. No matter which way he looked at it however, there was no denying one clear fact. "Your endgame changed after that."

"To be fair, I had no idea it would be that easy for you to fix me. I hadn't even considered you could. If you'd murdered me, the shock may have been enough to unlock my emotions for my final breaths, but I didn't think there was a high chance of it. And I had no way of knowing that once I could feel again, I would no longer want to die at all."

"Why didn't you just go back to the bridge sooner if you wanted to end your life that badly?" Why drag Sila into his mess? Why make him experience—He let out a low growl, cutting that thought short.

"I've been back there dozens of times over the past two years," he admitted. "Seemed like whenever I stood there, looking down at the water, that was the only time the guilt came back. I felt horrible for even considering taking the life my grandmother had spent so much time and energy raising. No matter how dead inside I already felt, I couldn't do it."

"So, you were going to have me do it for you." Sila clenched his hands into fists. "That's it then? You were just using me."

"I never used you," Bay disagreed, pursing

his lips. "At least, not any more than you used me. It felt good having an outlet, didn't it? Having someone willing to share the shadows with you? You could cut me, beat me, fuck me without lube, anything you wanted without fear of repercussions."

"What exactly do you call this?"

"This?" Bay held his gaze. "This is a confession."

Sila had to have misheard. "What?"

"I told you once already. Try not to forget it this time," Bay said before taking a deep breath. "I love you."

CHAPTER 32:

"You," Sila finally knew what dumbfounded felt like, "are certifiably insane."

"So you've told me," Bay nodded. "You like that though."

"Do I?"

"Yes."

"You sound incredibly sure of yourself, Professor."

"I wasn't before," he admitted. "But after what we went through here?"

"You mean all the stuff I have no recollection of what-so-ever?" Sila snorted. "Nothing I said to you while poisoned counts."

"That's why I have this." He held his hands out to the screen.

He was definitely angry now, because he felt played and he wasn't used to that, but... The confusion was also still there, right alongside something Sila was pretty sure he shouldn't be experiencing at the moment.

Something he refused to acknowledge was hope and *pride*.

Because then they'd *both* be insane.

"Footage of me committing murder," Sila drawled.

"Proof that you won't find me on that bridge ever again," Bay corrected. "That I won't ever try to leave you."

He still wasn't getting it.

"You have all those compromising videos of me," Bay said. "I just borrowed a page from your playbook."

"As in, we both destroy the videos and—"

"I don't want you to destroy them," he stated. "Keep them. I know you like watching them when you're alone. You probably planned on us watching them together in this room, didn't you?"

Sila had. The fact that Bay was able to guess that...

Interesting.

And kind of hot.

"You mixed the photos of me and my brother on purpose?" He should have paid more attention to that detail, but he'd been too pissed off and bewildered before. "How?"

"How could I tell you apart?" Bay asked. "It was so obvious after that day the two of you got involved with the Devils in the East Quad. There was a moment, though brief, where the Imperial Prince had you pinned by the throat and your mask dropped ever so slightly. The second your brother showed up it snapped back into place, but he wasn't as quick fixing his own."

"He's hot headed," Sila agreed.

"The opposite of you."

"In this moment?" He shook his head. "I wouldn't be so certain, Kitten."

Bay tipped his head. "Want to kill me?"

Sila's eyes narrowed.

"Want to chase me to the bedroom and—"

"Stop."

"Why?"

"I don't like being a pawn, Bay Delmar. You're playing a dangerous game right now."

"I'm playing the same game you started, Sila," he corrected. "With the same set of rules. People with psychopathy tend to believe they're above the rest of us, that they're always five steps head. It was simple enough to let you think that, since for the most part it was true. Only, the second you revealed your true nature to me, you should have realized you'd given me a leg up in this game of ours."

Bay taught Criminal Psychology.

"You were luring me in," Sila realized.

"Psychopaths are just like everyone else in one regard," Bay continued. "They have the same need to be loved and cared for. Even if you didn't think love was an emotion you're personally capable of, that doesn't stop you from craving it from others. That's why you cling so strongly to your twin. He loves and accepts you for who you are, no matter what twisted urges or thoughts run through that vicious head of yours.

"I let you do whatever you pleased to me, and in the process, I showed you you're not alone in your darkness. You like owning? That's great. I like being owned. I like that you covered me in your marks and the way you warned your brother off when he got too close. You want to feel understood and I want to feel wanted. We're a perfect match. I want you to keep me forever, Sila. That's all. I just want to be with you. I played my hand and I'm out of cards. It's your move, Varun."

"And August?" Sila's eyes narrowed. "Did you know I would go after him?"

"I couldn't tell if you were watching me once school started, or how invested you were prior to the start of the new semester," Bay said. "The only reason I knew you came to the cinema is because the worker told me if you were there whenever I arrived."

"What about the fact I was filming you?"

"I had a hunch, since you were never in the room with me, and since you kept coming back you'd clearly found a way to watch from somewhere else. But I didn't know if you were recording."

"And if I'd gone straight to the police?"

Bay lifted a brow. "To show them you illegally filmed someone at a sex theater?"

Right.

"I'd hoped you'd hear that something had happened to August and, since you knew I liked you, you'd maybe put two and two together. Then you'd come ask me about it and we could...I don't know, honestly. I wasn't anticipating anything really happening between us. But I wanted an excuse to talk to you. Then August ended up disappearing... I didn't realize it might have been you until I saw that slipup in the East Quad."

"You didn't care that I might have killed him?"

"Not even a little bit."

"That's not very professional of you, Professor. He was one of your students."

"I couldn't feel anything at the time," he reminded. "It didn't really matter to me."

"And now?"

"Now that I can feel?" Bay shrugged. "You said he was an asshole. What do I care if he's dead then?"

This was...a lot. Even his brother didn't like it when Sila got blood under his fingernails.

"You could take that to the police right now and get your house back," he pointed out.

"And expose you?" Bay shook his head. "I would never do that. There's no way to splice the footage to keep anyone from discovering how the night ended either."

That was true. Since Haroon was currently dead and Kelevra's Retinue had disposed of the body, there'd be a lame investigation put on by someone in the Imperial Prince's pocket. And that was only once Haroon's family or friends realized he was missing and reported him. If this video was presented however, it would be obvious something had gone down. They'd suspect Bay first, forcing the professor to either give Sila up and expose the rest of the footage, or take the blame and end up behind bars himself.

Neither of those scenarios sounded fun.

Bay had another choice here it seemed. His grandmother or Sila.

Was he really going to choose Sila though?

"That still doesn't explain what you *do* plan on doing with the video," Sila pointed out, though he was fairly certain he'd caught on. He wanted to hear it though. If they were going to stand here like this, Bay was going to have to air all his dirty laundry for Sila to even consider moving forward.

The fact that he was spoke volumes about who he was as a person, but damn the professor for being right.

He'd poked and prodded all the correct buttons where Sila was concerned. It'd been a while since he'd recognized the signs he was becoming dependent on the older guy. Whenever he didn't know where Bay was or what he was doing, Sila felt anxious. Bay was to blame for some of this, of course, but Sila wasn't innocent. He'd known something was happening to him, and he'd made the decision not to end things.

On some subconscious level, he'd even been aware what the professor might be up to. He'd turned a blind eye so that later, if he decided he no longer wanted Bay after all, he could claim he'd had no idea.

But even if he hadn't. No one had ever managed to get the upper hand on him before. Instead of enraging him or bruising his ego, Sila found himself going the other direction. It was sexy as all hell that Bay was that clever and manipulative.

"It's leverage," Bay told him. "Same as the footage you have of the Seaside. Now I can't leave you, and you can't leave me. If either of us try, we'll blow up our own lives."

"Can't leave you, huh?"

"You could kill me," he said. "But Berga knows we're involved now, and did you notice the way he was looking at me before he left the hospital? If anything happens, he'll suspect you first and foremost and then you'll have the entire Brumal to contend with. You really think the Imperial Prince will be able to protect you?"

Kelevra might try, considering Rin, but that would only result in chaos, and not the fun kind, because there was no way his brother would be able to walk out of it unscathed.

"What happens if you decide to leave me?" Sila asked. "Sure, I could leak your videos, but what's to stop you from then releasing mine?"

"I'm never going to leave you," Bay stated. "I said it before, but you didn't believe me. You also told me you weren't going to leave me, but I didn't believe you either. This takes care of that for the both of us. Puts us at ease, don't you think?"

That was all sorts of fucked up brilliance and Sila...He was impressed. He didn't want to be. He wanted to snap the other man's neck so this would be over, but at the same time, even the thought of killing Bay had his chest tightening uncomfortably.

He couldn't do it. He didn't want him to die.

He didn't want to lose him.

"Touche." Sila felt his body relax, the imminent threat over. "You're very clever, Professor."

"I'm not the youngest member on staff at a place like Vail through luck."

"Clearly."

"Are you still mad?"

"Yes."

"Are you going to—"

"Let's clarify a few things," Sila cut him off. "It's cute that you've been topping from the bottom, baby, and I don't really mind. But it's still the bottom. I'm still the one in charge here."

"I promise not to ever try to manipulate you again," Bay said, only for Sila to cluck his tongue disapprovingly.

"Where would the fun be in that? Keep doing what you've doing. Forever is a long time. Want me to want you that long? Make me."

"So long as you constantly breathe life into my undead body?" Bay smiled. "Deal."

"I make you keep feeling, you make me want you back." It wasn't bad. He didn't come out short and he got what he wanted out of it.

"Do you love me?"

Sila considered. "I like you. You're mine."

"Maybe one day then?"

"Maybe." He wasn't sure, but prior to now, he would have said there was no chance of anyone pulling a fast one on him, and yet here they were. Anything was possible. "Would it change your mind if I never do?"

"No," Bay replied without any hesitation.

They'd both realized something important on the bridge that day.

Bay never wanted to lose Sila.

And Sila never wanted to lose Bay.

"Bay Delmar," he rolled the sound of his name off his tongue, testing it like he had all those months back when they'd first started this. Then he met his gaze and grinned. "Run."

There was no hesitation there either. Bay immediately spun on his heels and took off down the hall like his life depended on it.

But the smile on his lips gave him away.

Interesting.

Sila gave himself one more moment alone to process everything he'd just learned. That possessiveness he felt toward his kitten didn't dwindle however, if anything, Bay felt more like his match now than he had even an hour ago.

Bay Delmar was his, and he was Bay Delmar's.

With an excited growl, Sila stalked forward,

the look on his face no less devilish than the one still frozen on the hover screen.

A Devil of Vitality always caught his prey.

EPILOGUE:

Three Years Later

"Lick it clean. You want to come, Kitten? Make it hard again."

Bay mewled but dutifully stuck out his tongue, the tie Sila had used to blindfold him preventing him from being able to locate Sila's cock on his own. He was bent over the saddle of his hoverbike, already naked and so needy that he'd leaked all over the leather seat.

They'd just gotten back from a race and he'd been riding the high of another win when Sila had jumped him in the garage of their home and stripped him bare. He'd been carrying the tie with him all night, one of the ones he'd bought Bay for a birthday gift sometime in the three years they'd been together, had been fantasizing about this for hours, to the point he'd been semi-hard during the entire race.

They weren't just celebrating Pandaveer's win though.

Sila had finally graduated from Vail, which meant Bay no longer had a reason to stay there despite hating teaching. The only reason he'd lasted at all was because he complained if he left too soon, he wouldn't get to see Sila on campus every day. Even though they hadn't had a class together since the first semester of his sophomore year.

It was cute.

Kind of clingy, but Sila was okay with that, since he didn't like it when Bay was out of his sight for longer than a few hours either. If anything, the years had strengthened this warped thing between them, tying them more tightly to one another. It was to the point the knot that bound them was so complex, Sila was pretty sure he wouldn't be able to untangle it even if he wanted to.

Which he did not.

It would have been enough for them to go public with their relationship after Sila was no longer a student, but Bay still hadn't wanted to stick around. The day after the graduation ceremony, he'd given his resignation letter. When asked what he planned to pursue next, he'd shrugged and said he'd figure it out eventually.

They weren't in any rush. They'd made enough money off the races to live comfortably and Sila's eventual paycheck from the hospital would only add to that. His residency started in less than a week and, even though Bay had been good and hadn't complained, it'd been obvious he was dreading how busy that was going to make

Sila.

Tonight was also meant to reassure him. His kitten was needy and required an abundance of care and attention.

And discipline.

Sila eased himself forward and slipped his cock between Bay's lips, groaning when the professor—or, ex-professor—eagerly sucked him down. He'd removed his own clothing as well, and his skin felt flushed and hot in the closed garage which was all metal, cement, and one way glass. The glass was to allow them to see out but prevent anyone else from accidentally peeking in.

Which was good, considering he had Bay's wrists bound at his narrow back with a zip tie he'd found earlier in the other guy's tool box.

Sila reached for it now, slipping a finger beneath the plastic to tug at his wrists so it bit into Bay's skin. The move also seated him more firmly within the hot cavern of his greedy mouth, causing them both to moan.

He'd jerked himself off to the sight of his kitten trussed up for him, painting Bay's face with his come. That was less than five minutes ago, but Sila was already achingly hard again, the crown of his cock bumping wildly against the back of Bay's throat, trying to get in even deeper.

He slipped free from Bay's mouth and his kitten whimpered. Ignoring him, Sila rounded the bike, coming to a stop at his back so he could take in the rounded globes of Bay's firm ass.

"What's this?" Sila had noticed the tiny object protruding from Bay's hole when he'd taken off his pants and bound him, but he'd purposefully overlooked it. Now, he reached forward and rolled the three small beads connected by a string around his pointer finger. "This for me, Kitten?"

Bay made a sound of agreement. "Everything's for you."

He stilled, liking that. But then, throughout their time together, it'd become abundantly clear that Bay always knew exactly what to say and do to call to the devil within him. "Everything, huh."

"Yes."

Without further warning, Sila grabbed onto the end of the toy and yanked it out of Bay's hole with one swift tug.

Bay cried and floundered over the bike, but a whack against his ass had him stilling as the last bead popped free.

Holding it up to the light, Sila took a second to inspect it. He hadn't purchased the toy himself, which meant it was something Bay had bought on his own. The string of pearls were uniform, and the anal beads stretched at least a foot in length from the first to last.

"Looks like I'm not the only one who was looking forward to celebrating," Sila laughed, moving to rest the toy on the work bench behind him. They were too pretty to drop to the floor and risk stepping on and ruining.

Besides, later, they'd look even better

wrapped tightly around Bay's throat...

Using both hands, Sila spread Bay's cheeks, grinning when his hole fluttered imploringly at the attention.

"Was it uncomfortable riding with those shoved up there?" Sila asked curiously. He was actually impressed that Bay hadn't been too distracted by it to lose.

"Yes," Bay admitted. "Especially since I kept pretending your fingers were inside of me instead."

"Trying to manage me again, baby?" Clearly he was trying to get Sila to pick up the pace and opting for pretty words to do it.

"You can punish me for it later," Bay offered.

"That won't be necessary," Sila said, chuckling when Bay made a sound of disappointment. "Don't whine. The reason it won't be necessary," he lined himself up with his entrance, "is because I'm going to punish you now."

Bay hissed as Sila drove forward, spearing into him in one hard thrust that had the bike shaking beneath them. He struggled against his bindings, but with how tightly the zip tie was done, there was no chance of him slipping free.

"Shh," Sila hushed when he started to rail him and Bay's gasps turned to full blown wails. There wasn't really a reason to since the garage was sound proof, but they both liked it when he gave orders, even small ones. "Be quiet and take it like you should."

Bay clamped his mouth shut, his shoulders quaking with strain.

In turn, Sila fucked him harder for his effort, trying to slip him up despite the fact he was the reason his kitten had gone silent in the first place. But then, that was also part of it. It was a battle of wills between them, a game to see which of the two would come out on top. Bay was a worthy opponent. There was no one else in the entire universe who could make a claim like that.

That was probably what had convinced Sila to forgive him for the deception that night he'd admitted to everything. If anyone else had threatened to hold a video of him murdering someone over his head, he would done away with them and destroyed the evidence. But Bay was right. Every day Sila knew he kept that footage was another day he was certain the older man loved him. Hell, he'd chosen to give up justice for his grandmother in order to ensure Sila stayed safe.

He'd had a choice, a real one, and he'd chosen Sila all on his own.

It wasn't even just that. Bay was his perfect match through and through. He not only understood Sila's devilish nature, he actually stroked its ego and begged it to come out and play. This game between them was always entertaining, and truly never-ending, though there were multiple rounds. More often than not, Sila was still victorious, but every now and again Bay would beat him.

He wasn't going to allow today to make it onto that short list.

Sila pulled back to the tip and then waited a beat, just long enough for Bay to start to squirm, then he pounded back into that tight heat, simultaneously spanking him. The sound of skin hitting skin mingled with Bay's loud sob and Sila's following laughter.

"Pretty sure I told you to be quiet," Sila said, draping himself over Bay. He bit at his ear lobe, hard enough to draw blood and then lapped at it, relishing when that had his kitten moaning all over again. "That's not quiet either, baby."

"Please." Bay pushed back into him, lifting his ass to help drive his cock in deeper.

"Oh no," he pressed a palm to his right cheek and forced him down, pulling out to the tip a second time teasingly. "You snared the Devil. Deal with the consequences." He didn't wait for him to respond, driving back home. He kept the tempo of his thrusts steady and deep, sure that Bay could feel every inch of him as he entered and retreated.

"Sila, please!" Bay begged. "I'm so close!"

"Yeah?" he brought his mouth to Bay's ear, stilling inside of him. Then he whispered in a low growl, "I love you, Bay Delmar."

Bay sucked in a sharp breath and then shook, his entire body like a livewire beneath Sila.

"Did you just come?" Sila asked once the tremors had subsided, peeling Bay off the bike, careful to keep him impaled on his cock all the while. He tore the blindfold off and then bent Bay over the workbench.

"That wasn't fair," Bay complained.

It wasn't.

He hadn't hidden his feelings. The moment Sila had realized the thing in his chest he felt toward the professor was love, he'd been forthright with that information.

And Bay had come in his pants.

In the middle of the class room.

Right before he was about to start another class.

Since then, any time Sila said it he either came or got hard.

"How about this," he tugged at the loop of the leather collar around Bay's neck, "I'll count to ten. You make it to our bedroom before I can catch you and I'll let you take a bath before we continue this. I catch you before then, and I fuck you so far past oversensitivity you'll be crying and begging me for mercy."

"The Devil shows no mercy."

Sila smirked behind him.

Bay swallowed and considered. "What about my wrists?"

"What about them?" There was no way he was unbinding him. That would ruin the fun.

He inhaled shakily. "All right."

Sila straightened him from the table and turned him toward the door that led up to the living part of the house. Then he slapped him on the ass. "Get running, Kitten. One."

Bay raced for the stairs, not bothering to be quiet as he stomped up them.

"Two!" Sila moseyed over toward the doorway. "Three!"

He heard Bay stumble into the kitchen.

"Ten!"

Bay's curse greeted his ears as he took the steps two at a time, but they'd both known it was coming.

The Devil didn't show any mercy *or* play fair.

And the man that he loved wouldn't have it any other way.

Chani Lynn Feener has wanted to be a writer since the age of ten during fifth grade story time. She majored in Creative Writing at Johnson State College in Vermont. To pay her bills, she has worked many odd jobs, including, but not limited to, telemarketing, order picking in a warehouse, and filling ink cartridges. When she isn't writing, she's binging TV shows, drawing, or frequenting zoos/aquariums. Chani is also the author of teen paranormal series, *The Underworld Saga*, originally written under the penname Tempest C. Avery. She currently resides in Connecticut, but lives on Goodreads.com.

Chani Lynn Feener can be found on Goodreads.com, as well as on Twitter and Instagram @TempestChani.

Printed in Poland
by Amazon Fulfillment
Poland Sp. z o.o., Wrocław